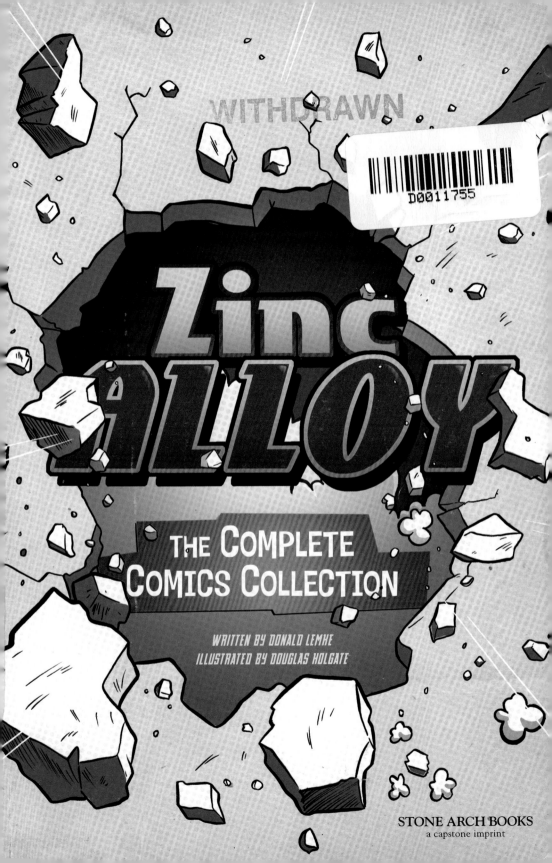

WITHDRAWN

D0011755

Zinc ALLOY

THE COMPLETE COMICS COLLECTION

WRITTEN BY DONALD LEMKE
ILLUSTRATED BY DOUGLAS HOLGATE

STONE ARCH BOOKS
a capstone imprint

Zinc Alloy

WRITTEN BY DONALD LEMKE
ILLUSTRATED BY DOUGLAS HOLGATE

DESIGNER: HILARY WACHOLZ
EDITOR: CHRISTOPHER HARBO

Stone Arch Graphic Novels are published
by Stone Arch Books, an imprint of Capstone.
1710 Roe Crest Drive, North Mankato, Minnesota 56003
www.capstonepub.com

Library of Congress Cataloging-in-Publication Data is available
on the Library of Congress website.
ISBN: 978-1-4965-8733-6 (library binding)
ISBN: 978-1-4965-9322-1 (paperback)
ISBN: 978-1-4965-8737-4 (eBook PDF)

Summary: Zack Allen loves comic books, but this wimpy kid is nothing like his favorite superheroes. He's always getting picked on by bullies at school. Then one day, Zack builds a powerful suit of armor and becomes . . . Zinc Alloy, the Invincible Boy-Bot!

Printed and bound in China.
2493

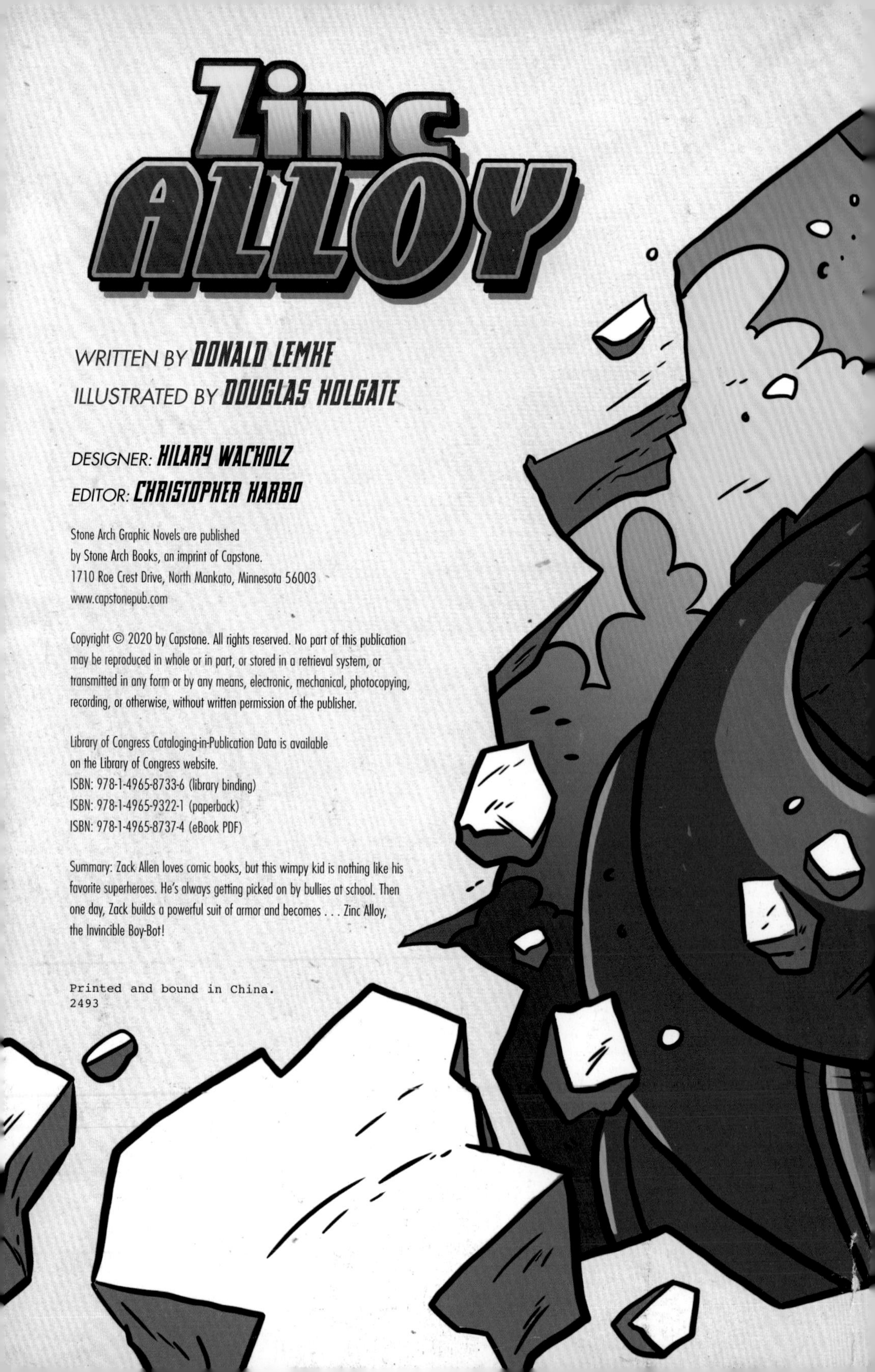

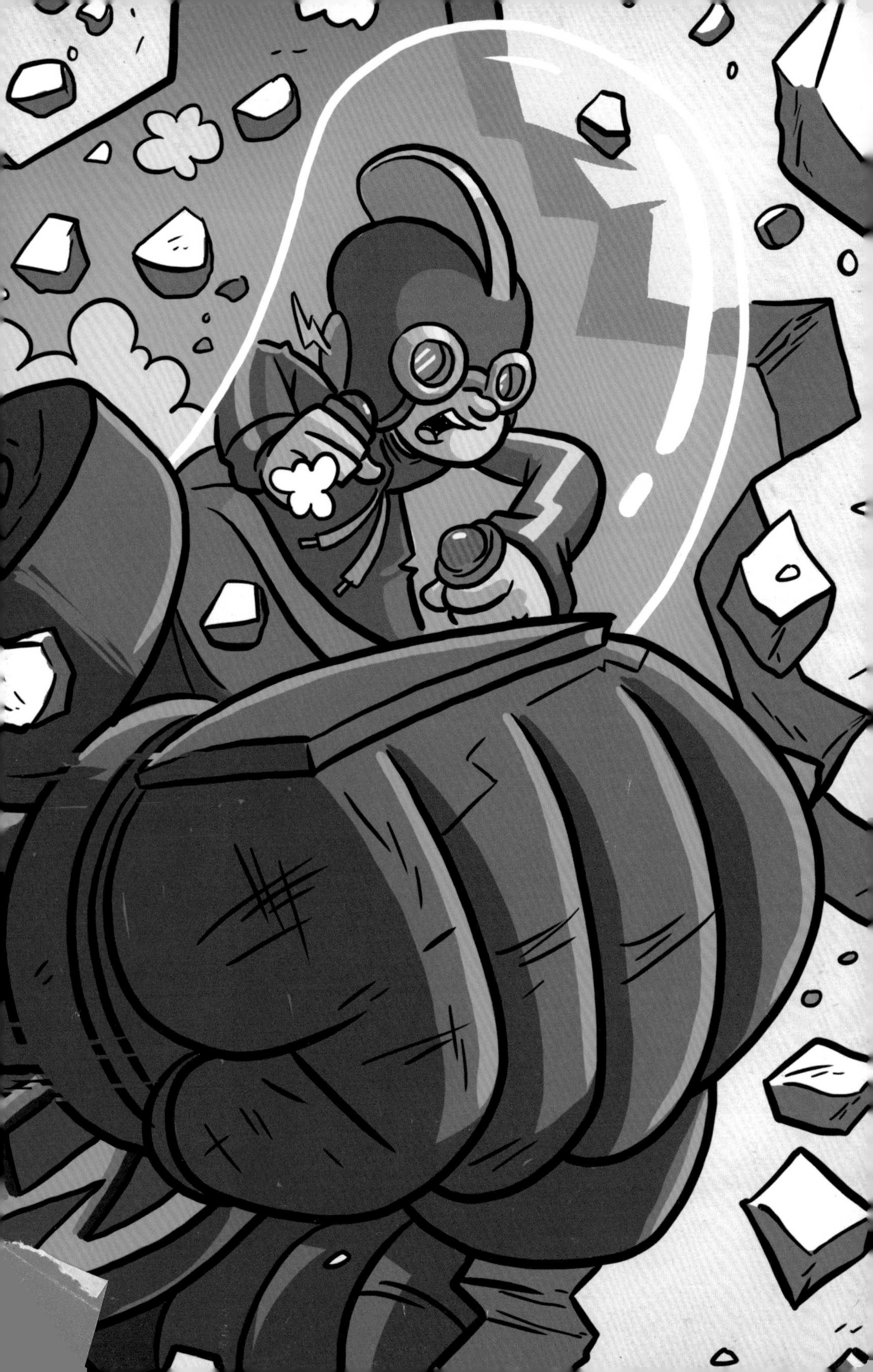

TABLE OF CONTENTS

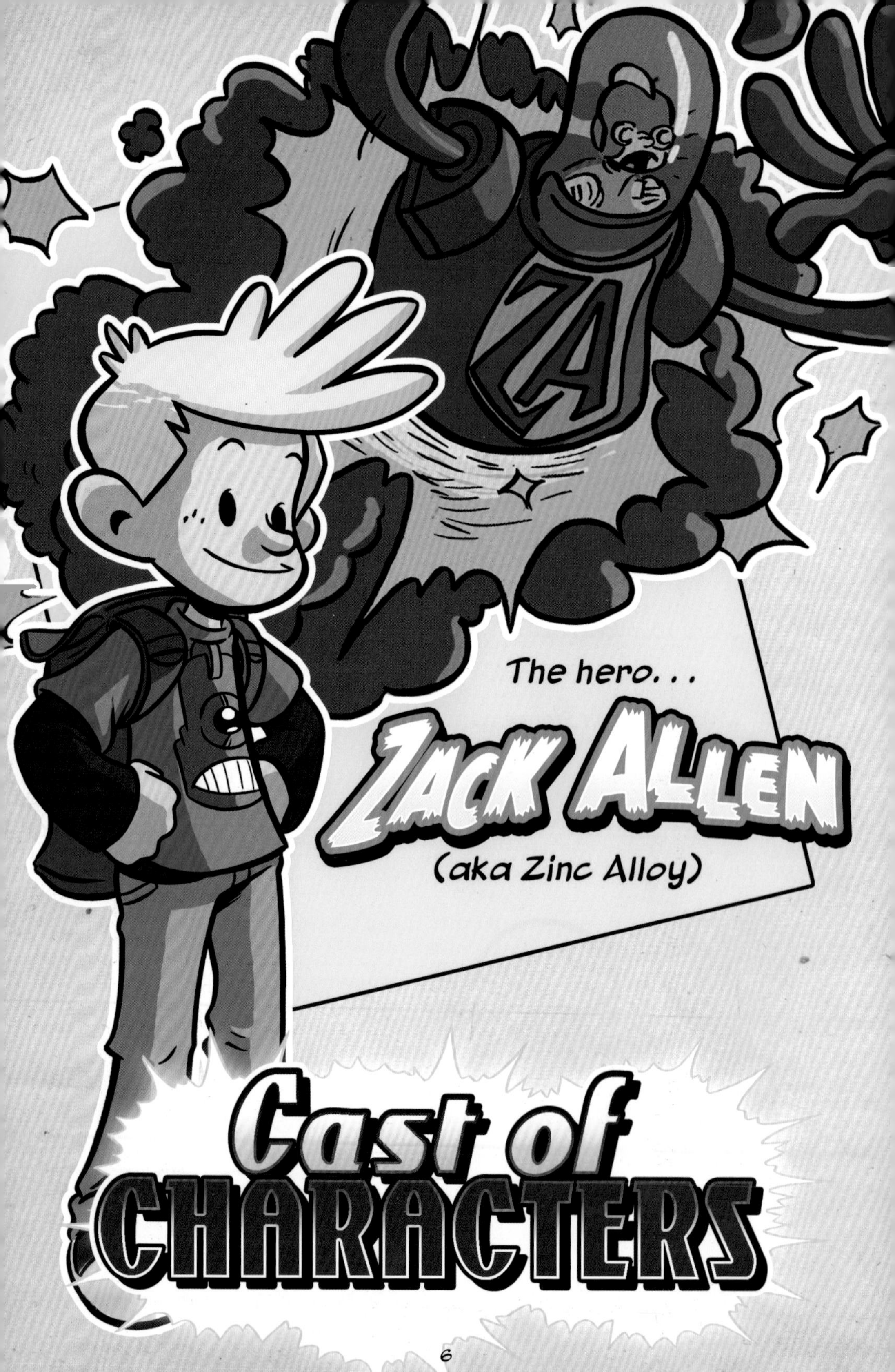
The hero...
ZACK ALLEN
(aka Zinc Alloy)
Cast of
CHARACTERS

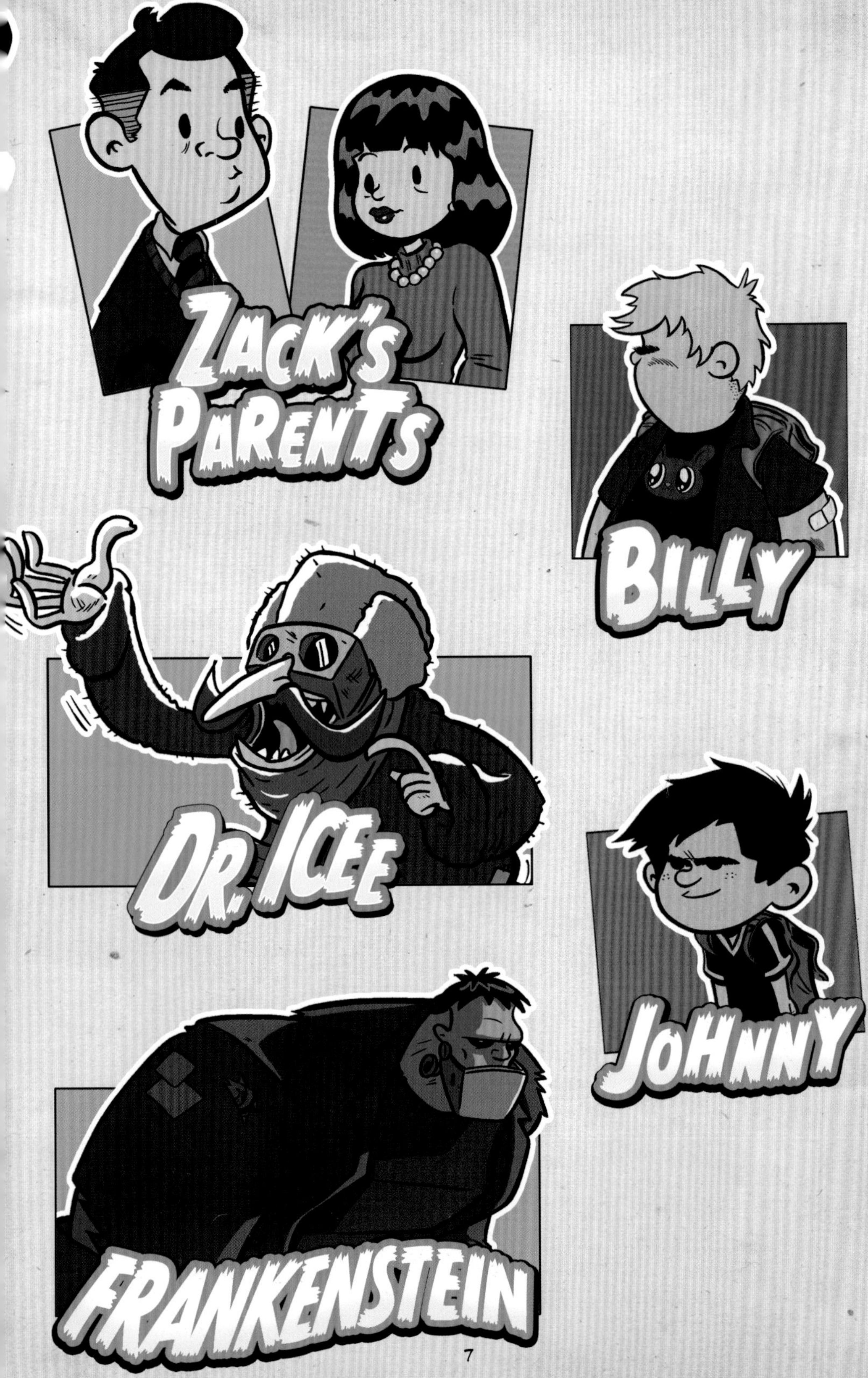
ZACK'S PARENTS
BILLY
DR. ICEE
JOHNNY
FRANKENSTEIN

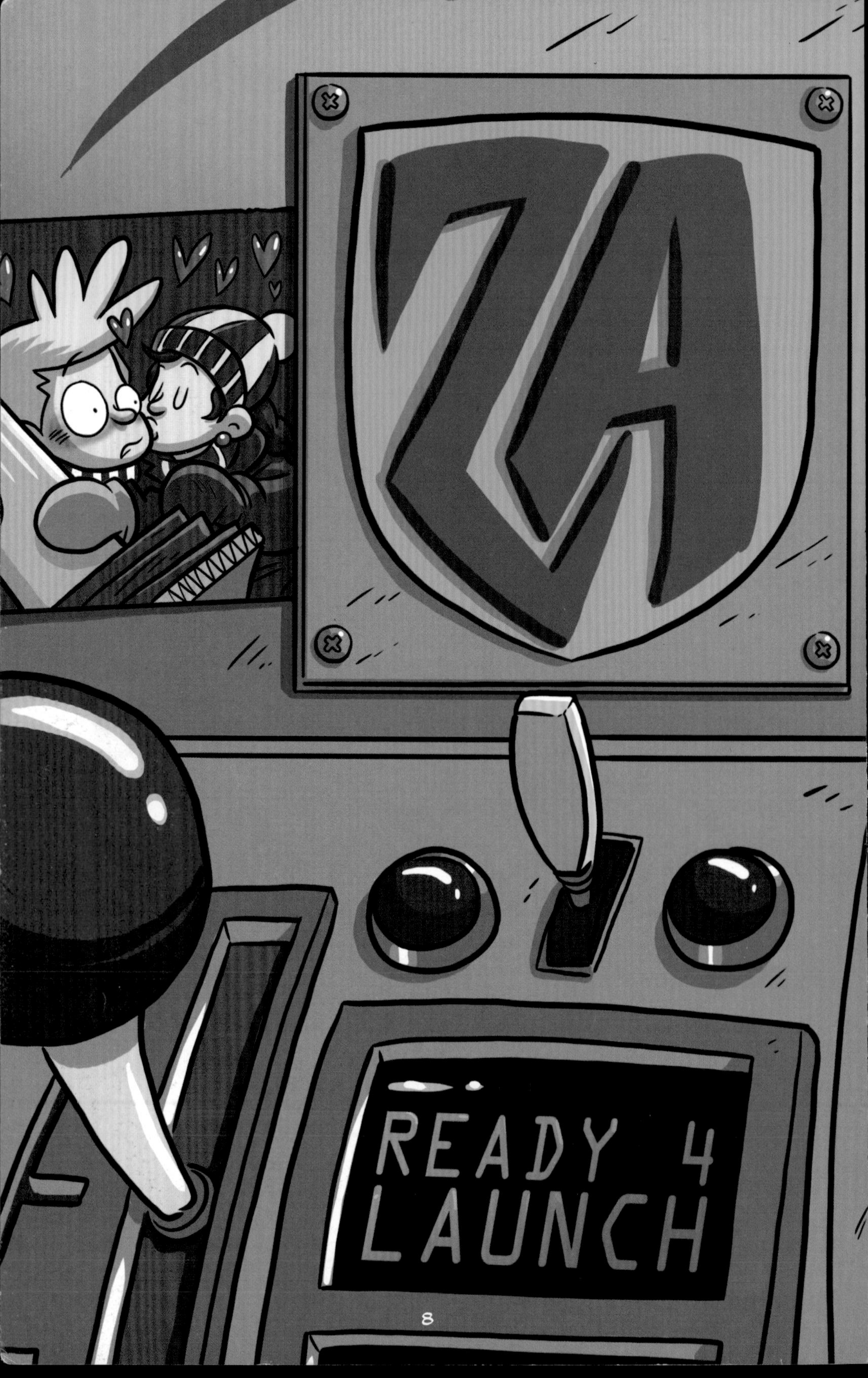
ZA
READY 4 LAUNCH

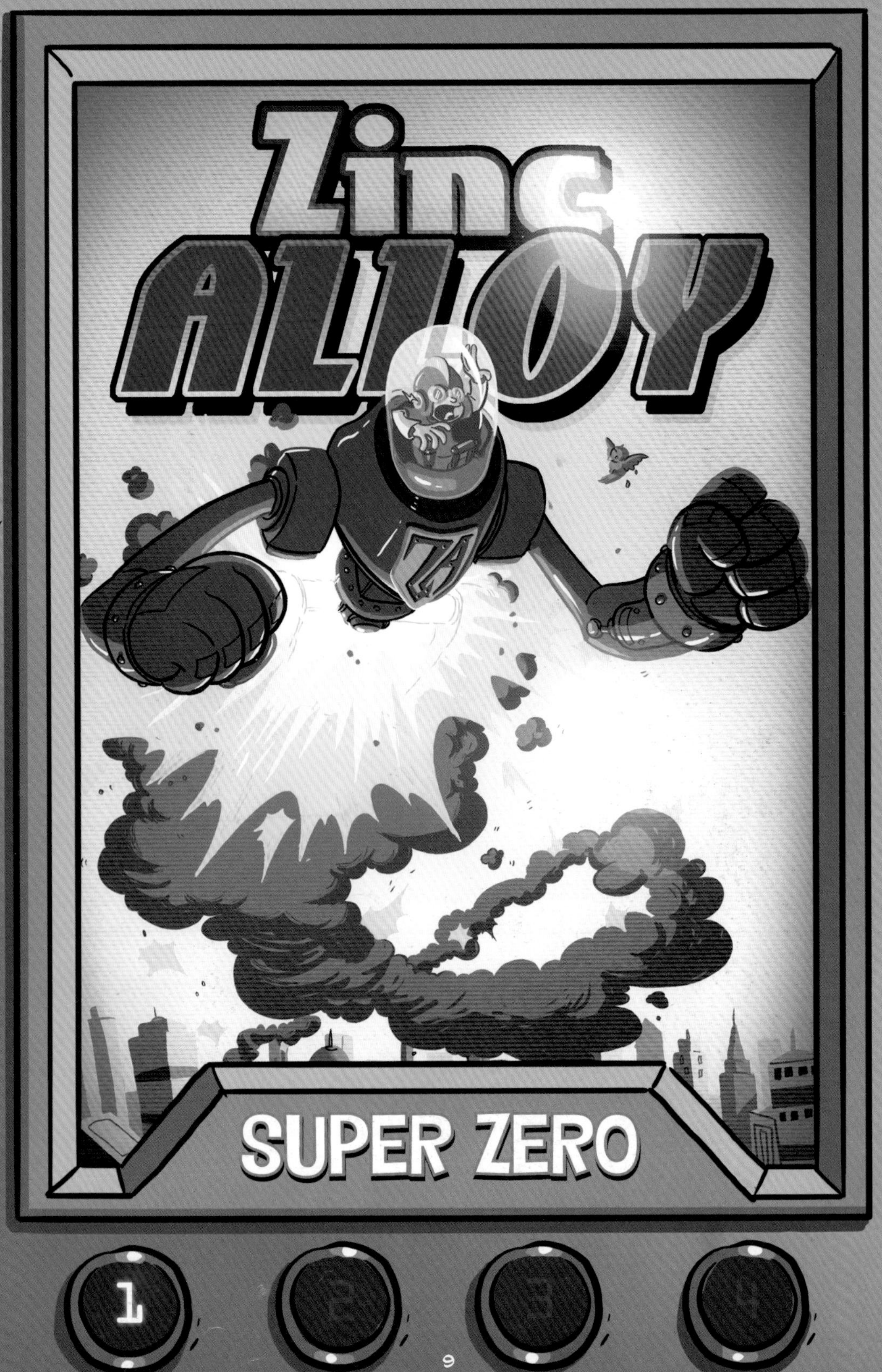
Zinc ALLOY
SUPER ZERO
1
2
3
4

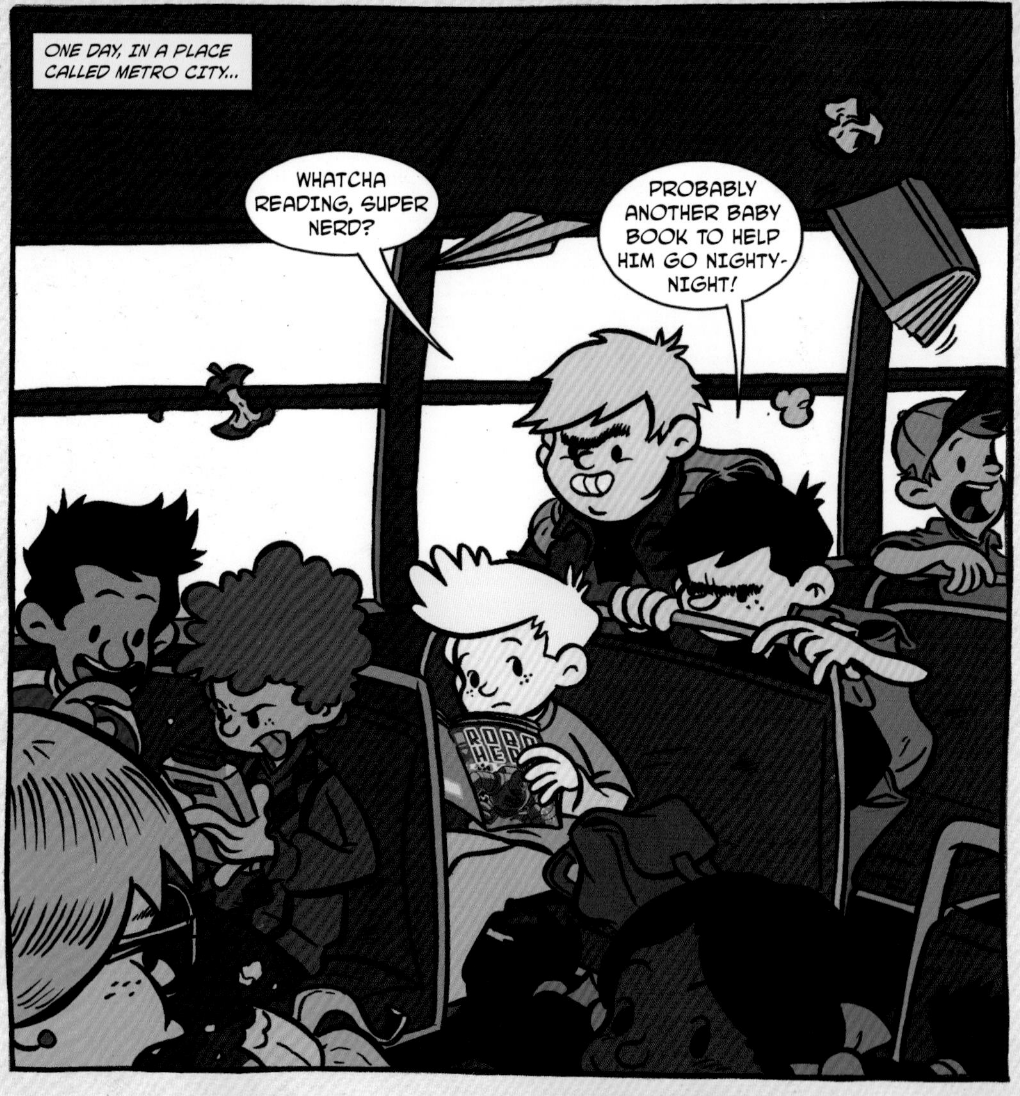
ONE DAY, IN A PLACE CALLED METRO CITY...
WHATCHA READING, SUPER NERD?
PROBABLY ANOTHER BABY BOOK TO HELP HIM GO NIGHTY-NIGHT!

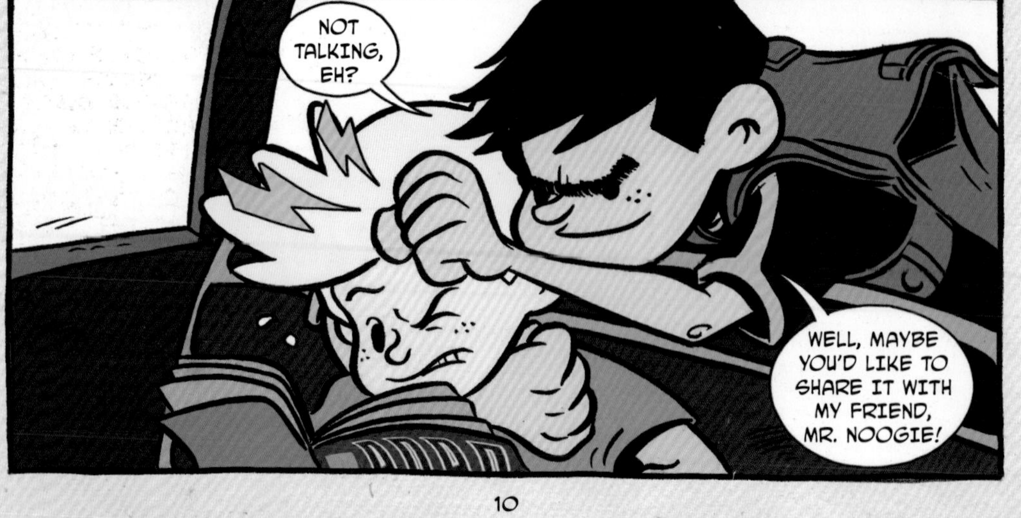
NOT TALKING, EH?
WELL, MAYBE YOU'D LIKE TO SHARE IT WITH MY FRIEND, MR. NOOGIE!

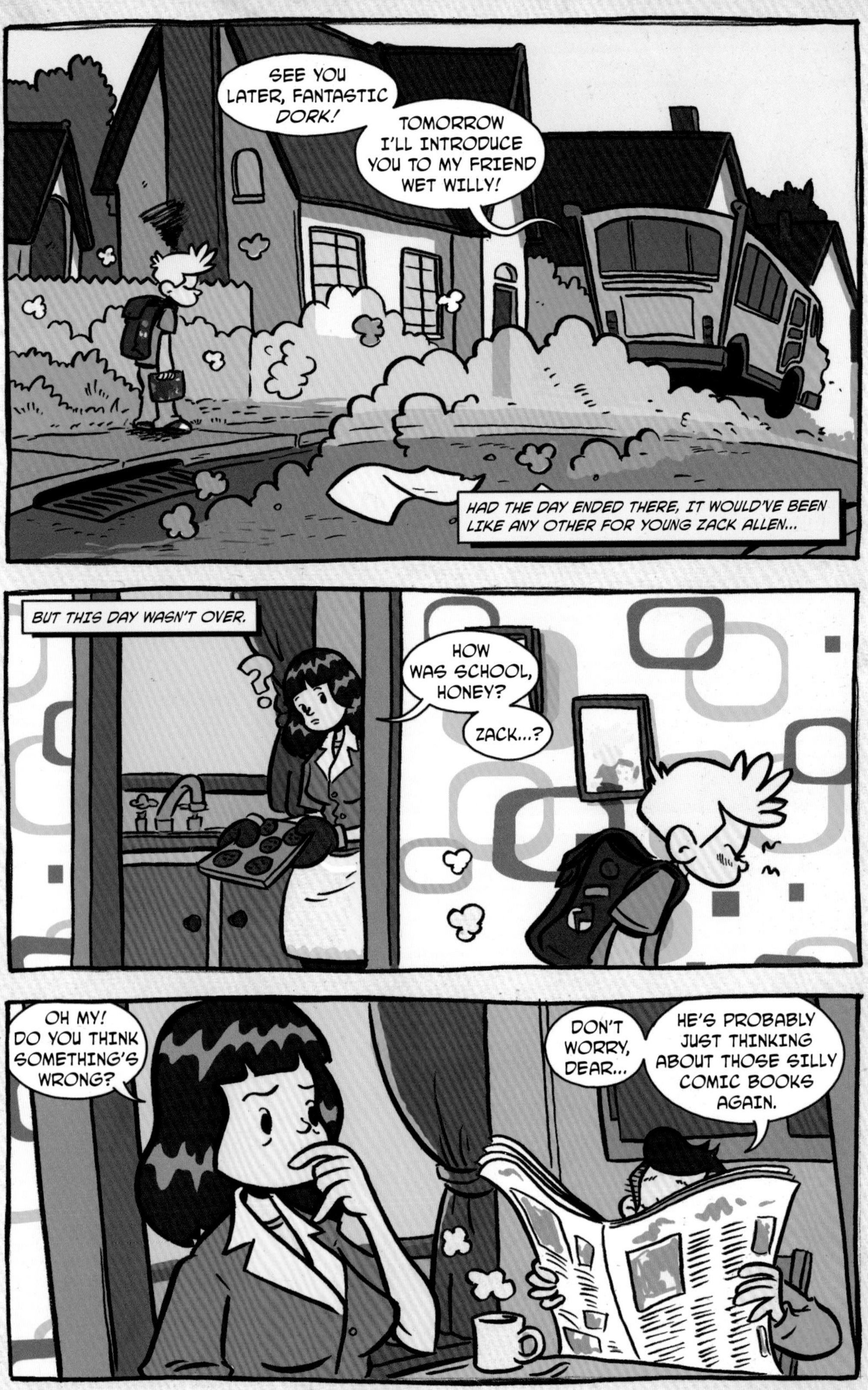

SEE YOU LATER, FANTASTIC *DORK!*
TOMORROW I'LL INTRODUCE YOU TO MY FRIEND WET WILLY!
HAD THE DAY ENDED THERE, IT WOULD'VE BEEN LIKE ANY OTHER FOR YOUNG ZACK ALLEN...
BUT THIS DAY WASN'T OVER.
HOW WAS SCHOOL, HONEY?
ZACK...?
OH MY! DO YOU THINK SOMETHING'S WRONG?
DON'T WORRY, DEAR...
HE'S PROBABLY JUST THINKING ABOUT THOSE SILLY COMIC BOOKS AGAIN.

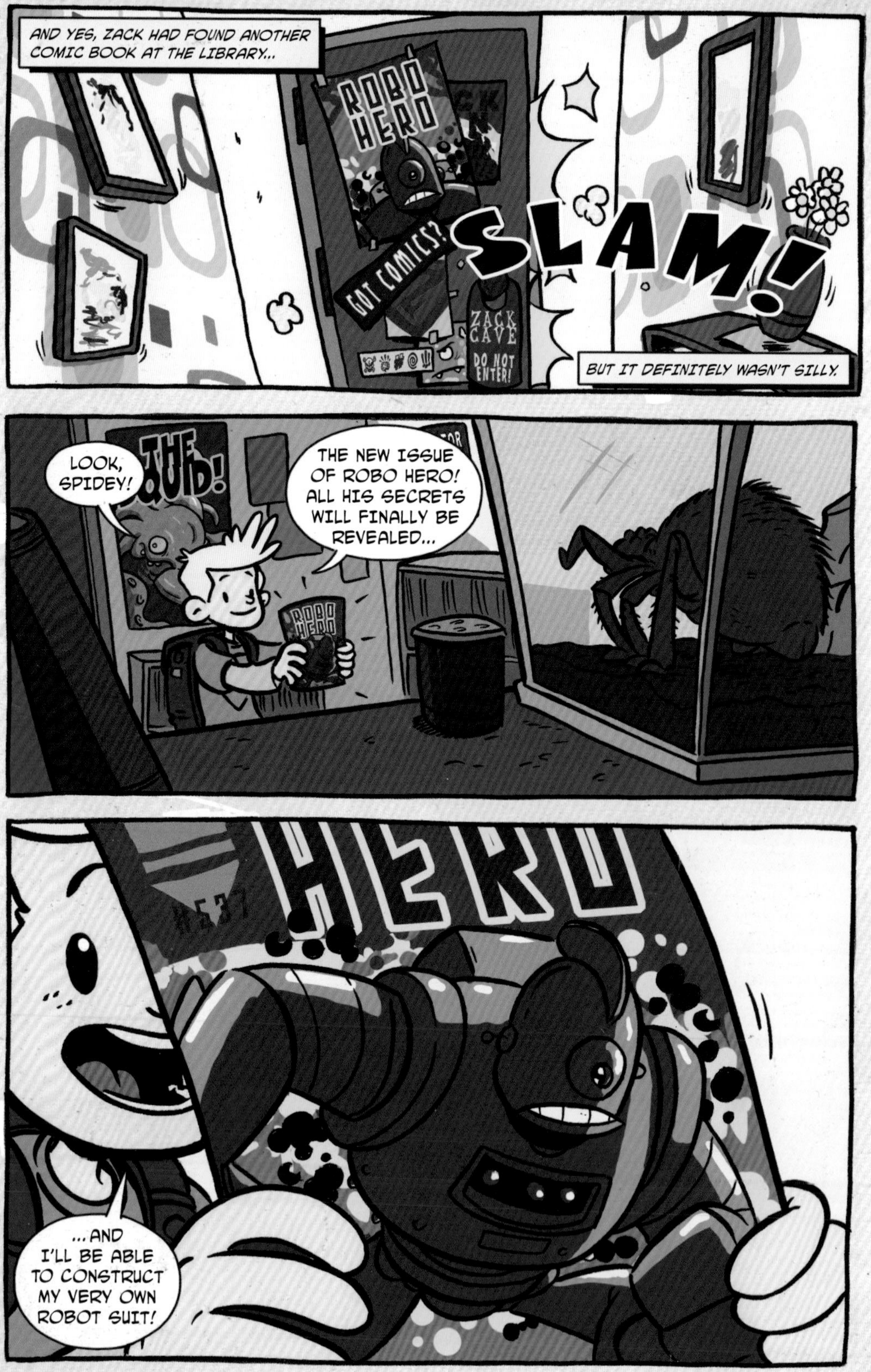

AND YES, ZACK HAD FOUND ANOTHER COMIC BOOK AT THE LIBRARY...
ROBO HERO
GOT COMICS?
ZACK CAVE DO NOT ENTER!
SLAM!
BUT IT DEFINITELY WASN'T SILLY.
LOOK, SPIDEY!
THE NEW ISSUE OF ROBO HERO! ALL HIS SECRETS WILL FINALLY BE REVEALED...
ROBO HERO
HERO
...AND I'LL BE ABLE TO CONSTRUCT MY VERY OWN ROBOT SUIT!

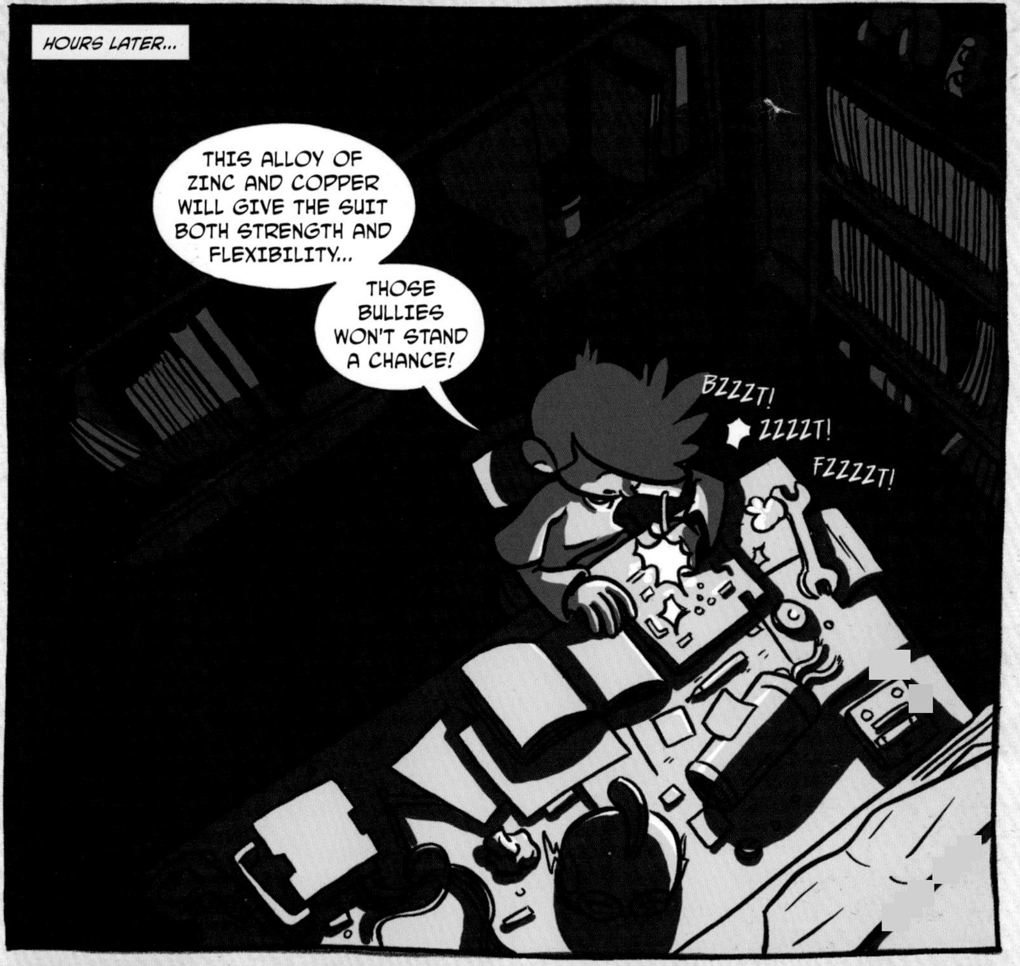
HOURS LATER...
THIS ALLOY OF ZINC AND COPPER WILL GIVE THE SUIT BOTH STRENGTH AND FLEXIBILITY...
THOSE BULLIES WON'T STAND A CHANCE!
BZZZT!
ZZZZT!
FZZZZT!

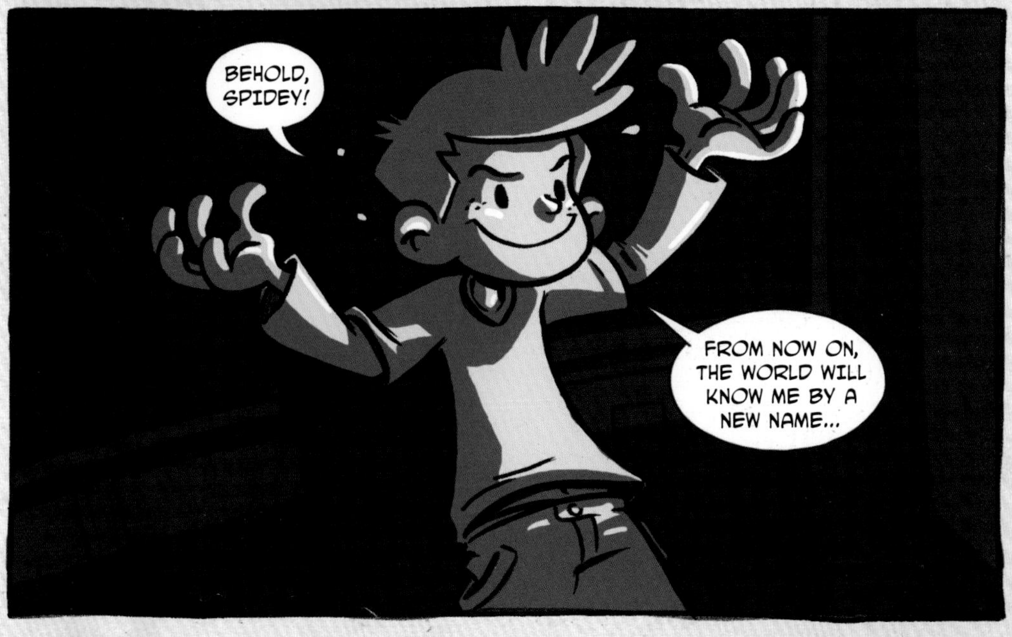
BEHOLD, SPIDEY!
FROM NOW ON, THE WORLD WILL KNOW ME BY A NEW NAME...

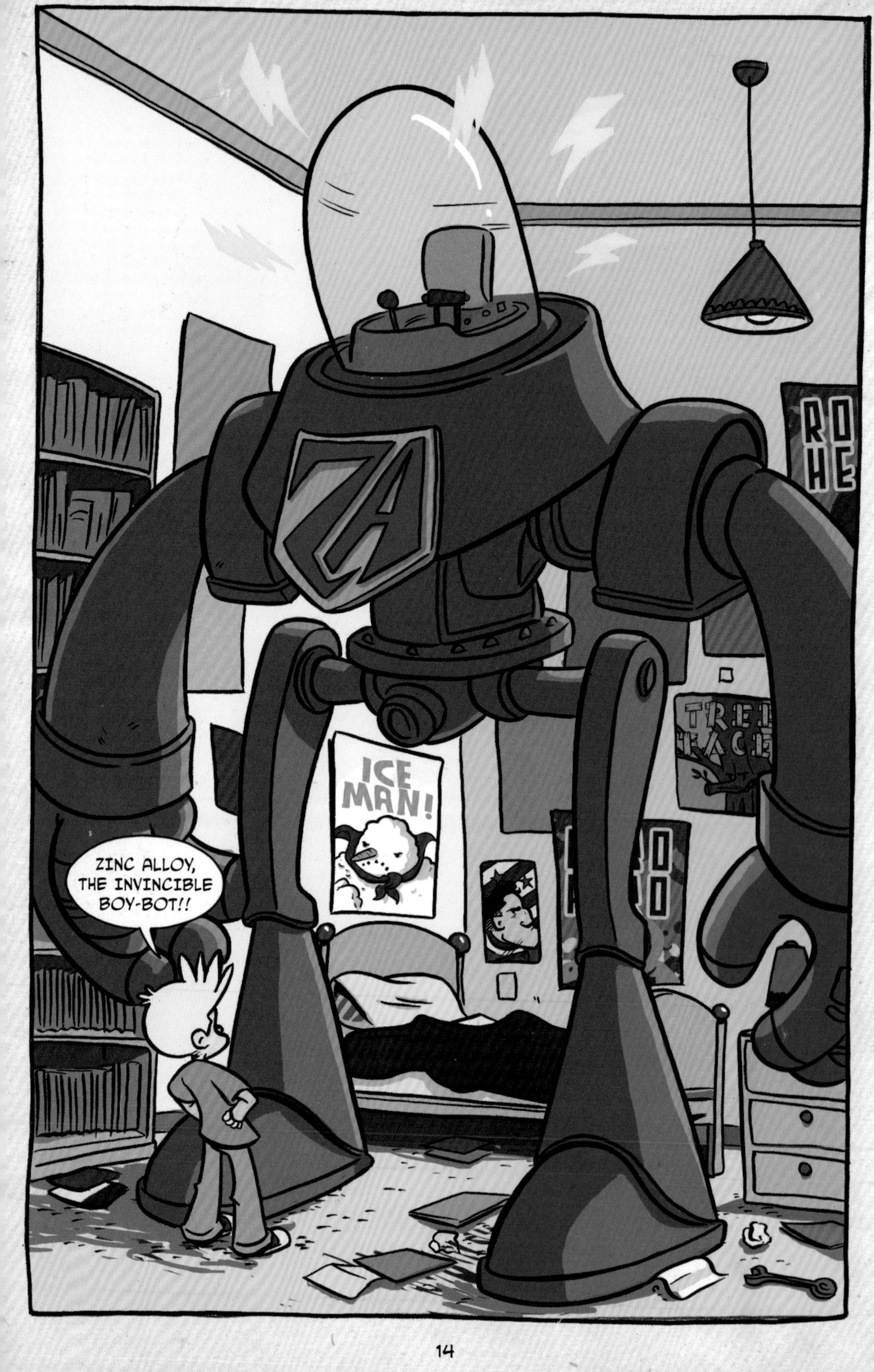
ZINC ALLOY, THE INVINCIBLE BOY-BOT!!
ICE MAN!

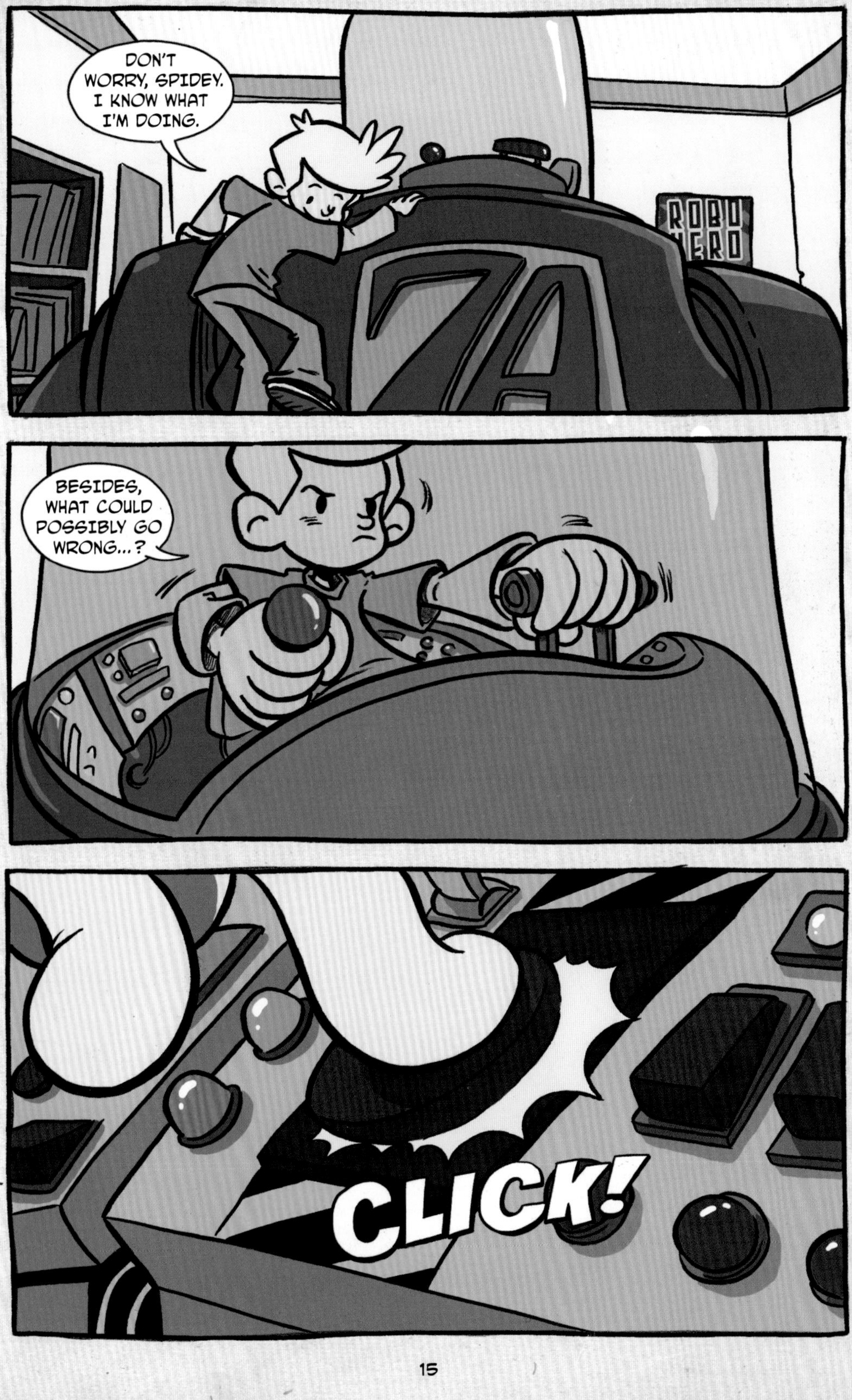
DON'T WORRY, SPIDEY. I KNOW WHAT I'M DOING.
ROBU
BESIDES, WHAT COULD POSSIBLY GO WRONG...?
CLICK!

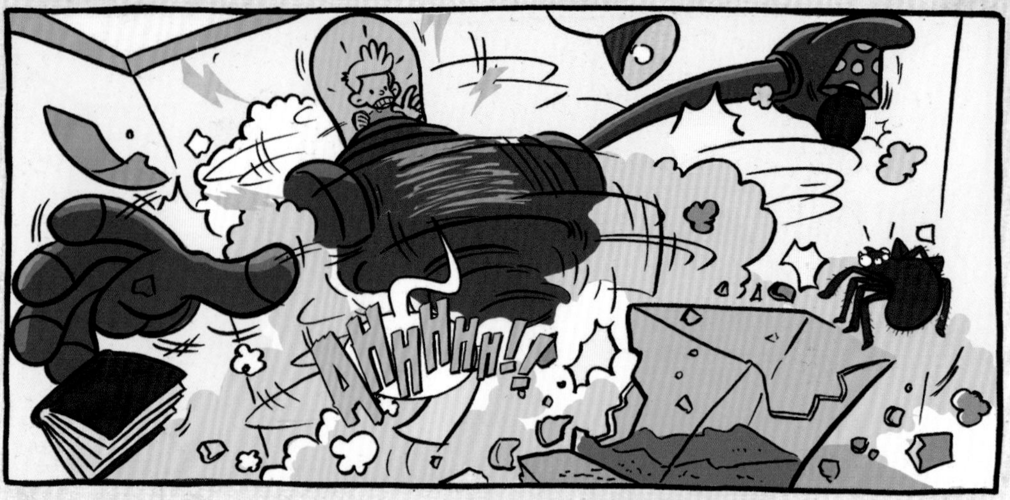
AHHHHH!!

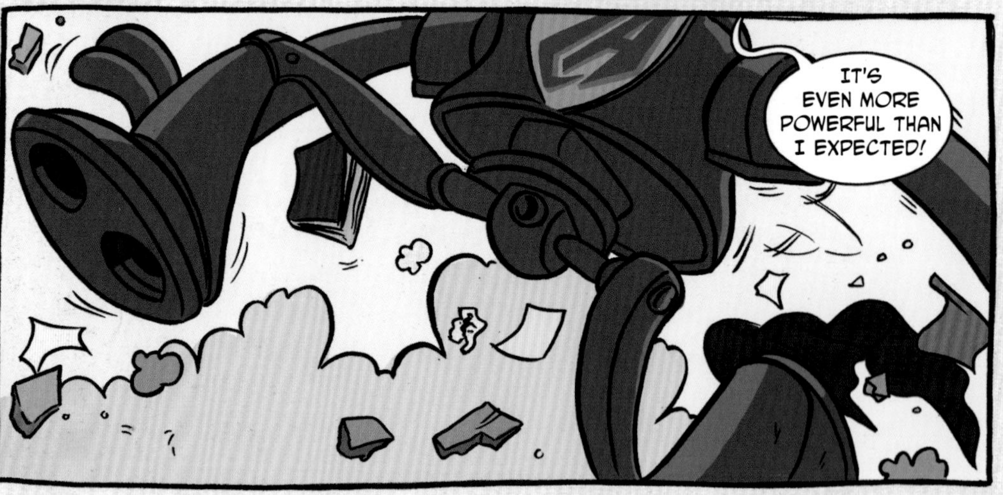
IT'S EVEN MORE POWERFUL THAN I EXPECTED!

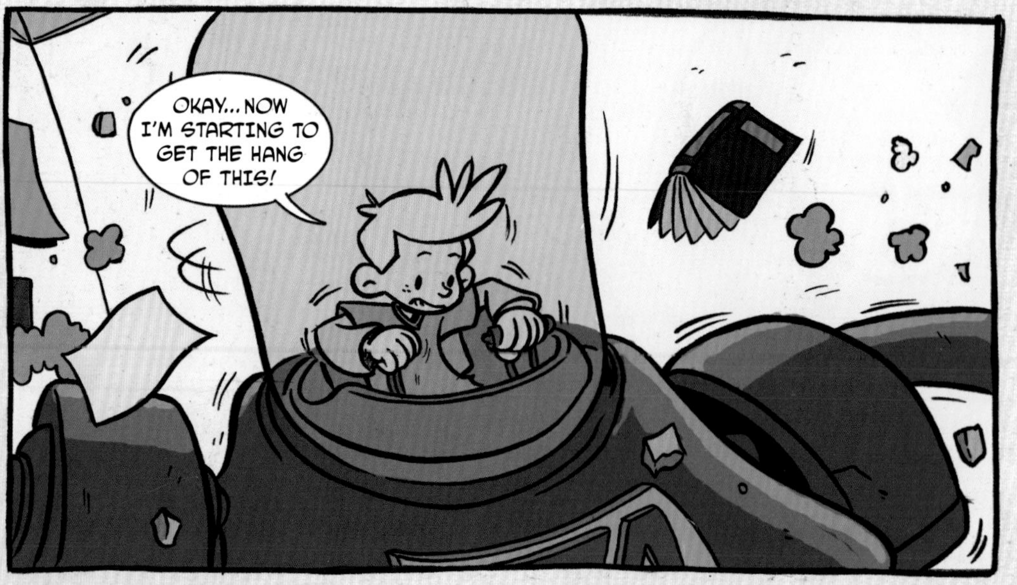
OKAY... NOW I'M STARTING TO GET THE HANG OF THIS!

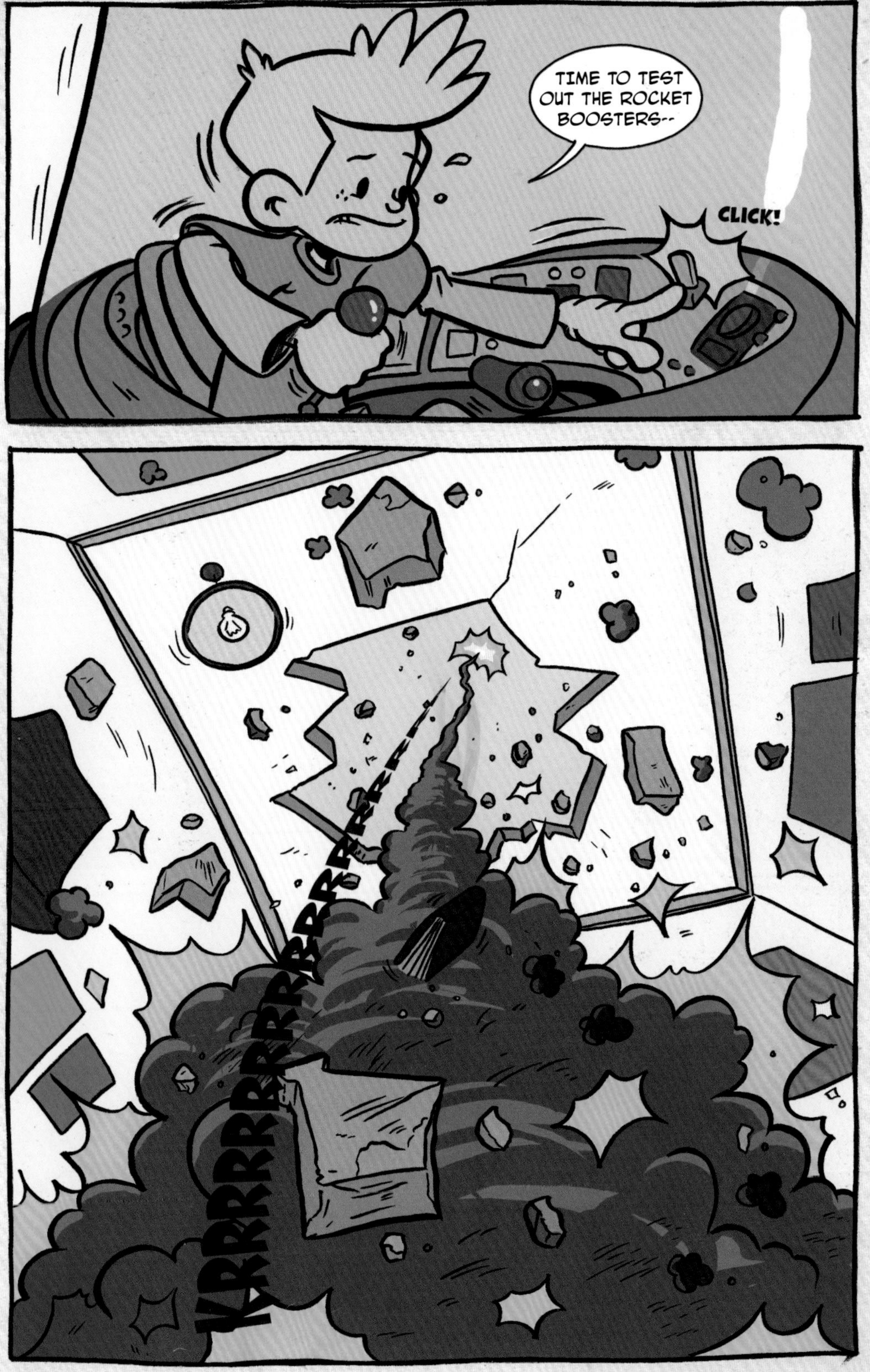
TIME TO TEST OUT THE ROCKET BOOSTERS--
CLICK!

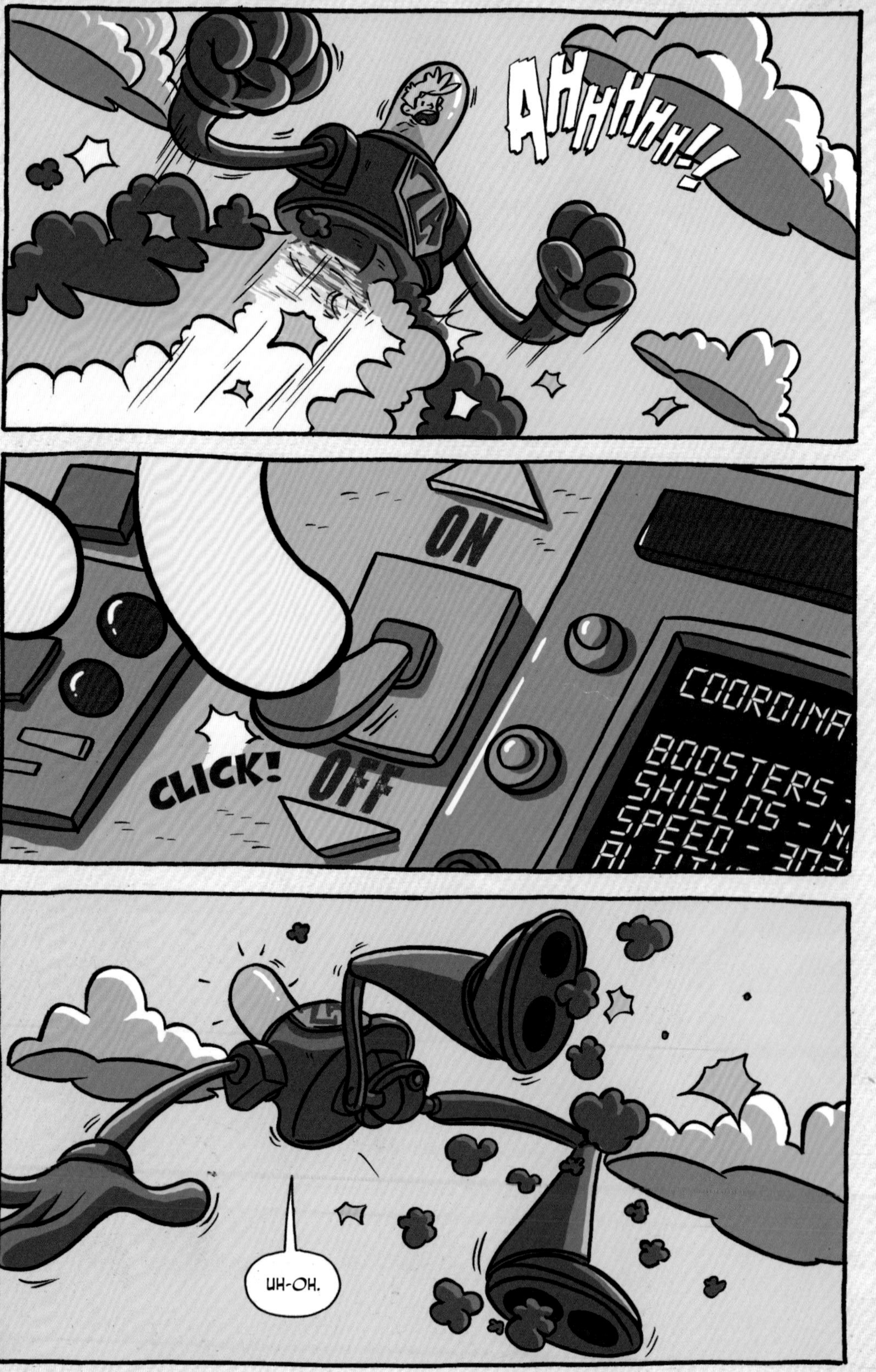
AHHHHHH!!
ON
OFF
CLICK!
COORDINA
BOOSTERS -
SHIELDS -
SPEED -
UH-OH.

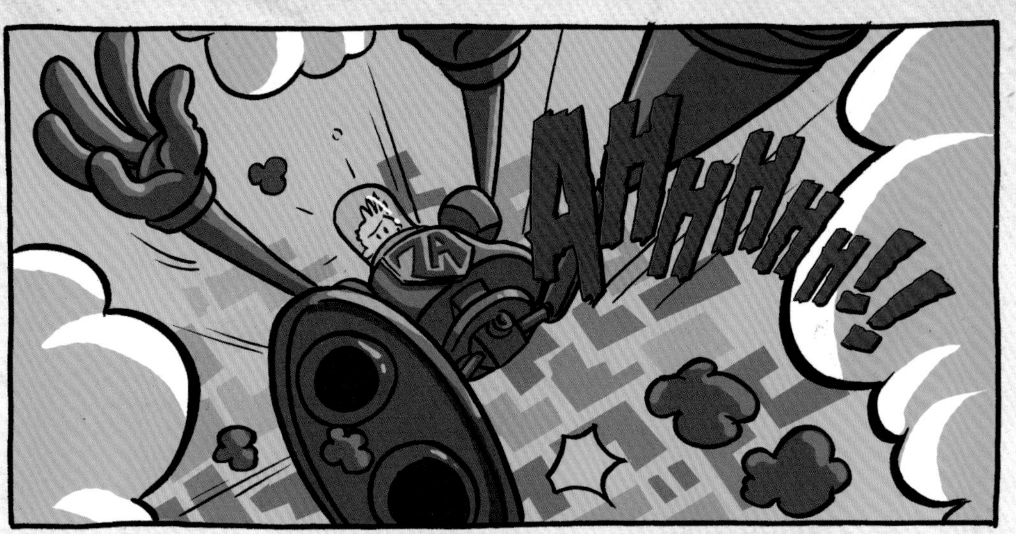
AHHHHH!!!

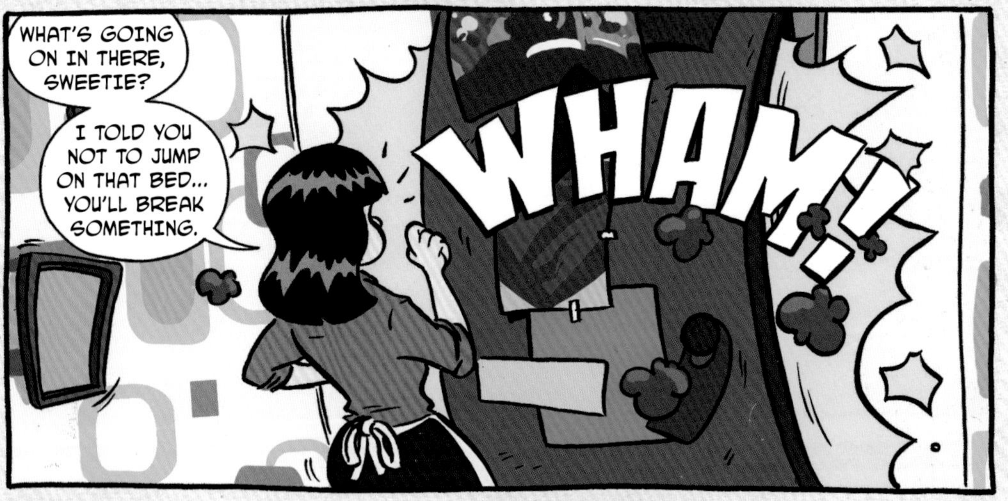
WHAT'S GOING ON IN THERE, SWEETIE?
I TOLD YOU NOT TO JUMP ON THAT BED... YOU'LL BREAK SOMETHING.
WHAM!!

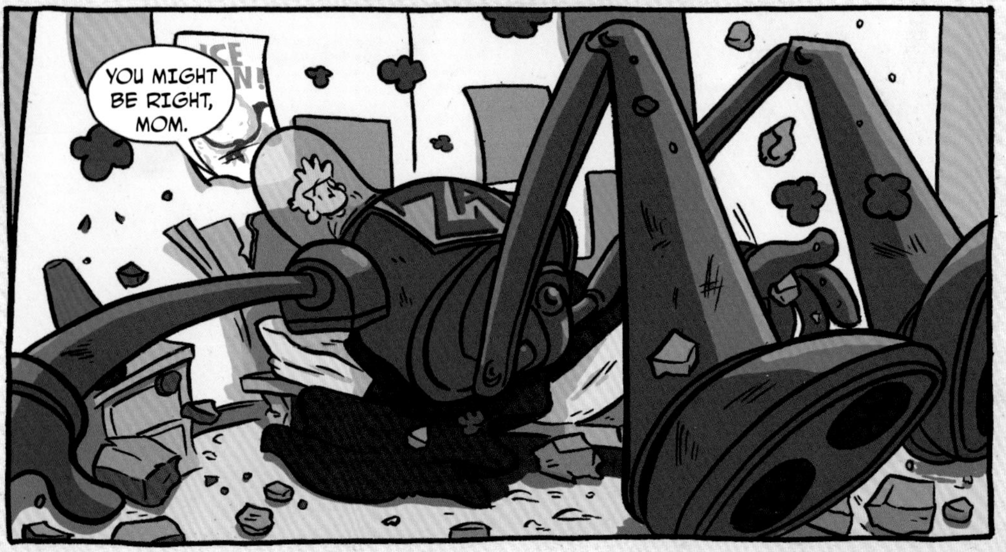
YOU MIGHT BE RIGHT, MOM.

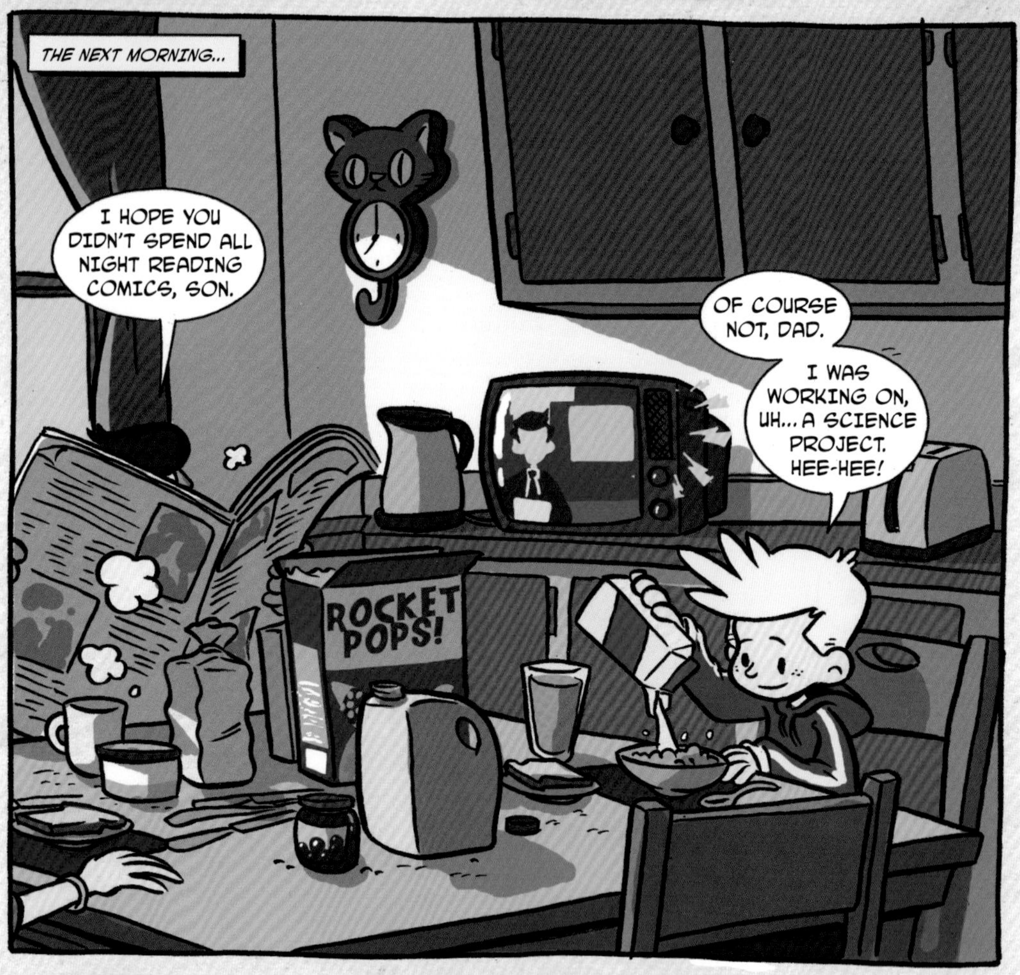
THE NEXT MORNING...
I HOPE YOU DIDN'T SPEND ALL NIGHT READING COMICS, SON.
OF COURSE NOT, DAD.
I WAS WORKING ON, UH... A SCIENCE PROJECT. HEE-HEE!
ROCKET POPS!

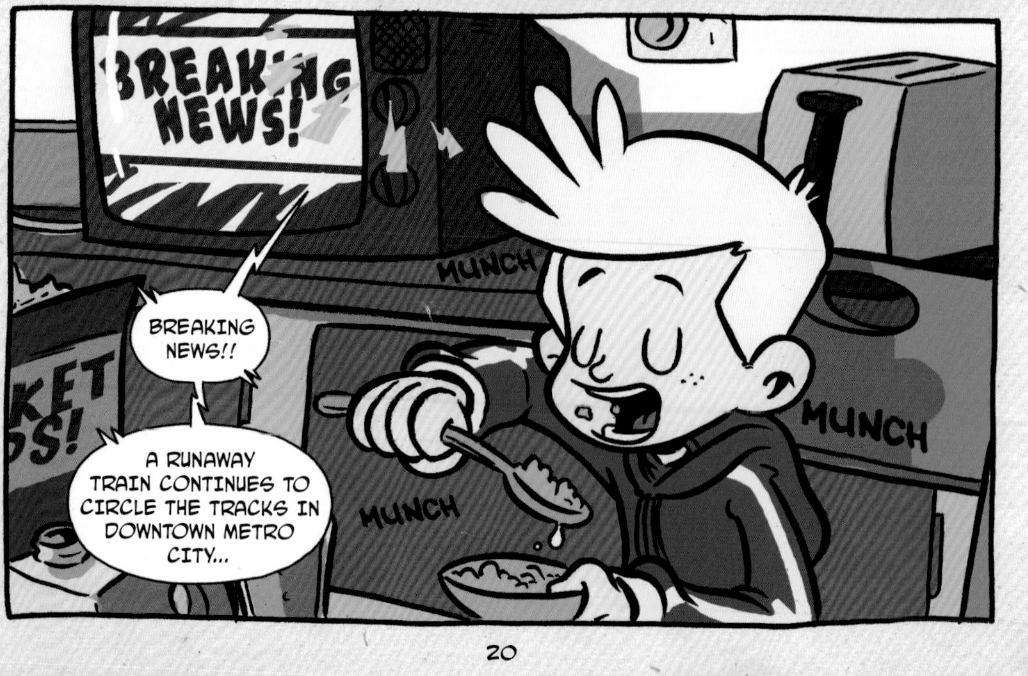
BREAKING NEWS!
MUNCH
BREAKING NEWS!!
MUNCH
A RUNAWAY TRAIN CONTINUES TO CIRCLE THE TRACKS IN DOWNTOWN METRO CITY...
MUNCH

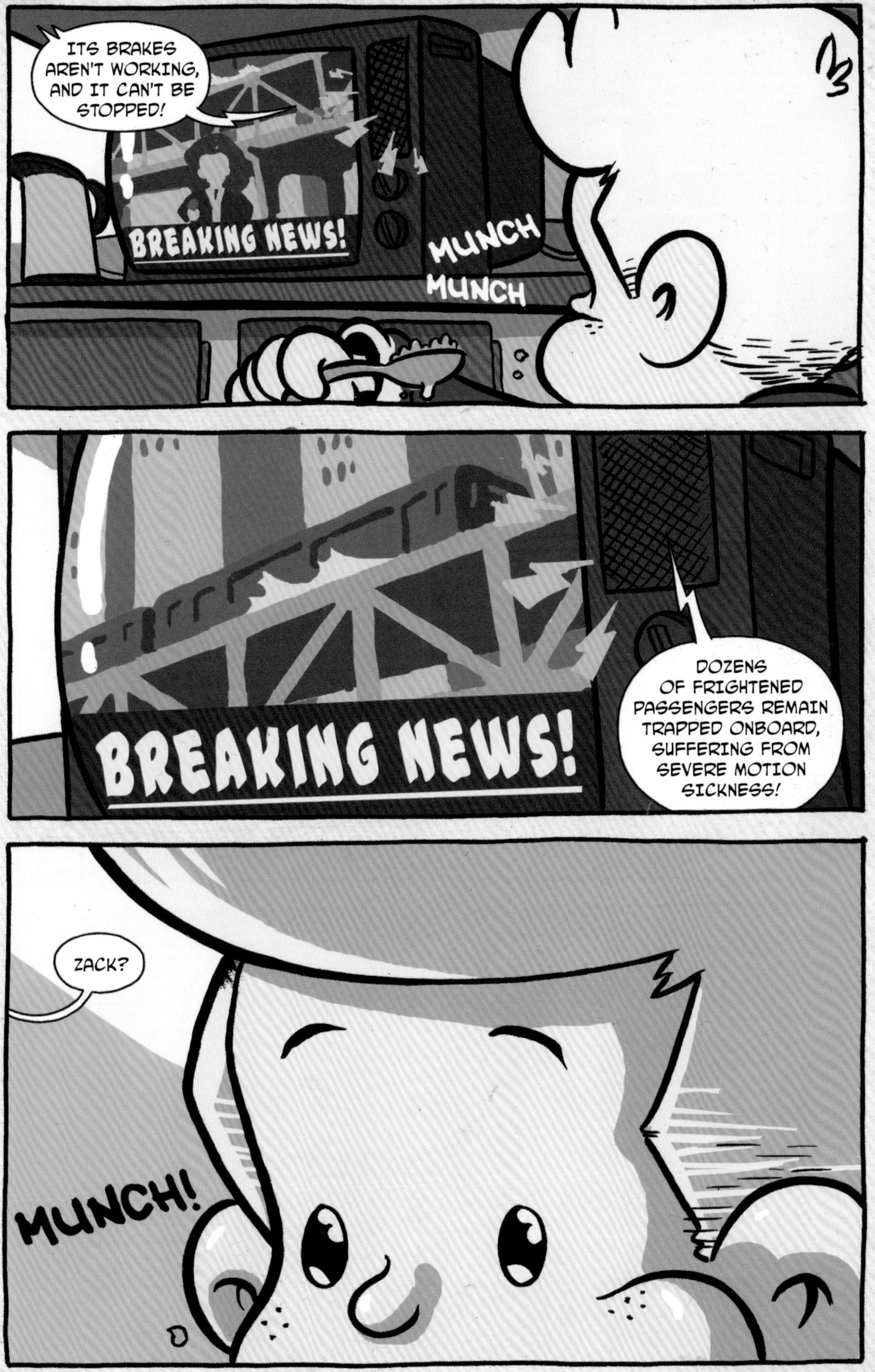
ITS BRAKES AREN'T WORKING, AND IT CAN'T BE STOPPED!
BREAKING NEWS!
MUNCH
MUNCH
BREAKING NEWS!
DOZENS OF FRIGHTENED PASSENGERS REMAIN TRAPPED ONBOARD, SUFFERING FROM SEVERE MOTION SICKNESS!
ZACK?
MUNCH!

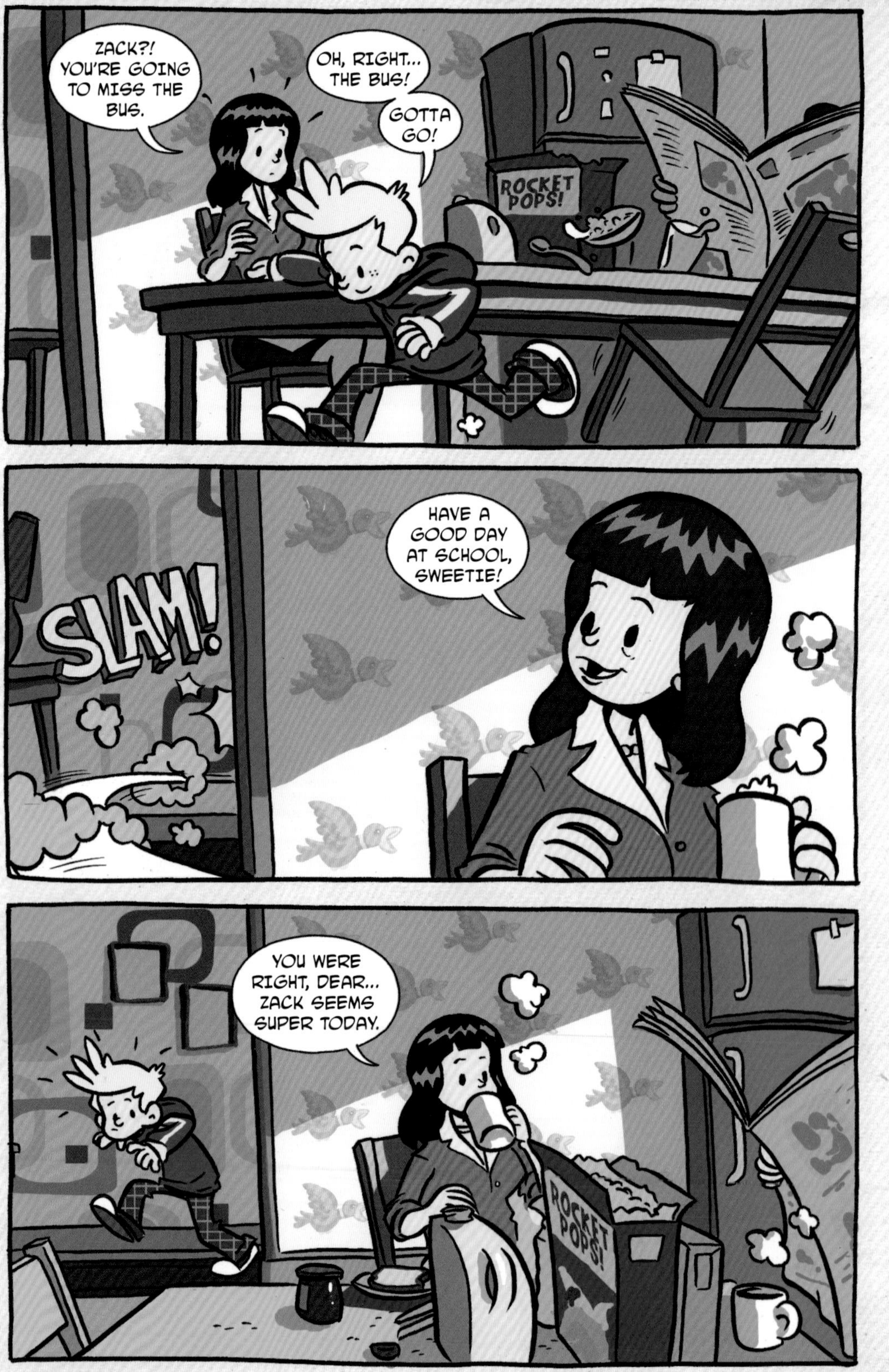
ZACK?! YOU'RE GOING TO MISS THE BUS.
OH, RIGHT... THE BUS!
GOTTA GO!
ROCKET POPS!
SLAM!
HAVE A GOOD DAY AT SCHOOL, SWEETIE!
YOU WERE RIGHT, DEAR... ZACK SEEMS SUPER TODAY.
ROCKET POPS!

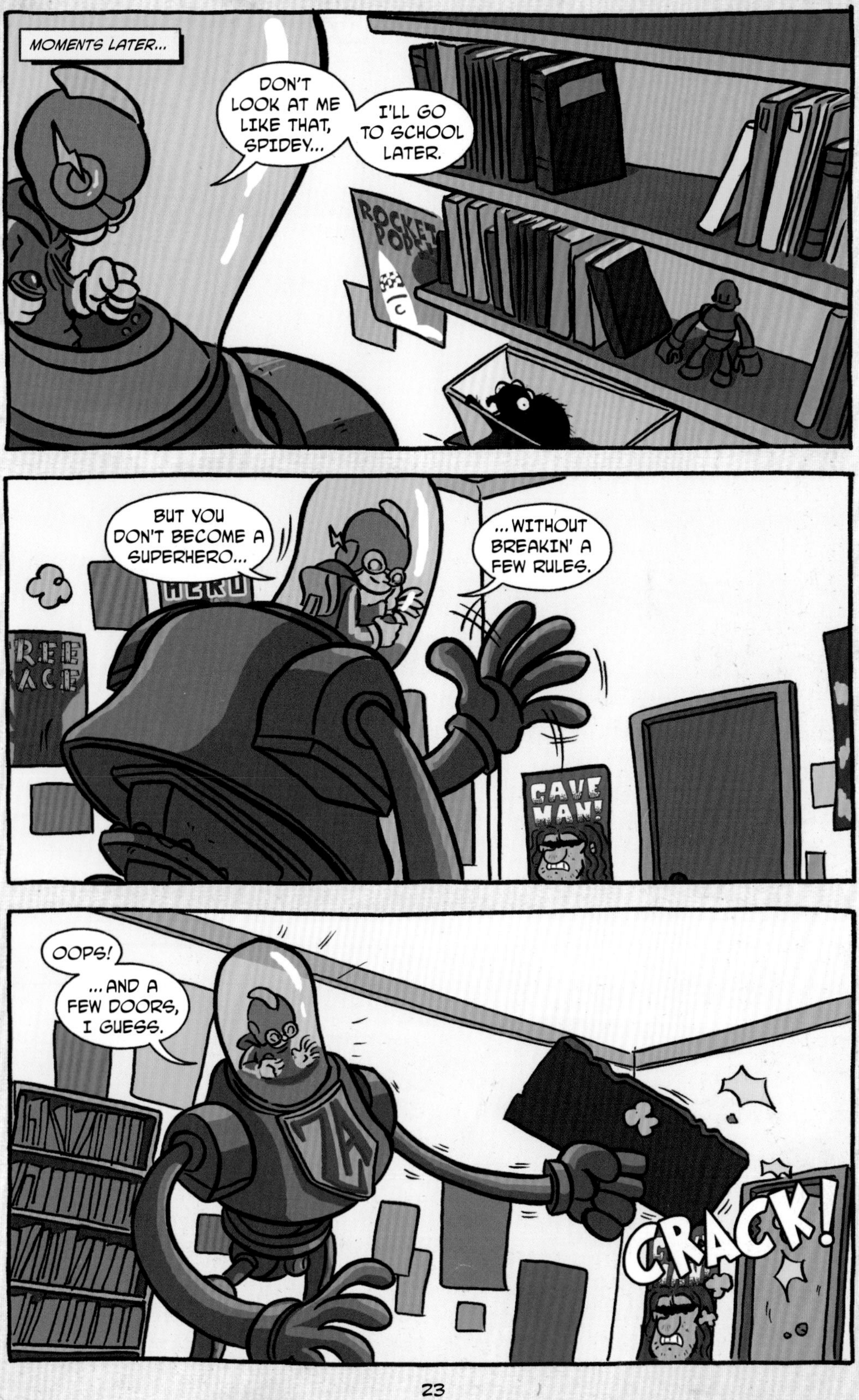
MOMENTS LATER...
DON'T LOOK AT ME LIKE THAT, SPIDEY...
I'LL GO TO SCHOOL LATER.
ROCKET POPS
BUT YOU DON'T BECOME A SUPERHERO...
...WITHOUT BREAKIN' A FEW RULES.
HERO
CAVE MAN!
OOPS!
...AND A FEW DOORS, I GUESS.
7A
CRACK!

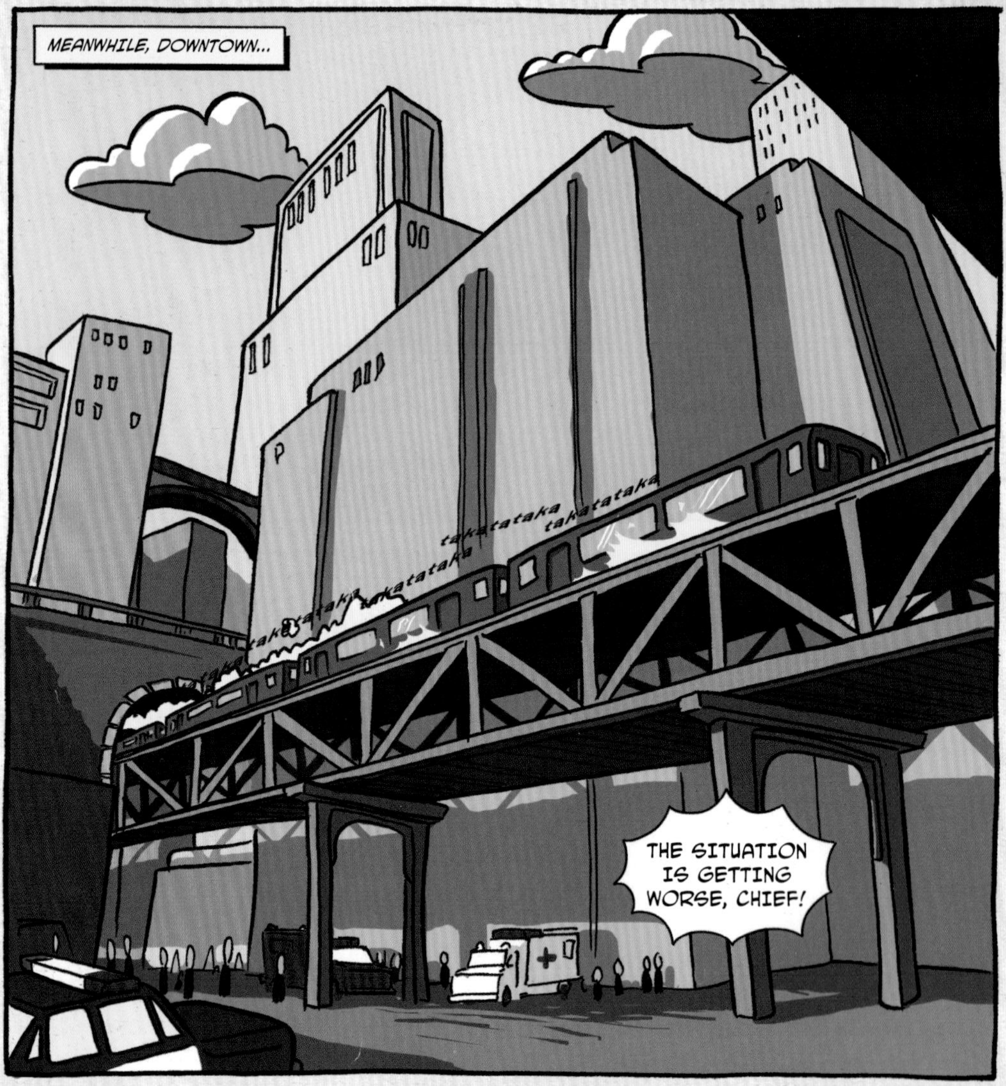
MEANWHILE, DOWNTOWN...
takatataka
THE SITUATION IS GETTING WORSE, CHIEF!

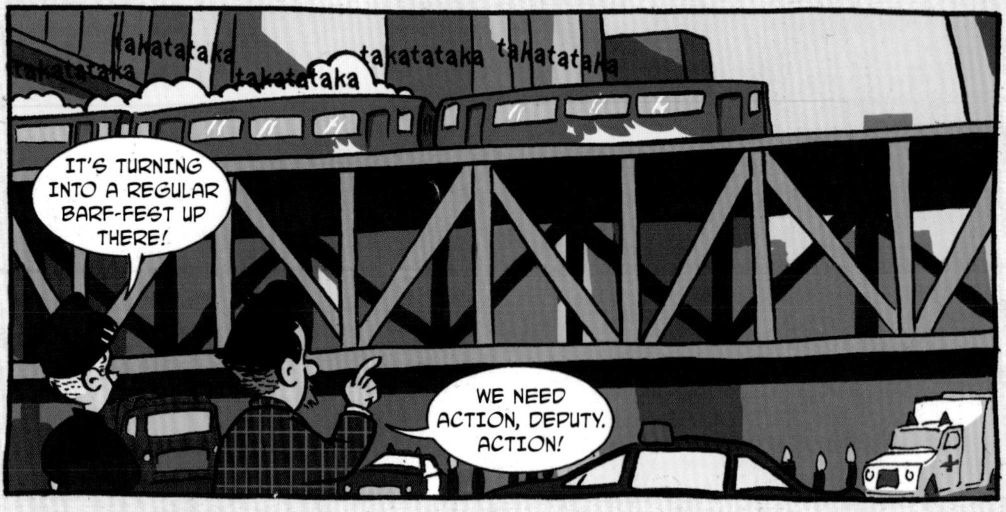
takatataka
IT'S TURNING INTO A REGULAR BARF-FEST UP THERE!
WE NEED ACTION, DEPUTY. ACTION!

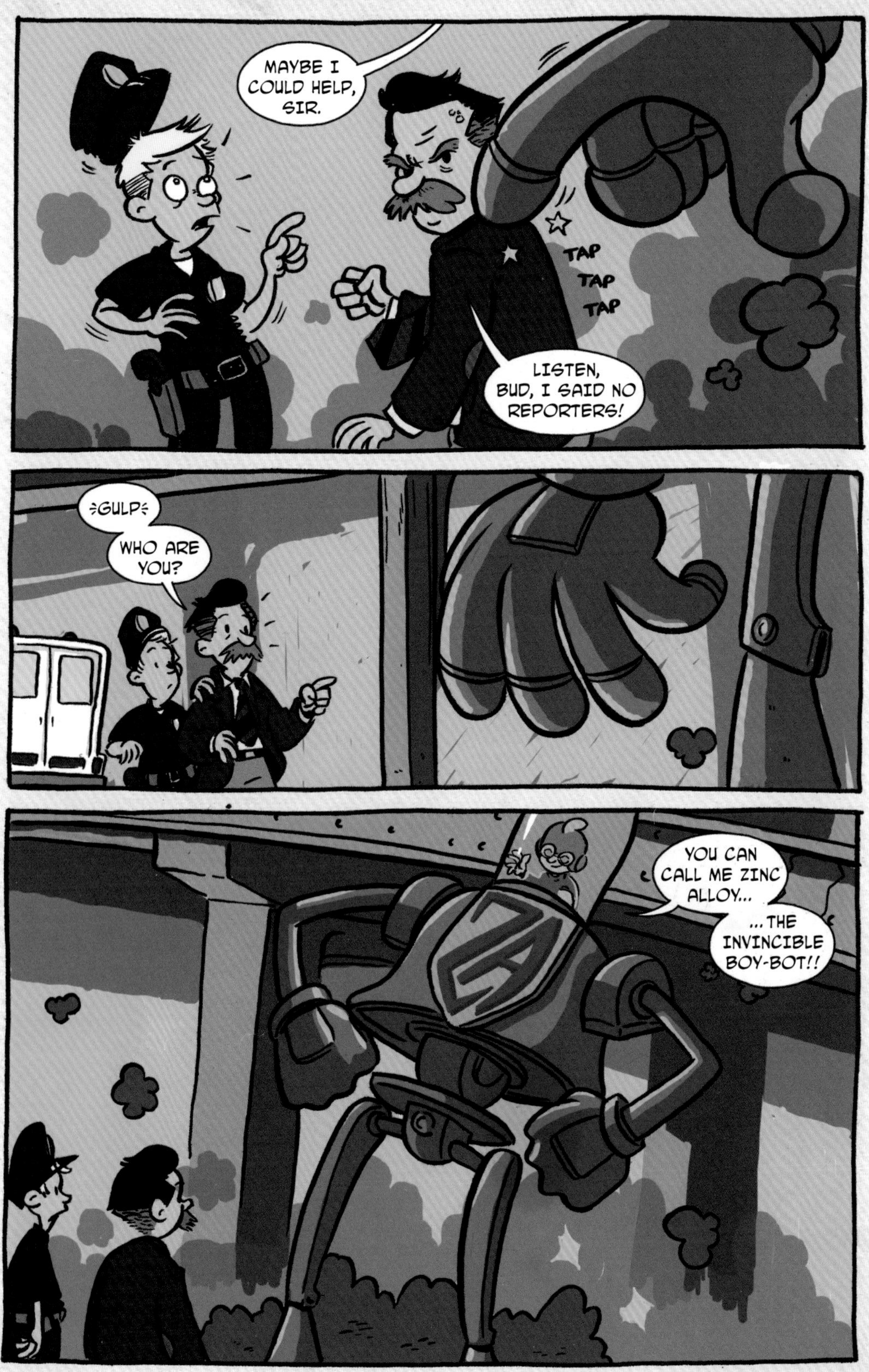
MAYBE I COULD HELP, SIR.
TAP
TAP
TAP
LISTEN, BUD, I SAID NO REPORTERS!
GULP
WHO ARE YOU?
YOU CAN CALL ME ZINC ALLOY...
...THE INVINCIBLE BOY-BOT!!

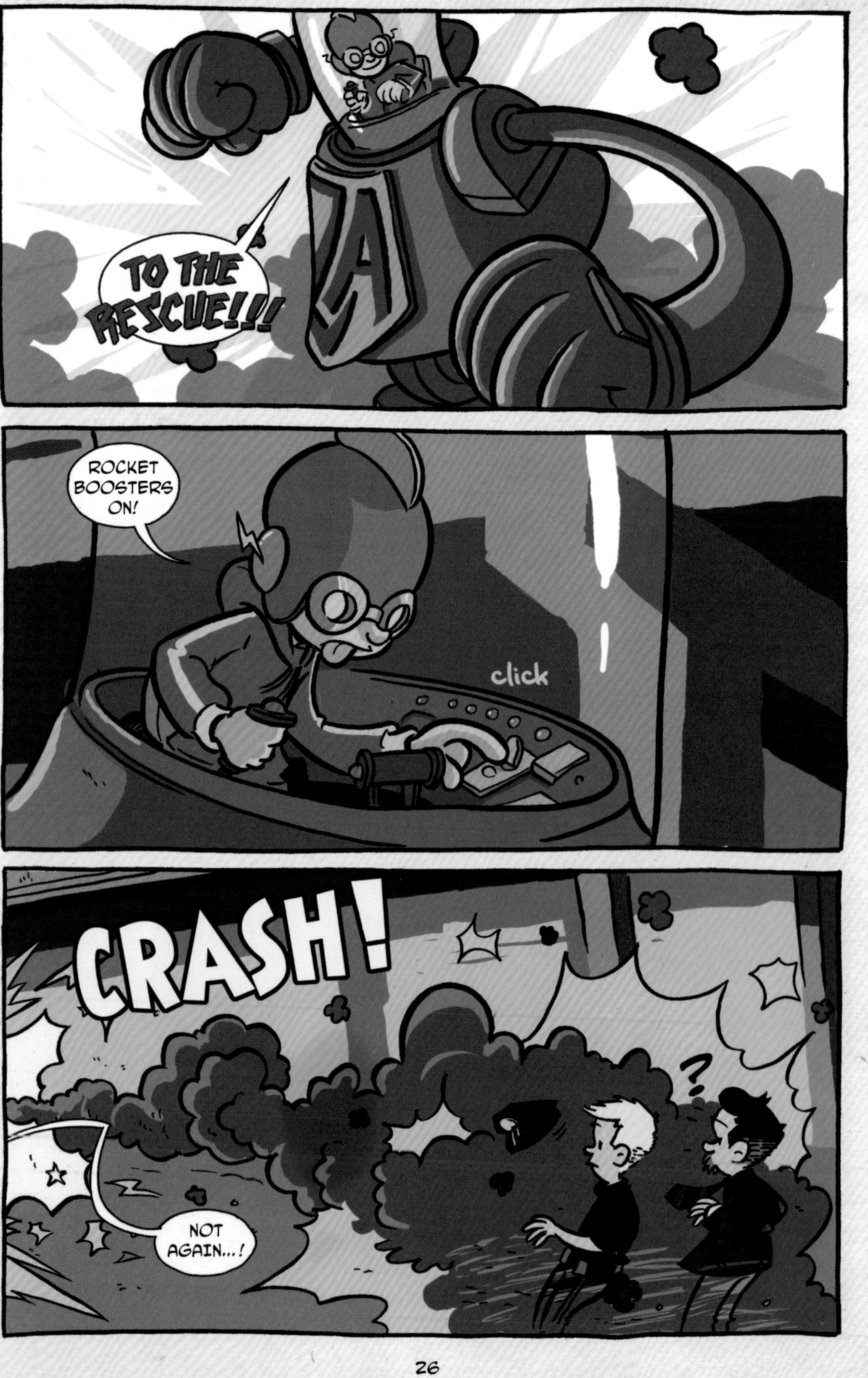

TO THE RESCUE!!!
ROCKET BOOSTERS ON!
click
CRASH!
?
NOT AGAIN...!

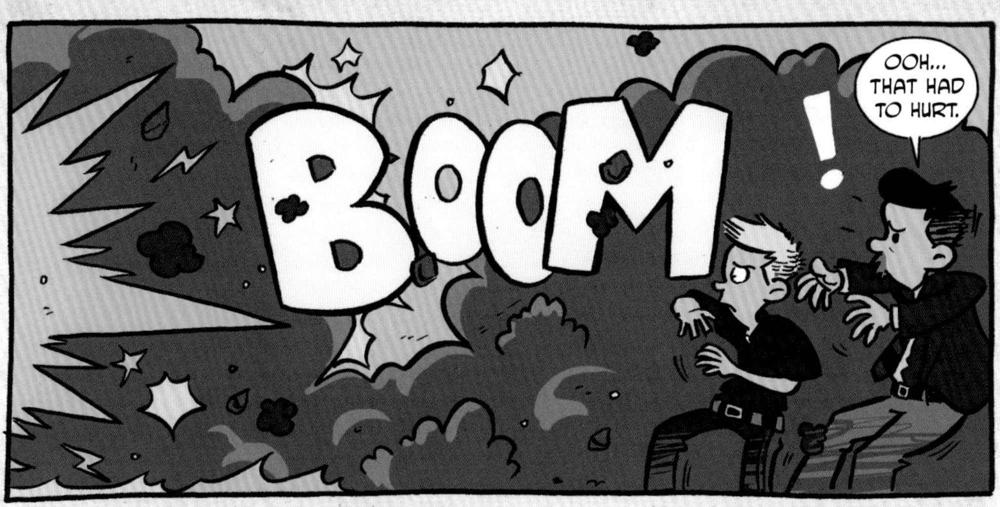
BOOM!
OOH... THAT HAD TO HURT.

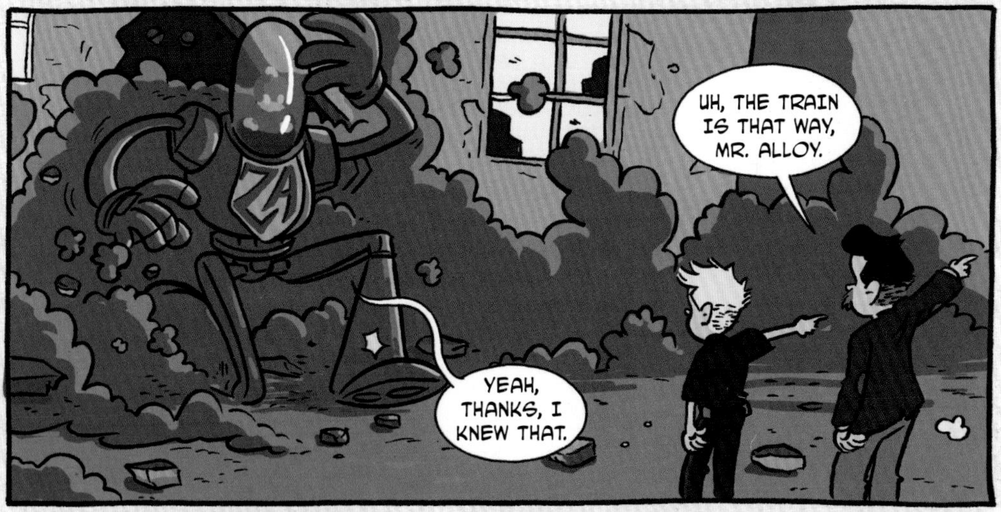
UH, THE TRAIN IS THAT WAY, MR. ALLOY.
YEAH, THANKS, I KNEW THAT.

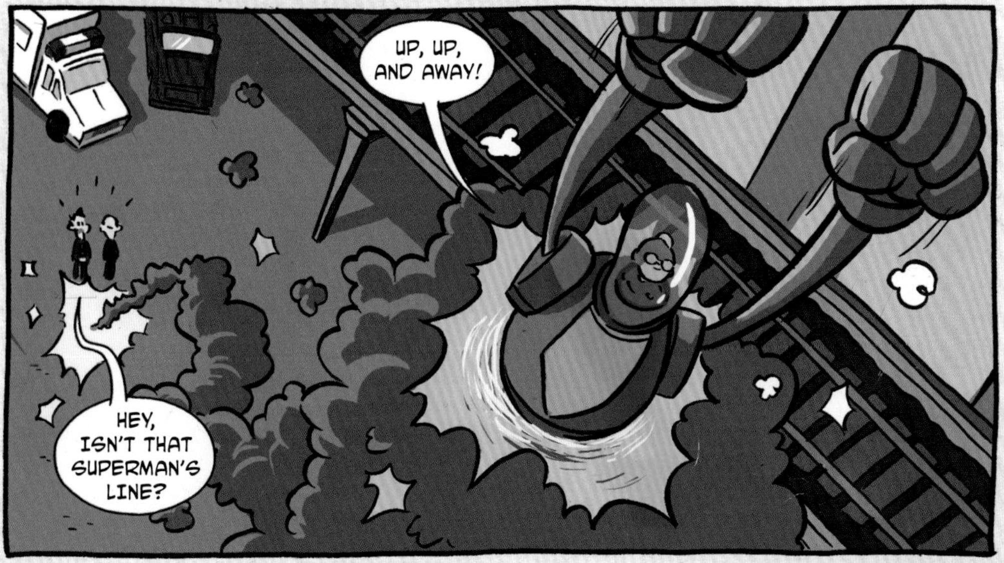
UP, UP, AND AWAY!
HEY, ISN'T THAT SUPERMAN'S LINE?

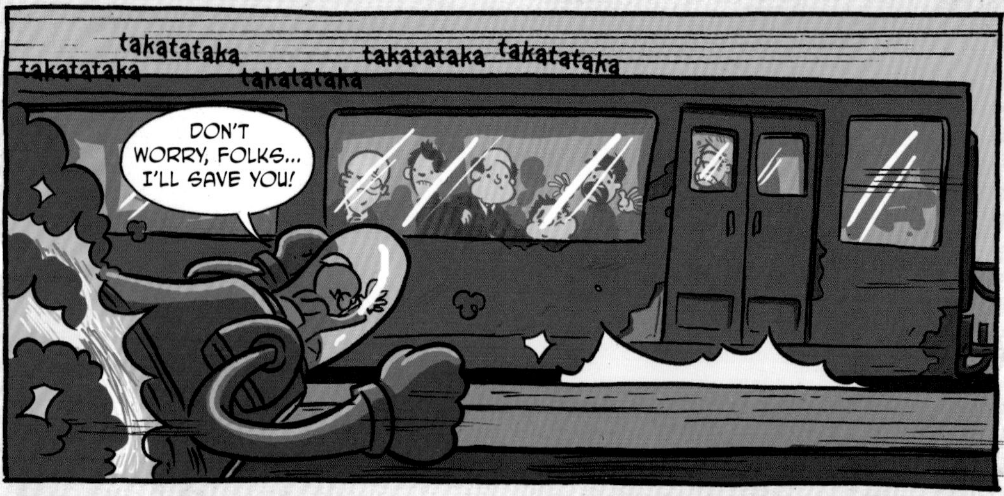
takatataka
takatataka
takatataka
takatataka
takatataka
DON'T WORRY, FOLKS... I'LL SAVE YOU!

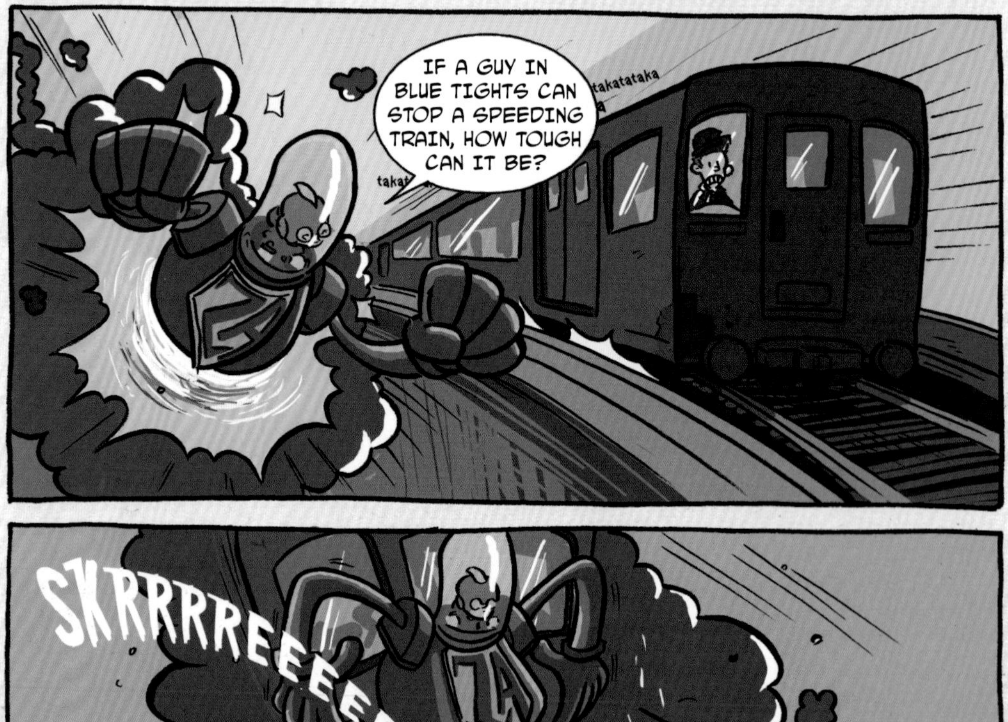
IF A GUY IN BLUE TIGHTS CAN STOP A SPEEDING TRAIN, HOW TOUGH CAN IT BE?
takatataka

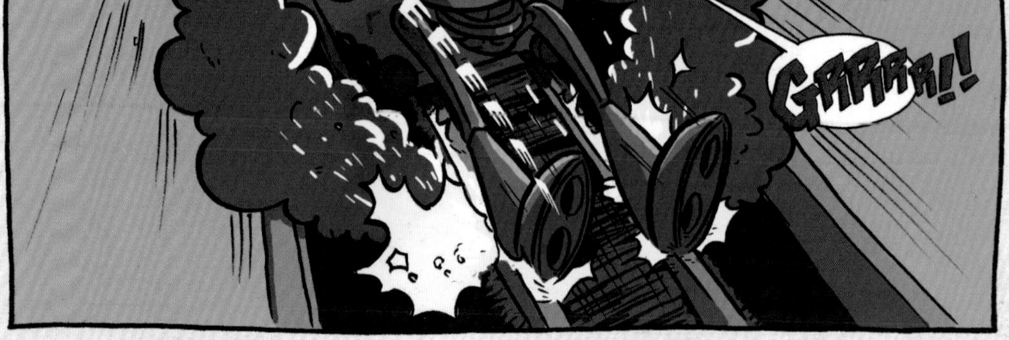
SKRRRRREEEEEEEEE
GRRRR!!

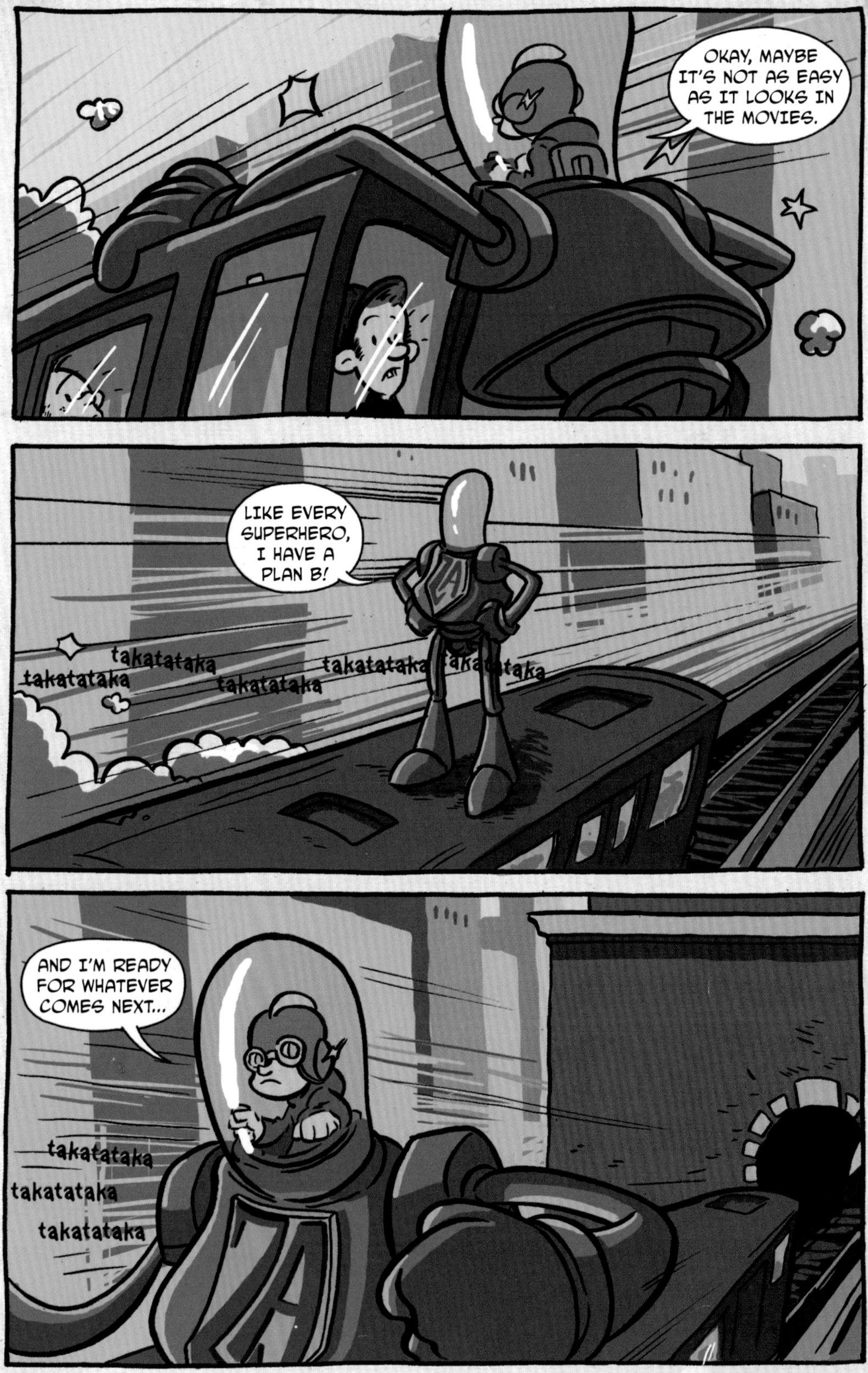
OKAY, MAYBE IT'S NOT AS EASY AS IT LOOKS IN THE MOVIES.
LIKE EVERY SUPERHERO, I HAVE A PLAN B!
takatataka
takatataka
takatataka
takatataka
takatataka
AND I'M READY FOR WHATEVER COMES NEXT...
takatataka
takatataka
takatataka

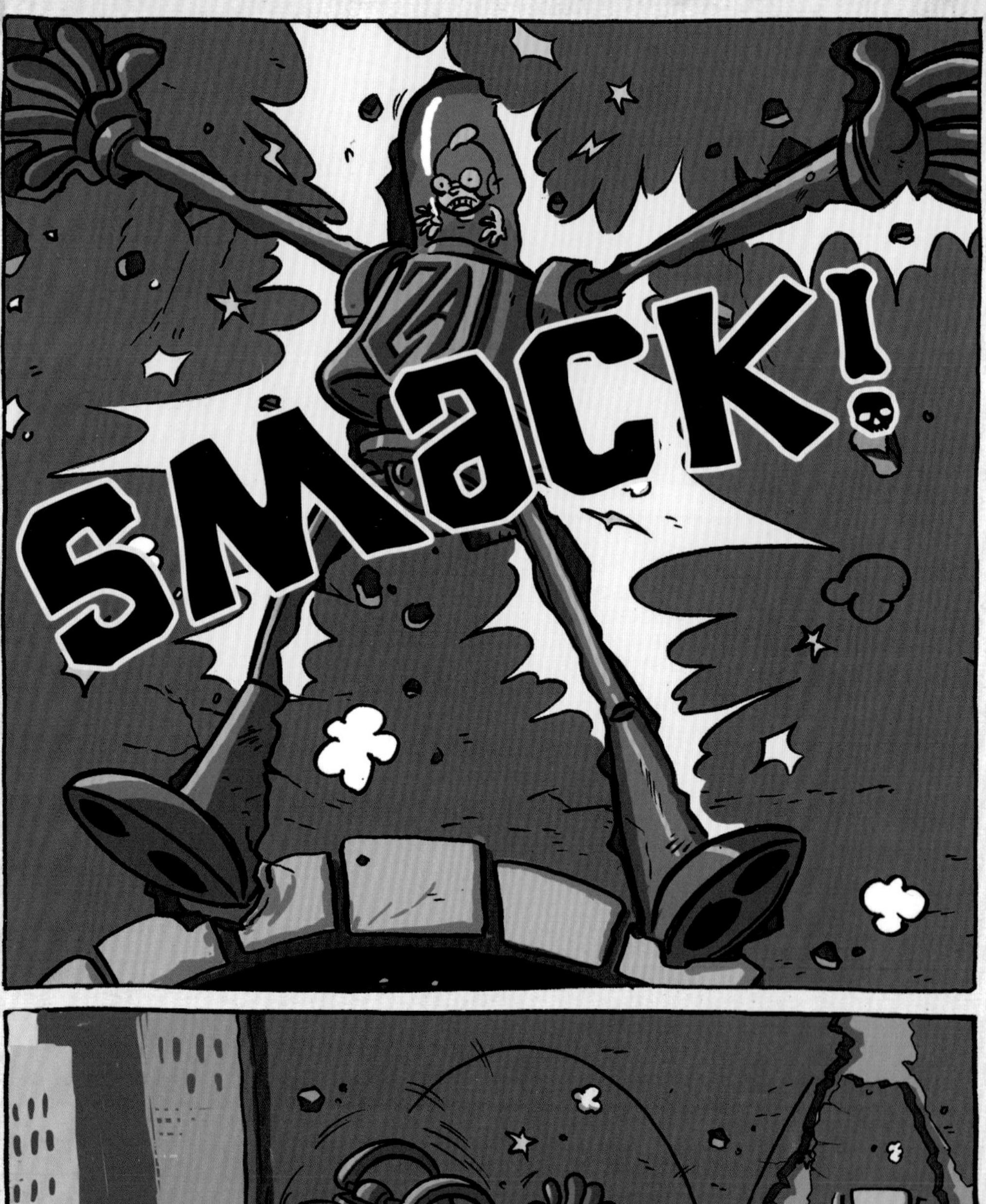
SMACK!

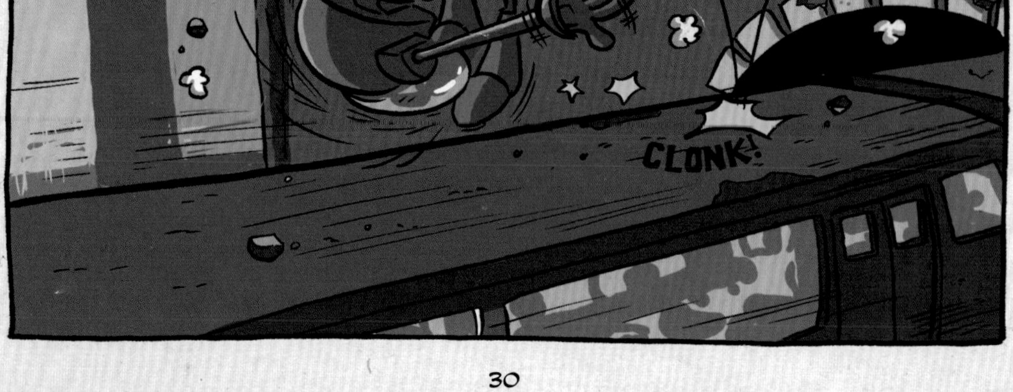
CLONK!

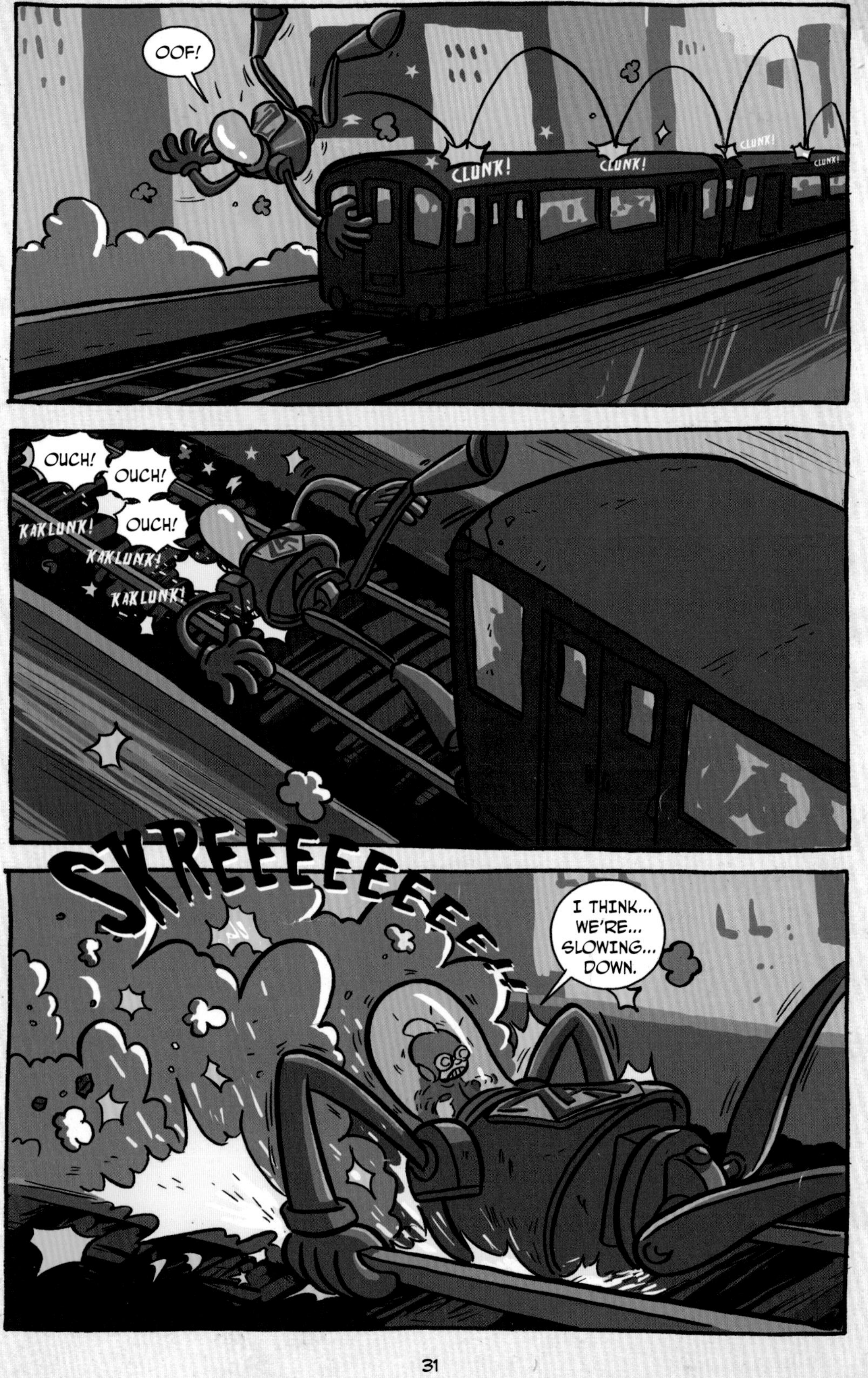
OOF!
CLUNK!
CLUNK!
CLUNK!
CLUNK!
OUCH!
OUCH!
OUCH!
KAKLUNK!
KAKLUNK!
KAKLUNK!
SKREEEEEEEEEE
I THINK... WE'RE... SLOWING... DOWN.

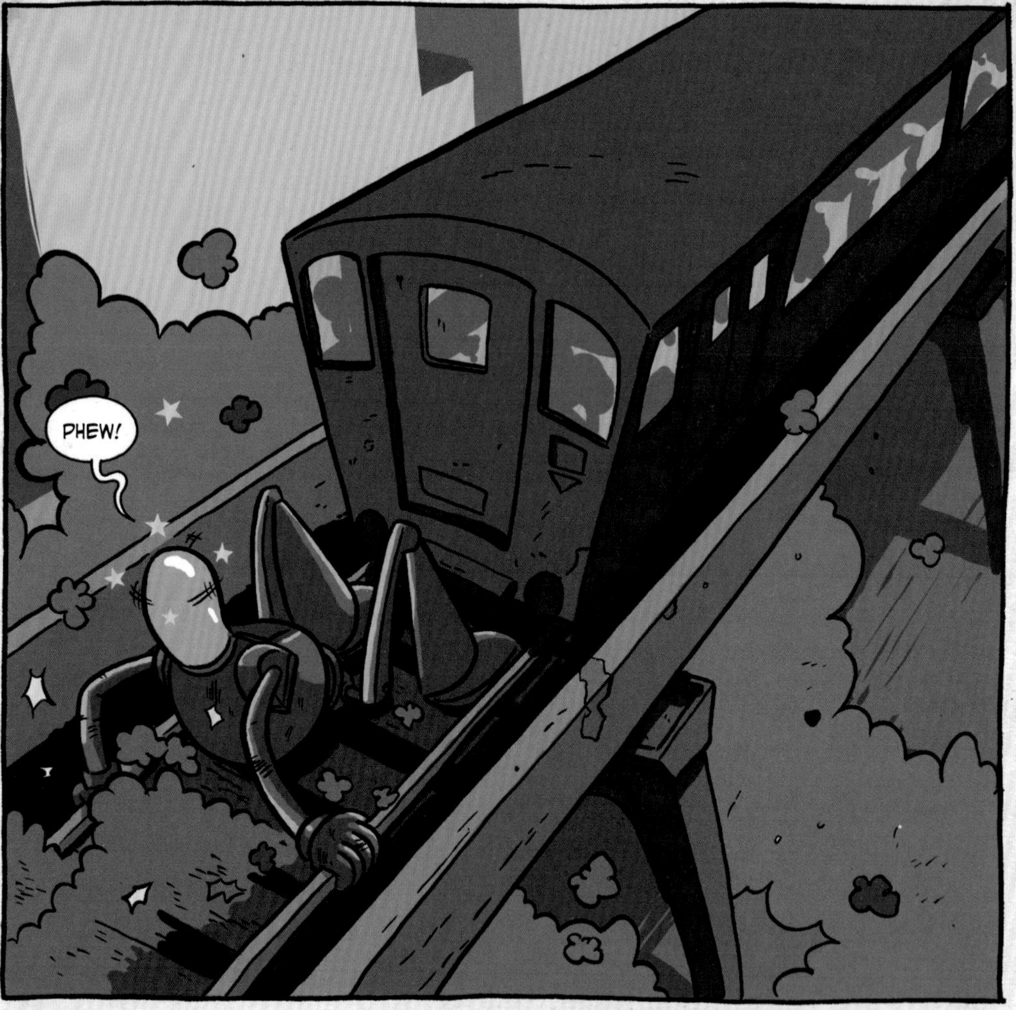
PHEW!

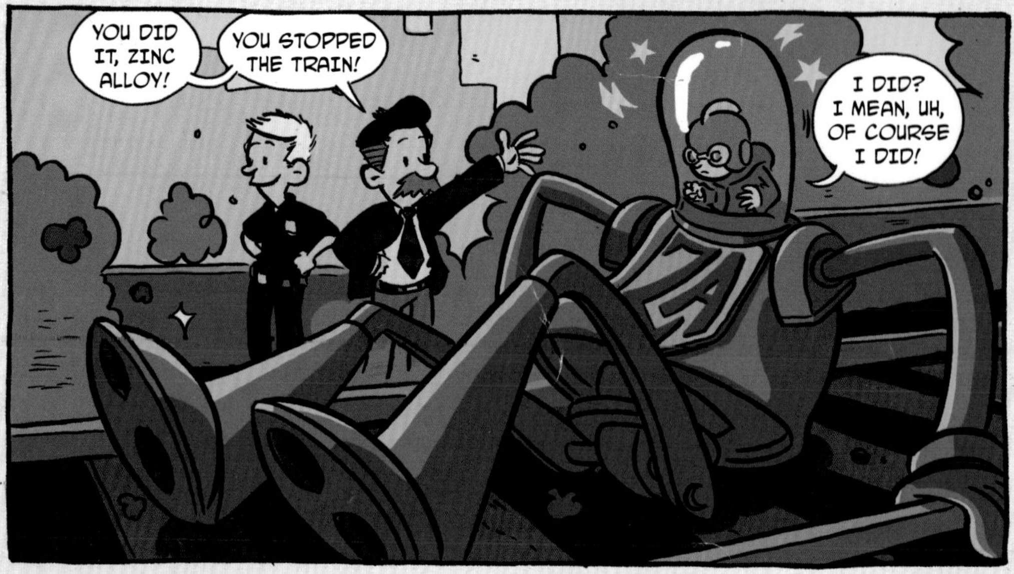
YOU DID IT, ZINC ALLOY!
YOU STOPPED THE TRAIN!
I DID? I MEAN, UH, OF COURSE I DID!

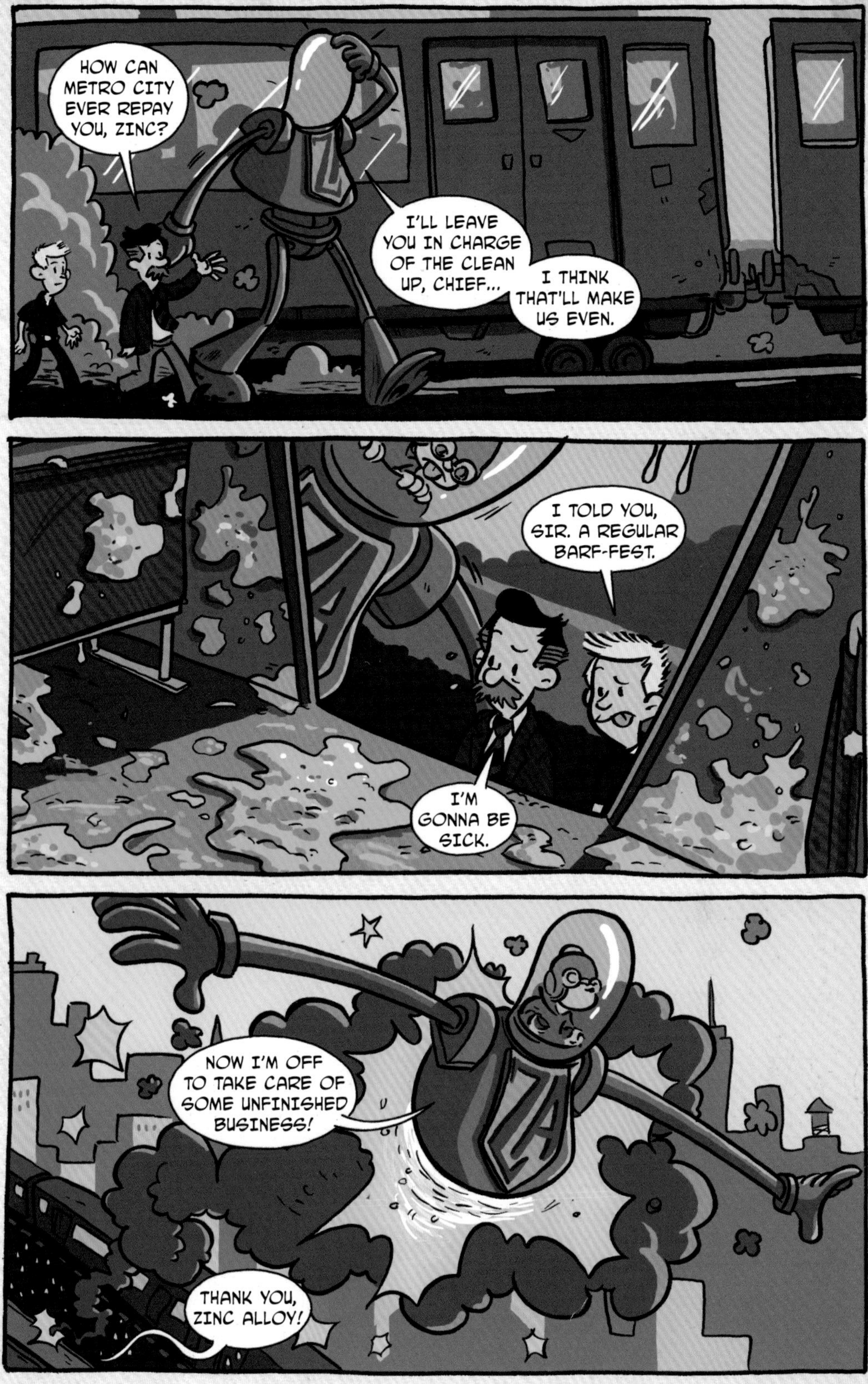
HOW CAN METRO CITY EVER REPAY YOU, ZINC?
I'LL LEAVE YOU IN CHARGE OF THE CLEAN UP, CHIEF...
I THINK THAT'LL MAKE US EVEN.
I TOLD YOU, SIR. A REGULAR BARF-FEST.
I'M GONNA BE SICK.
NOW I'M OFF TO TAKE CARE OF SOME UNFINISHED BUSINESS!
THANK YOU, ZINC ALLOY!

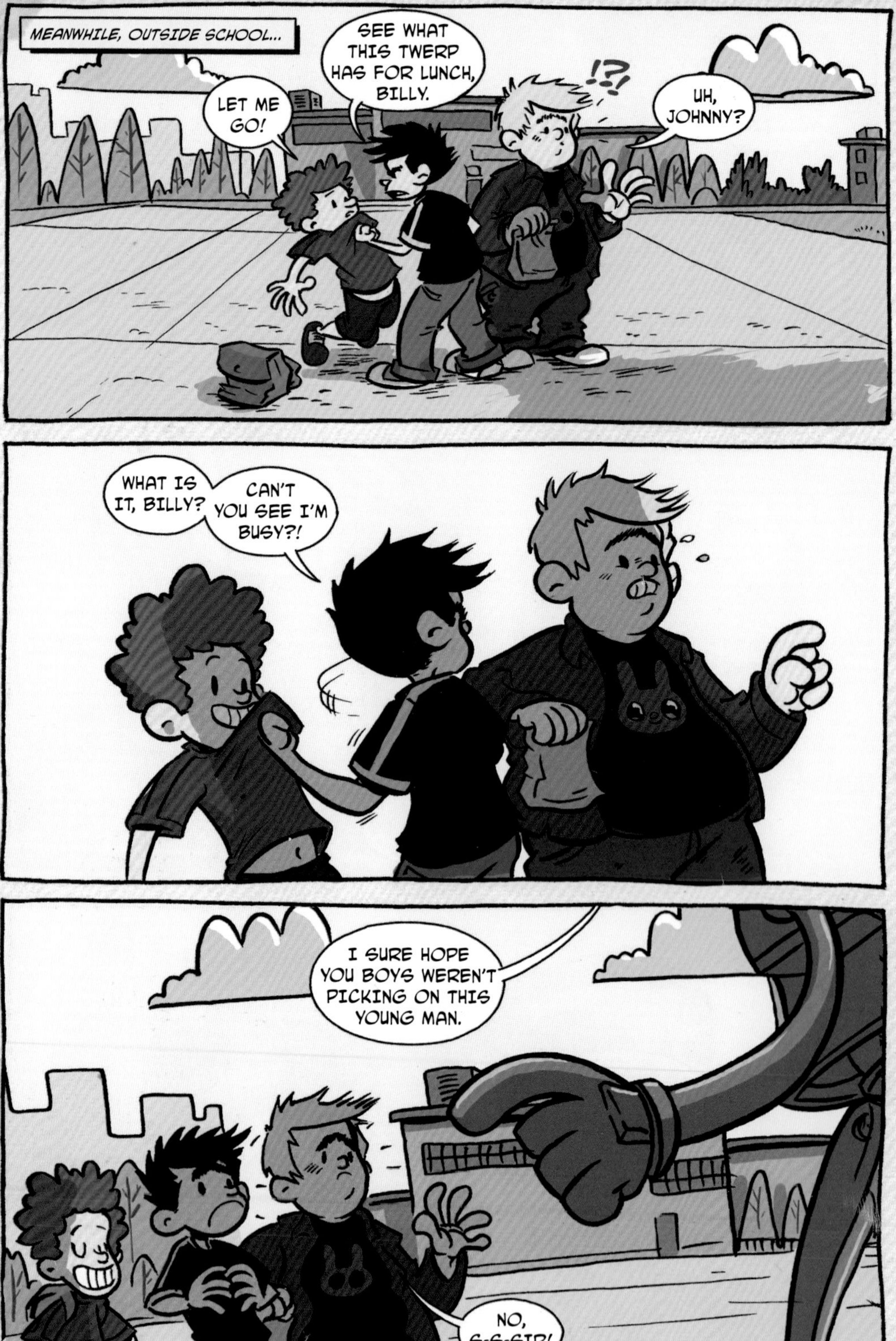
MEANWHILE, OUTSIDE SCHOOL...
LET ME GO!
SEE WHAT THIS TWERP HAS FOR LUNCH, BILLY.
!?
UH, JOHNNY?
WHAT IS IT, BILLY?
CAN'T YOU SEE I'M BUSY?!
I SURE HOPE YOU BOYS WEREN'T PICKING ON THIS YOUNG MAN.
NO, S-S-SIR!

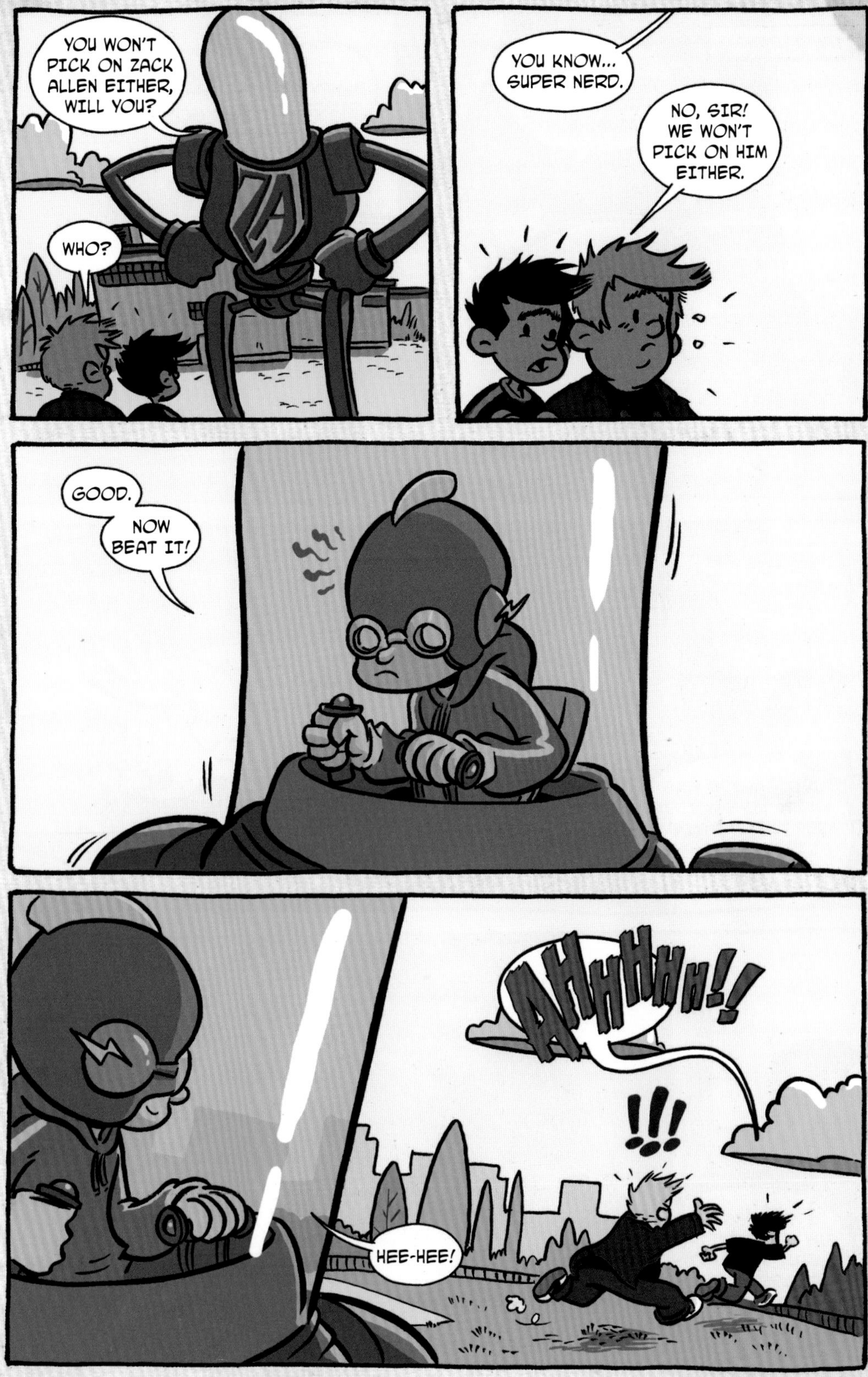
YOU WON'T PICK ON ZACK ALLEN EITHER, WILL YOU?
WHO?
YOU KNOW... SUPER NERD.
NO, SIR! WE WON'T PICK ON HIM EITHER.
GOOD.
NOW BEAT IT!
AHHHHH!!
!!!
HEE-HEE!

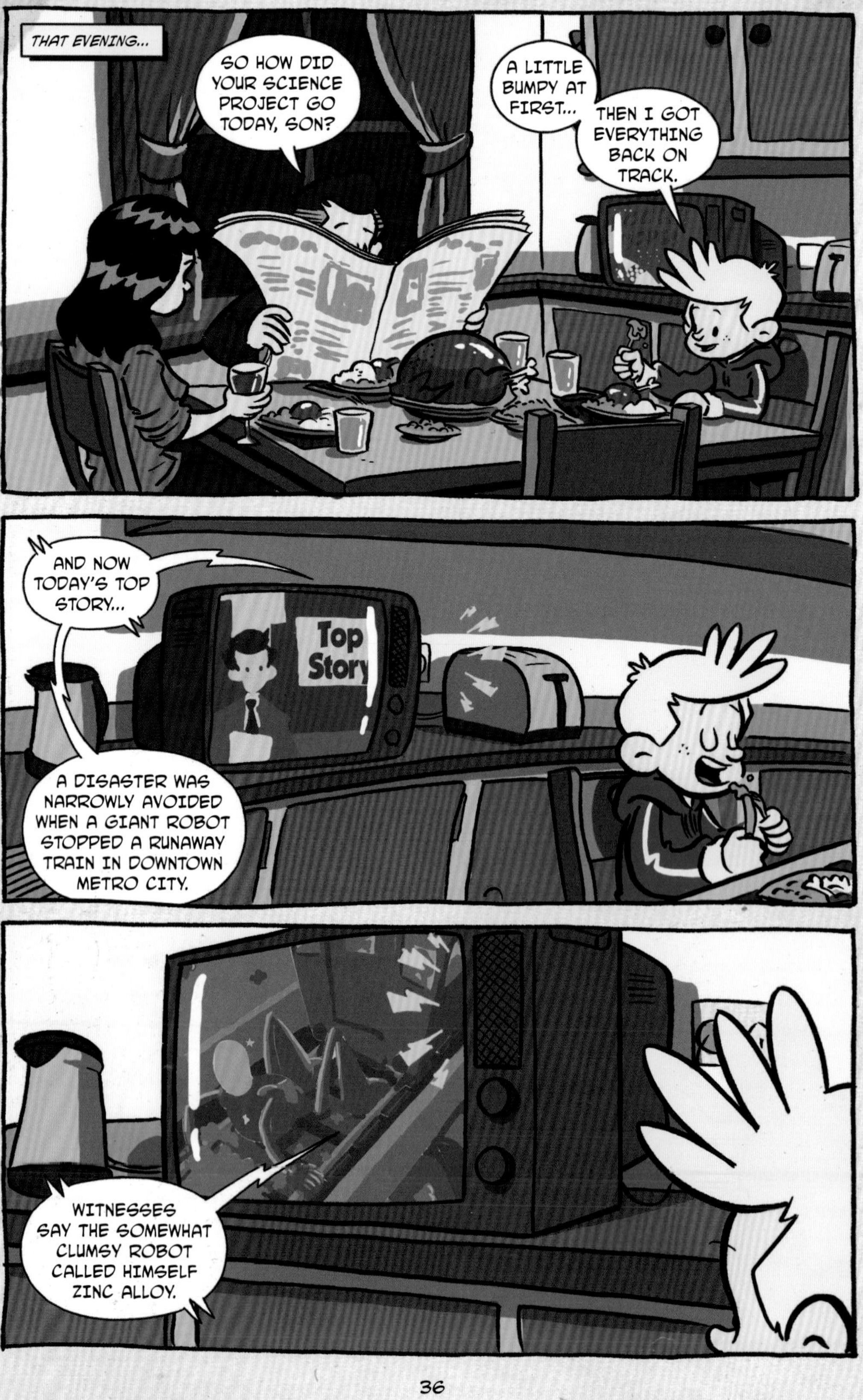
THAT EVENING...
SO HOW DID YOUR SCIENCE PROJECT GO TODAY, SON?
A LITTLE BUMPY AT FIRST...
THEN I GOT EVERYTHING BACK ON TRACK.
AND NOW TODAY'S TOP STORY...
Top Story
A DISASTER WAS NARROWLY AVOIDED WHEN A GIANT ROBOT STOPPED A RUNAWAY TRAIN IN DOWNTOWN METRO CITY.
WITNESSES SAY THE SOMEWHAT CLUMSY ROBOT CALLED HIMSELF ZINC ALLOY.

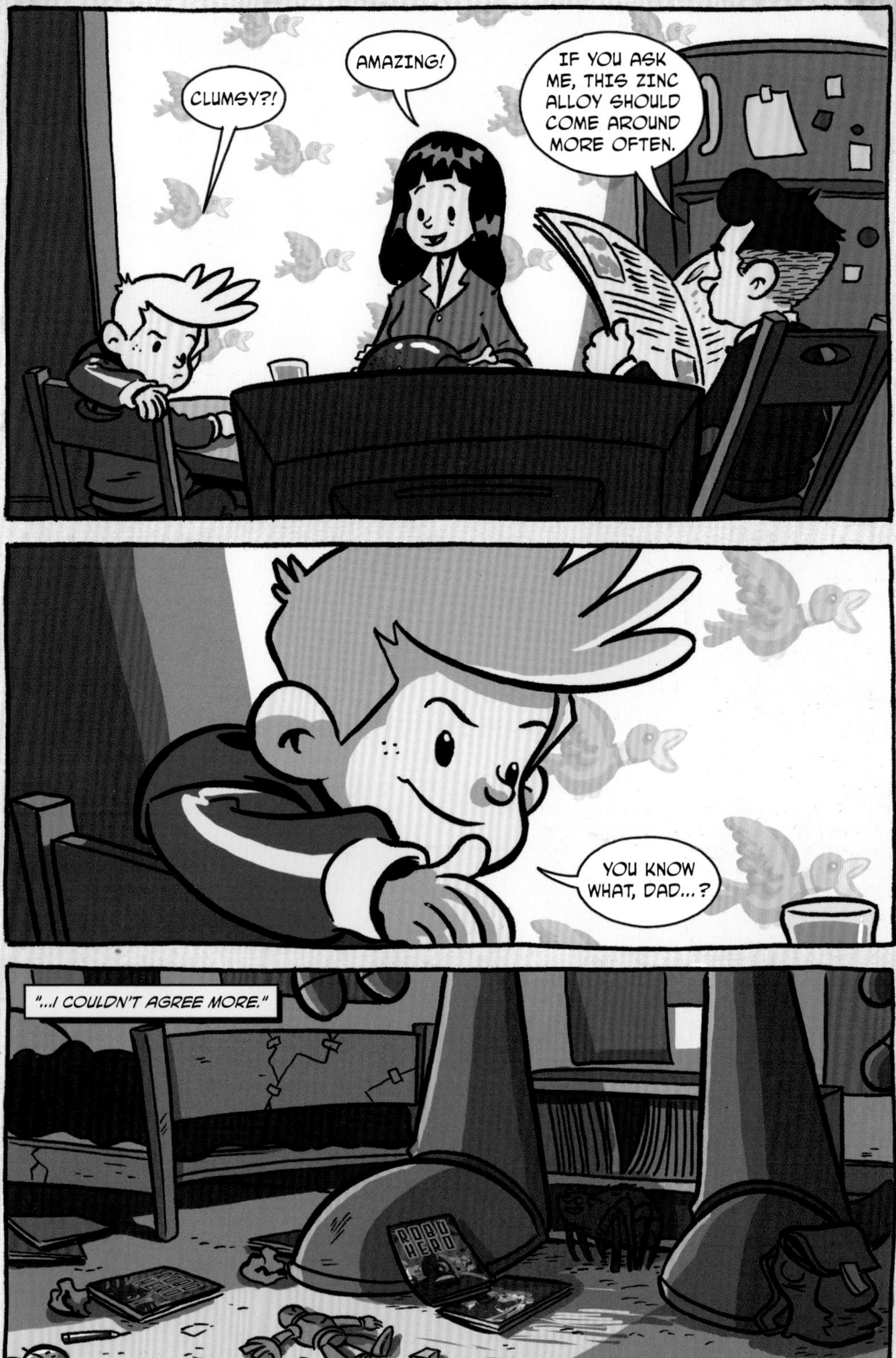
CLUMSY?!
AMAZING!
IF YOU ASK ME, THIS ZINC ALLOY SHOULD COME AROUND MORE OFTEN.
YOU KNOW WHAT, DAD...?
"...I COULDN'T AGREE MORE."
ROBO HERO

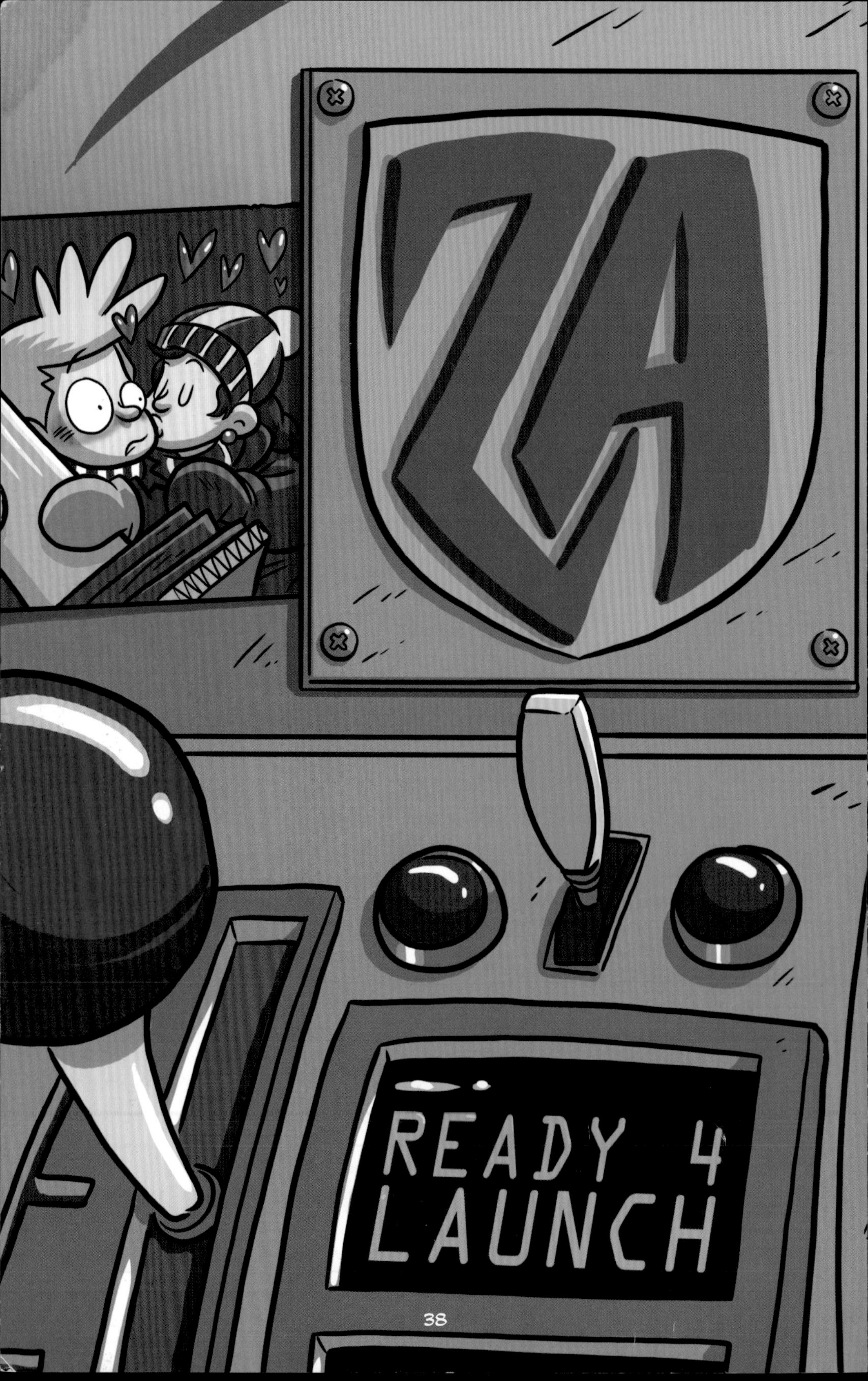
ZA
READY 4 LAUNCH

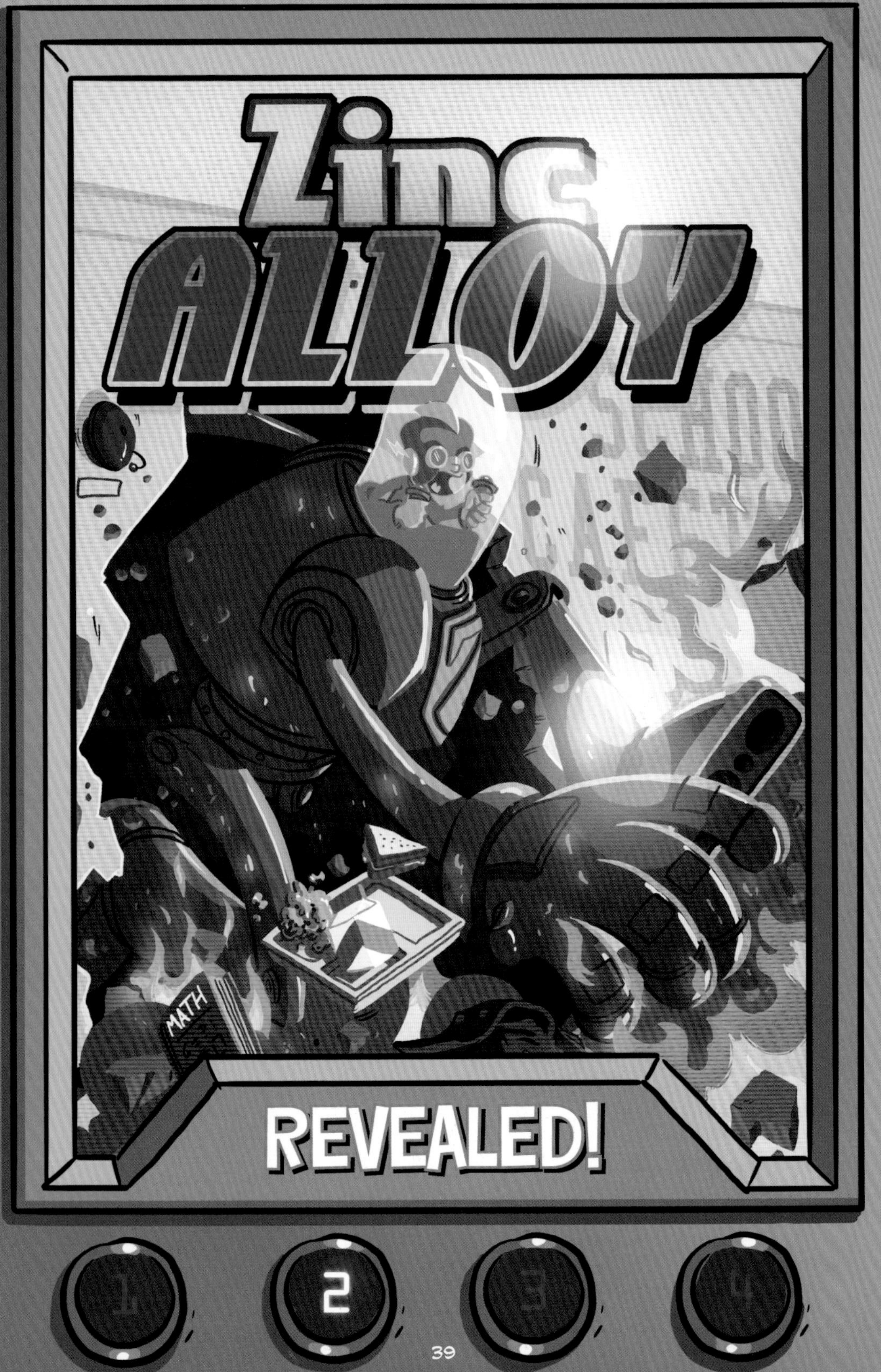
Zinc ALLOY
MATH
REVEALED!
1
2
3
4

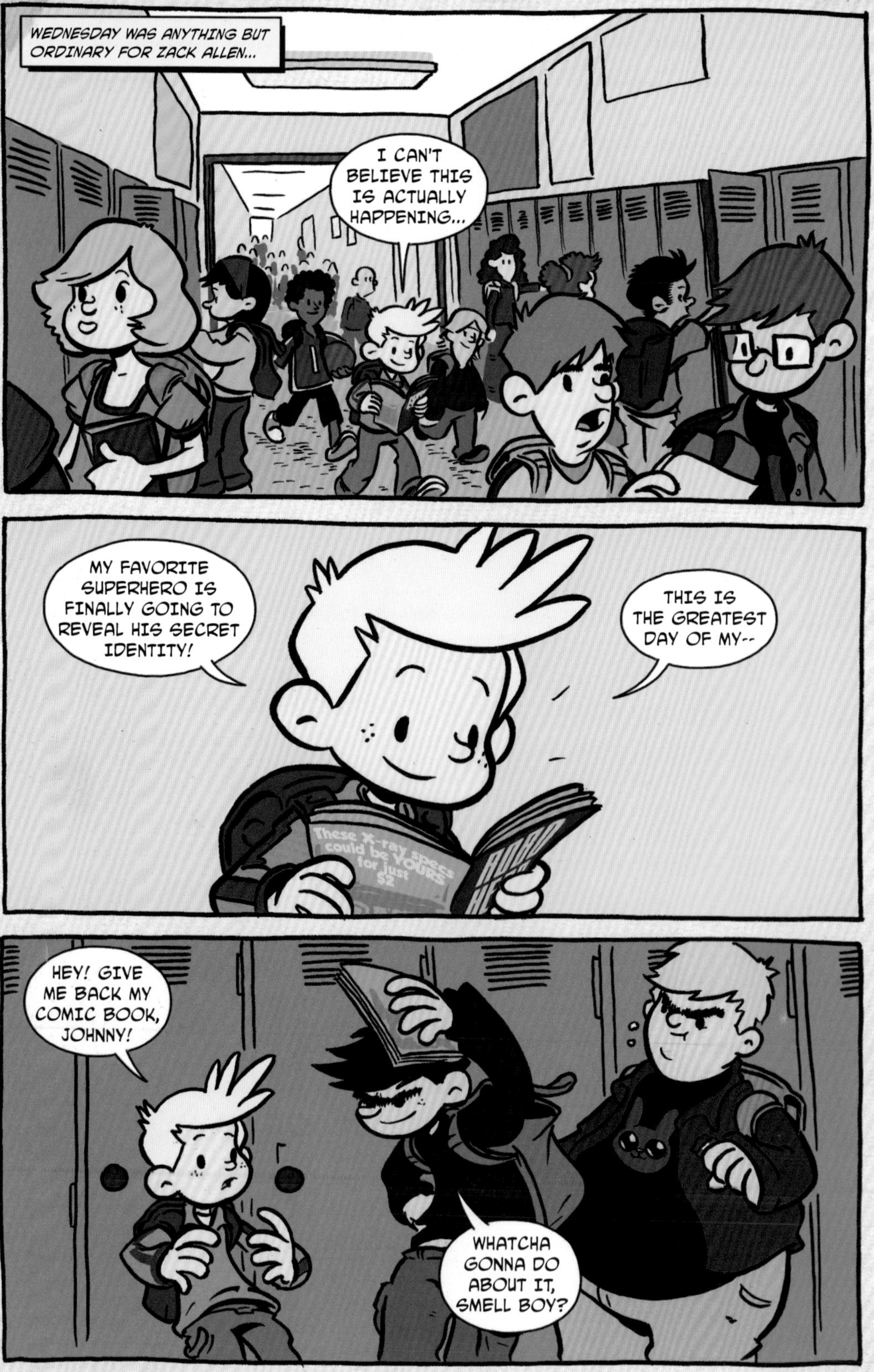
WEDNESDAY WAS ANYTHING BUT ORDINARY FOR ZACK ALLEN...
I CAN'T BELIEVE THIS IS ACTUALLY HAPPENING...
MY FAVORITE SUPERHERO IS FINALLY GOING TO REVEAL HIS SECRET IDENTITY!
THIS IS THE GREATEST DAY OF MY--
These X-ray specs could be YOURS for just $2
HEY! GIVE ME BACK MY COMIC BOOK, JOHNNY!
WHATCHA GONNA DO ABOUT IT, SMELL BOY?

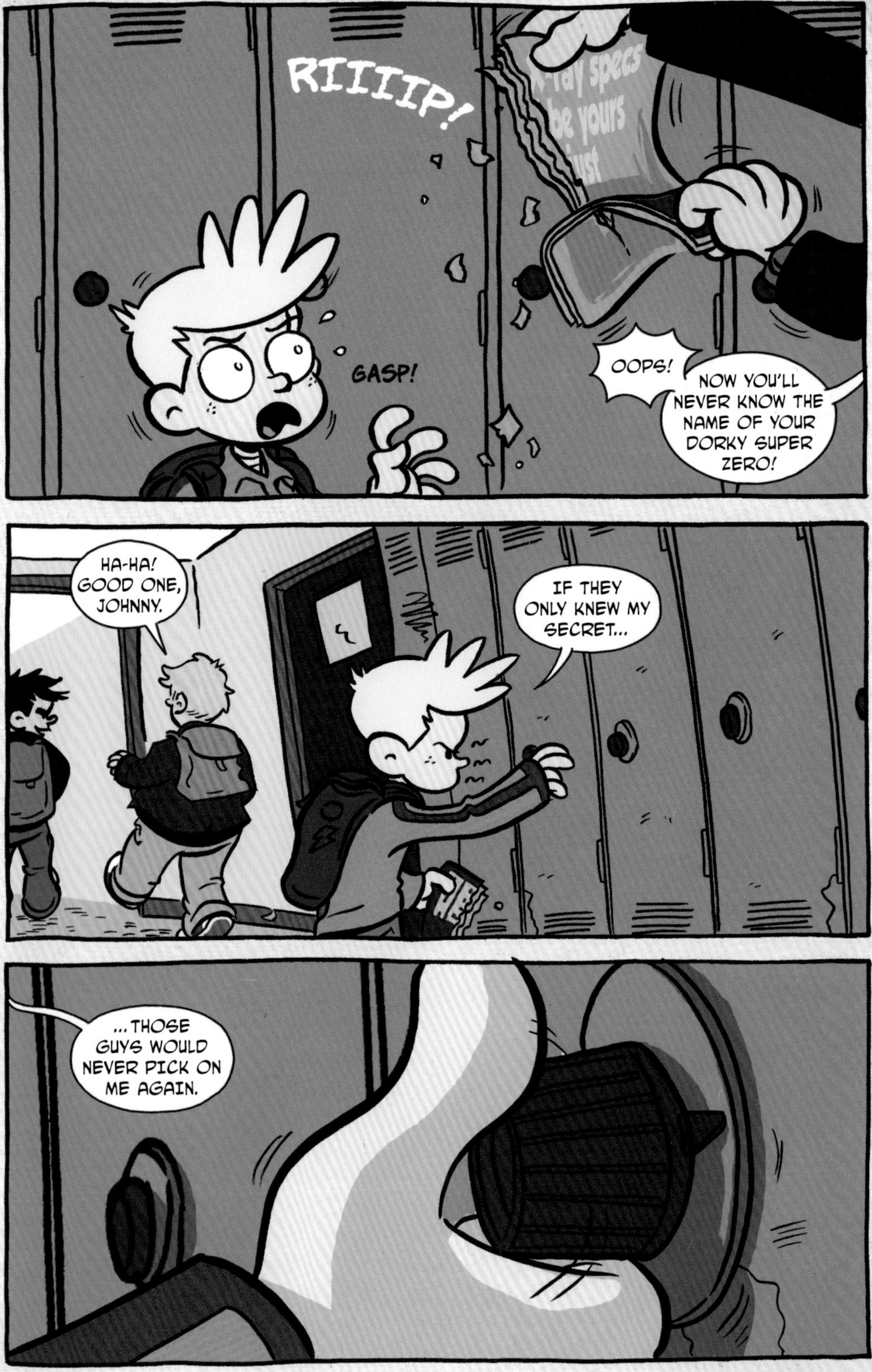
RIIIIP!
GASP!
OOPS!
NOW YOU'LL NEVER KNOW THE NAME OF YOUR DORKY SUPER ZERO!
HA-HA! GOOD ONE, JOHNNY.
IF THEY ONLY KNEW MY SECRET...
...THOSE GUYS WOULD NEVER PICK ON ME AGAIN.

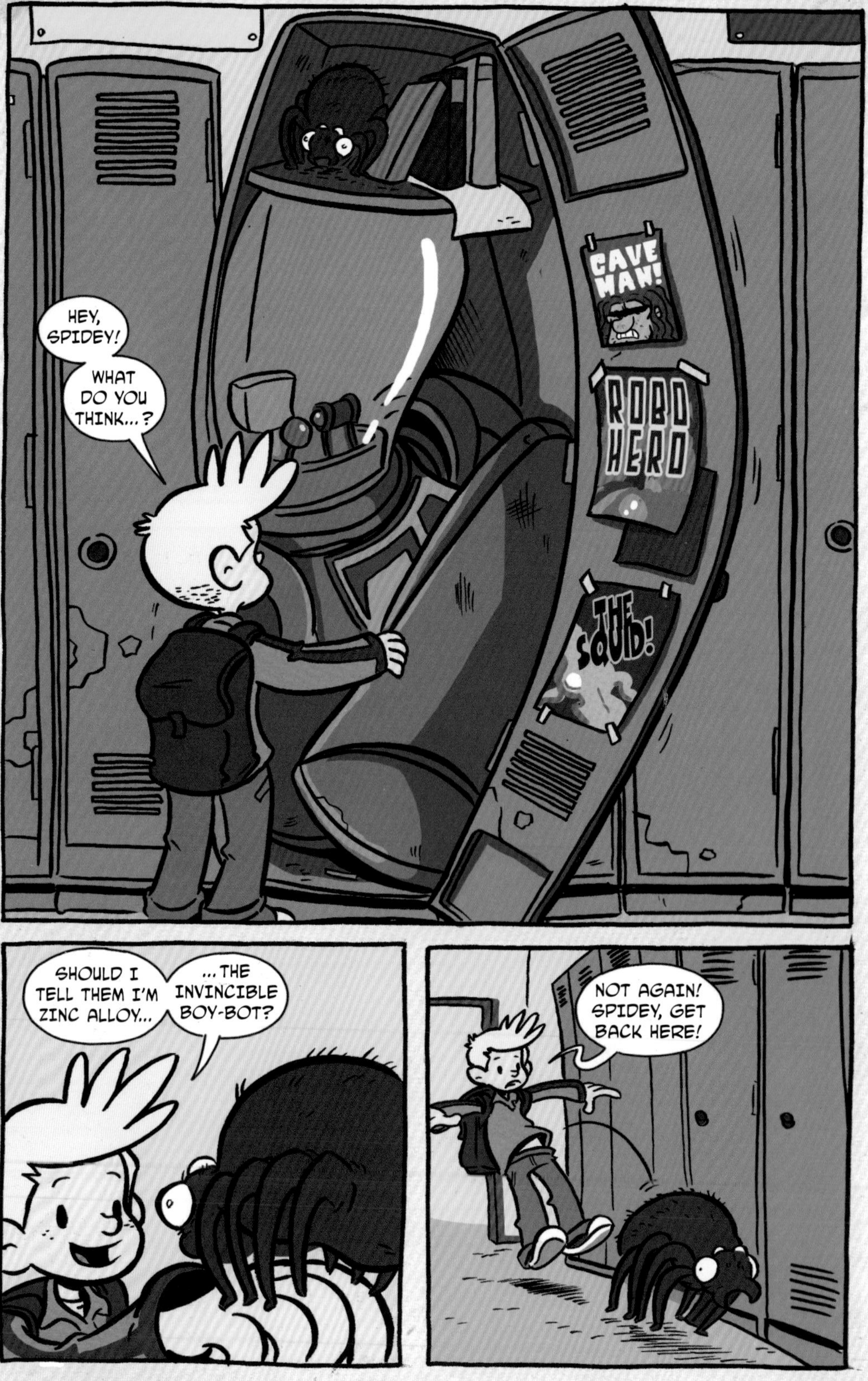
HEY, SPIDEY!
WHAT DO YOU THINK...?
CAVE MAN!
ROBO HERO
THE SQUID!
SHOULD I TELL THEM I'M ZINC ALLOY...
...THE INVINCIBLE BOY-BOT?
NOT AGAIN! SPIDEY, GET BACK HERE!

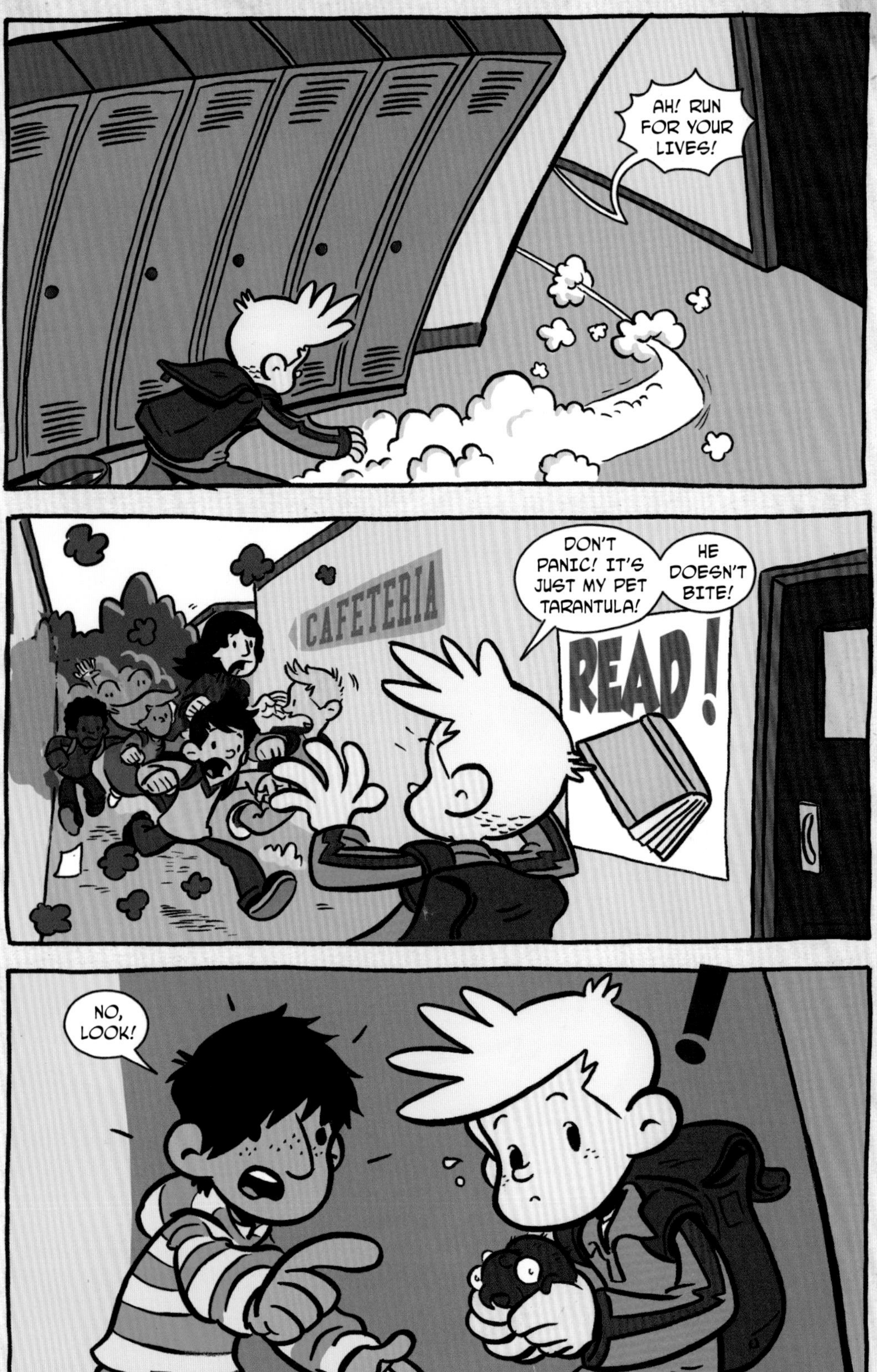
AH! RUN FOR YOUR LIVES!
CAFETERIA
DON'T PANIC! IT'S JUST MY PET TARANTULA!
HE DOESN'T BITE!
READ!
NO, LOOK!
!

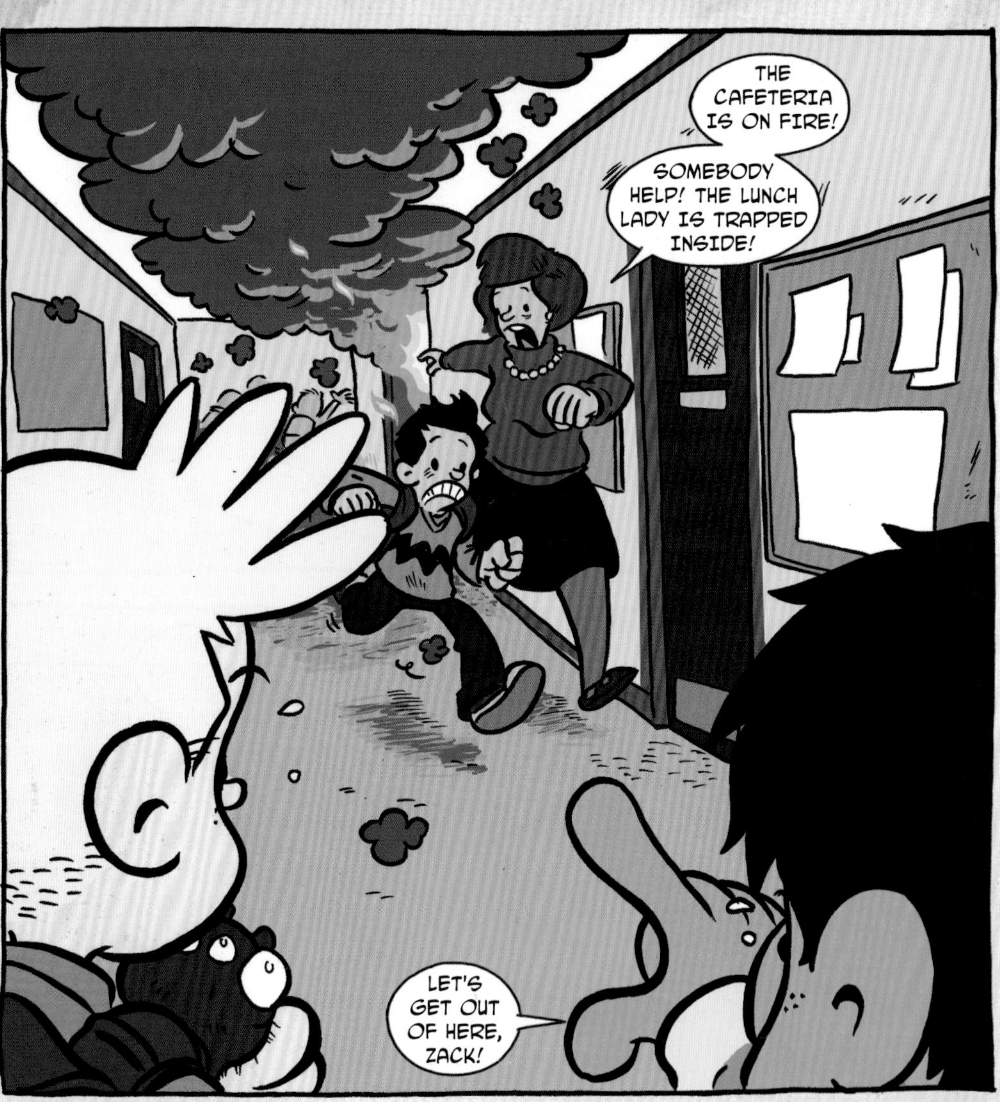
THE CAFETERIA IS ON FIRE!
SOMEBODY HELP! THE LUNCH LADY IS TRAPPED INSIDE!
LET'S GET OUT OF HERE, ZACK!

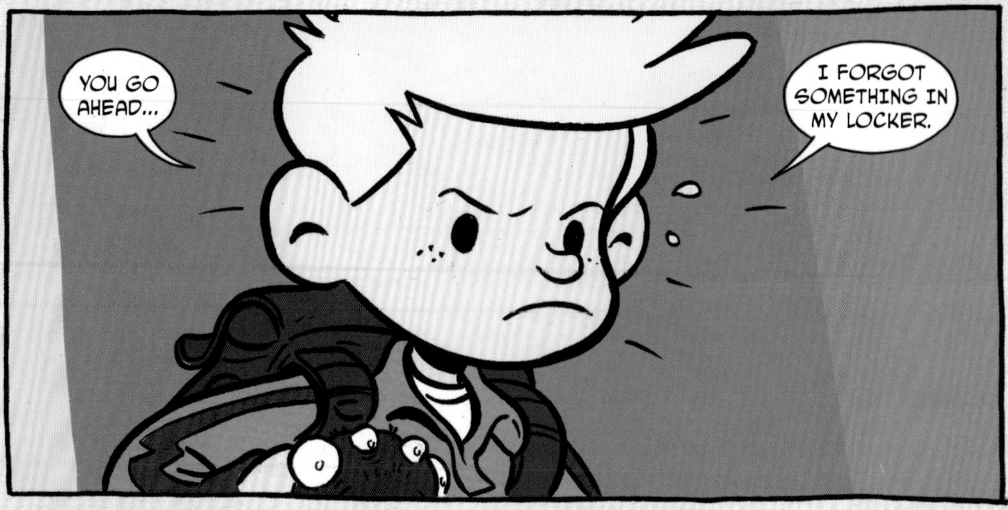
YOU GO AHEAD...
I FORGOT SOMETHING IN MY LOCKER.

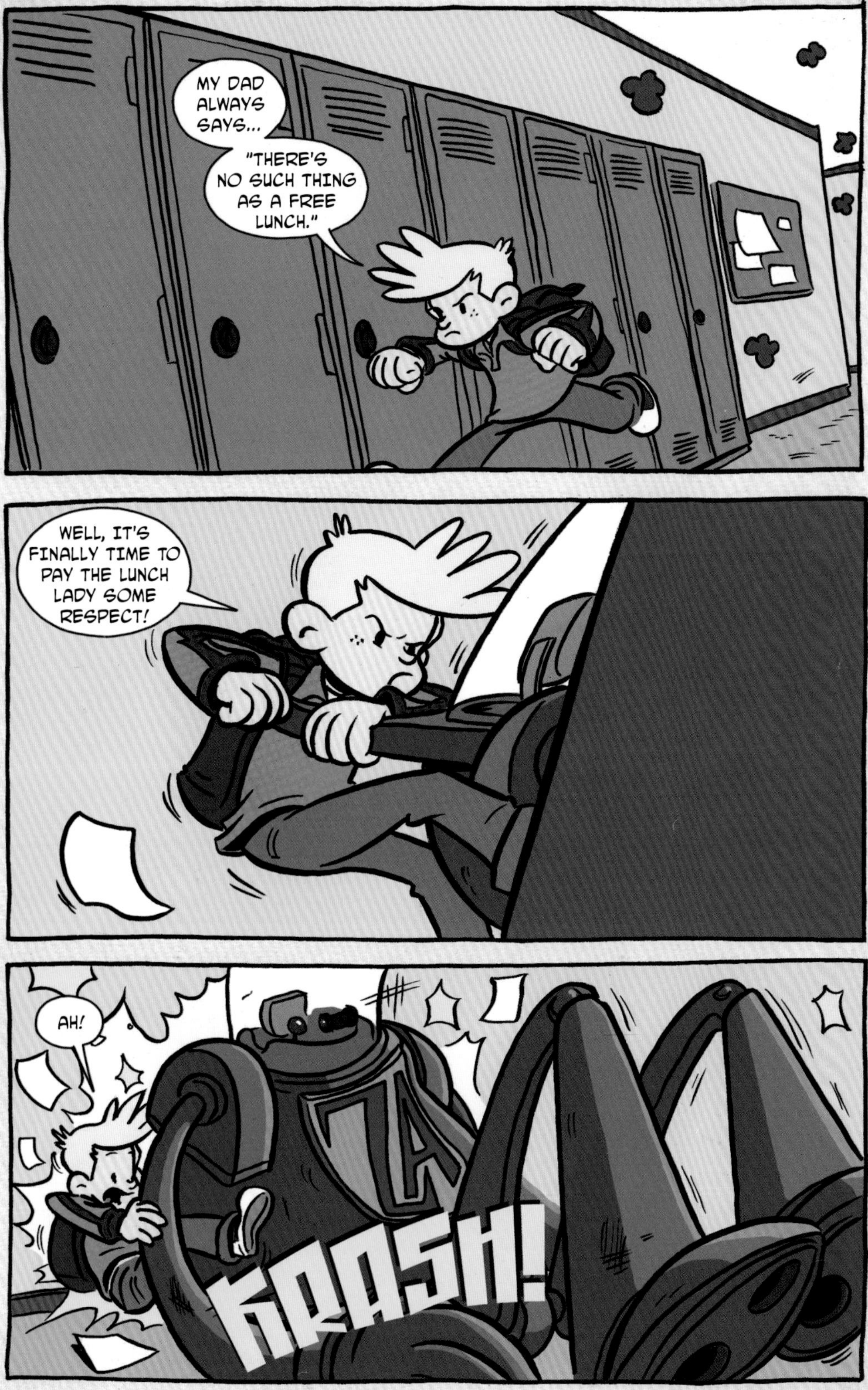
MY DAD ALWAYS SAYS...
"THERE'S NO SUCH THING AS A FREE LUNCH."
WELL, IT'S FINALLY TIME TO PAY THE LUNCH LADY SOME RESPECT!
AH!
KRASH!

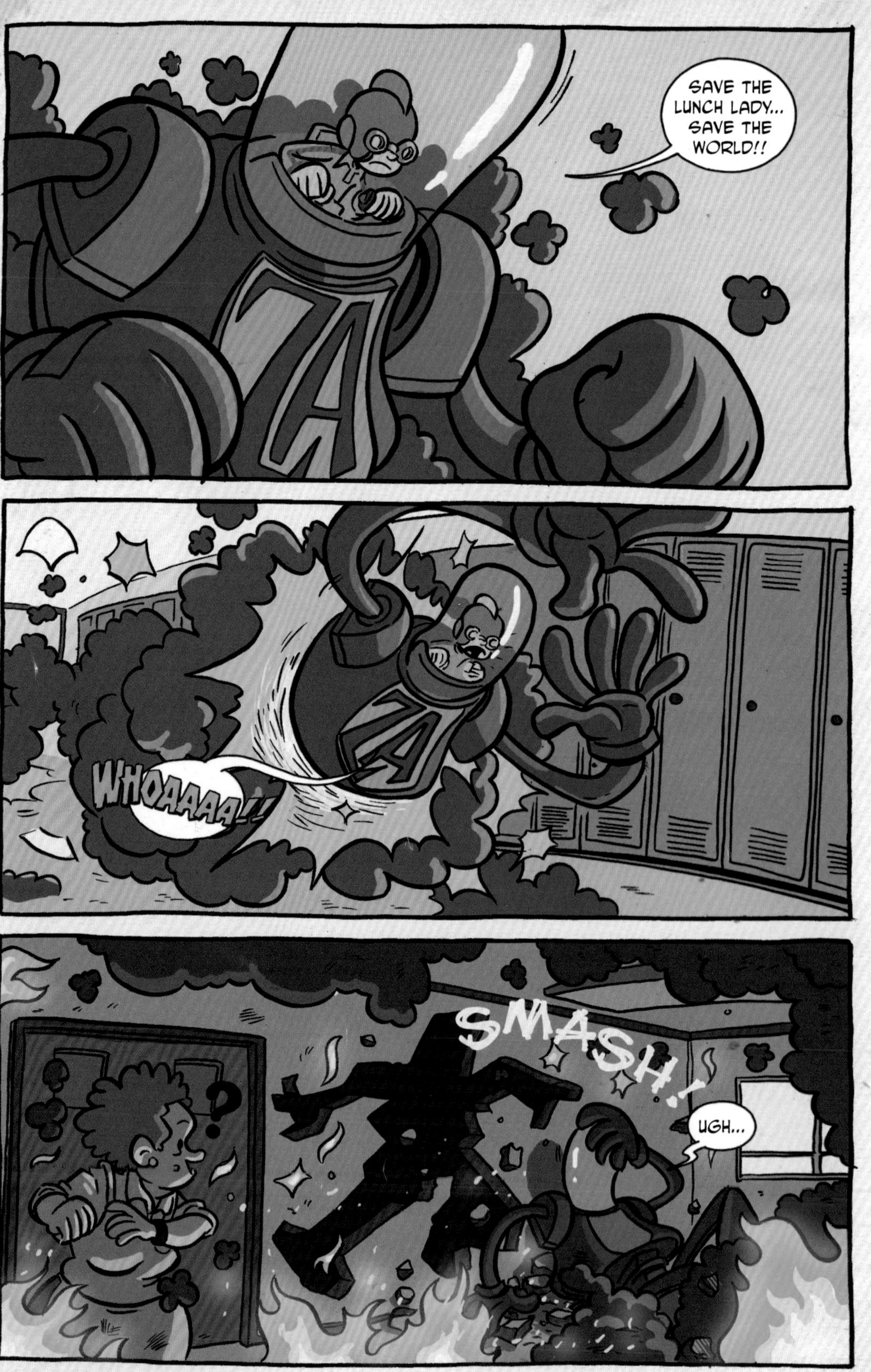
SAVE THE LUNCH LADY... SAVE THE WORLD!!
WHOAAAA!!
SMASH!
UGH...

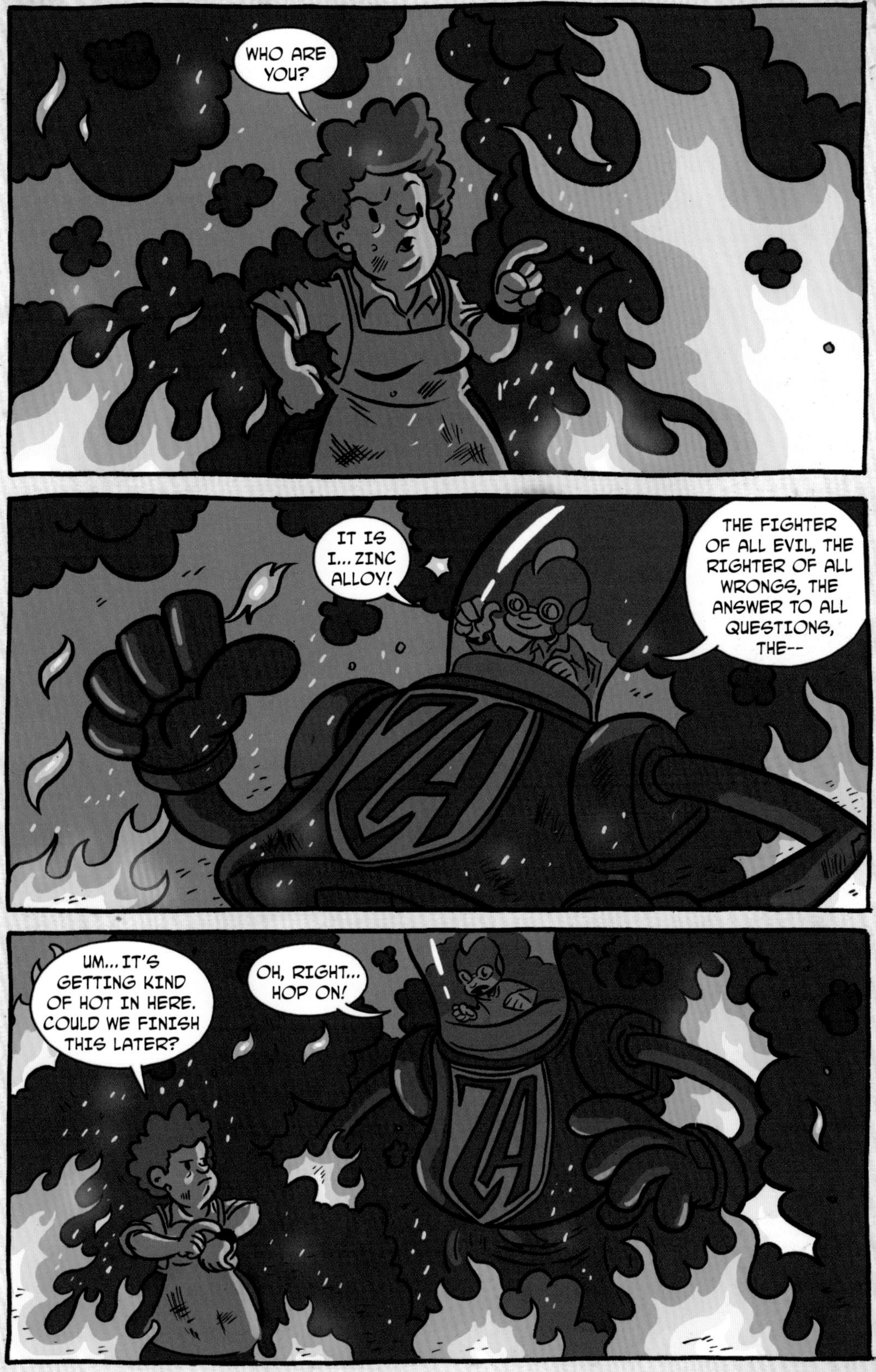
WHO ARE YOU?
IT IS I...ZINC ALLOY!
THE FIGHTER OF ALL EVIL, THE RIGHTER OF ALL WRONGS, THE ANSWER TO ALL QUESTIONS, THE--
UM...IT'S GETTING KIND OF HOT IN HERE. COULD WE FINISH THIS LATER?
OH, RIGHT... HOP ON!

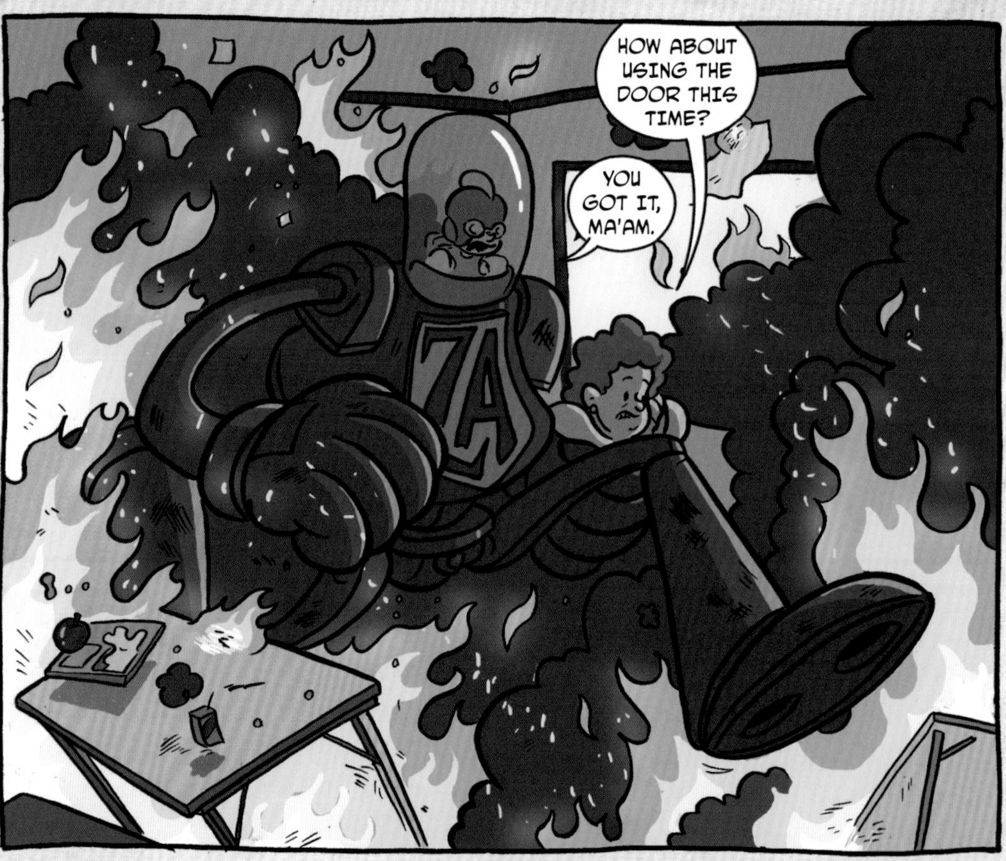
HOW ABOUT USING THE DOOR THIS TIME?
YOU GOT IT, MA'AM.

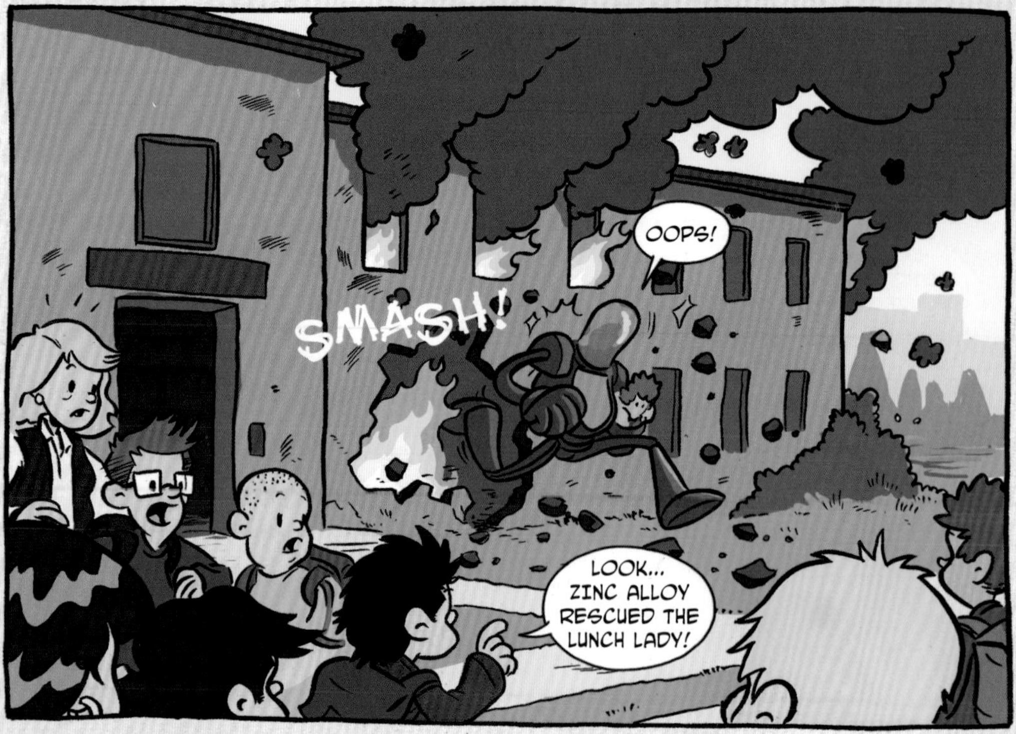
OOPS!
SMASH!
LOOK... ZINC ALLOY RESCUED THE LUNCH LADY!

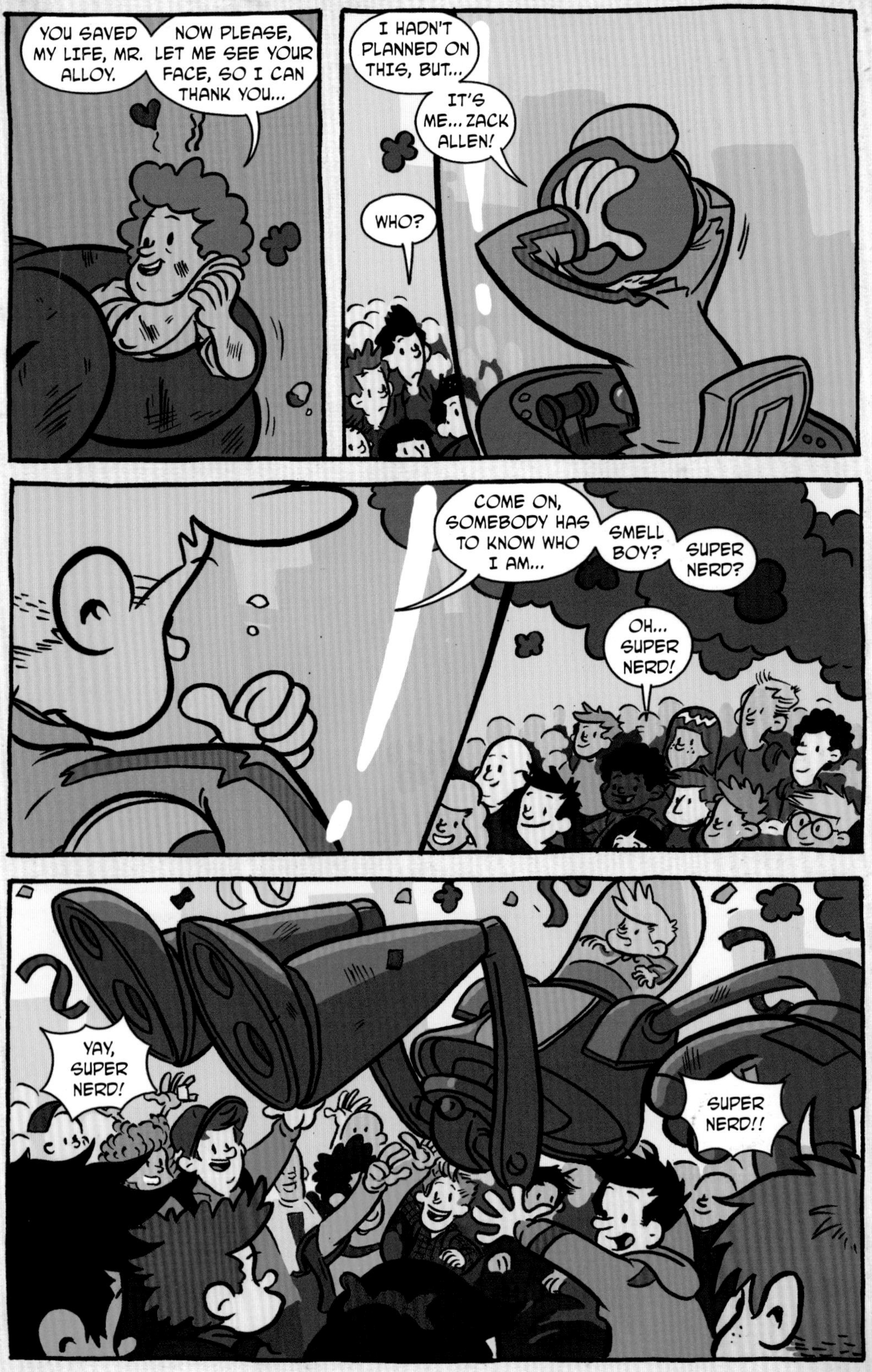
YOU SAVED MY LIFE, MR. ALLOY.
NOW PLEASE, LET ME SEE YOUR FACE, SO I CAN THANK YOU...
I HADN'T PLANNED ON THIS, BUT...
IT'S ME... ZACK ALLEN!
WHO?
COME ON, SOMEBODY HAS TO KNOW WHO I AM...
SMELL BOY?
SUPER NERD?
OH... SUPER NERD!
YAY, SUPER NERD!
SUPER NERD!!

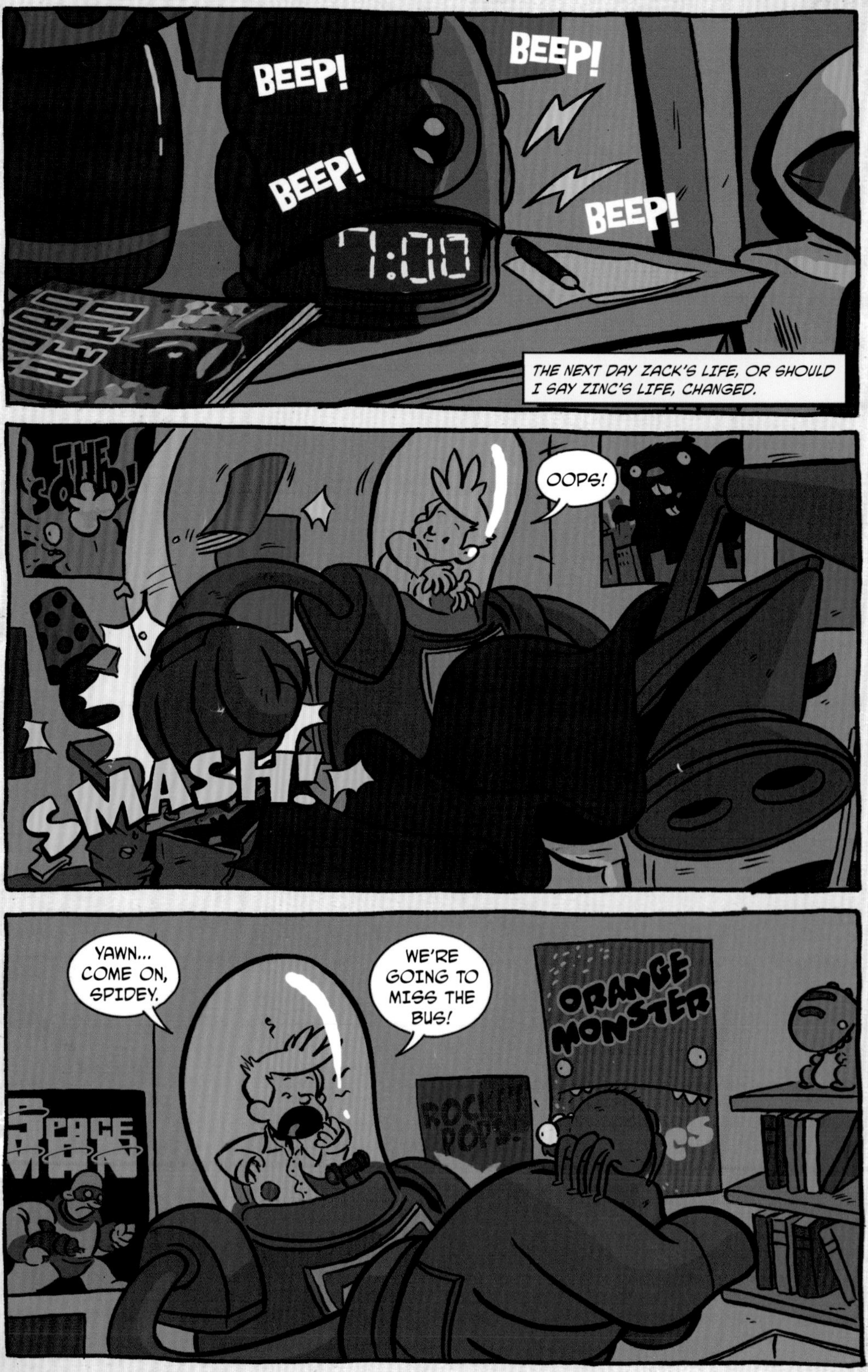
BEEP!
BEEP!
BEEP!
BEEP!
7:00
THE NEXT DAY ZACK'S LIFE, OR SHOULD I SAY ZINC'S LIFE, CHANGED.
THE SQUID!
OOPS!
SMASH!
YAWN... COME ON, SPIDEY.
WE'RE GOING TO MISS THE BUS!
ORANGE MONSTER
ROCKET POPS
SPACE MAN

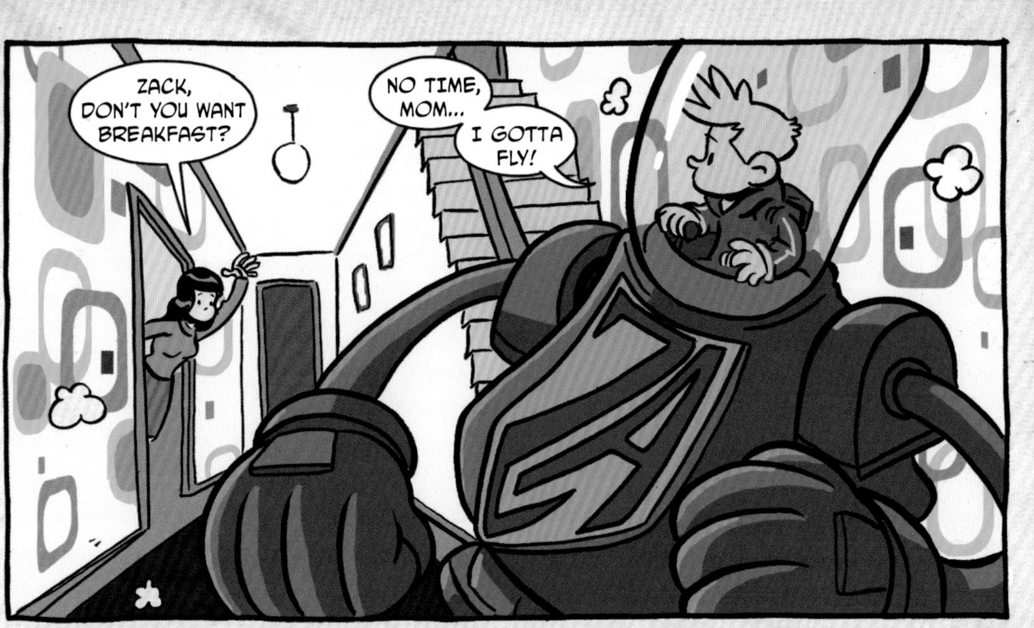
ZACK, DON'T YOU WANT BREAKFAST?
NO TIME, MOM...
I GOTTA FLY!

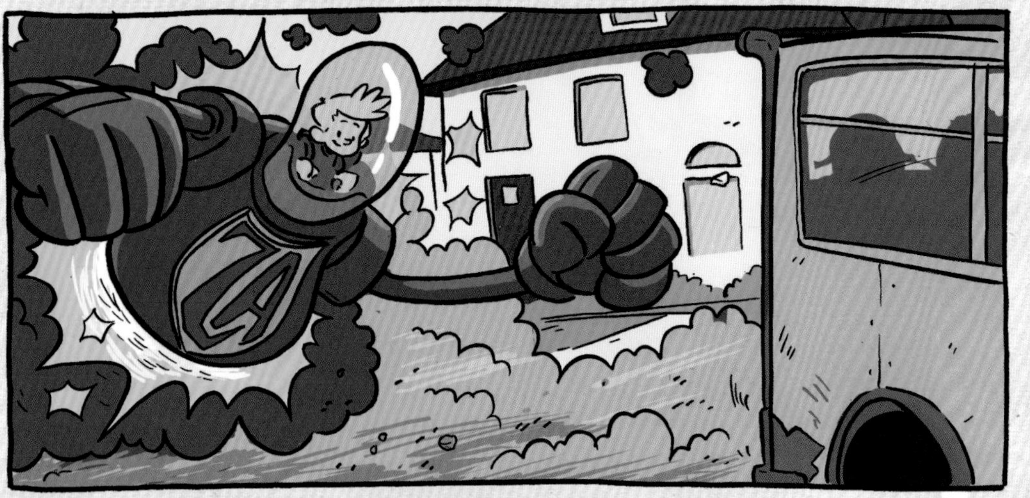

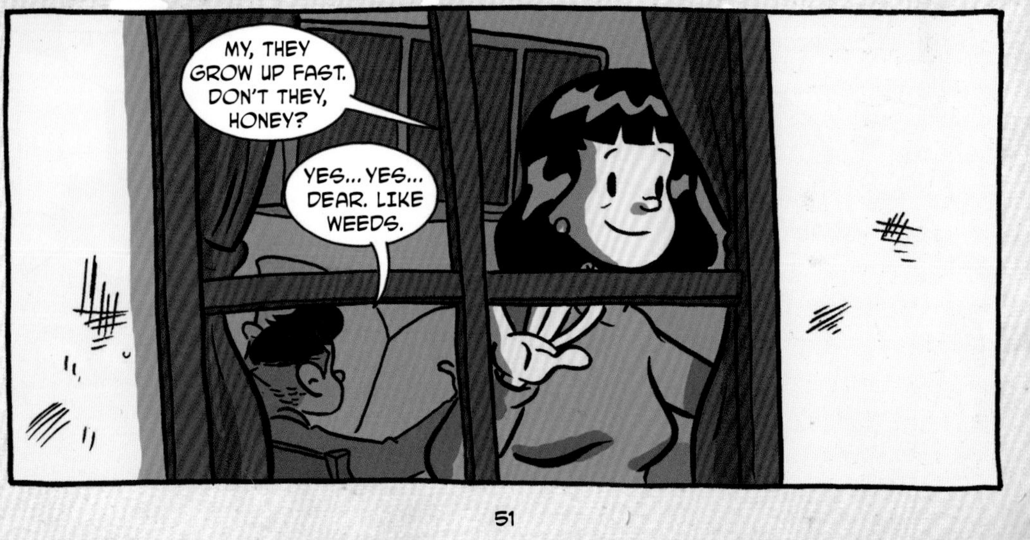
MY, THEY GROW UP FAST. DON'T THEY, HONEY?
YES...YES... DEAR. LIKE WEEDS.

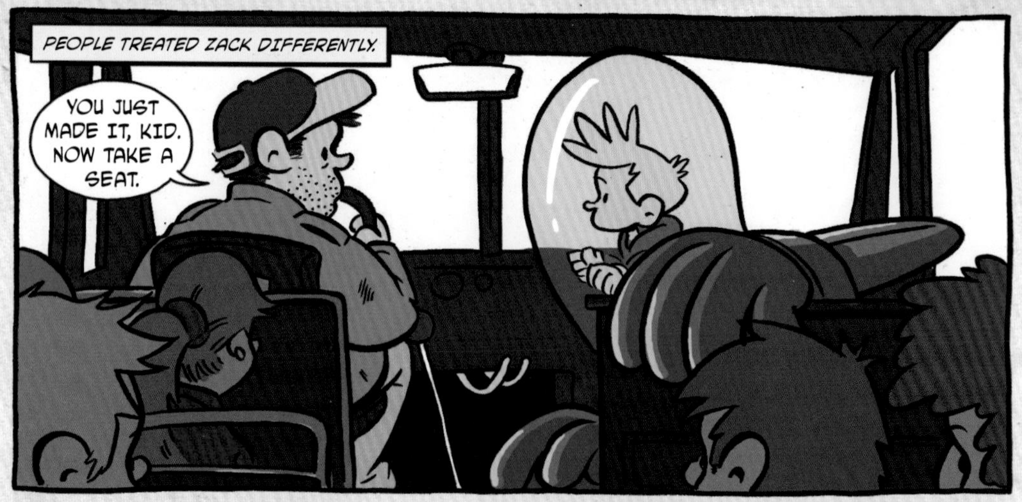
PEOPLE TREATED ZACK DIFFERENTLY.
YOU JUST MADE IT, KID. NOW TAKE A SEAT.

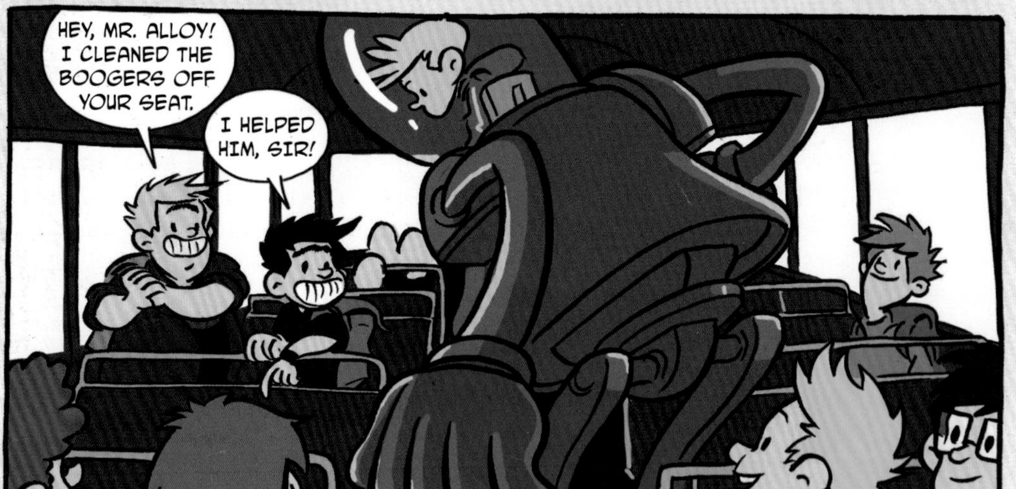
HEY, MR. ALLOY! I CLEANED THE BOOGERS OFF YOUR SEAT.
I HELPED HIM, SIR!

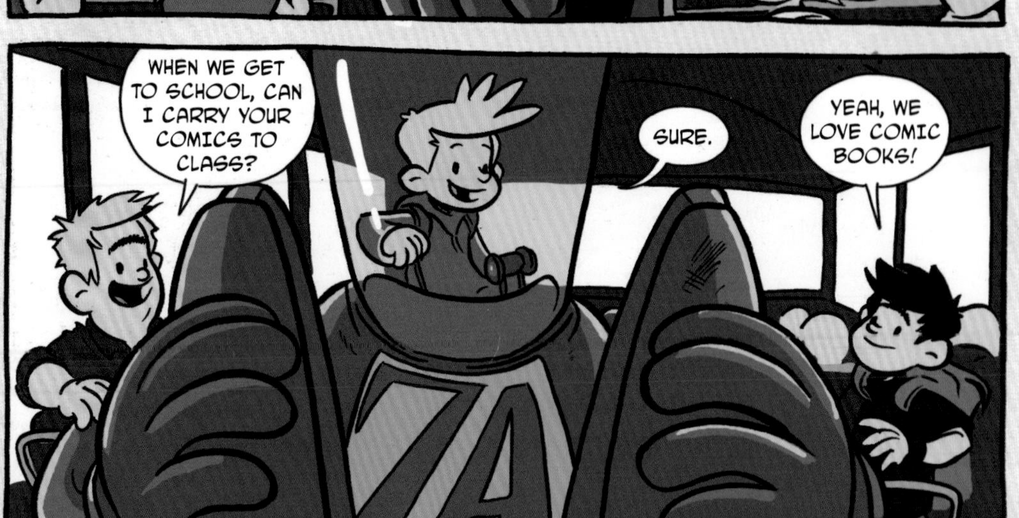
WHEN WE GET TO SCHOOL, CAN I CARRY YOUR COMICS TO CLASS?
SURE.
YEAH, WE LOVE COMIC BOOKS!

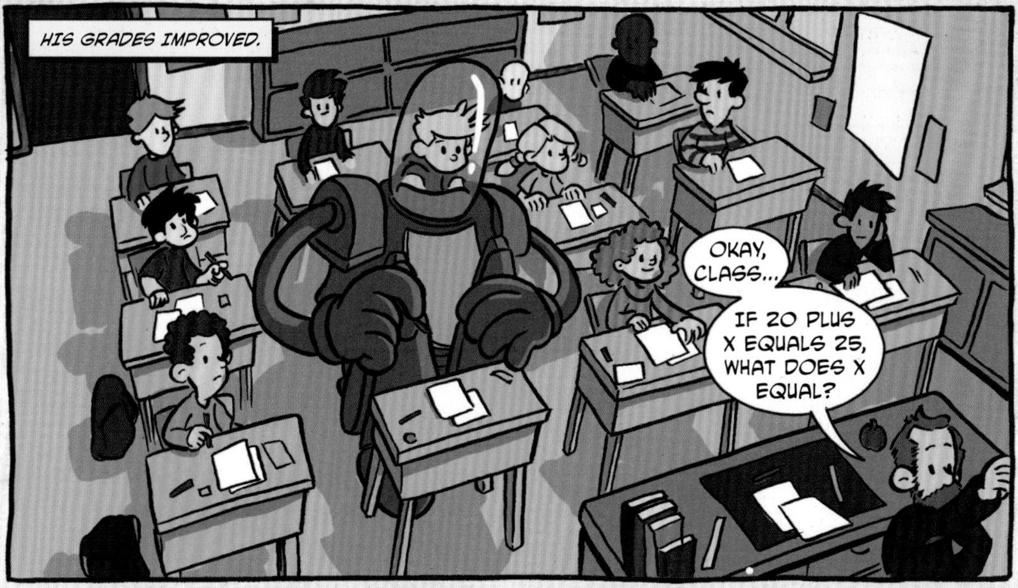
HIS GRADES IMPROVED.
OKAY, CLASS...
IF 20 PLUS X EQUALS 25, WHAT DOES X EQUAL?

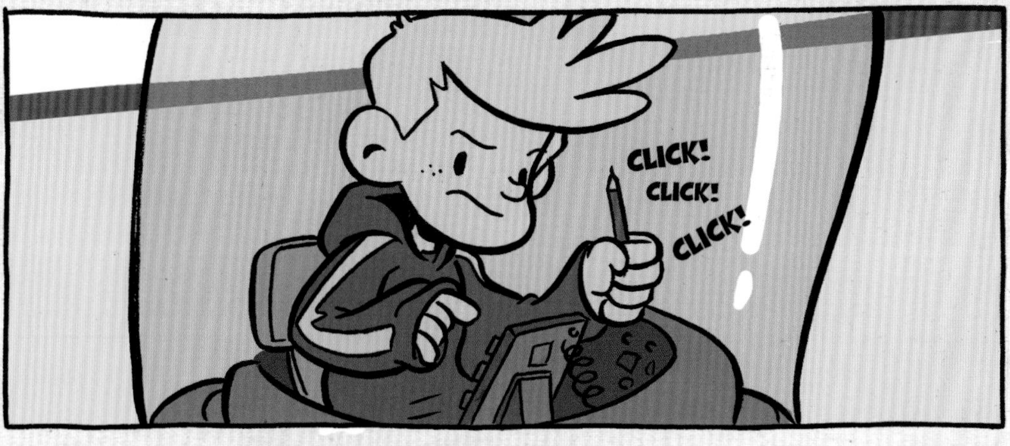
CLICK!
CLICK!
CLICK!

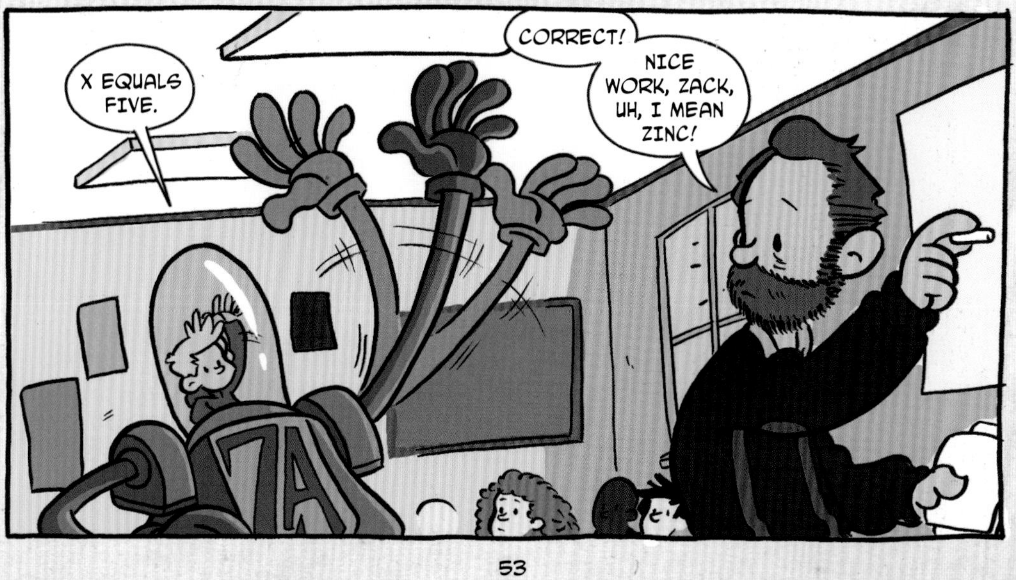
X EQUALS FIVE.
CORRECT!
NICE WORK, ZACK, UH, I MEAN ZINC!

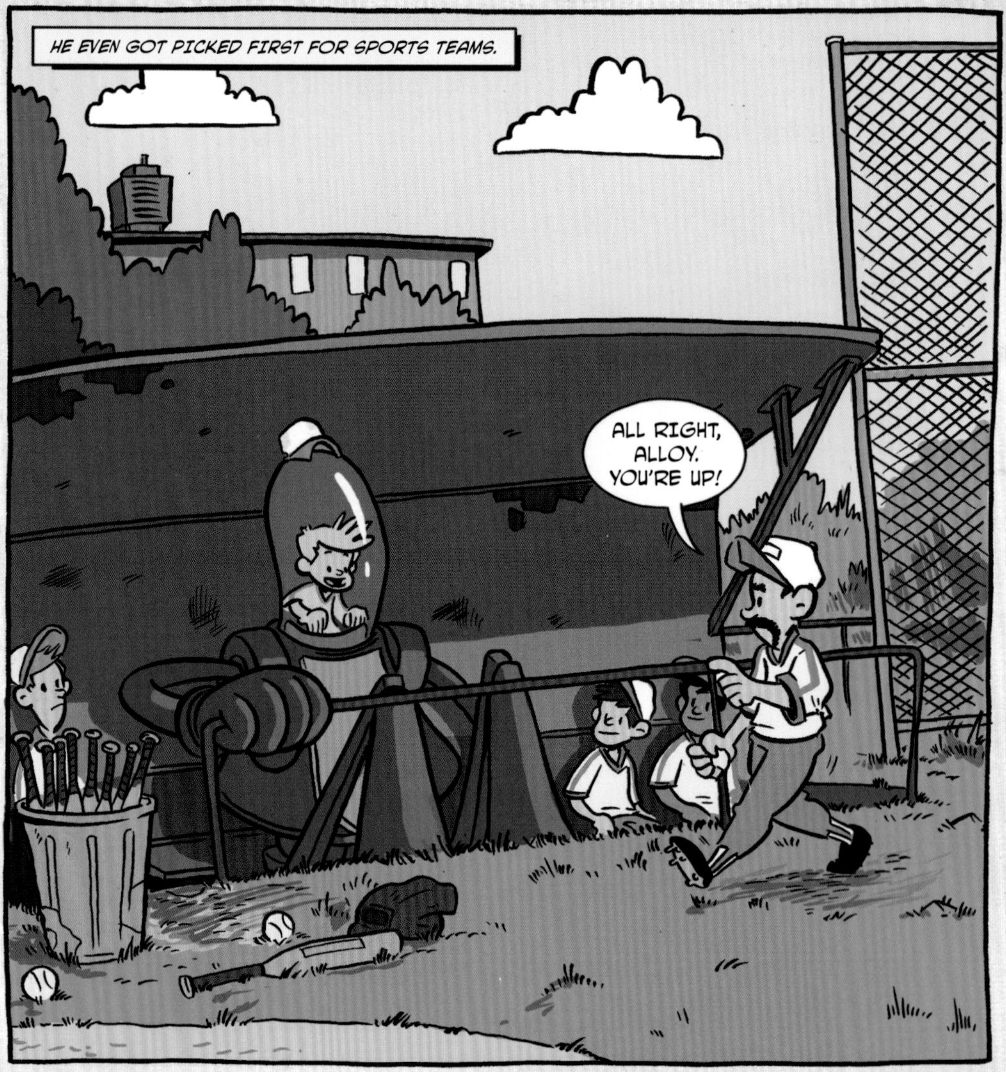
HE EVEN GOT PICKED FIRST FOR SPORTS TEAMS.
ALL RIGHT, ALLOY. YOU'RE UP!

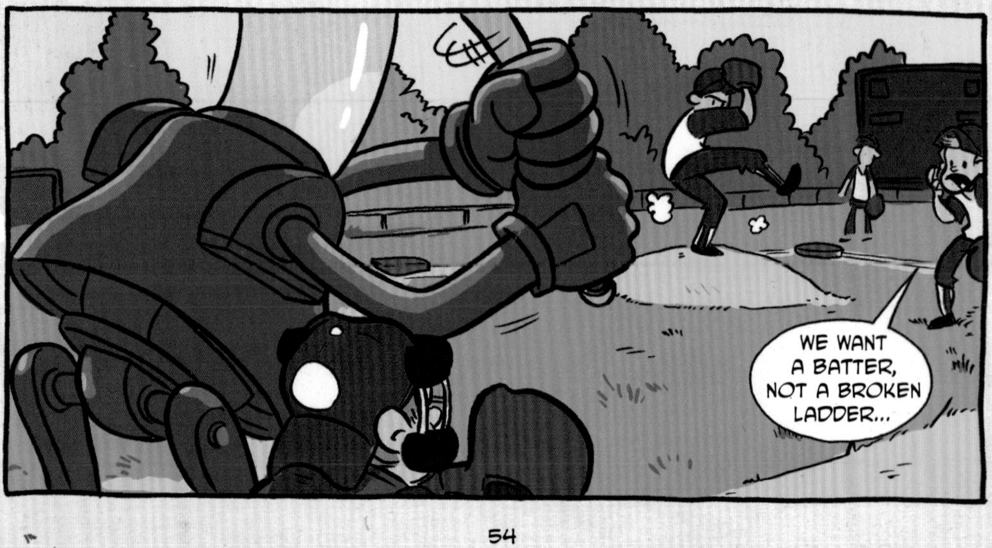
WE WANT A BATTER, NOT A BROKEN LADDER...

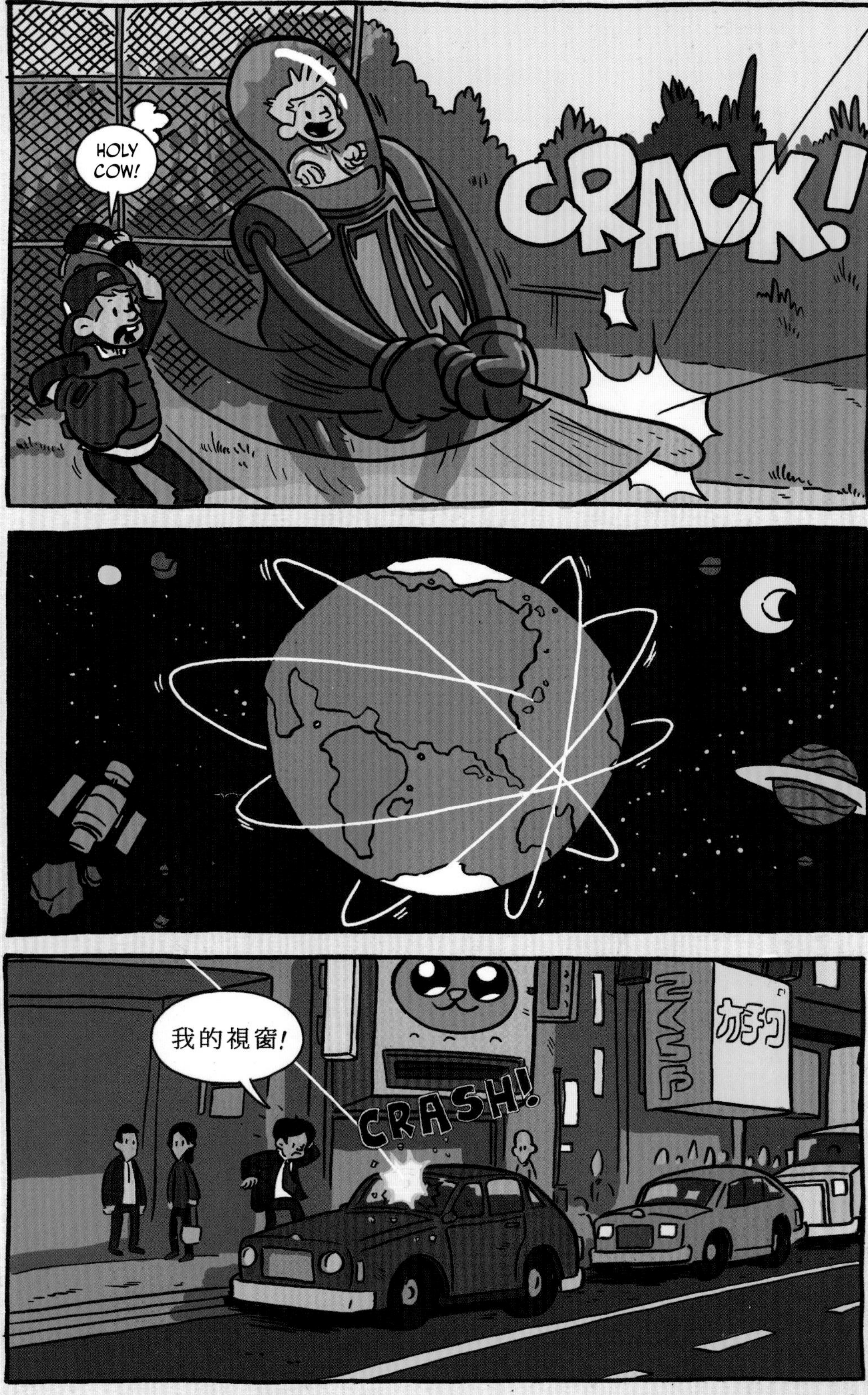
HOLY COW!
CRACK!
我的視窗!
CRASH!

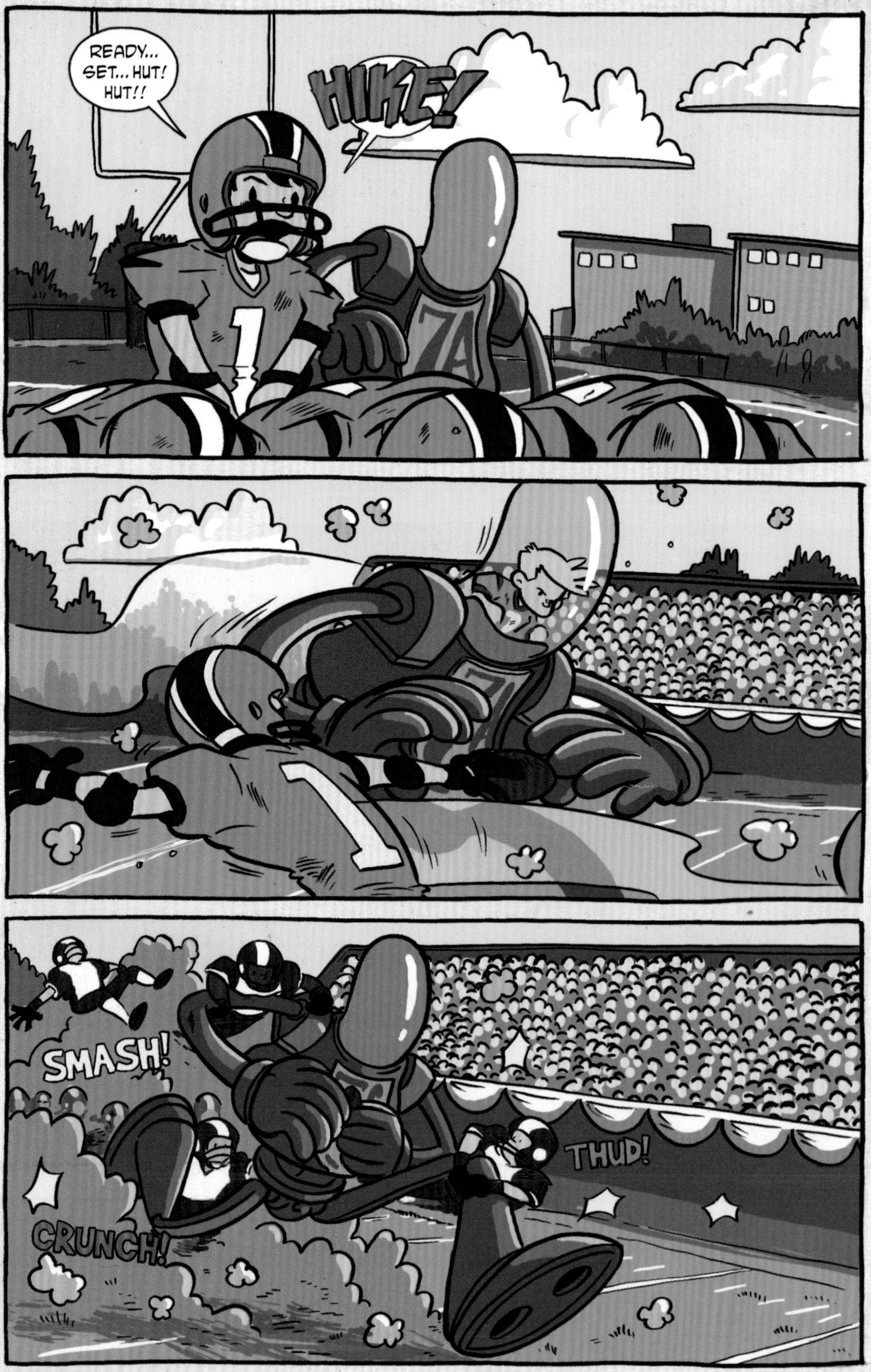
READY... SET... HUT! HUT!!
HIKE!
SMASH!
THUD!
CRUNCH!

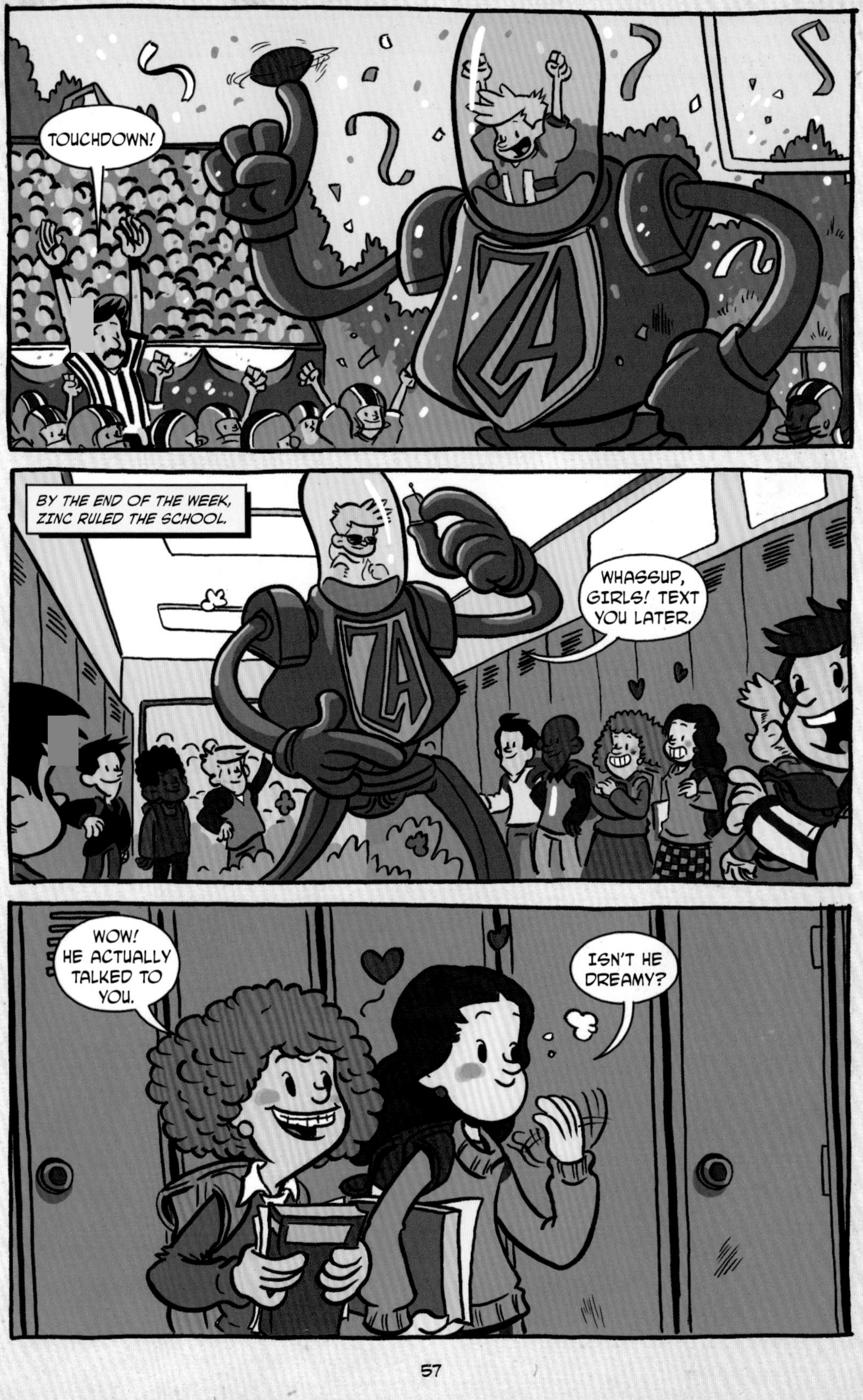
TOUCHDOWN!
BY THE END OF THE WEEK, ZINC RULED THE SCHOOL.
WHASSUP, GIRLS! TEXT YOU LATER.
WOW! HE ACTUALLY TALKED TO YOU.
ISN'T HE DREAMY?

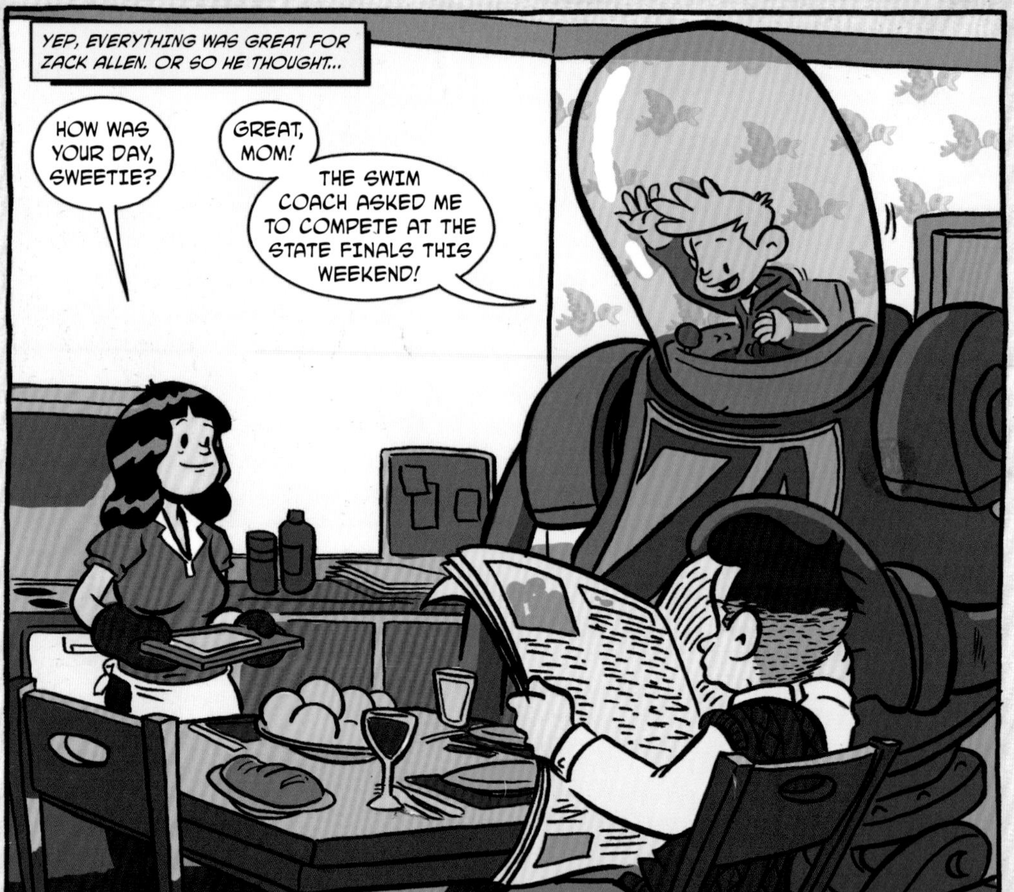
YEP, EVERYTHING WAS GREAT FOR ZACK ALLEN. OR SO HE THOUGHT...
HOW WAS YOUR DAY, SWEETIE?
GREAT, MOM!
THE SWIM COACH ASKED ME TO COMPETE AT THE STATE FINALS THIS WEEKEND!

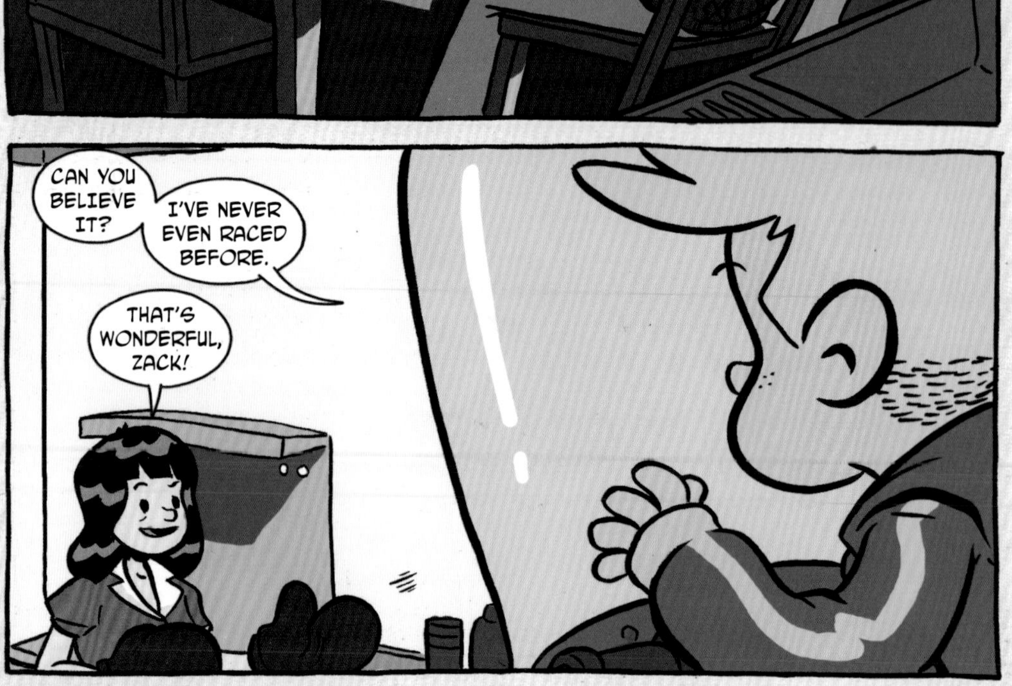
CAN YOU BELIEVE IT?
I'VE NEVER EVEN RACED BEFORE.
THAT'S WONDERFUL, ZACK!

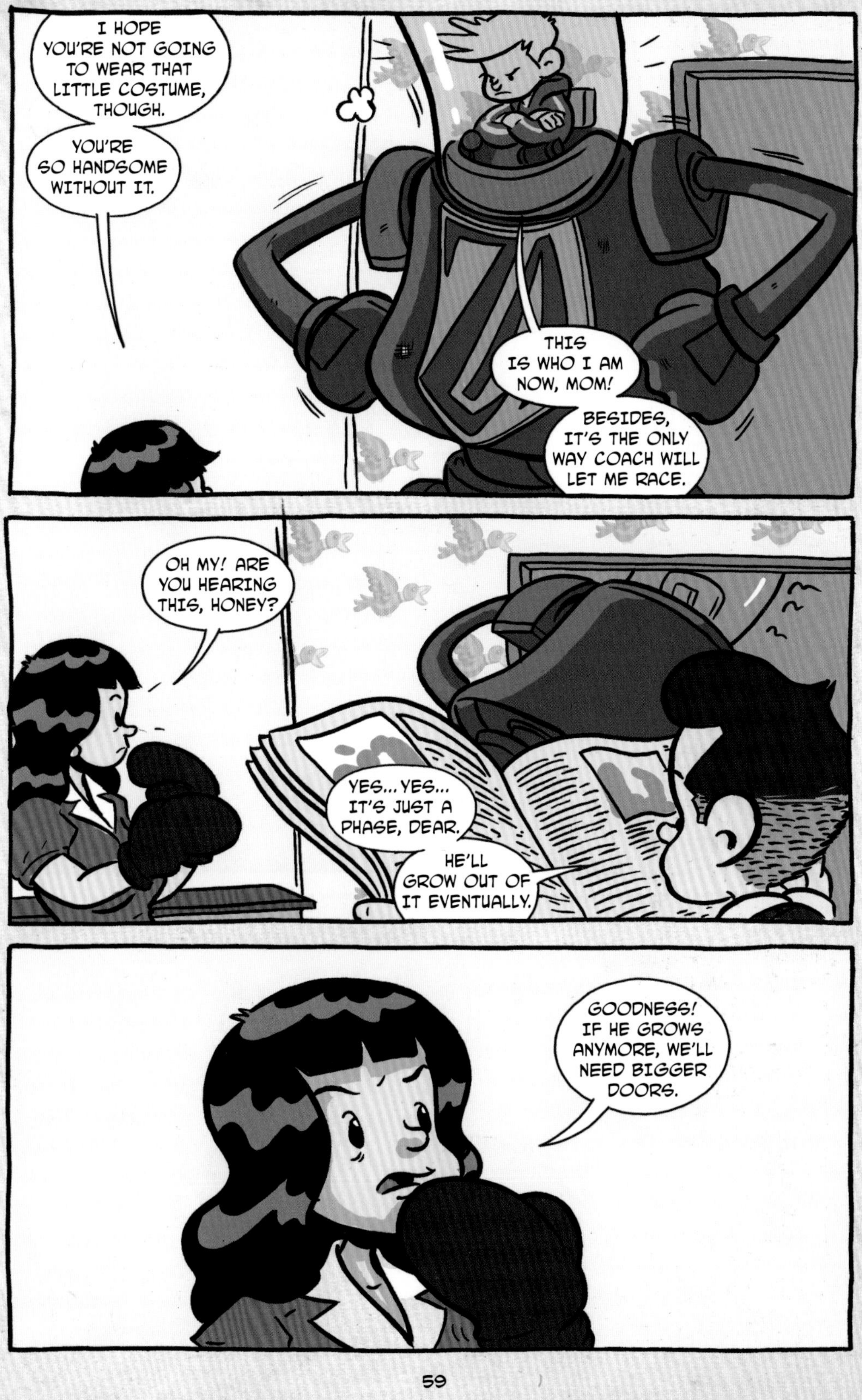
I HOPE YOU'RE NOT GOING TO WEAR THAT LITTLE COSTUME, THOUGH.
YOU'RE SO HANDSOME WITHOUT IT.
THIS IS WHO I AM NOW, MOM!
BESIDES, IT'S THE ONLY WAY COACH WILL LET ME RACE.
OH MY! ARE YOU HEARING THIS, HONEY?
YES... YES... IT'S JUST A PHASE, DEAR.
HE'LL GROW OUT OF IT EVENTUALLY.
GOODNESS! IF HE GROWS ANYMORE, WE'LL NEED BIGGER DOORS.

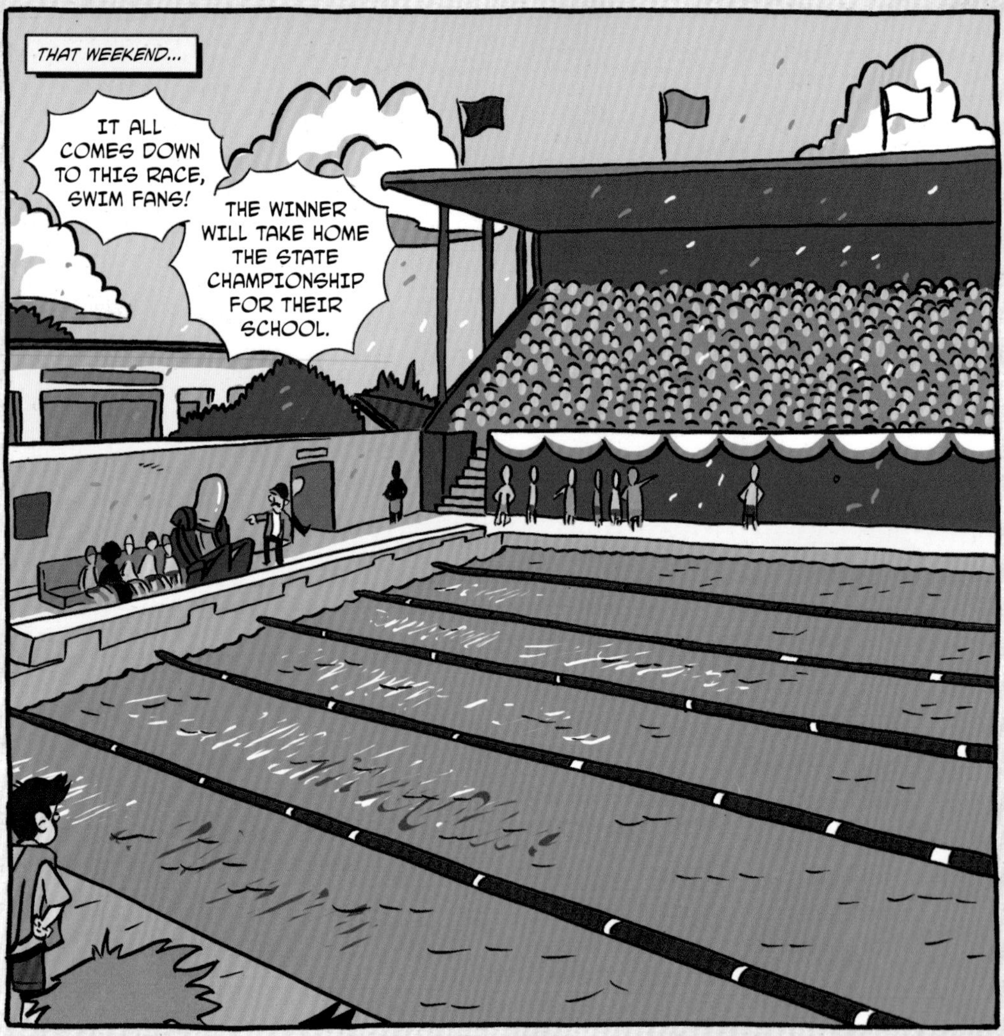
THAT WEEKEND...
IT ALL COMES DOWN TO THIS RACE, SWIM FANS!
THE WINNER WILL TAKE HOME THE STATE CHAMPIONSHIP FOR THEIR SCHOOL.

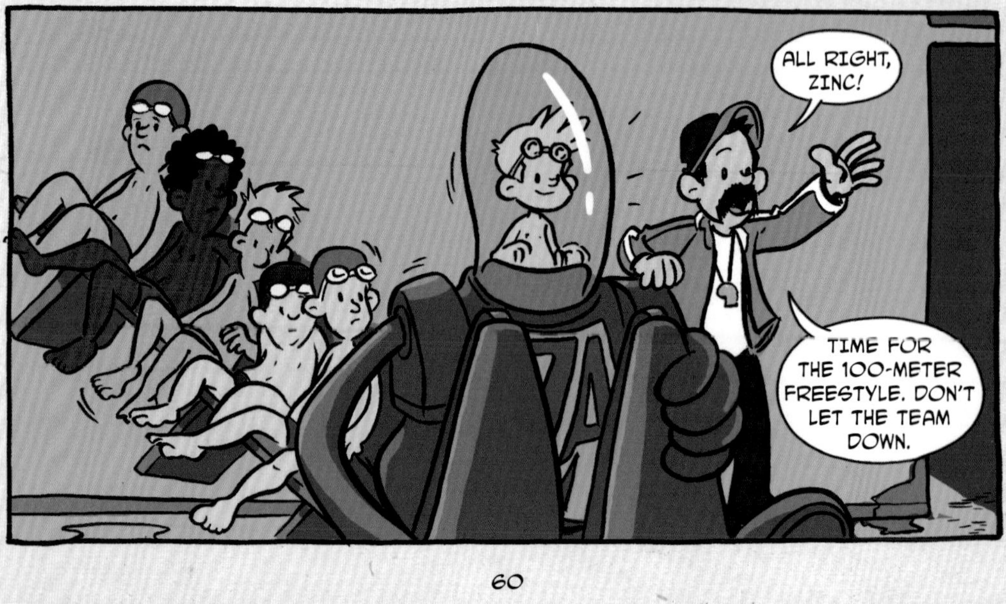
ALL RIGHT, ZINC!
TIME FOR THE 100-METER FREESTYLE. DON'T LET THE TEAM DOWN.

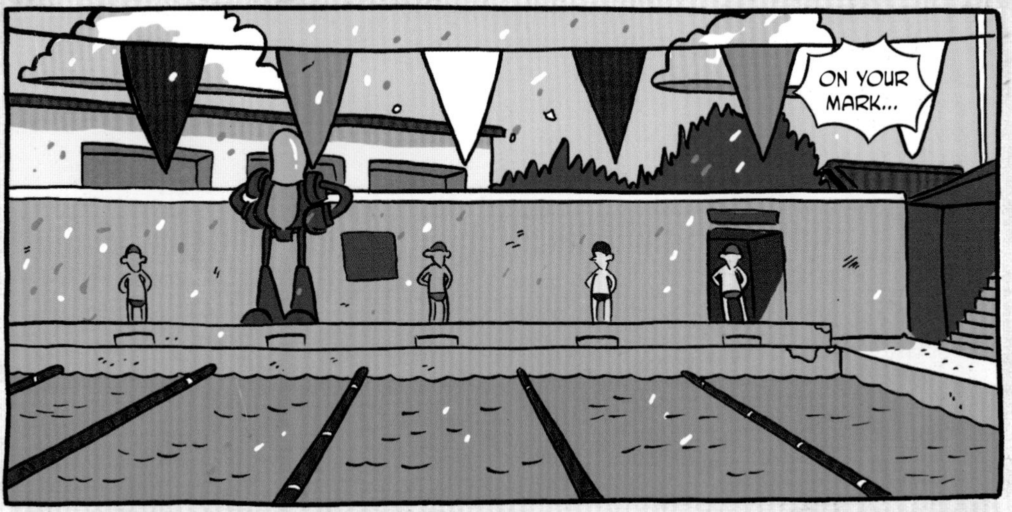
ON YOUR MARK...

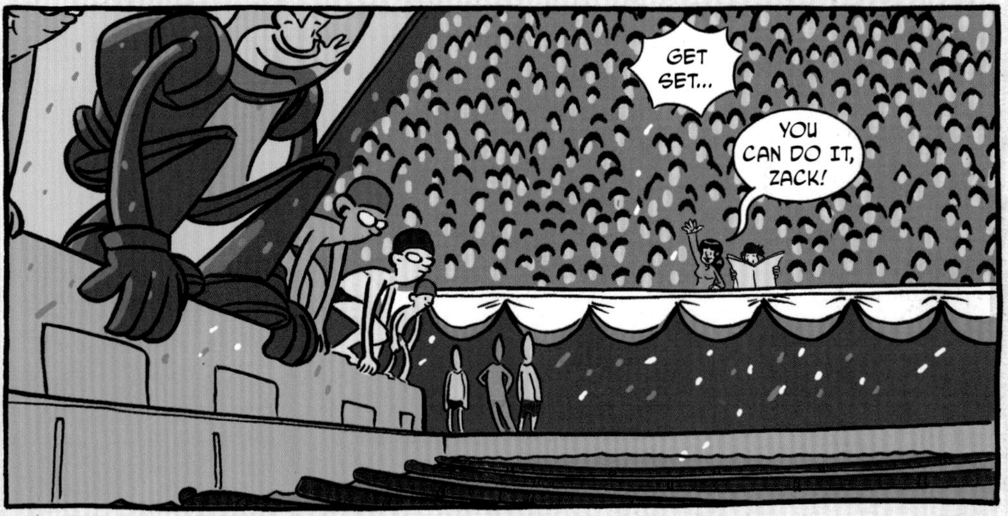
GET SET...
YOU CAN DO IT, ZACK!

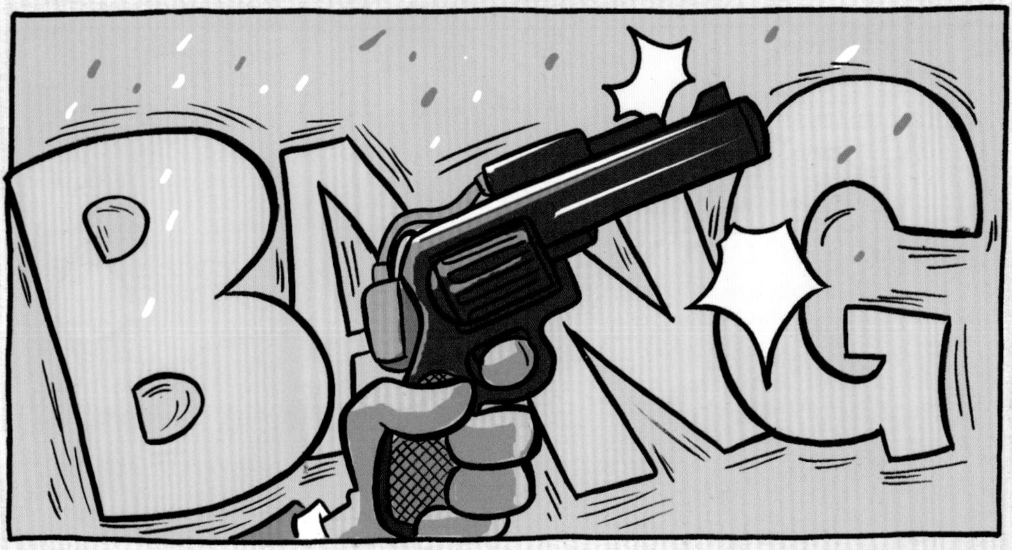
BANG

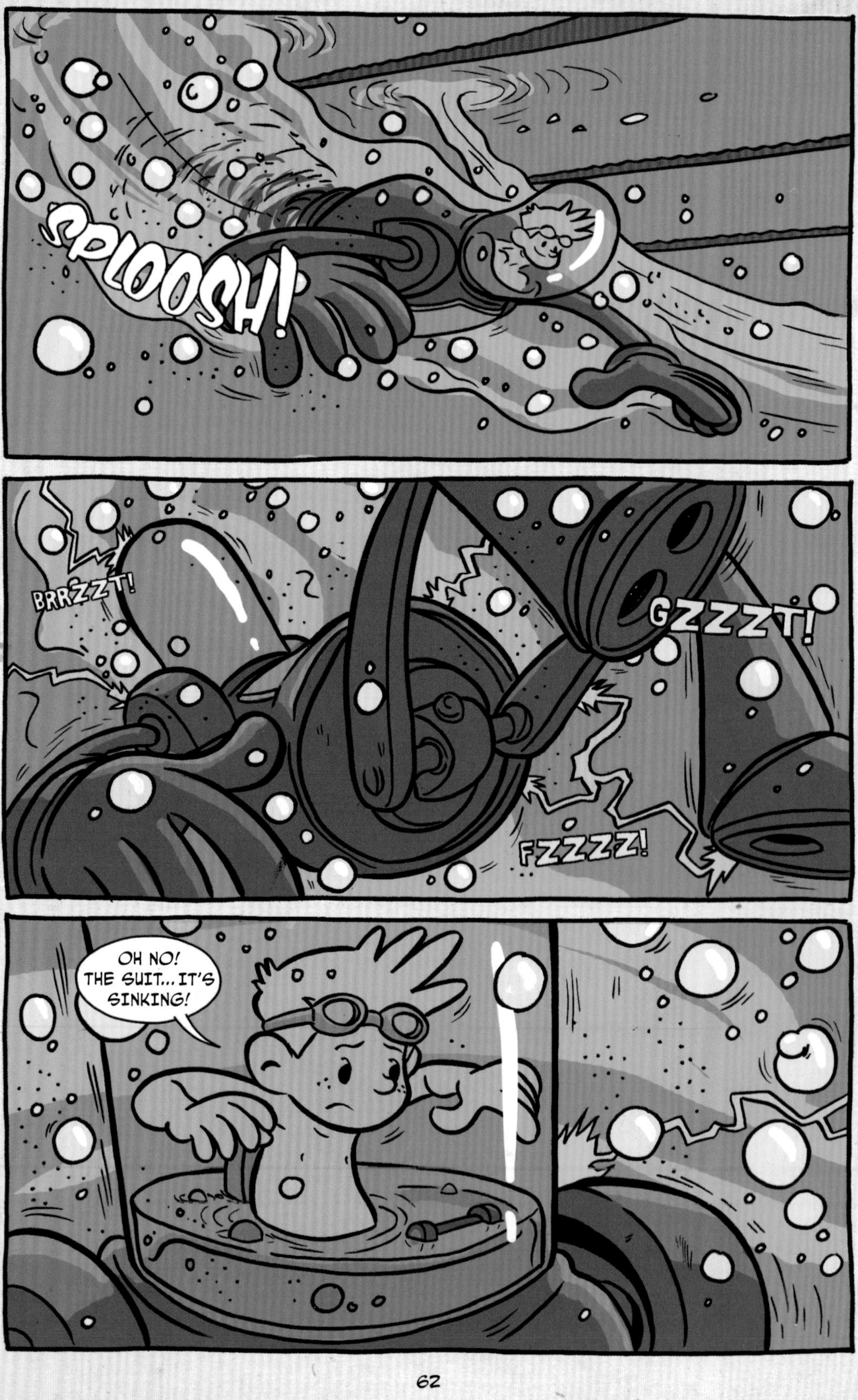
SPLOOSH!
BRRZZZT!
GZZZZT!
FZZZZZ!
OH NO! THE SUIT... IT'S SINKING!

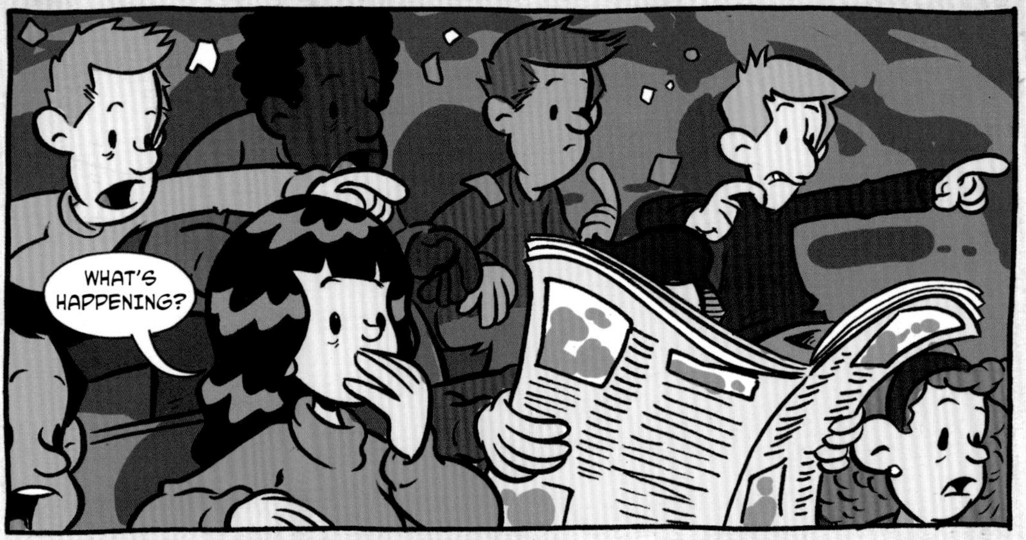
WHAT'S HAPPENING?

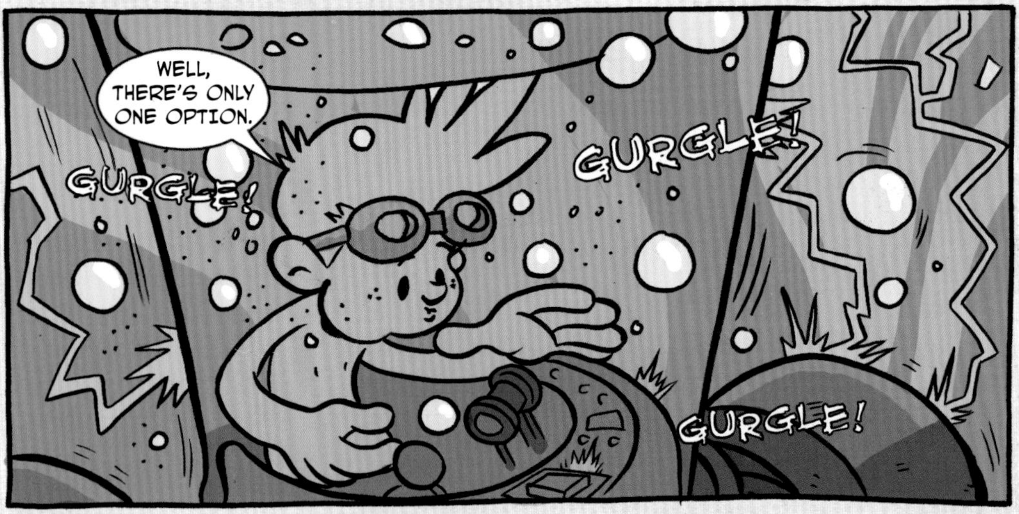
WELL, THERE'S ONLY ONE OPTION.
GURGLE!
GURGLE!
GURGLE!

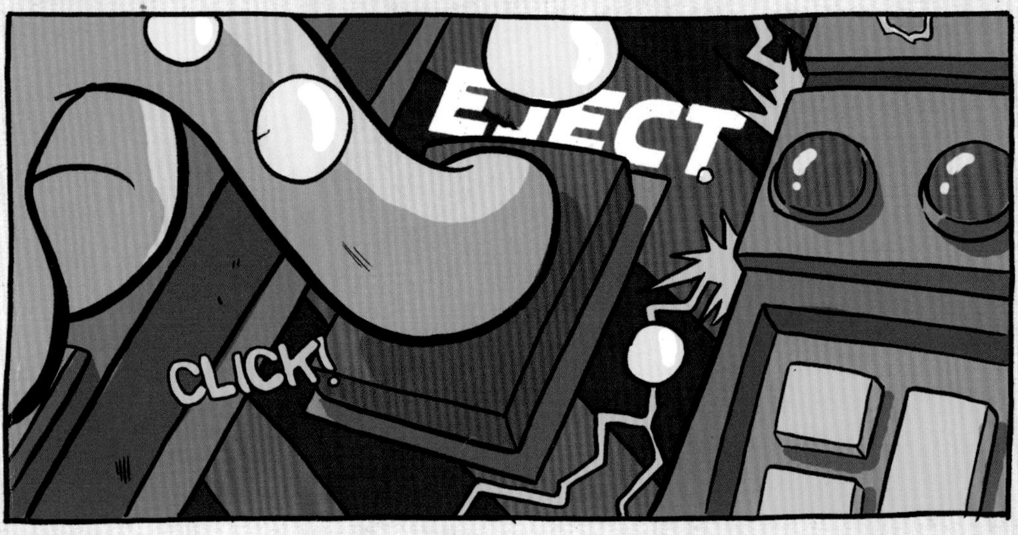
EJECT
CLICK!

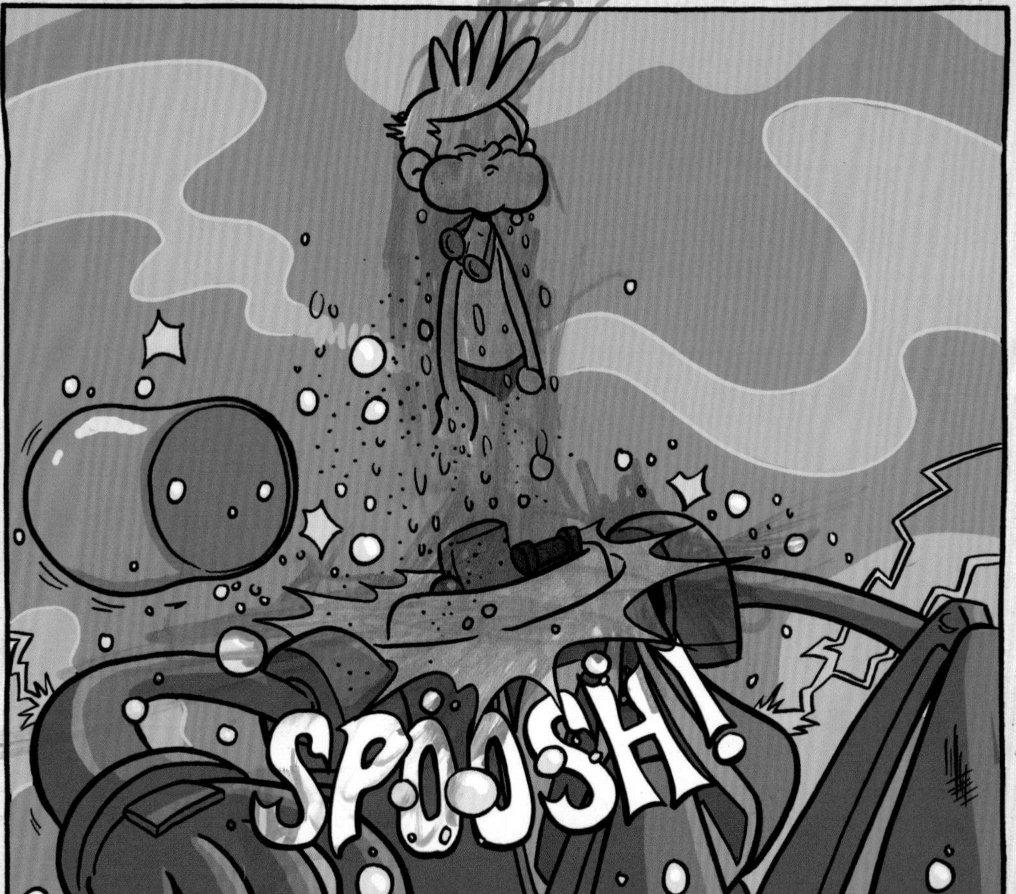
SPOOSH!

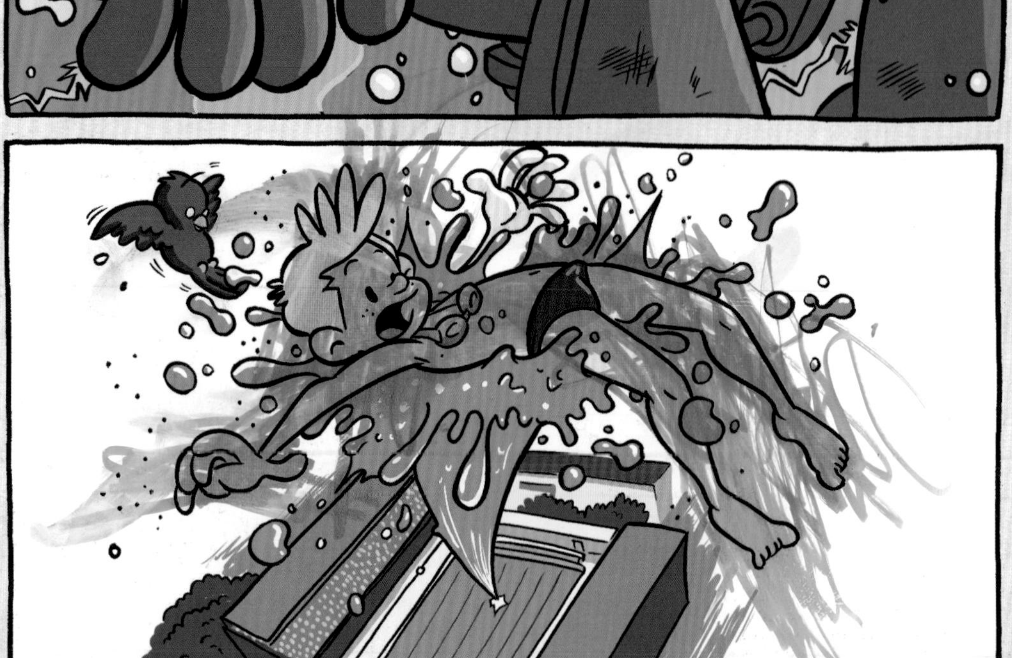

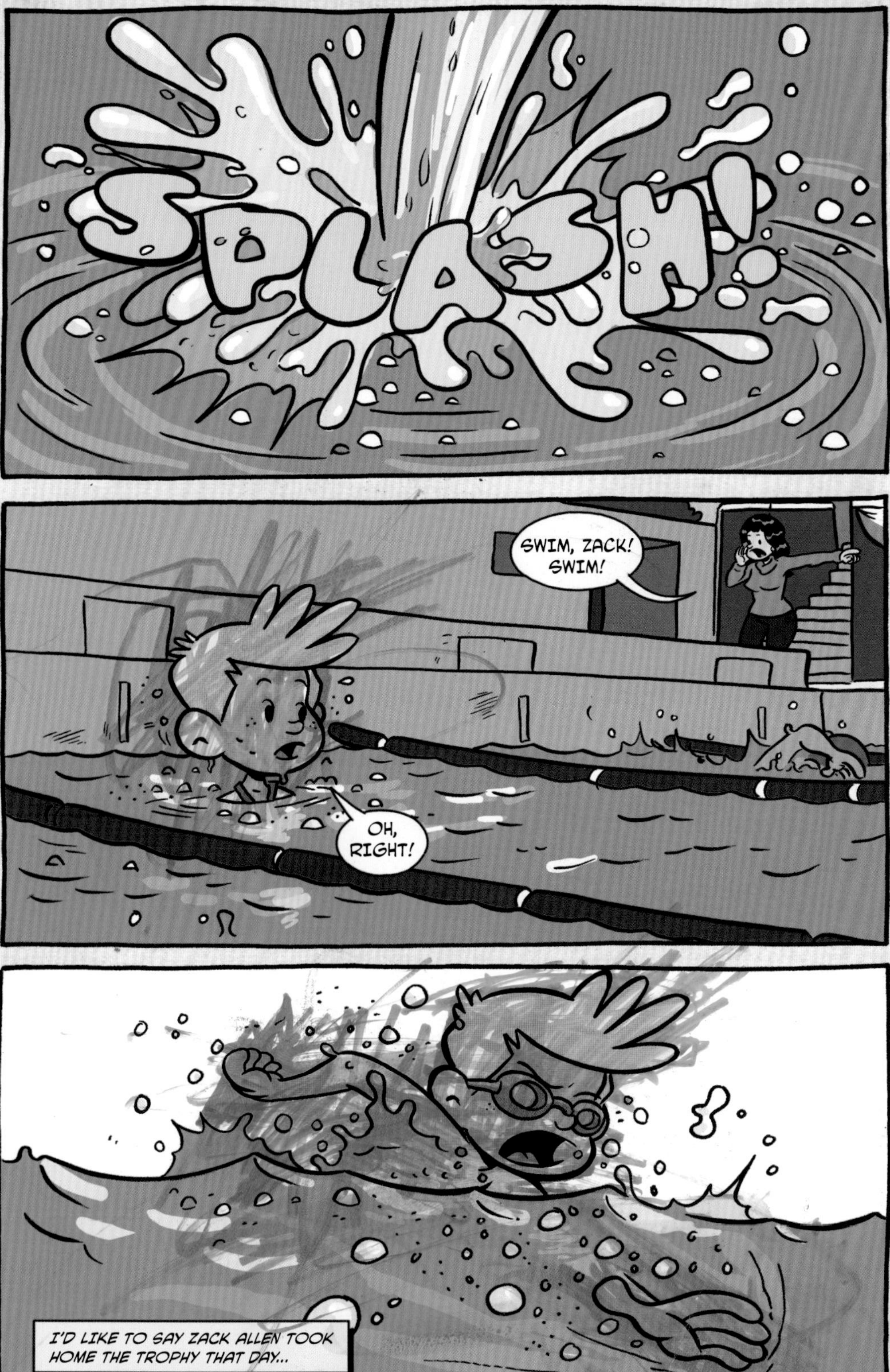
SPLASH!
SWIM, ZACK! SWIM!
OH, RIGHT!
I'D LIKE TO SAY ZACK ALLEN TOOK HOME THE TROPHY THAT DAY...

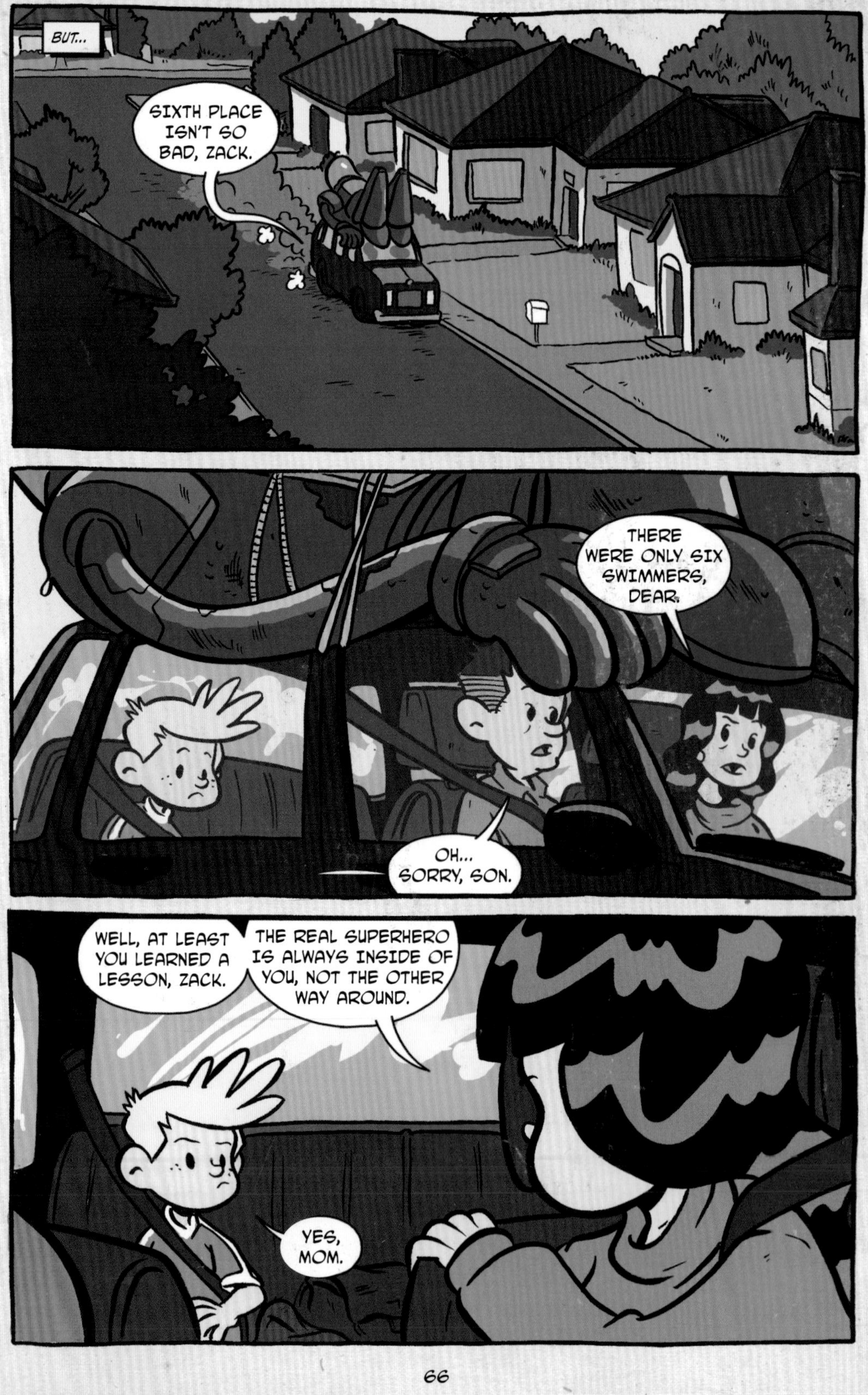
BUT...
SIXTH PLACE ISN'T SO BAD, ZACK.
THERE WERE ONLY SIX SWIMMERS, DEAR.
OH... SORRY, SON.
WELL, AT LEAST YOU LEARNED A LESSON, ZACK.
THE REAL SUPERHERO IS ALWAYS INSIDE OF YOU, NOT THE OTHER WAY AROUND.
YES, MOM.

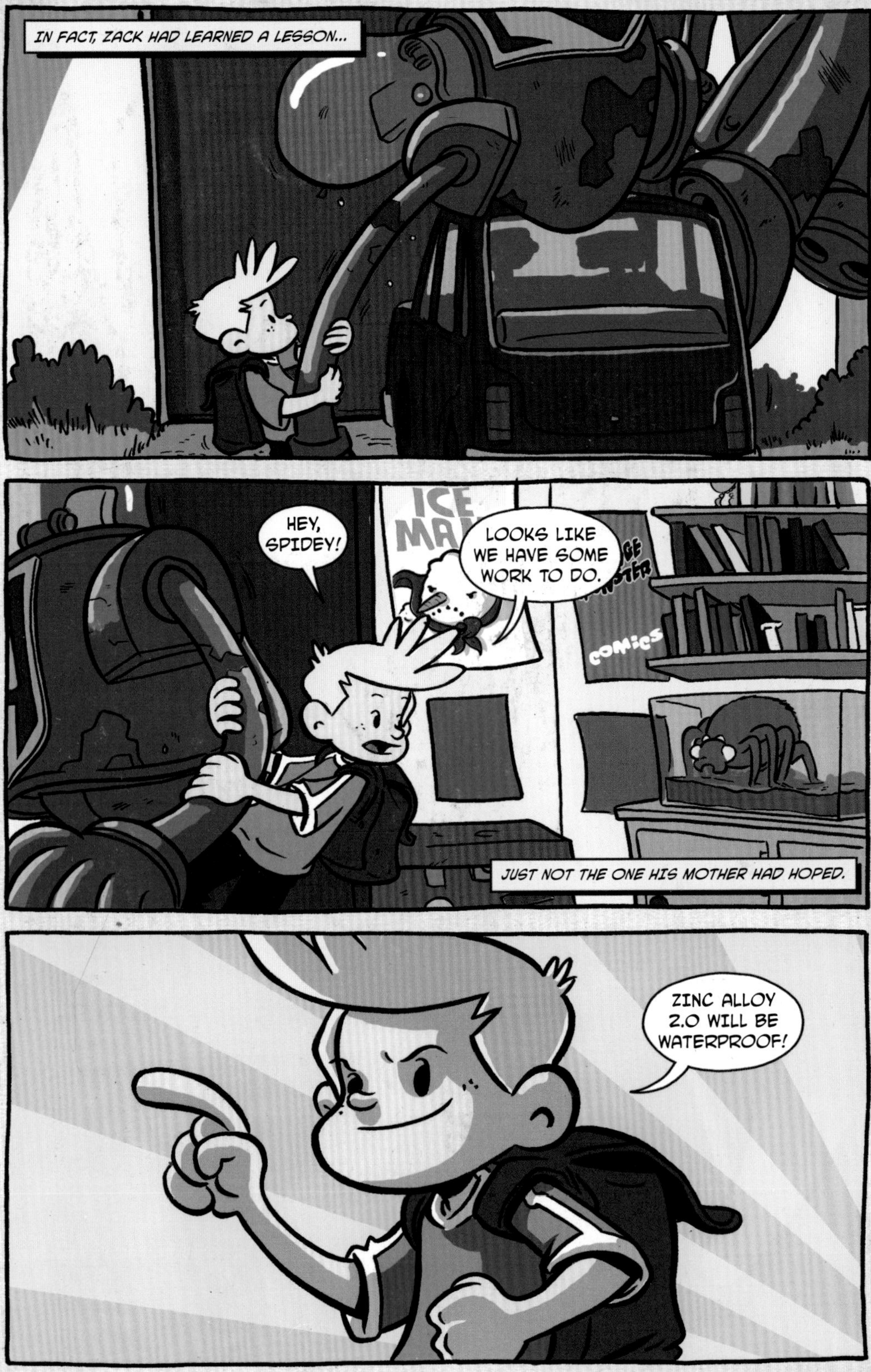
IN FACT, ZACK HAD LEARNED A LESSON...
HEY, SPIDEY!
LOOKS LIKE WE HAVE SOME WORK TO DO.
COMICS
JUST NOT THE ONE HIS MOTHER HAD HOPED.
ZINC ALLOY 2.0 WILL BE WATERPROOF!

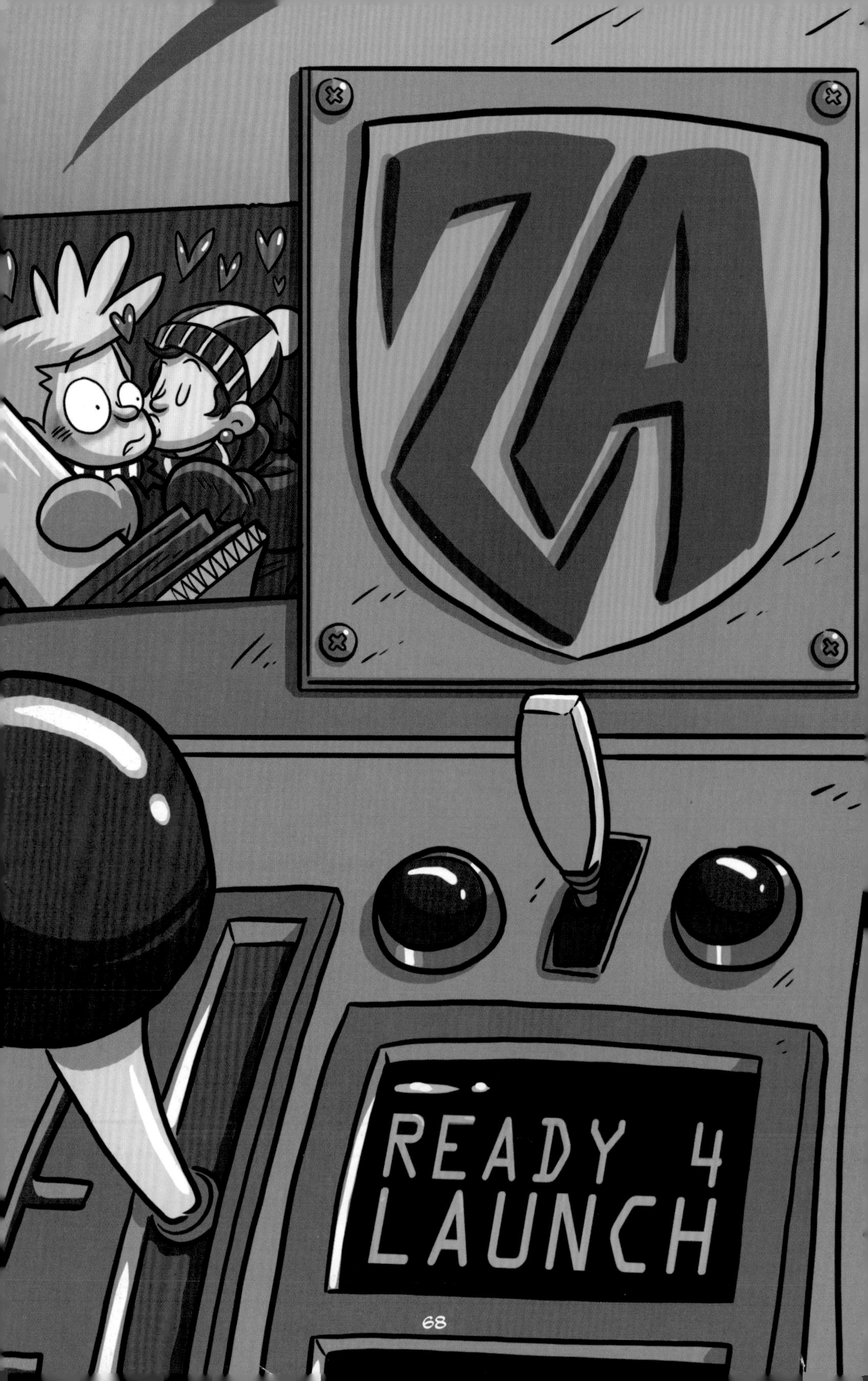
ZA
READY 4 LAUNCH

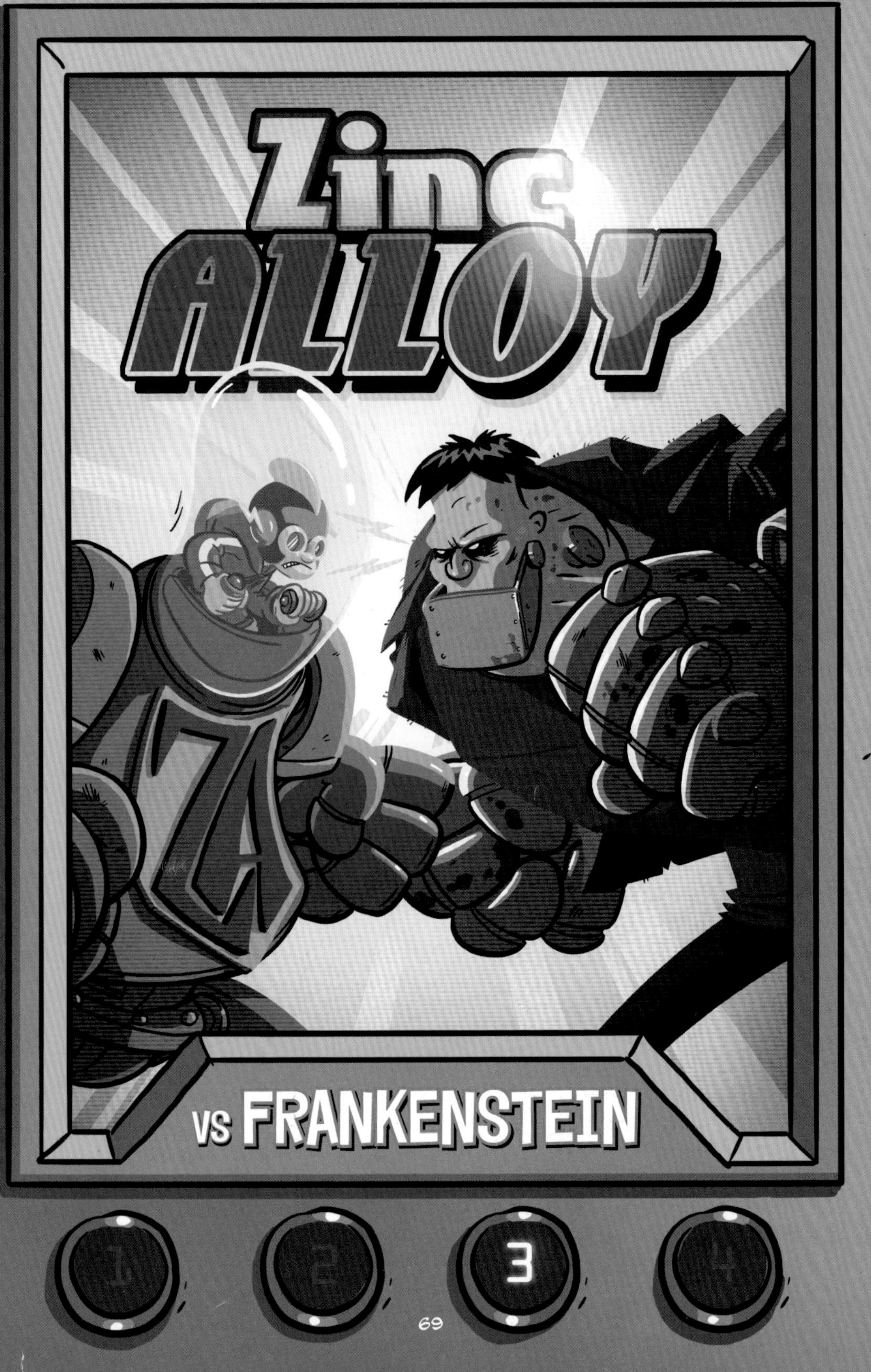
Zinc ALLOY
VS FRANKENSTEIN
1
2
3
4

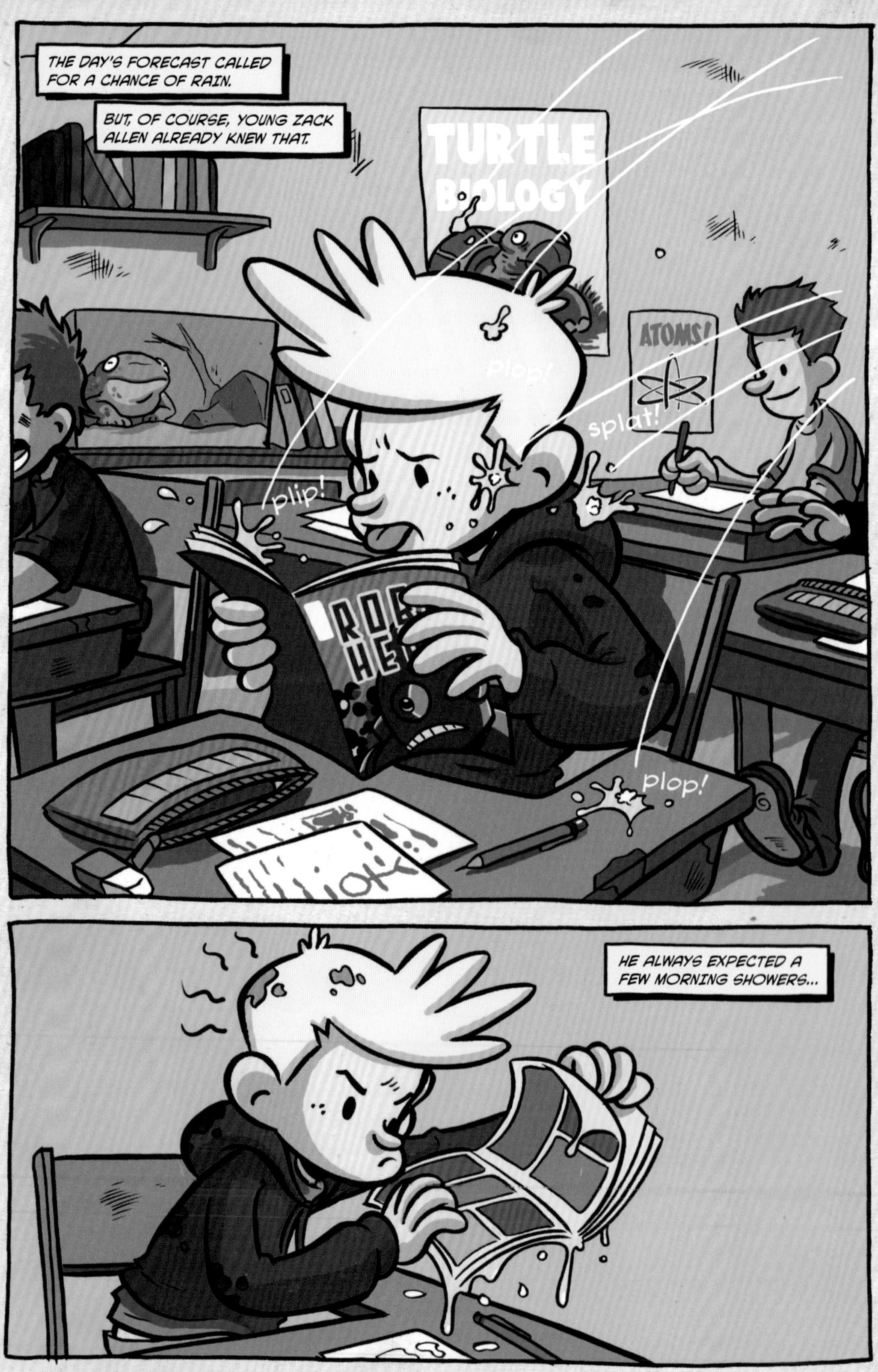

THE DAY'S FORECAST CALLED FOR A CHANCE OF RAIN.
BUT, OF COURSE, YOUNG ZACK ALLEN ALREADY KNEW THAT.
TURTLE BIOLOGY
ATOMS!
plop!
splat!
plip!
plop!
HE ALWAYS EXPECTED A FEW MORNING SHOWERS...

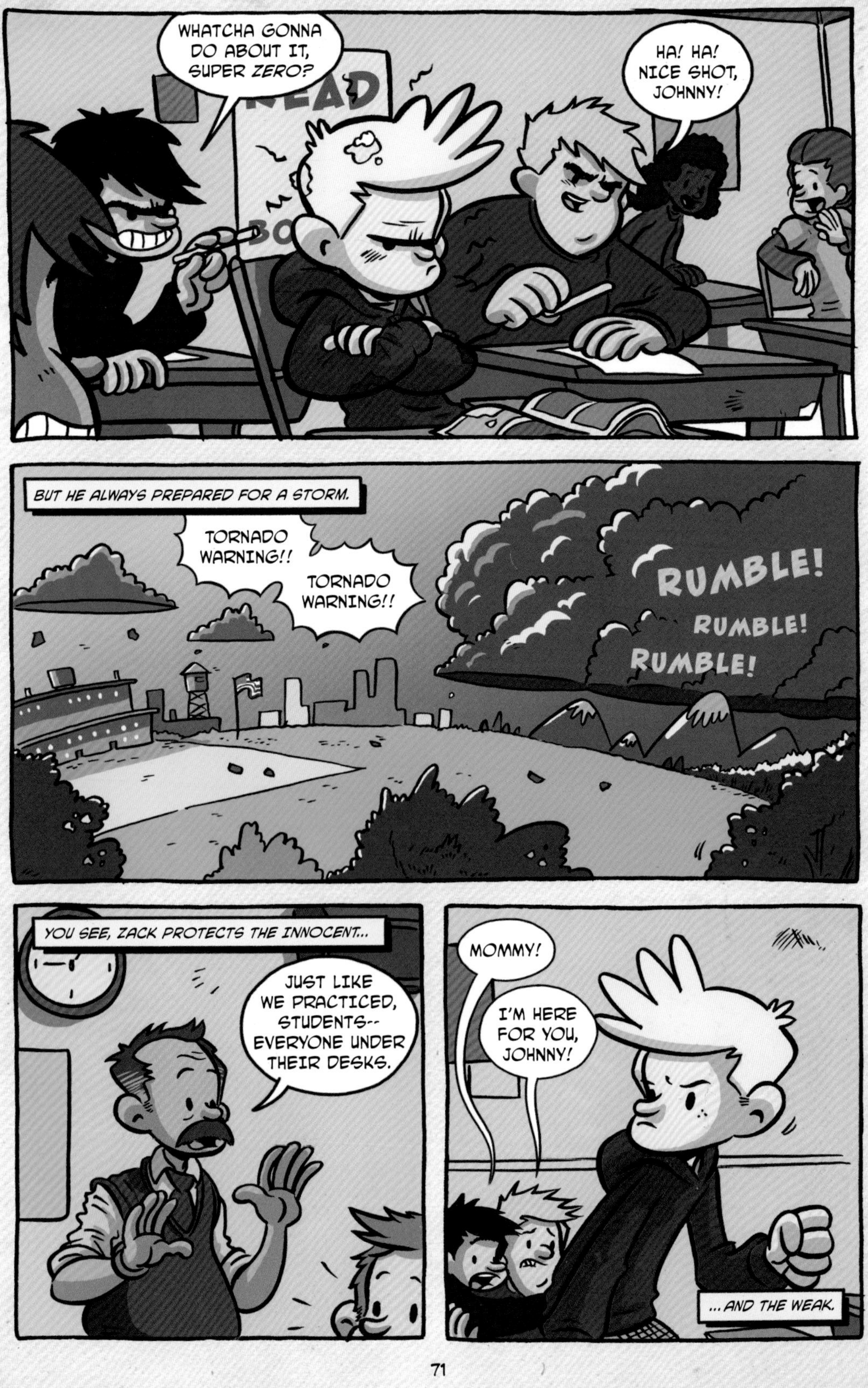
WHATCHA GONNA DO ABOUT IT, SUPER ZERO?
HA! HA! NICE SHOT, JOHNNY!
BUT HE ALWAYS PREPARED FOR A STORM.
TORNADO WARNING!!
TORNADO WARNING!!
RUMBLE!
RUMBLE!
RUMBLE!
YOU SEE, ZACK PROTECTS THE INNOCENT...
JUST LIKE WE PRACTICED, STUDENTS-- EVERYONE UNDER THEIR DESKS.
MOMMY!
I'M HERE FOR YOU, JOHNNY!
...AND THE WEAK.

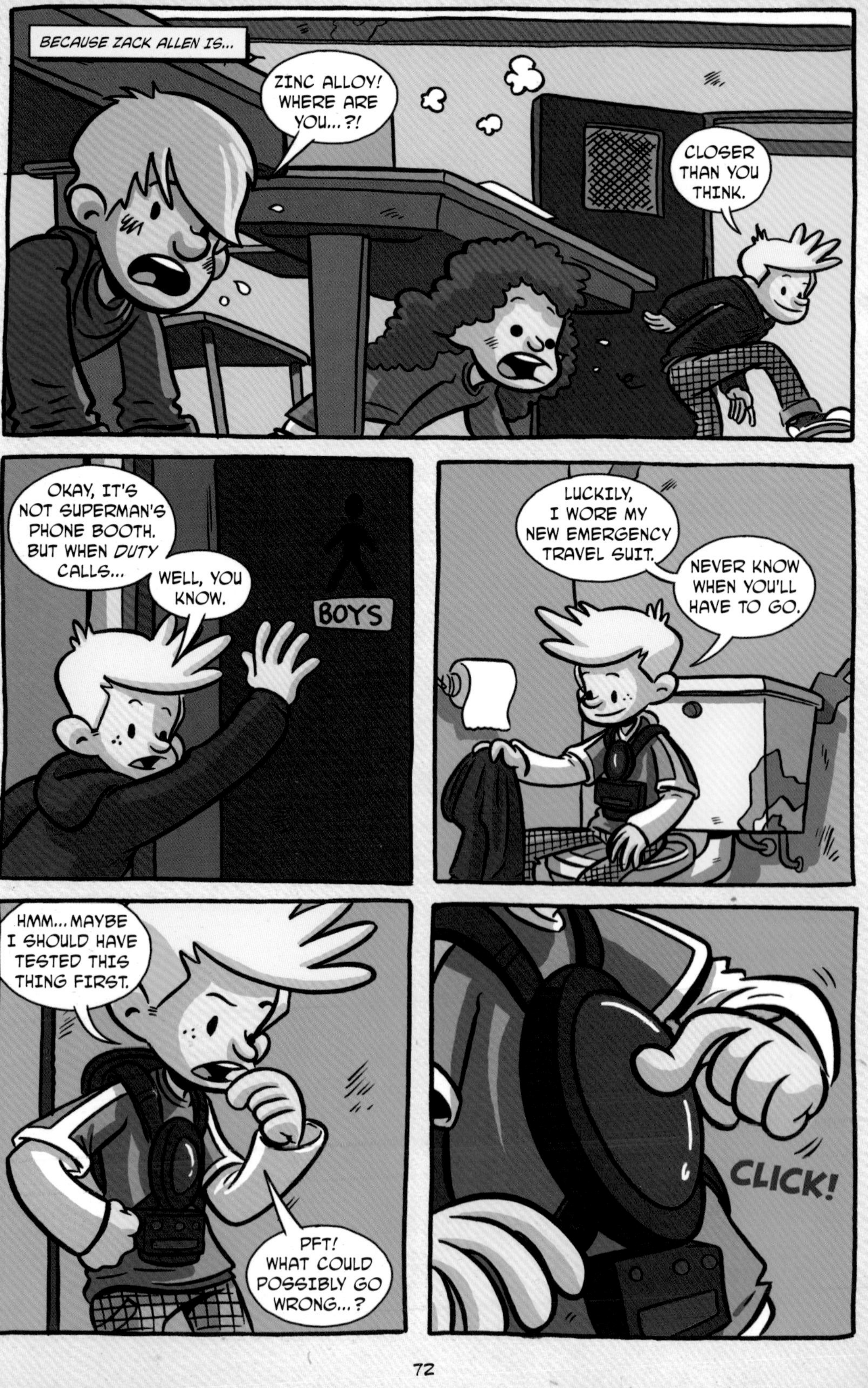

BECAUSE ZACK ALLEN IS...
ZINC ALLOY! WHERE ARE YOU...?!
CLOSER THAN YOU THINK.
OKAY, IT'S NOT SUPERMAN'S PHONE BOOTH. BUT WHEN *DUTY* CALLS...
WELL, YOU KNOW.
BOYS
LUCKILY, I WORE MY NEW EMERGENCY TRAVEL SUIT.
NEVER KNOW WHEN YOU'LL HAVE TO GO.
HMM... MAYBE I SHOULD HAVE TESTED THIS THING FIRST.
PFT! WHAT COULD POSSIBLY GO WRONG...?
CLICK!

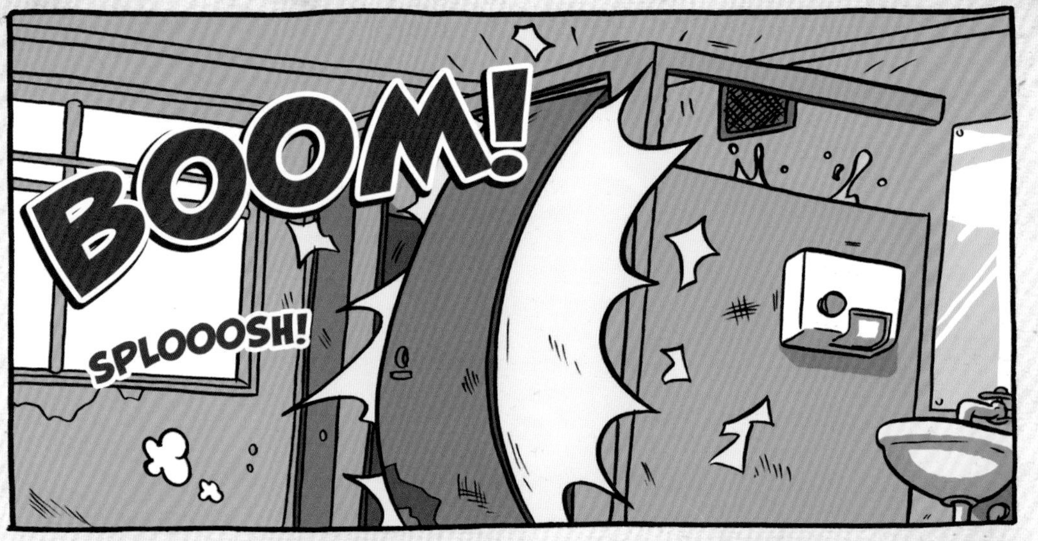
BOOM!
SPLOOOSH!

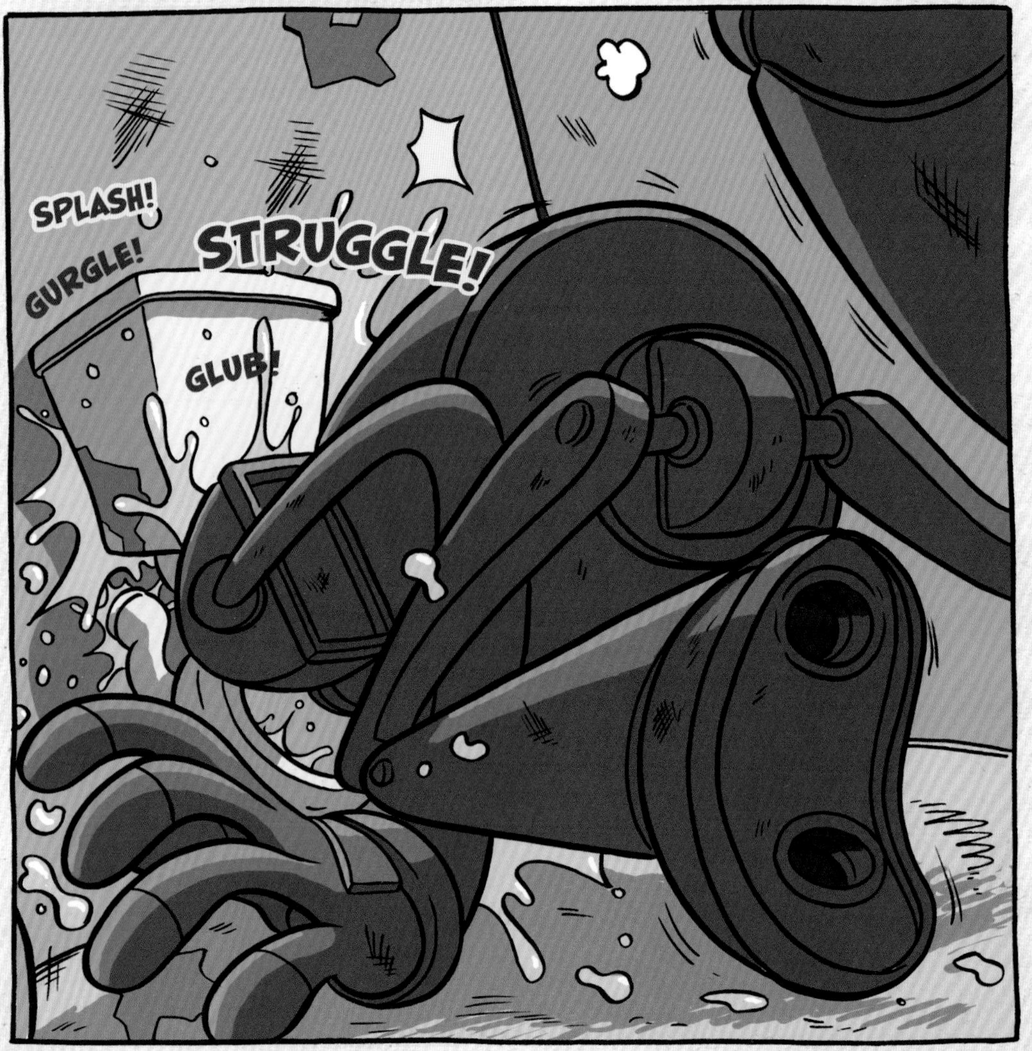
SPLASH!
GURGLE!
STRUGGLE!
GLUB!

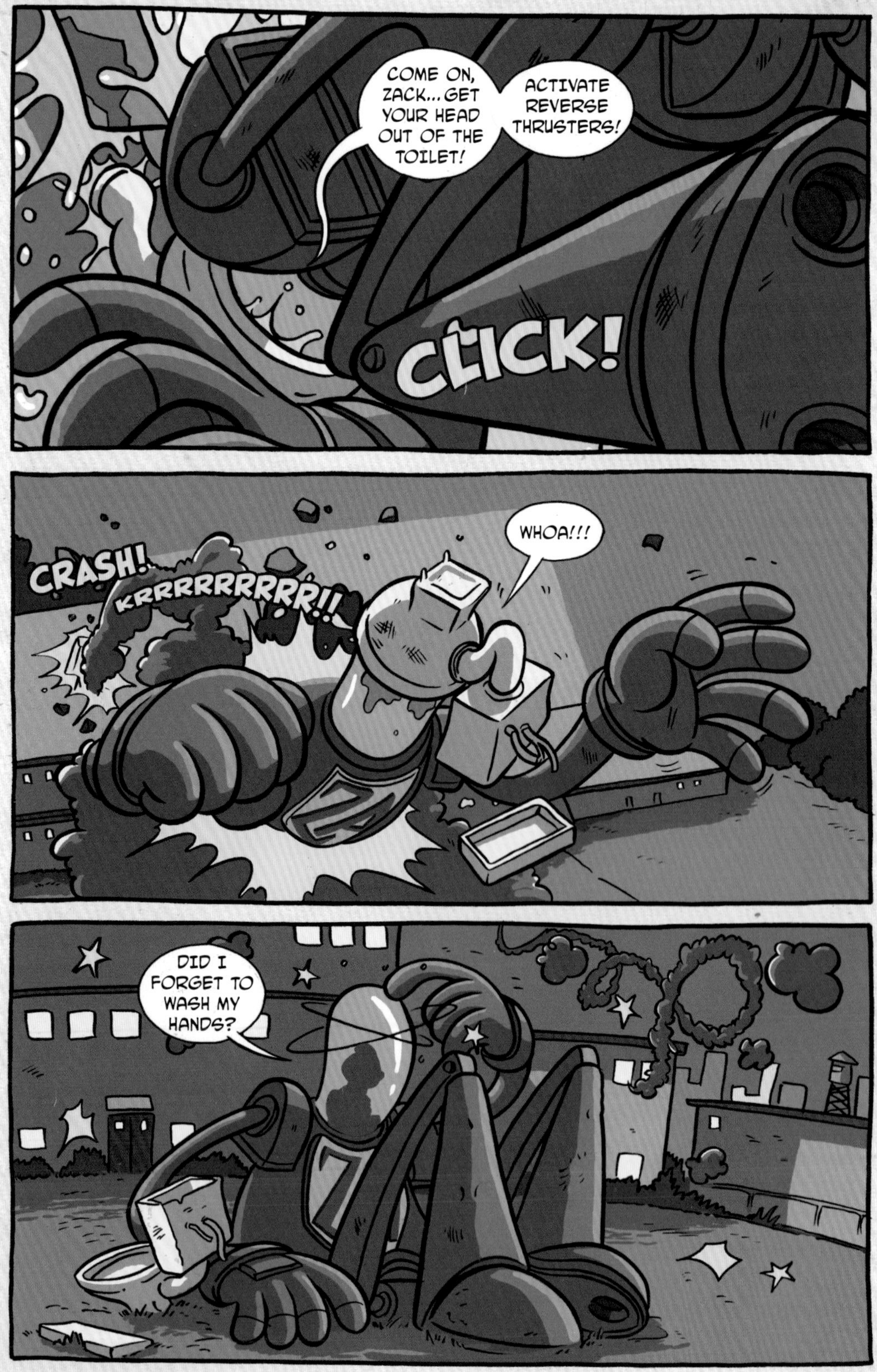
COME ON, ZACK... GET YOUR HEAD OUT OF THE TOILET!
ACTIVATE REVERSE THRUSTERS!
CLICK!
CRASH!
KRRRRRRRRR!!
WHOA!!!
DID I FORGET TO WASH MY HANDS?

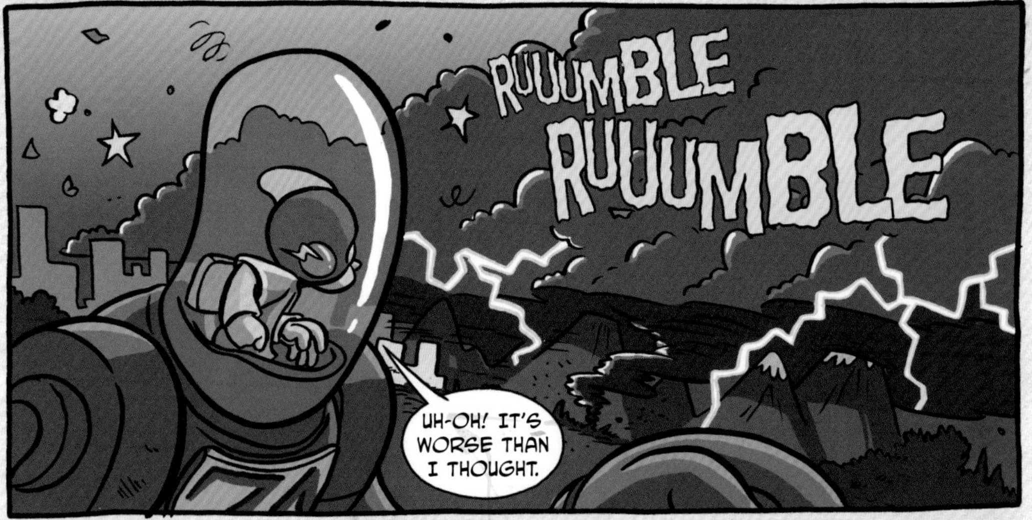
RUUUMBLE
RUUUMBLE
UH-OH! IT'S WORSE THAN I THOUGHT.

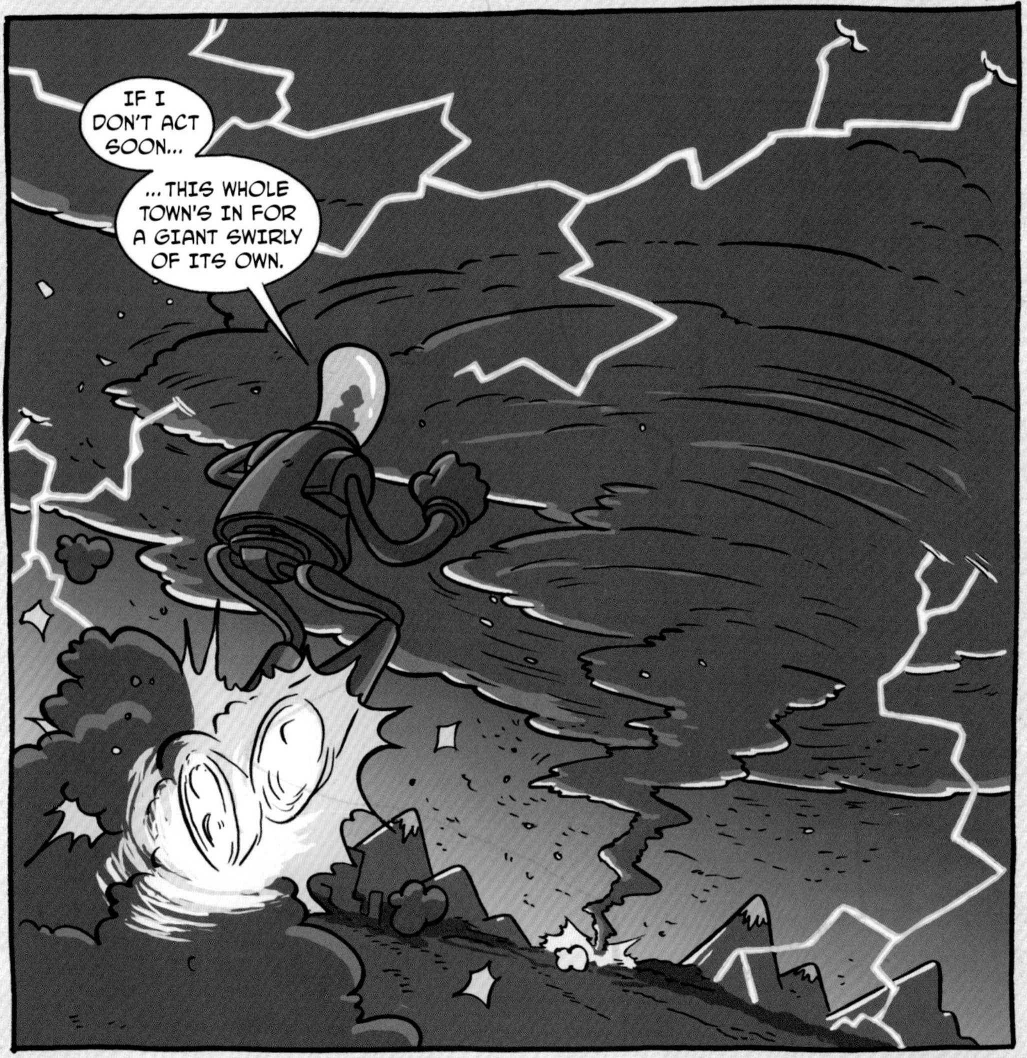
IF I DON'T ACT SOON...
...THIS WHOLE TOWN'S IN FOR A GIANT SWIRLY OF ITS OWN.

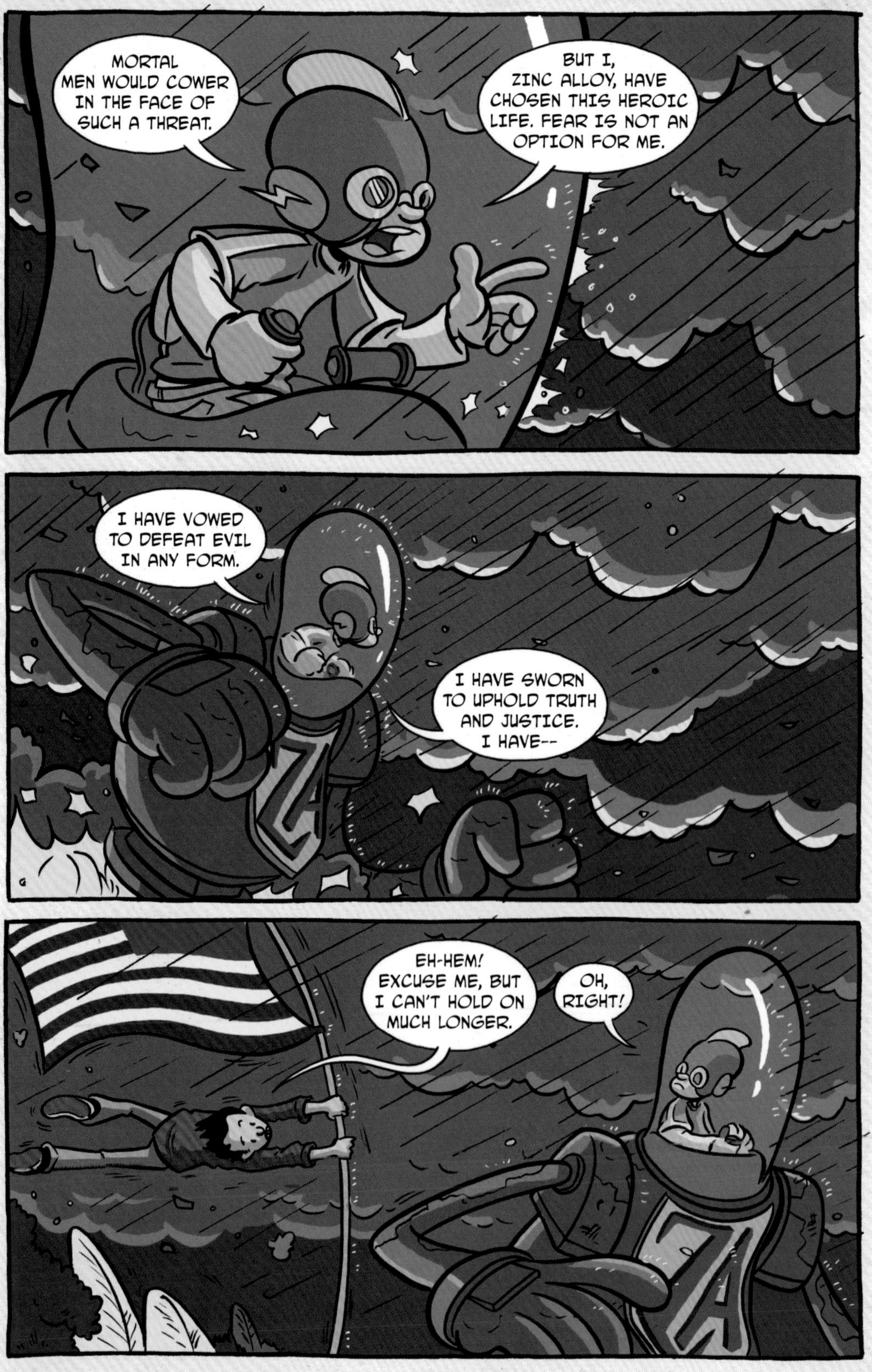
MORTAL MEN WOULD COWER IN THE FACE OF SUCH A THREAT.
BUT I, ZINC ALLOY, HAVE CHOSEN THIS HEROIC LIFE. FEAR IS NOT AN OPTION FOR ME.
I HAVE VOWED TO DEFEAT EVIL IN ANY FORM.
I HAVE SWORN TO UPHOLD TRUTH AND JUSTICE. I HAVE--
EH-HEM! EXCUSE ME, BUT I CAN'T HOLD ON MUCH LONGER.
OH, RIGHT!

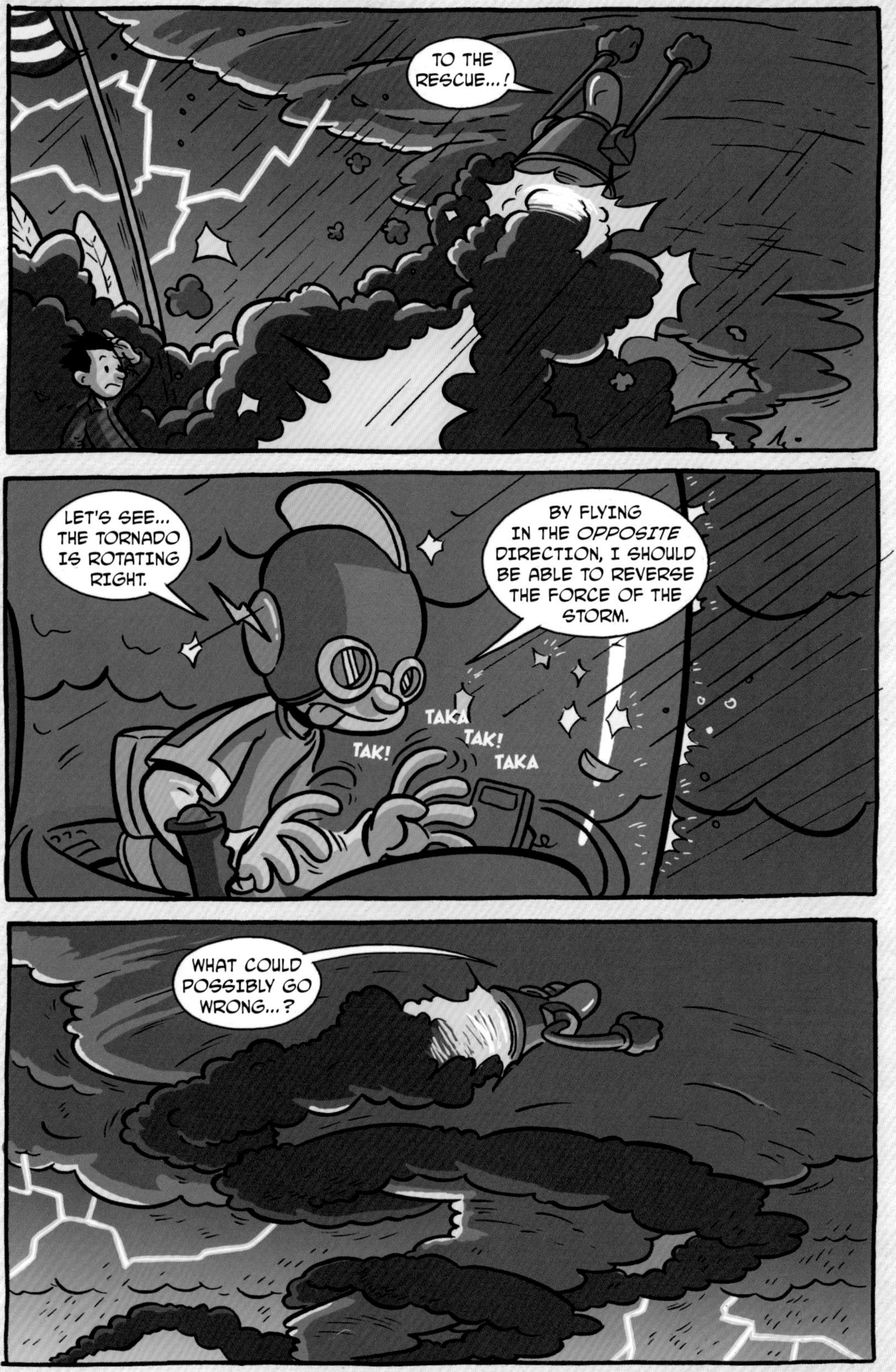
TO THE RESCUE...!
LET'S SEE... THE TORNADO IS ROTATING RIGHT.
BY FLYING IN THE *OPPOSITE* DIRECTION, I SHOULD BE ABLE TO REVERSE THE FORCE OF THE STORM.
TAKA
TAK!
TAK!
TAKA
WHAT COULD POSSIBLY GO WRONG...?

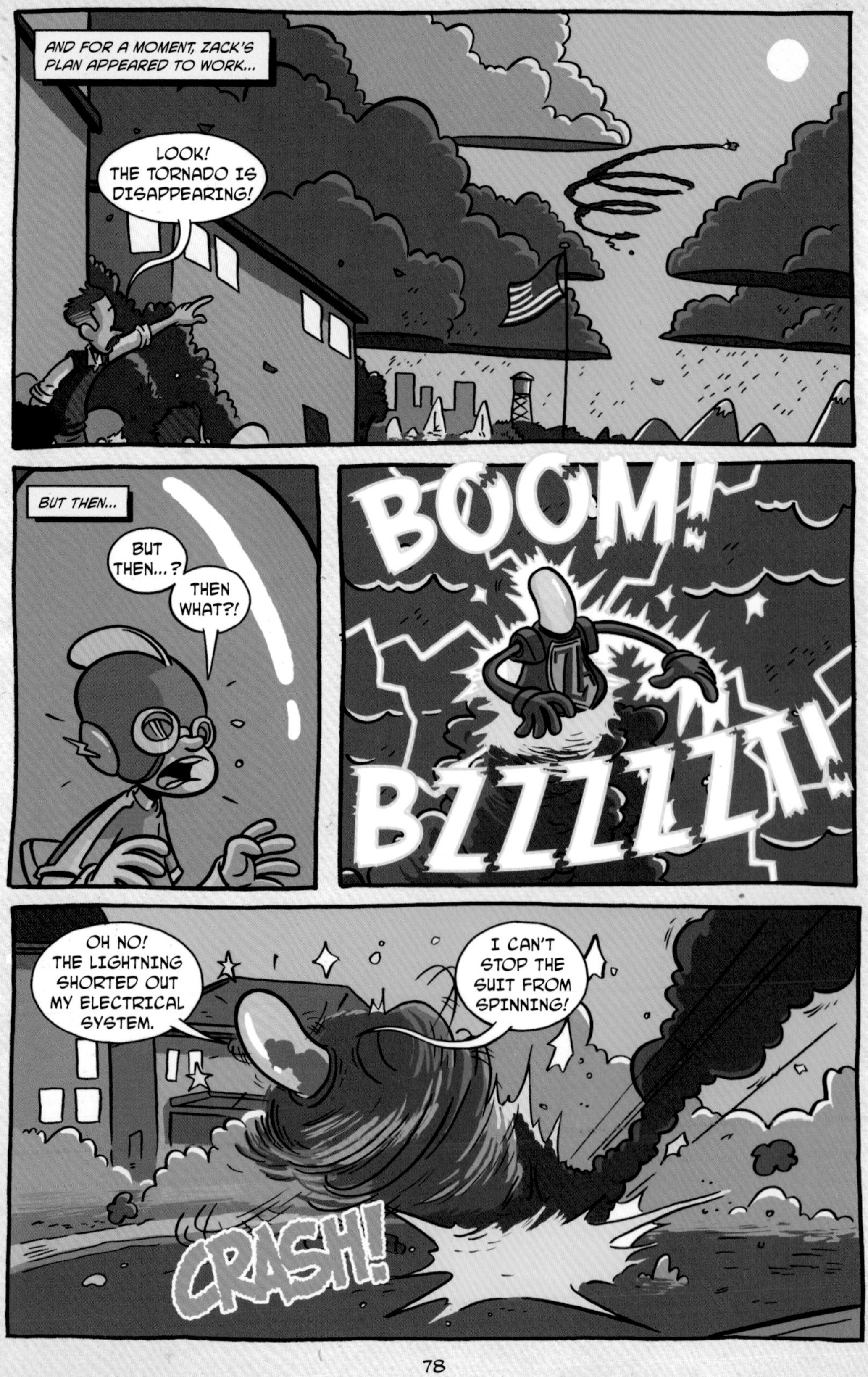
AND FOR A MOMENT, ZACK'S PLAN APPEARED TO WORK...
LOOK! THE TORNADO IS DISAPPEARING!
BUT THEN...
BUT THEN...?
THEN WHAT?!
BOOM!
BZZZZZT!
OH NO! THE LIGHTNING SHORTED OUT MY ELECTRICAL SYSTEM.
I CAN'T STOP THE SUIT FROM SPINNING!
CRASH!

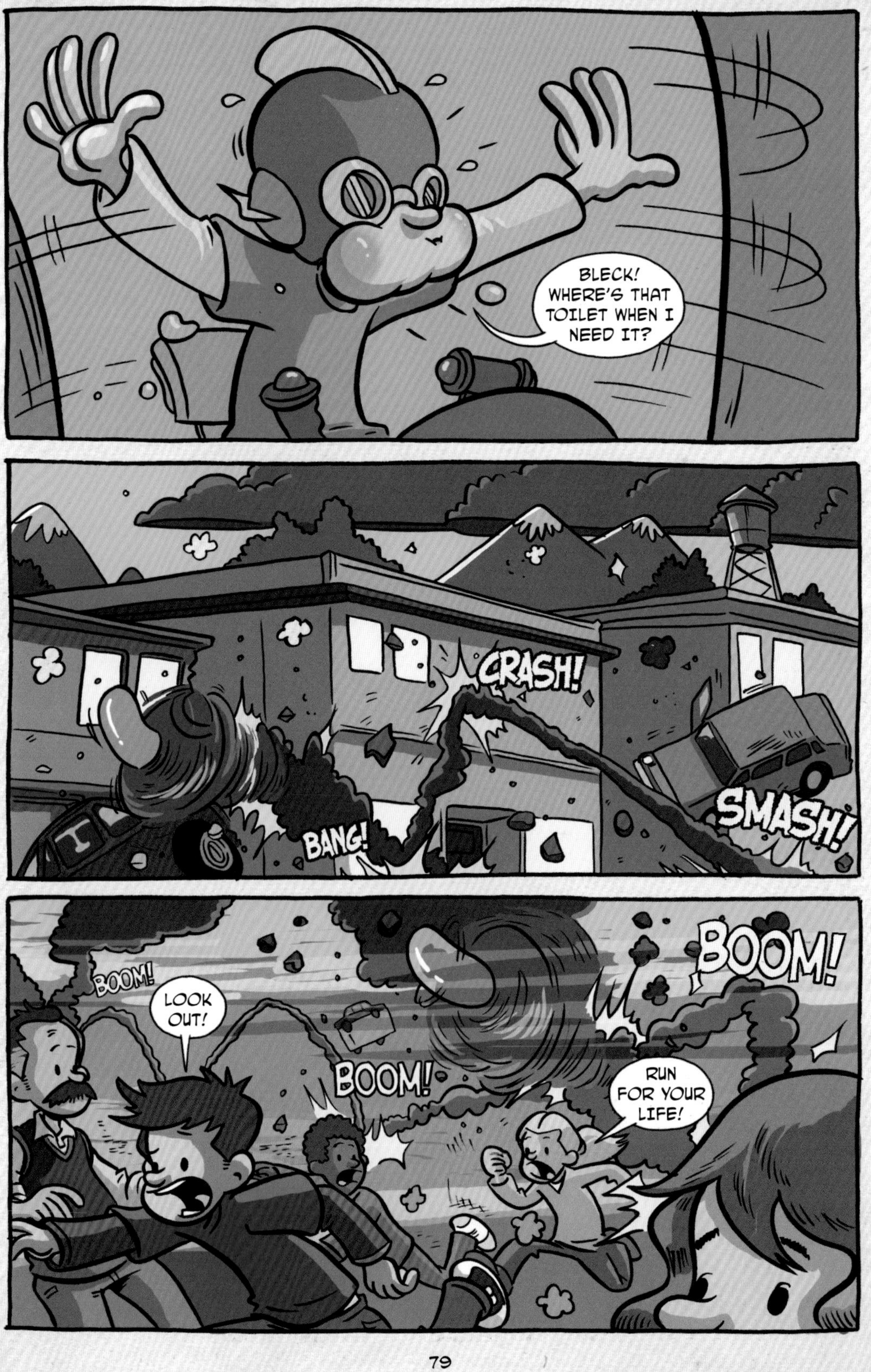
BLECK! WHERE'S THAT TOILET WHEN I NEED IT?
CRASH!
BANG!
SMASH!
BOOM!
LOOK OUT!
BOOM!
BOOM!
RUN FOR YOUR LIFE!

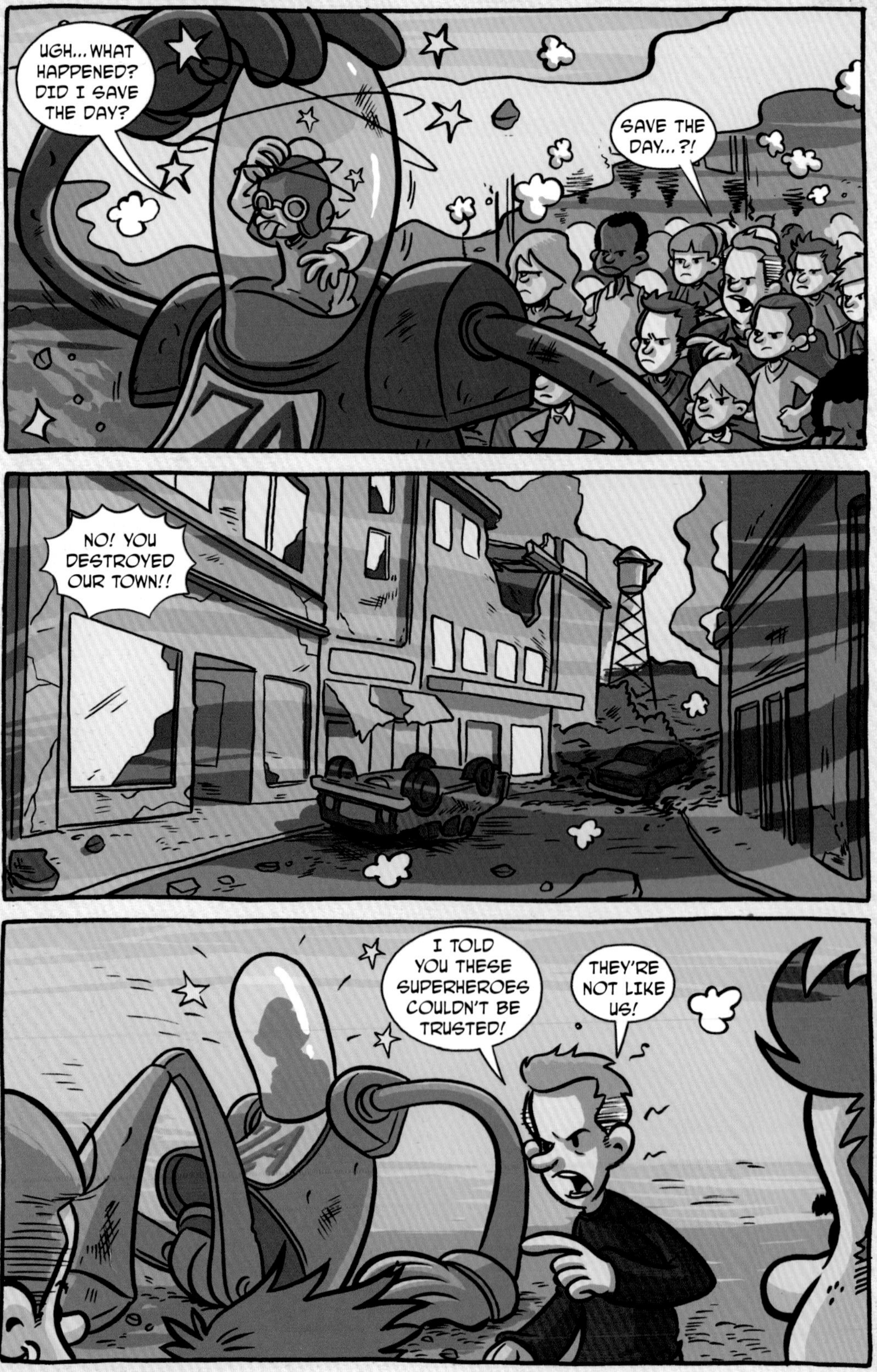
UGH... WHAT HAPPENED? DID I SAVE THE DAY?
SAVE THE DAY...?!
NO! YOU DESTROYED OUR TOWN!!
I TOLD YOU THESE SUPERHEROES COULDN'T BE TRUSTED!
THEY'RE NOT LIKE US!

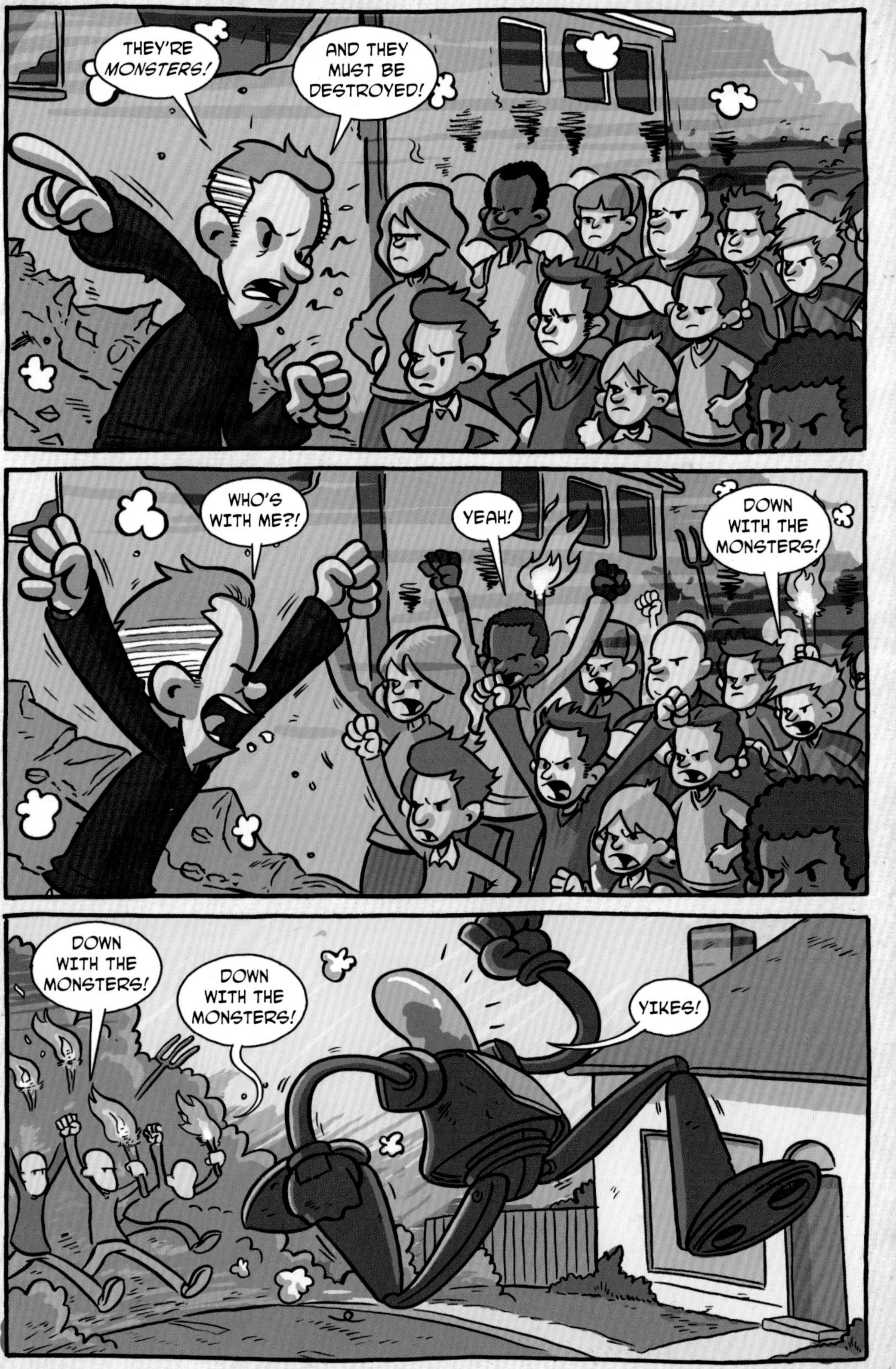
THEY'RE *MONSTERS!*
AND THEY MUST BE DESTROYED!
WHO'S WITH ME?!
YEAH!
DOWN WITH THE MONSTERS!
DOWN WITH THE MONSTERS!
DOWN WITH THE MONSTERS!
YIKES!

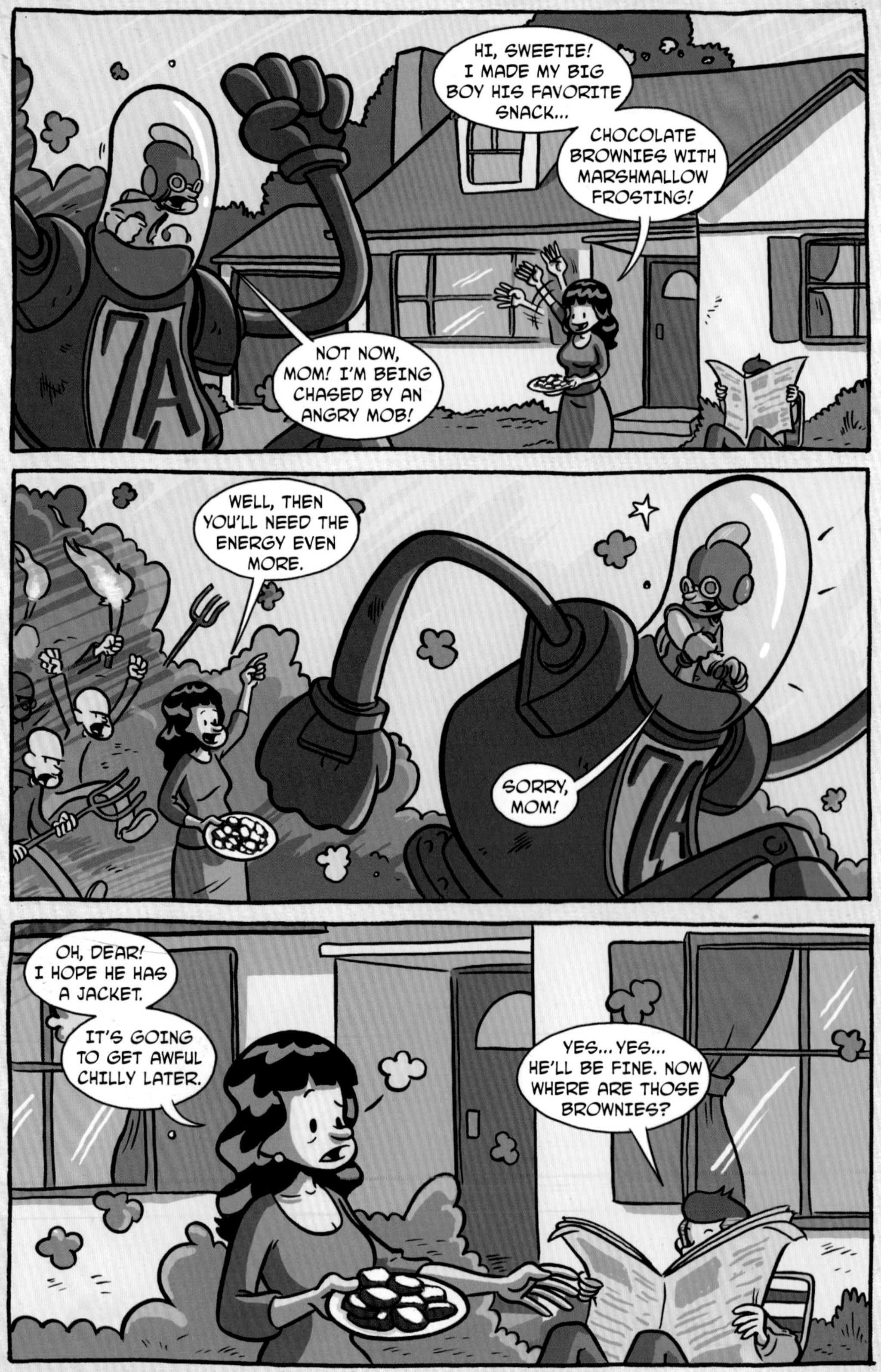
HI, SWEETIE! I MADE MY BIG BOY HIS FAVORITE SNACK...
CHOCOLATE BROWNIES WITH MARSHMALLOW FROSTING!
NOT NOW, MOM! I'M BEING CHASED BY AN ANGRY MOB!
WELL, THEN YOU'LL NEED THE ENERGY EVEN MORE.
SORRY, MOM!
OH, DEAR! I HOPE HE HAS A JACKET.
IT'S GOING TO GET AWFUL CHILLY LATER.
YES... YES... HE'LL BE FINE. NOW WHERE ARE THOSE BROWNIES?

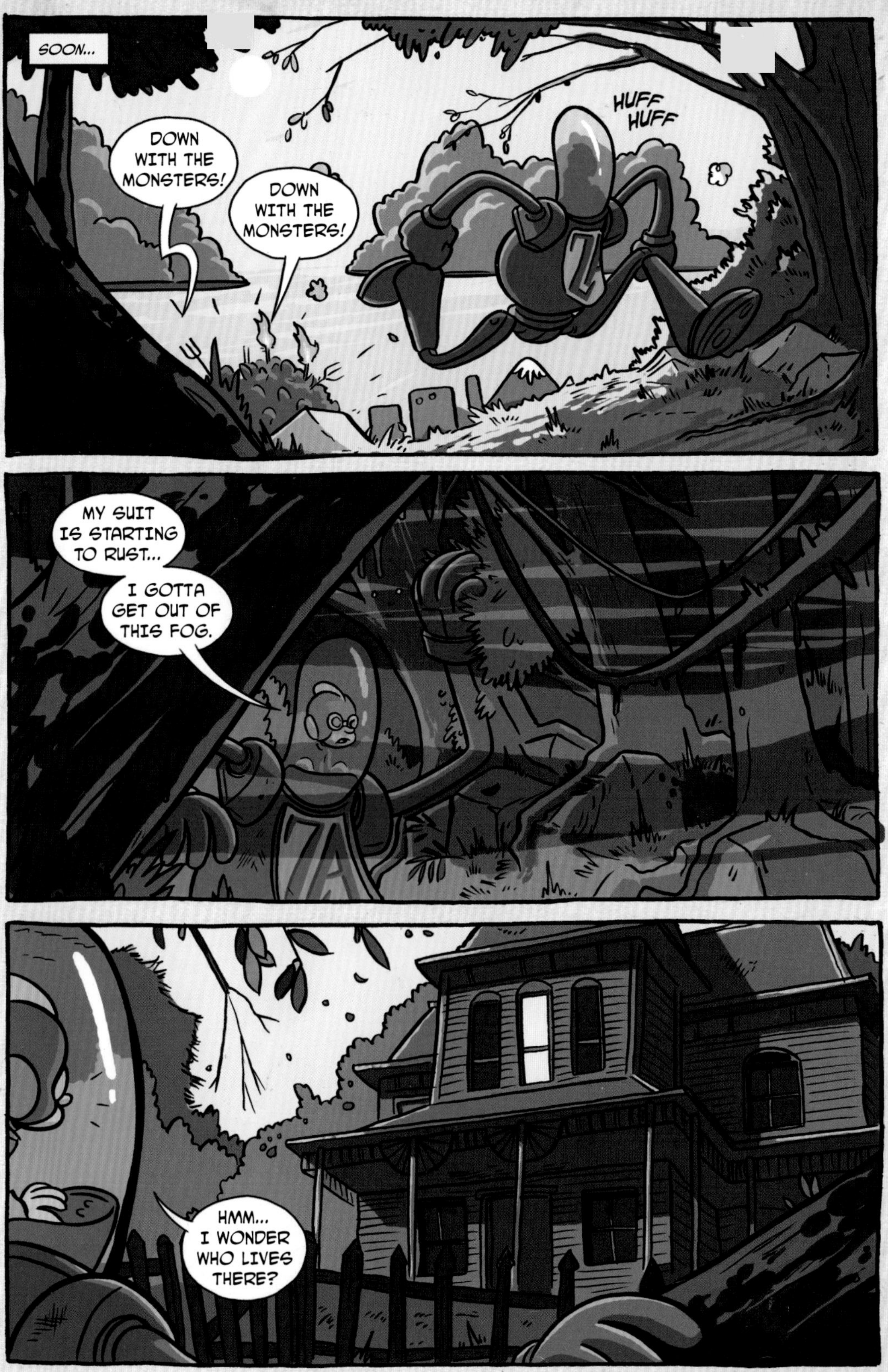
SOON...
DOWN WITH THE MONSTERS!
DOWN WITH THE MONSTERS!
HUFF HUFF
MY SUIT IS STARTING TO RUST...
I GOTTA GET OUT OF THIS FOG.
HMM... I WONDER WHO LIVES THERE?

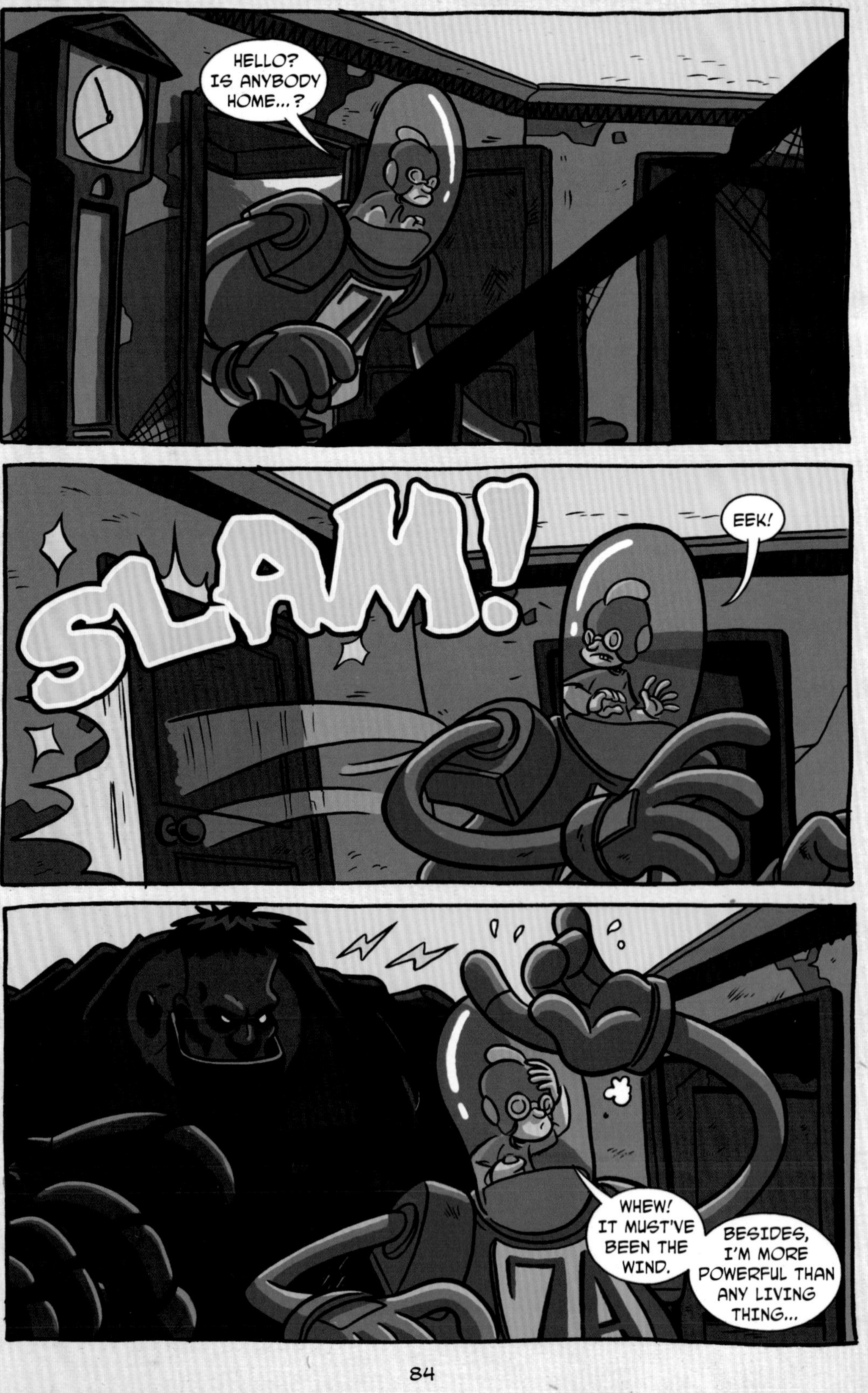
HELLO? IS ANYBODY HOME...?
SLAM!
EEK!
WHEW! IT MUST'VE BEEN THE WIND.
BESIDES, I'M MORE POWERFUL THAN ANY LIVING THING...

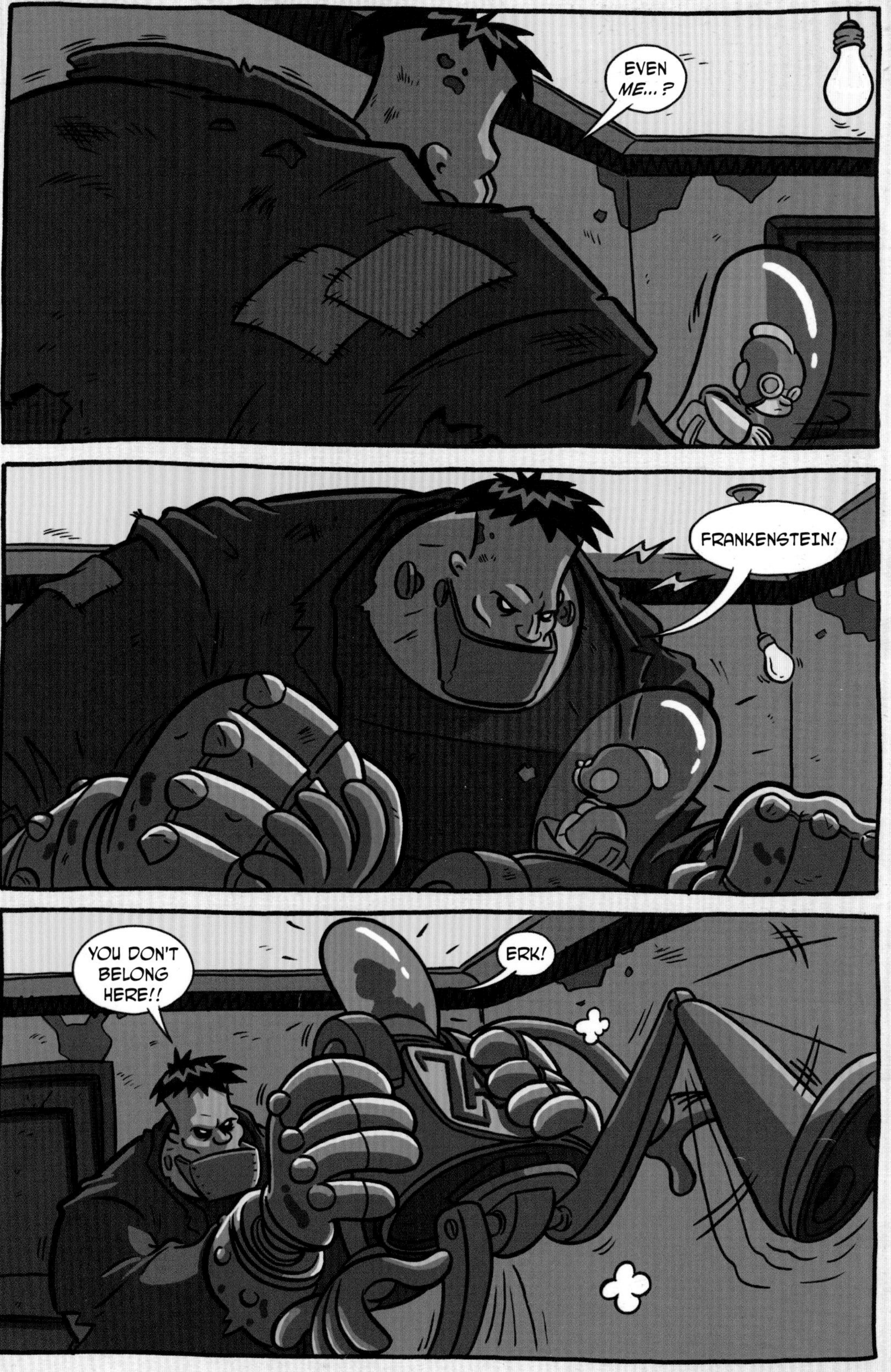
EVEN ME...?
FRANKENSTEIN!
YOU DON'T BELONG HERE!!
ERK!

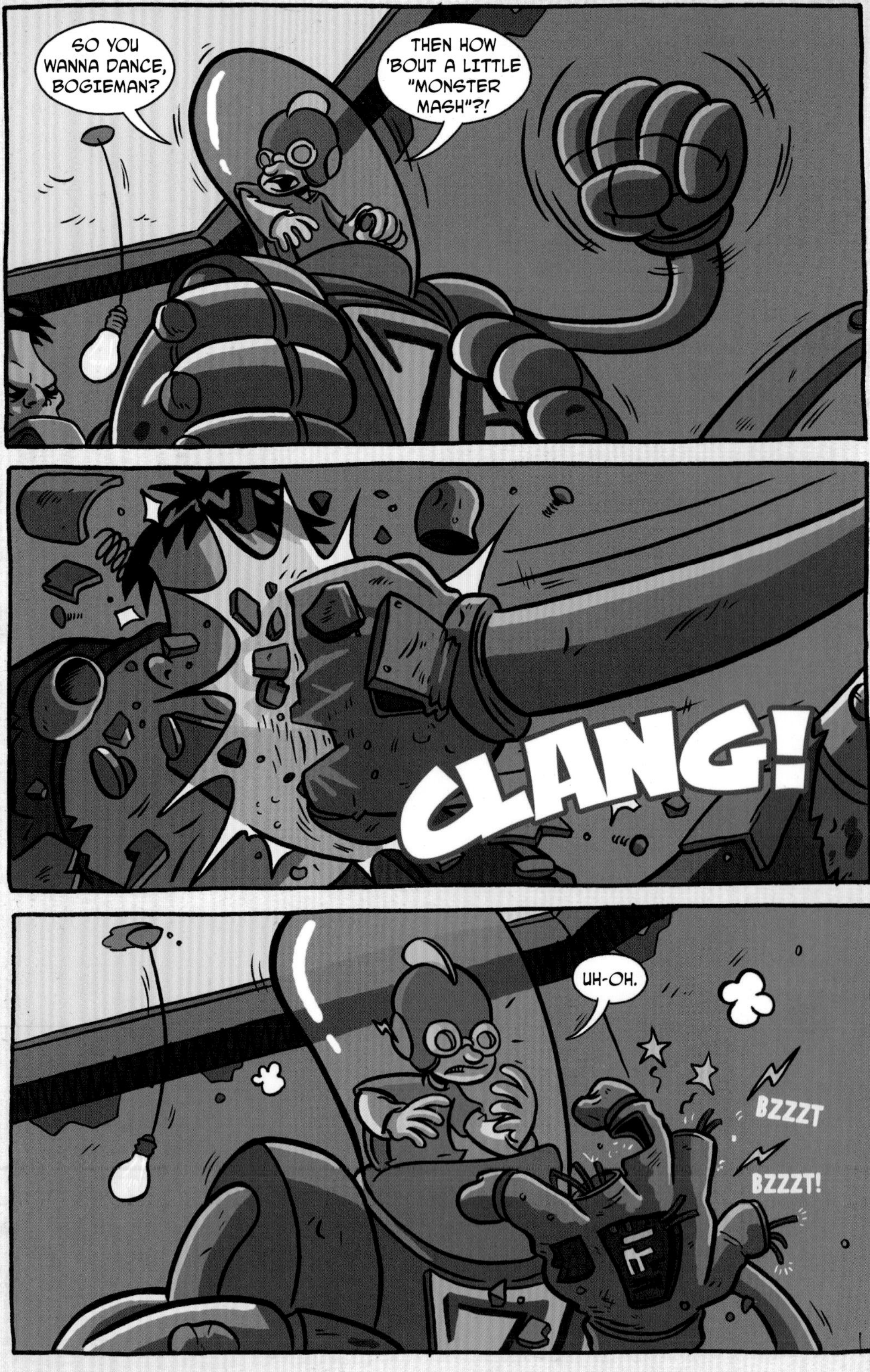
SO YOU WANNA DANCE, BOGIEMAN?
THEN HOW 'BOUT A LITTLE "MONSTER MASH"?!
CLANG!
UH-OH.
BZZZT
BZZZT!

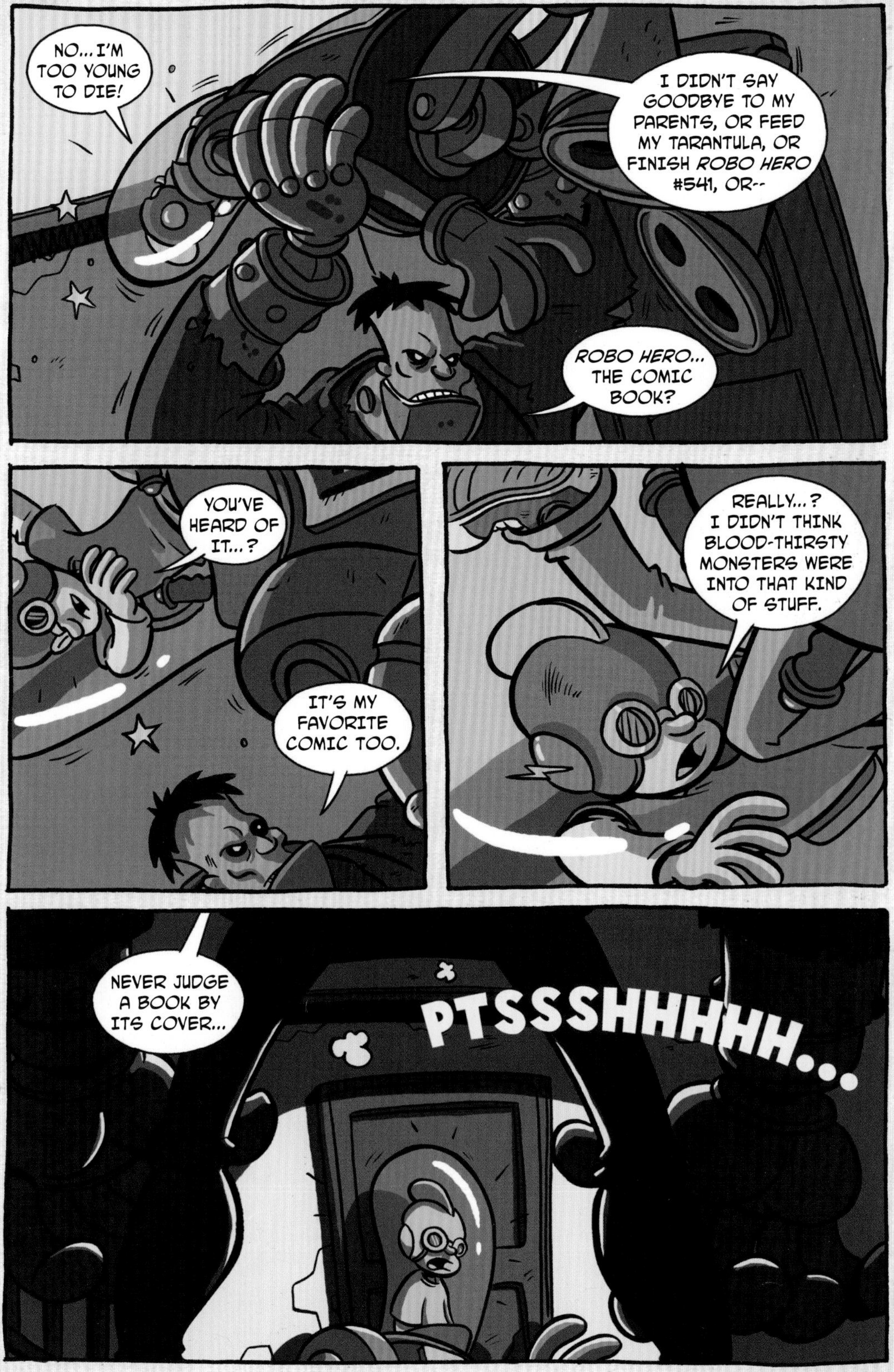
NO... I'M TOO YOUNG TO DIE!
I DIDN'T SAY GOODBYE TO MY PARENTS, OR FEED MY TARANTULA, OR FINISH *ROBO HERO* #541, OR--
ROBO HERO... THE COMIC BOOK?
YOU'VE HEARD OF IT...?
IT'S MY FAVORITE COMIC TOO.
REALLY...? I DIDN'T THINK BLOOD-THIRSTY MONSTERS WERE INTO THAT KIND OF STUFF.
NEVER JUDGE A BOOK BY ITS COVER...
PTSSSHHHHHH...

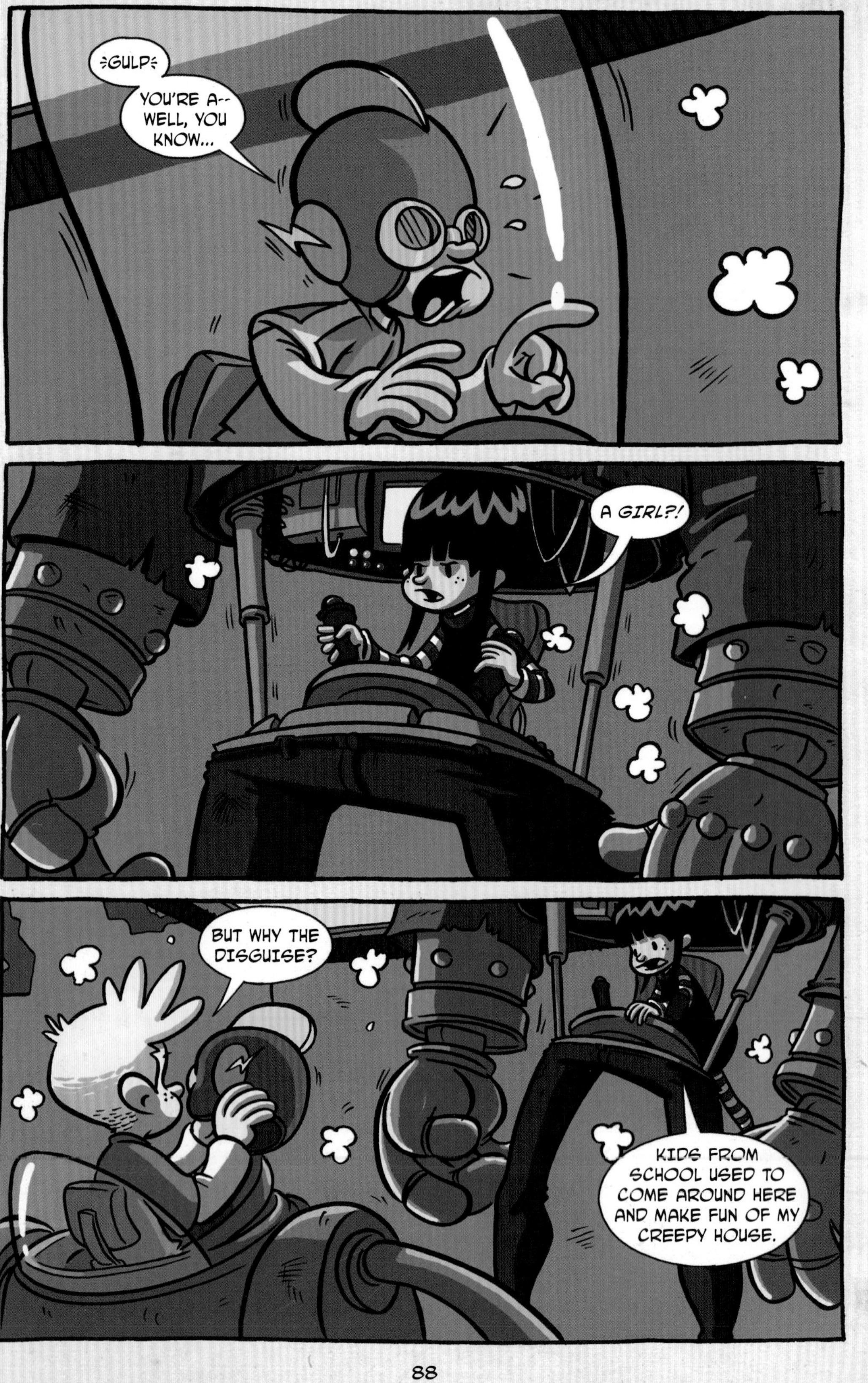
GULP
YOU'RE A-- WELL, YOU KNOW...
A GIRL?!
BUT WHY THE DISGUISE?
KIDS FROM SCHOOL USED TO COME AROUND HERE AND MAKE FUN OF MY CREEPY HOUSE.

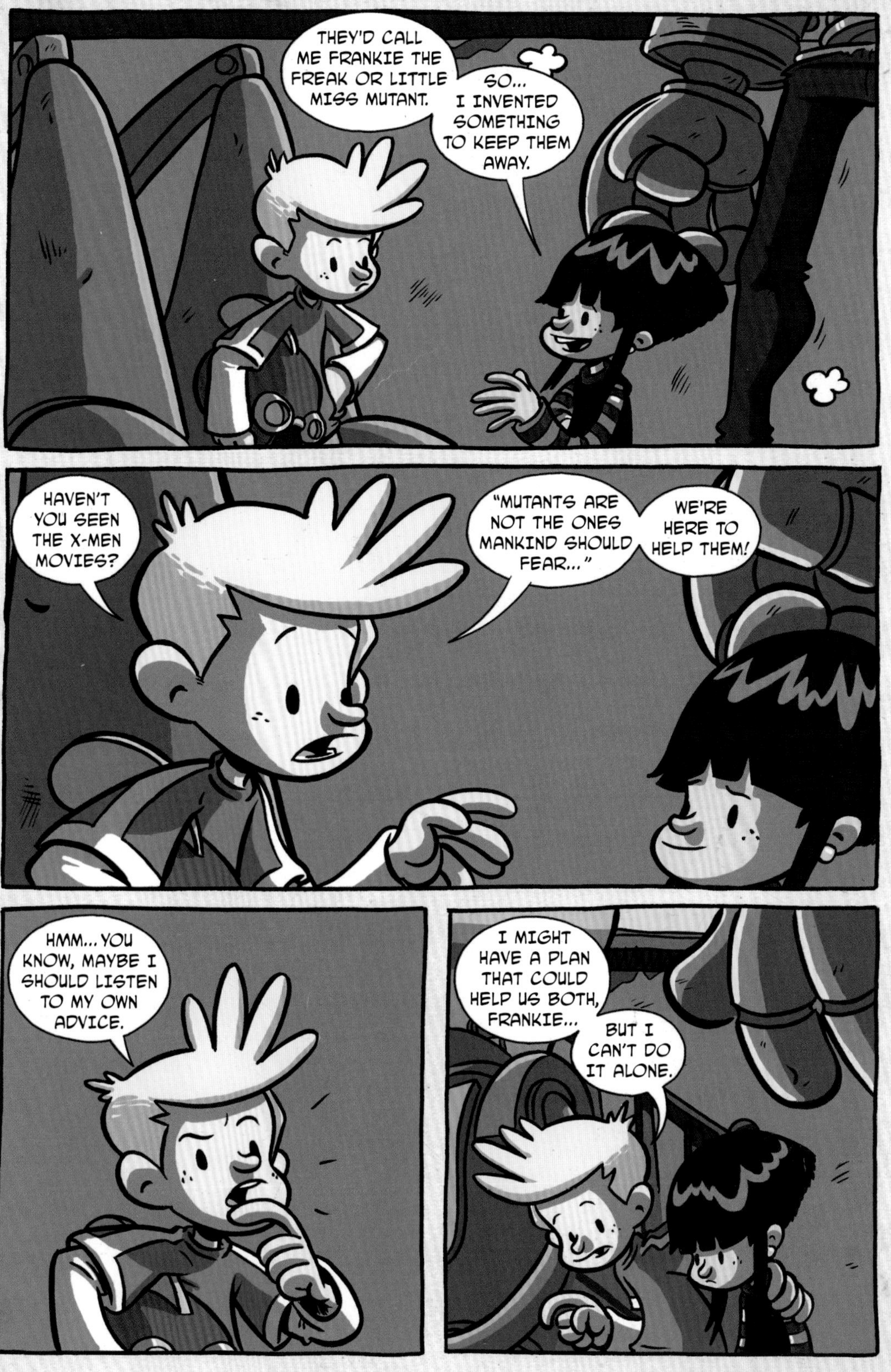
THEY'D CALL ME FRANKIE THE FREAK OR LITTLE MISS MUTANT.
SO... I INVENTED SOMETHING TO KEEP THEM AWAY.
HAVEN'T YOU SEEN THE X-MEN MOVIES?
"MUTANTS ARE NOT THE ONES MANKIND SHOULD FEAR..."
WE'RE HERE TO HELP THEM!
HMM... YOU KNOW, MAYBE I SHOULD LISTEN TO MY OWN ADVICE.
I MIGHT HAVE A PLAN THAT COULD HELP US BOTH, FRANKIE...
BUT I CAN'T DO IT ALONE.

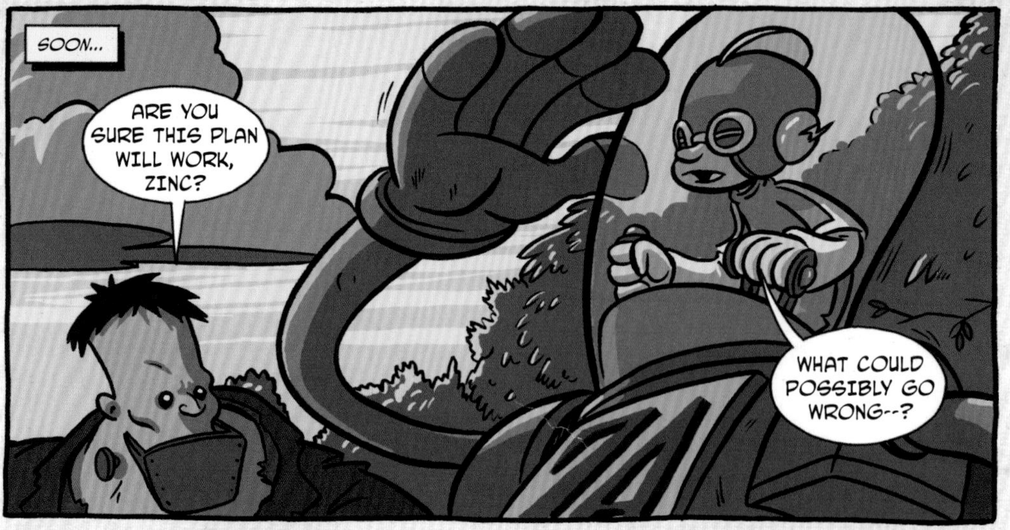
SOON...
ARE YOU SURE THIS PLAN WILL WORK, ZINC?
WHAT COULD POSSIBLY GO WRONG--?

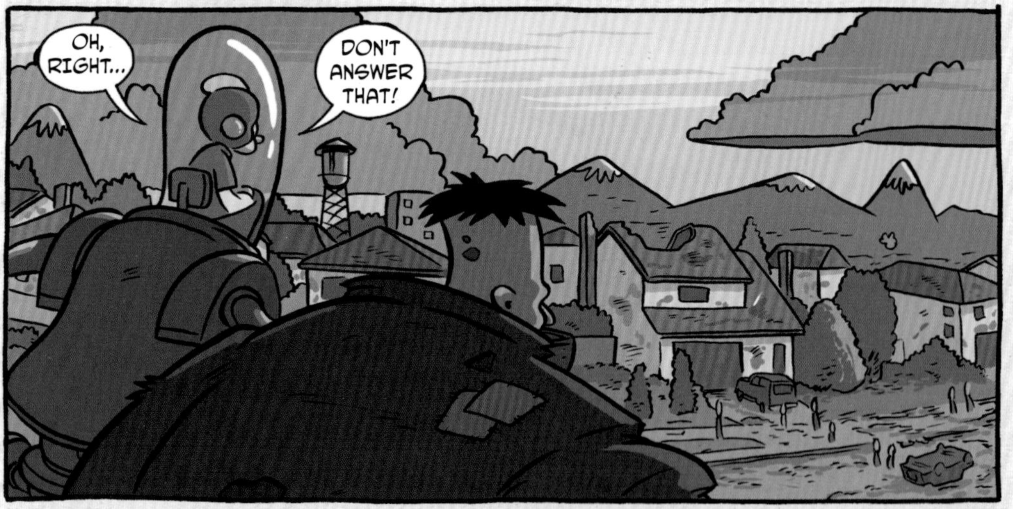
OH, RIGHT...
DON'T ANSWER THAT!

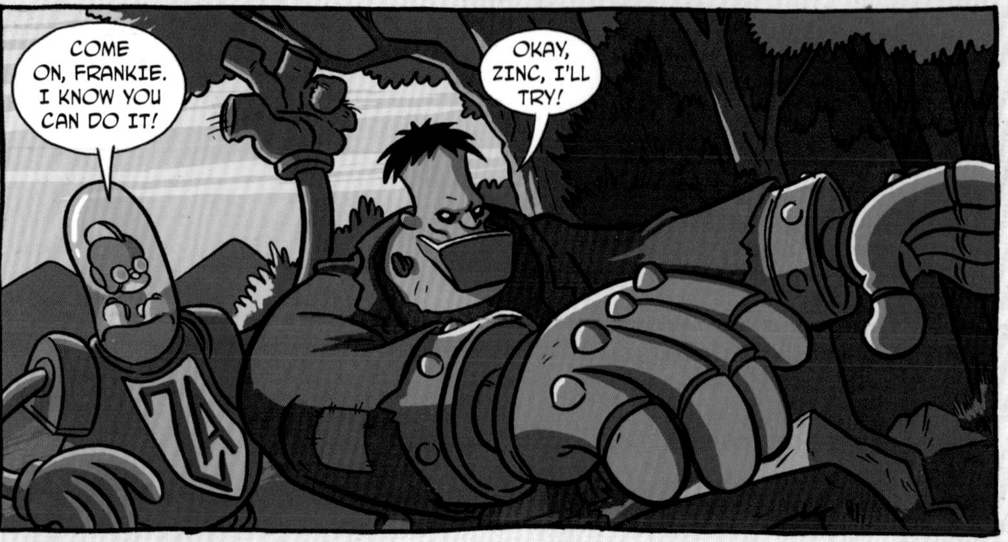
COME ON, FRANKIE. I KNOW YOU CAN DO IT!
OKAY, ZINC, I'LL TRY!

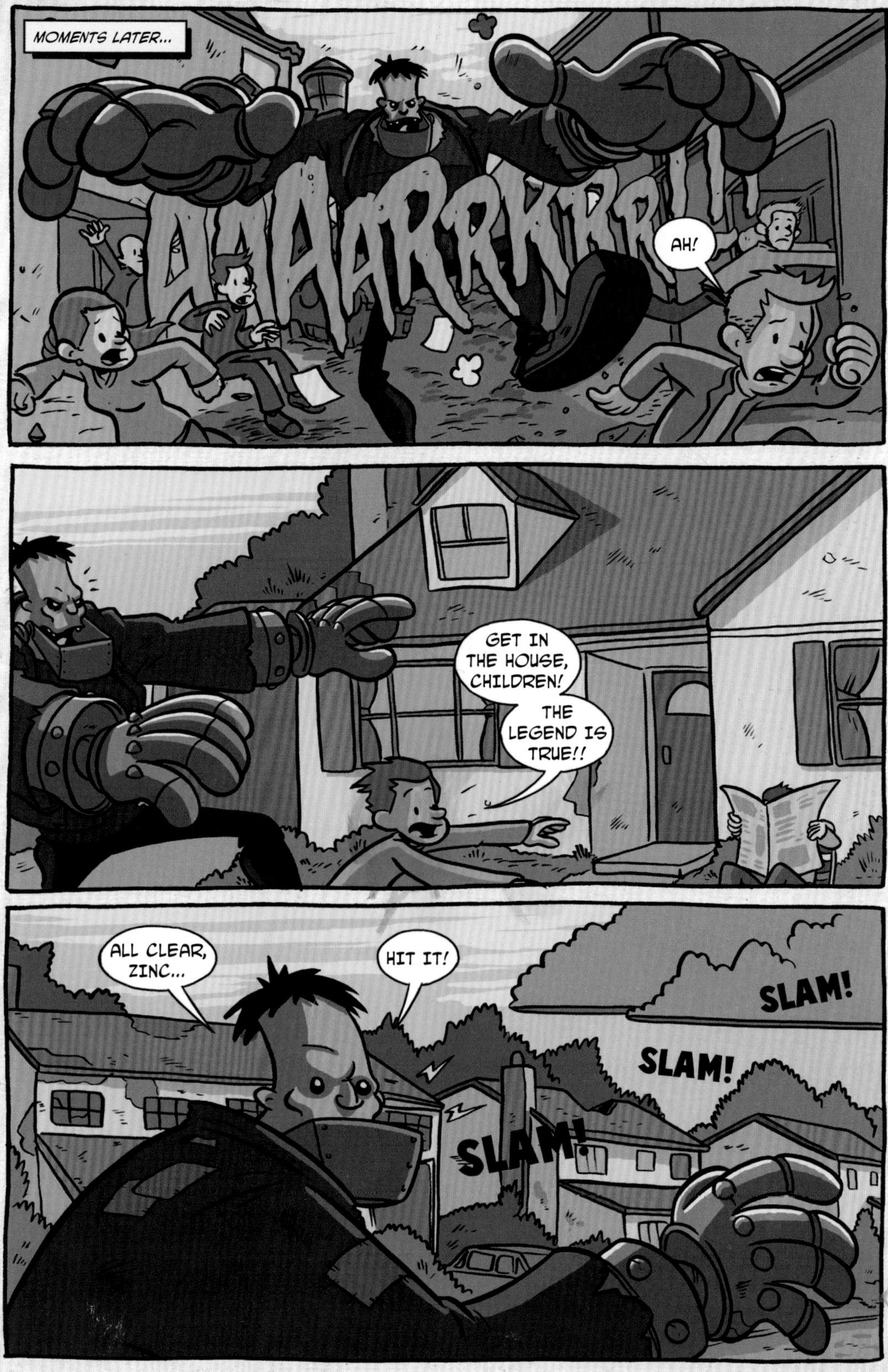
MOMENTS LATER...
AAARRKRR!!
AH!
GET IN THE HOUSE, CHILDREN!
THE LEGEND IS TRUE!!
ALL CLEAR, ZINC...
HIT IT!
SLAM!
SLAM!
SLAM!

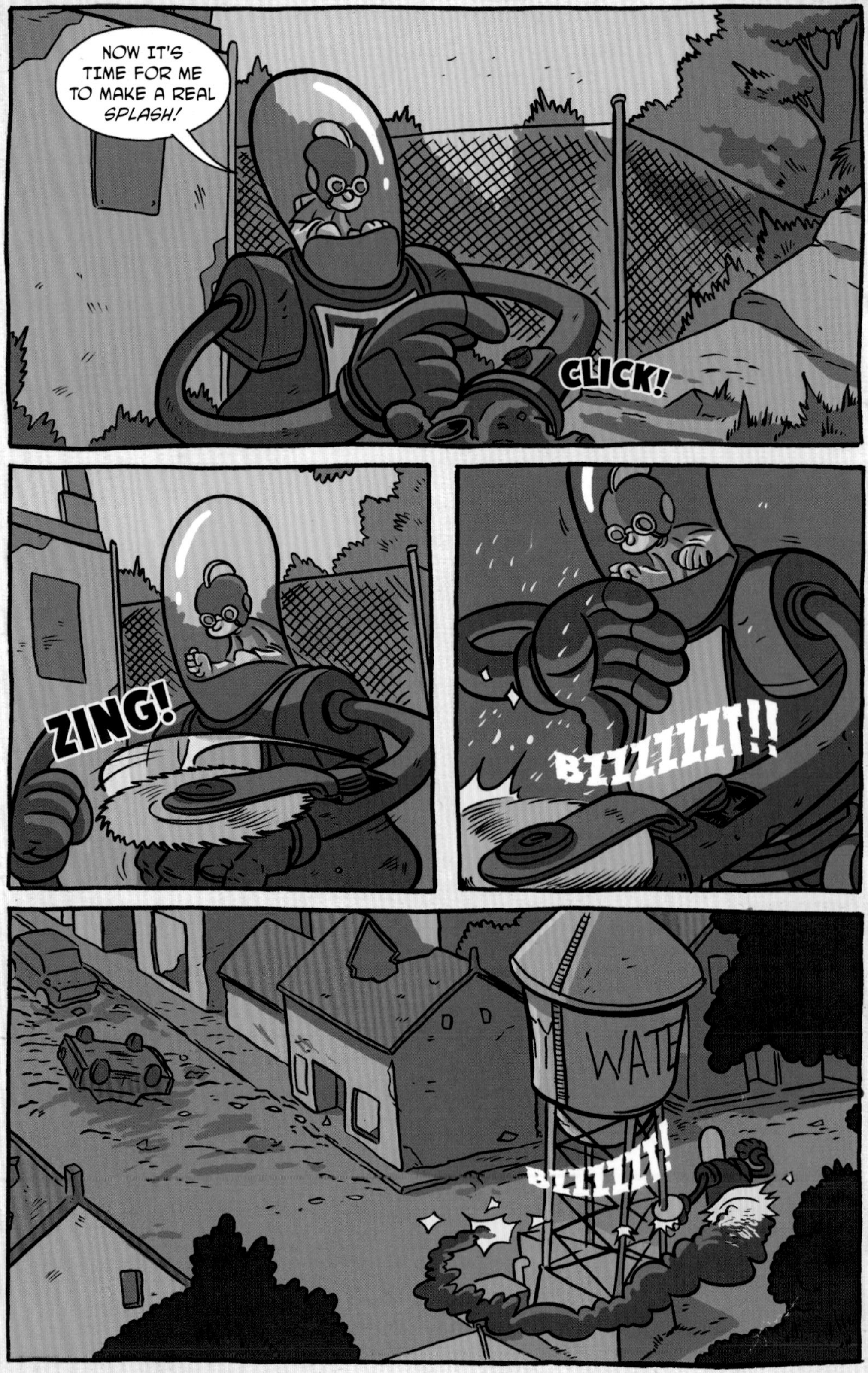
NOW IT'S TIME FOR ME TO MAKE A REAL *SPLASH!*
CLICK!
ZING!
BZZZZZT!!
BZZZZT!

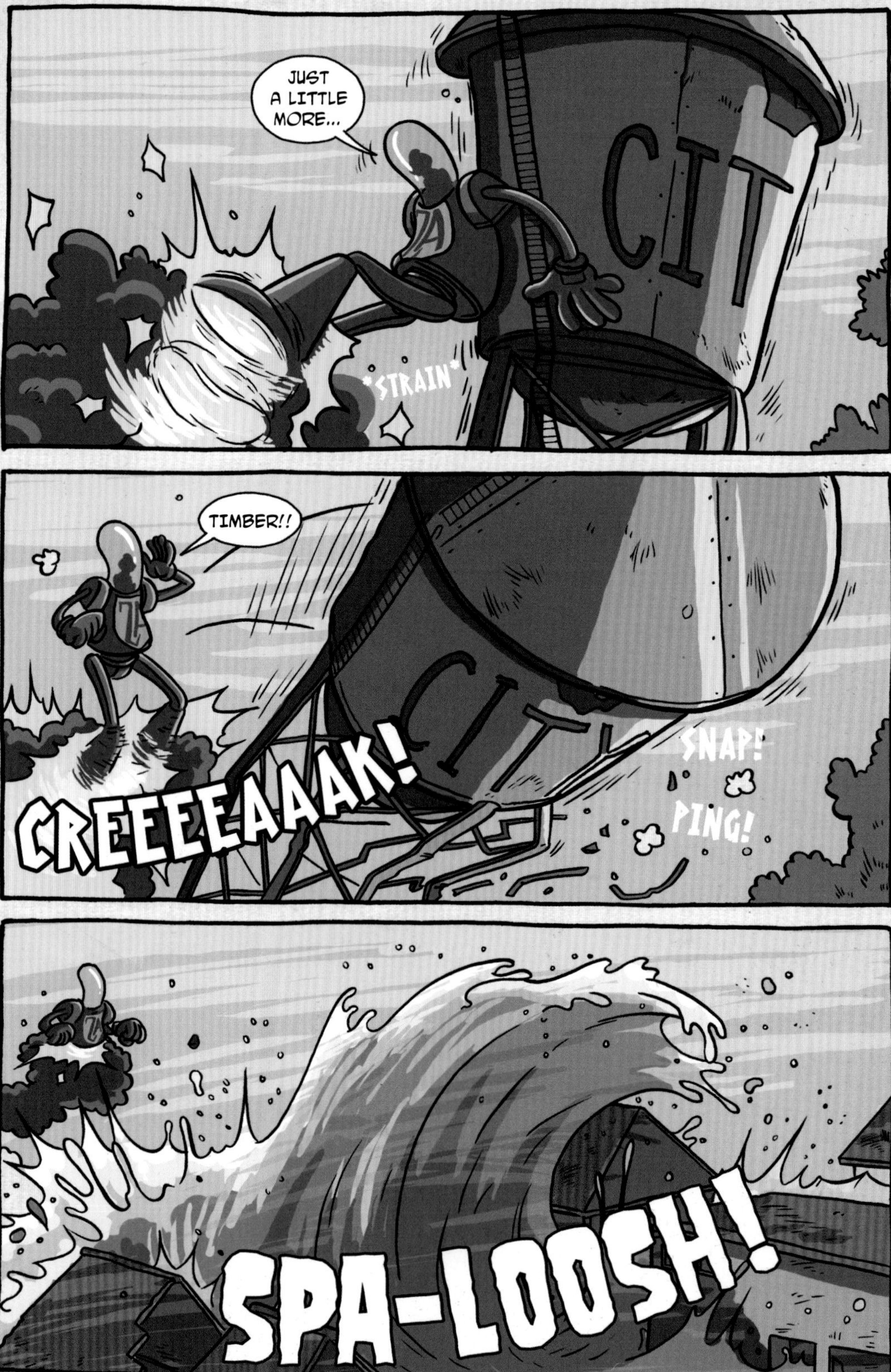
JUST A LITTLE MORE...
STRAIN
TIMBER!!
CREEEEAAAK!
SNAP!
PING!
SPA-LOOSH!

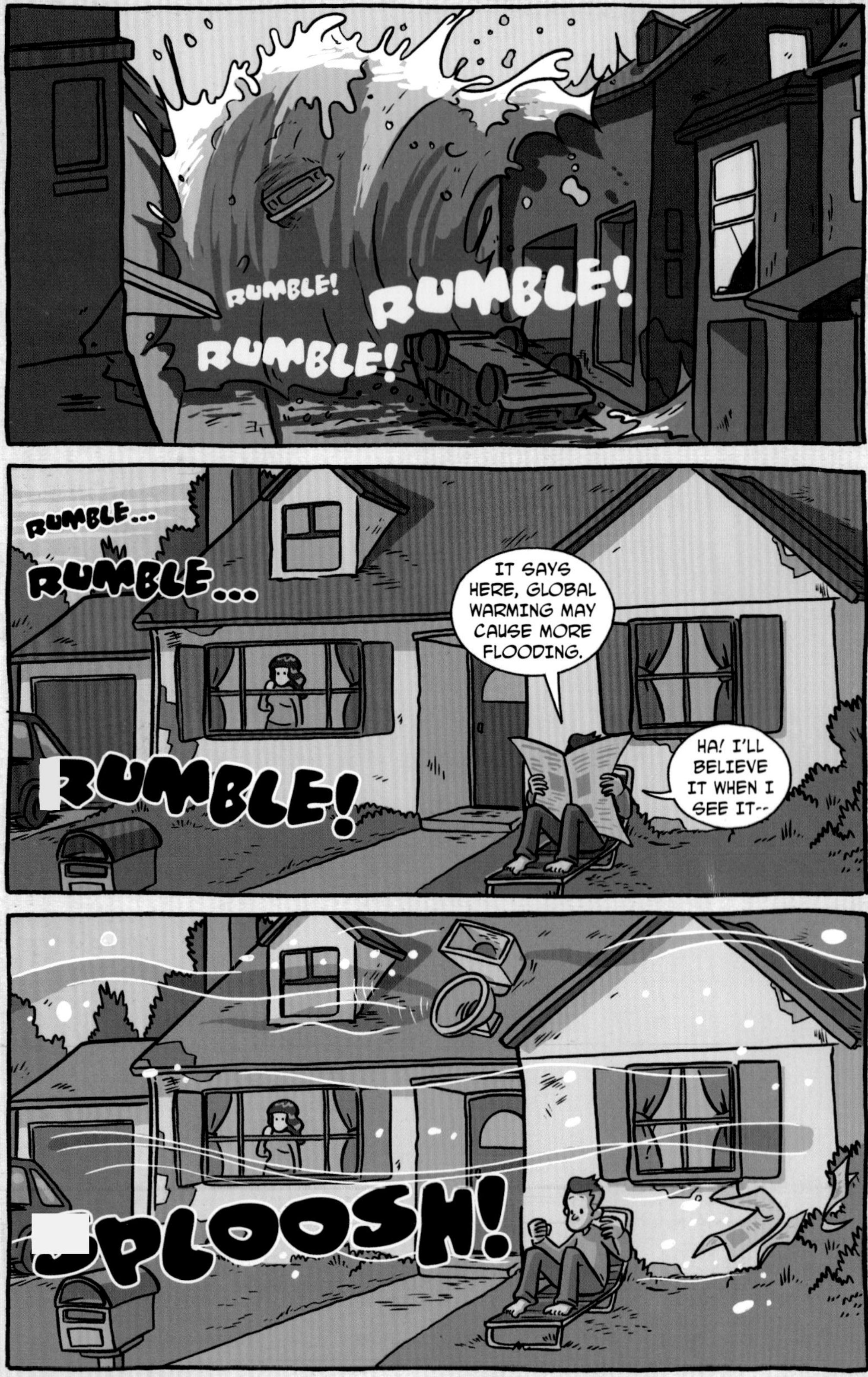

RUMBLE!
RUMBLE!
RUMBLE!
RUMBLE...
RUMBLE...
IT SAYS HERE, GLOBAL WARMING MAY CAUSE MORE FLOODING.
UMBLE!
HA! I'LL BELIEVE IT WHEN I SEE IT--
PLOOSH!

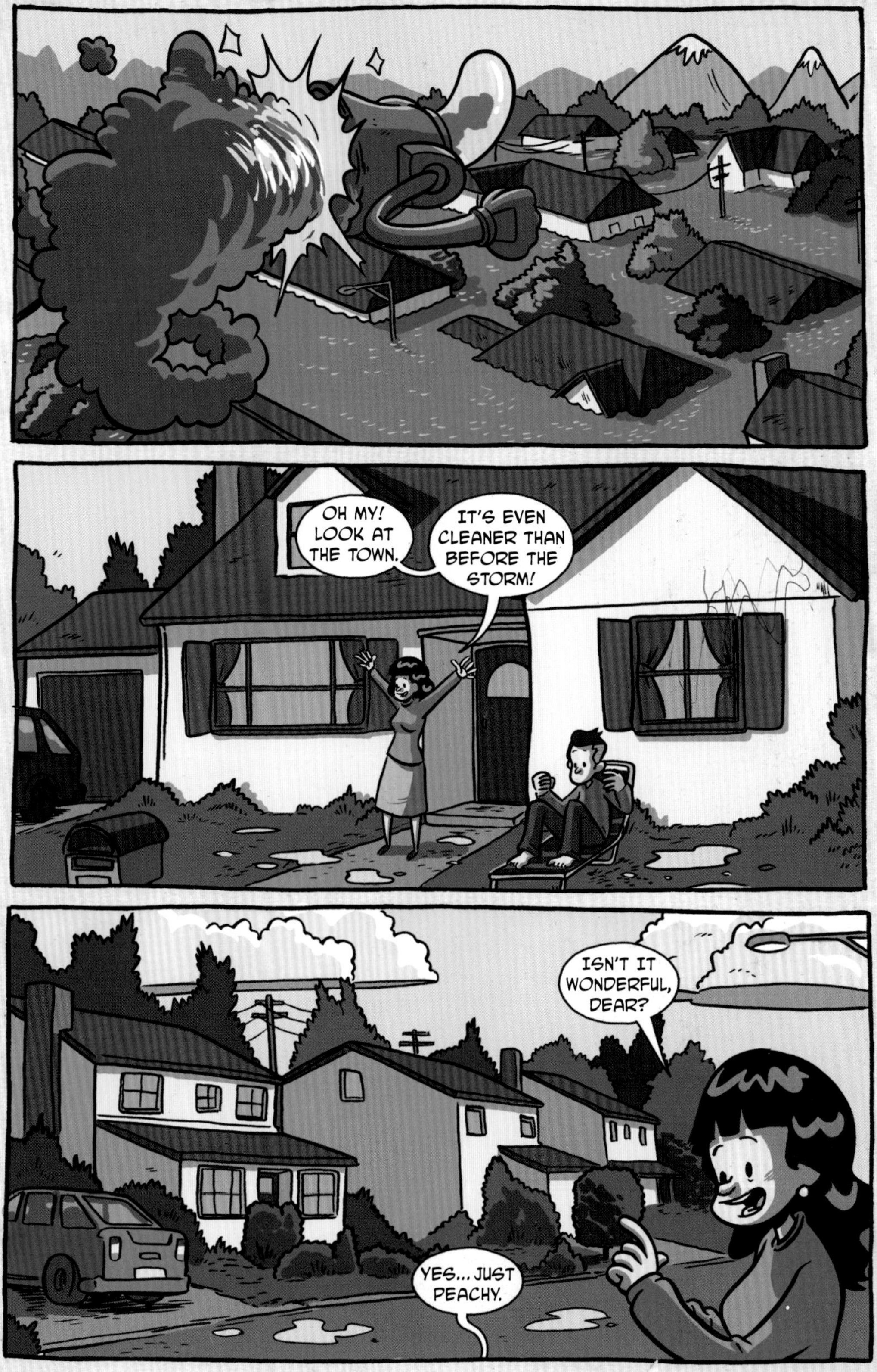
OH MY! LOOK AT THE TOWN.
IT'S EVEN CLEANER THAN BEFORE THE STORM!
ISN'T IT WONDERFUL, DEAR?
YES... JUST PEACHY.

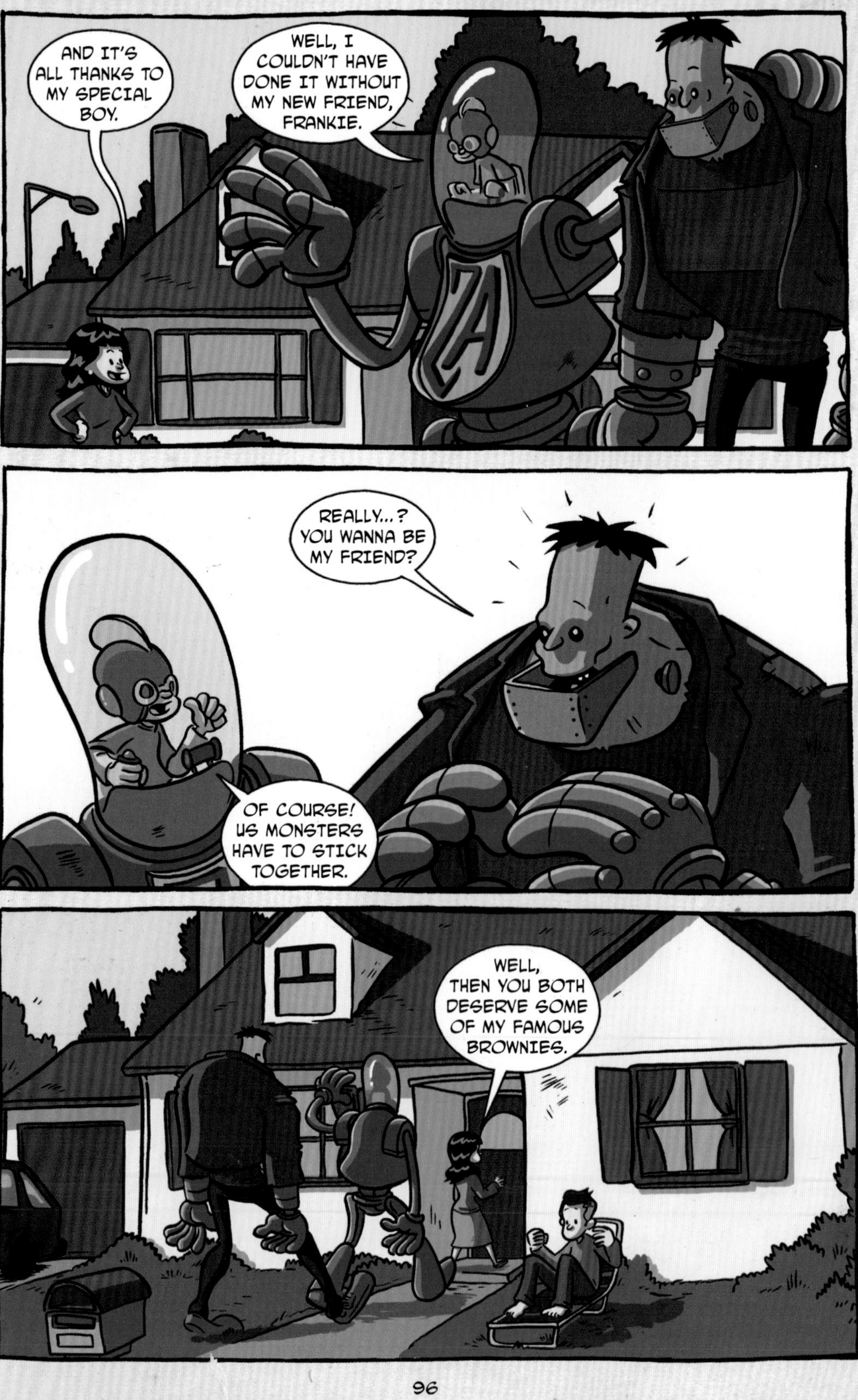
AND IT'S ALL THANKS TO MY SPECIAL BOY.
WELL, I COULDN'T HAVE DONE IT WITHOUT MY NEW FRIEND, FRANKIE.
REALLY...? YOU WANNA BE MY FRIEND?
OF COURSE! US MONSTERS HAVE TO STICK TOGETHER.
WELL, THEN YOU BOTH DESERVE SOME OF MY FAMOUS BROWNIES.

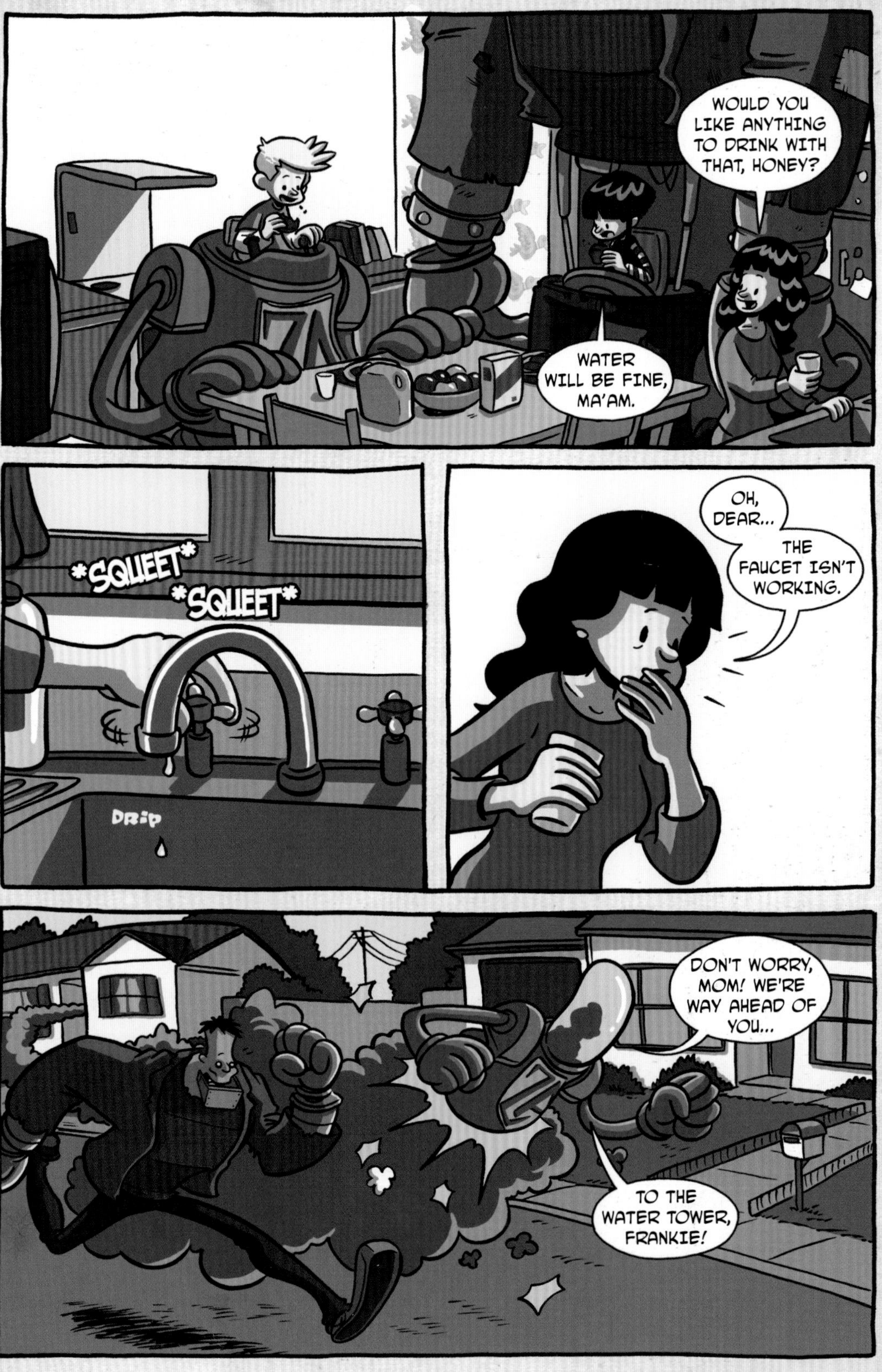
WOULD YOU LIKE ANYTHING TO DRINK WITH THAT, HONEY?
WATER WILL BE FINE, MA'AM.
SQUEET
SQUEET
DRIP
OH, DEAR...
THE FAUCET ISN'T WORKING.
DON'T WORRY, MOM! WE'RE WAY AHEAD OF YOU...
TO THE WATER TOWER, FRANKIE!

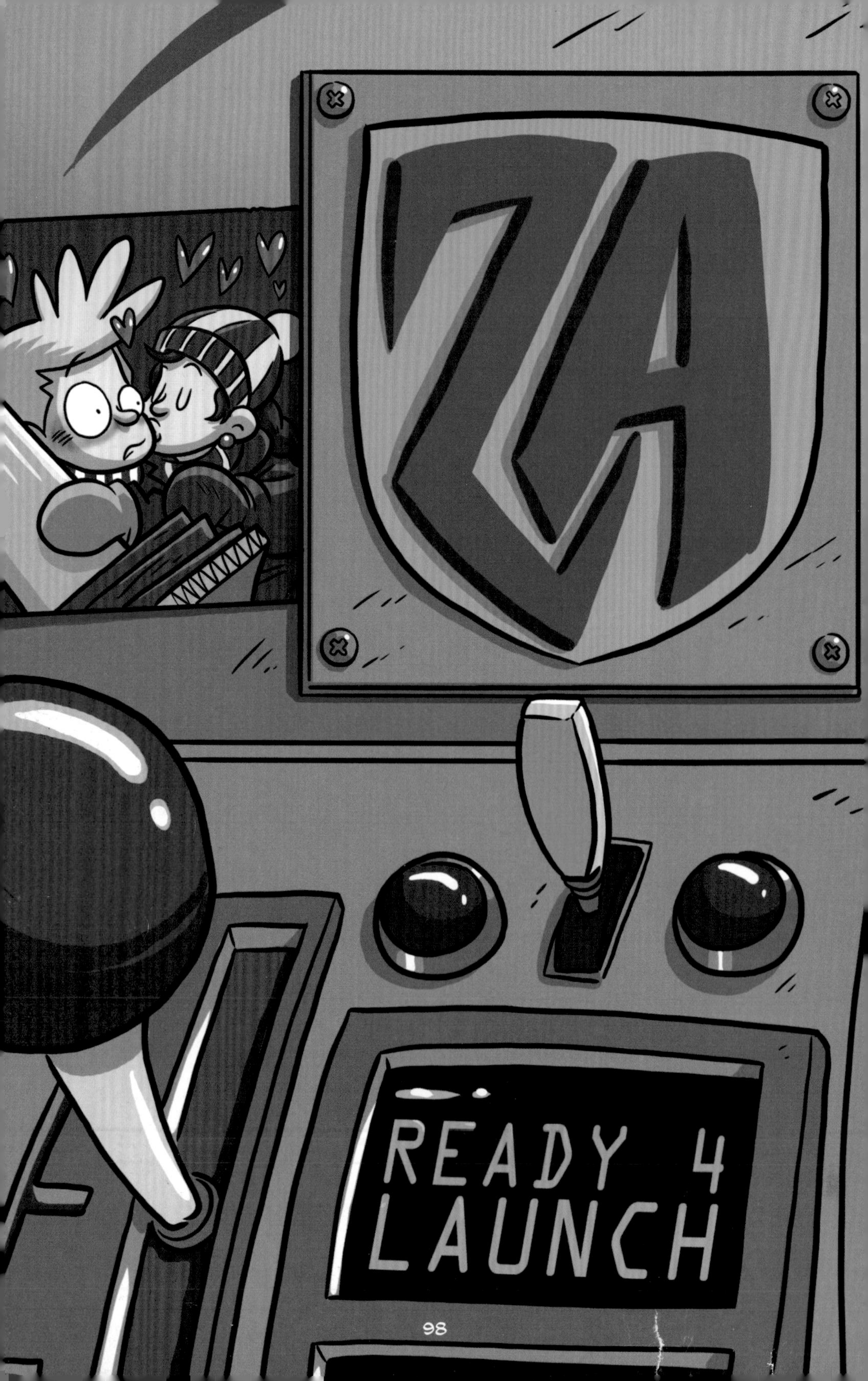
ZA
READY 4
LAUNCH

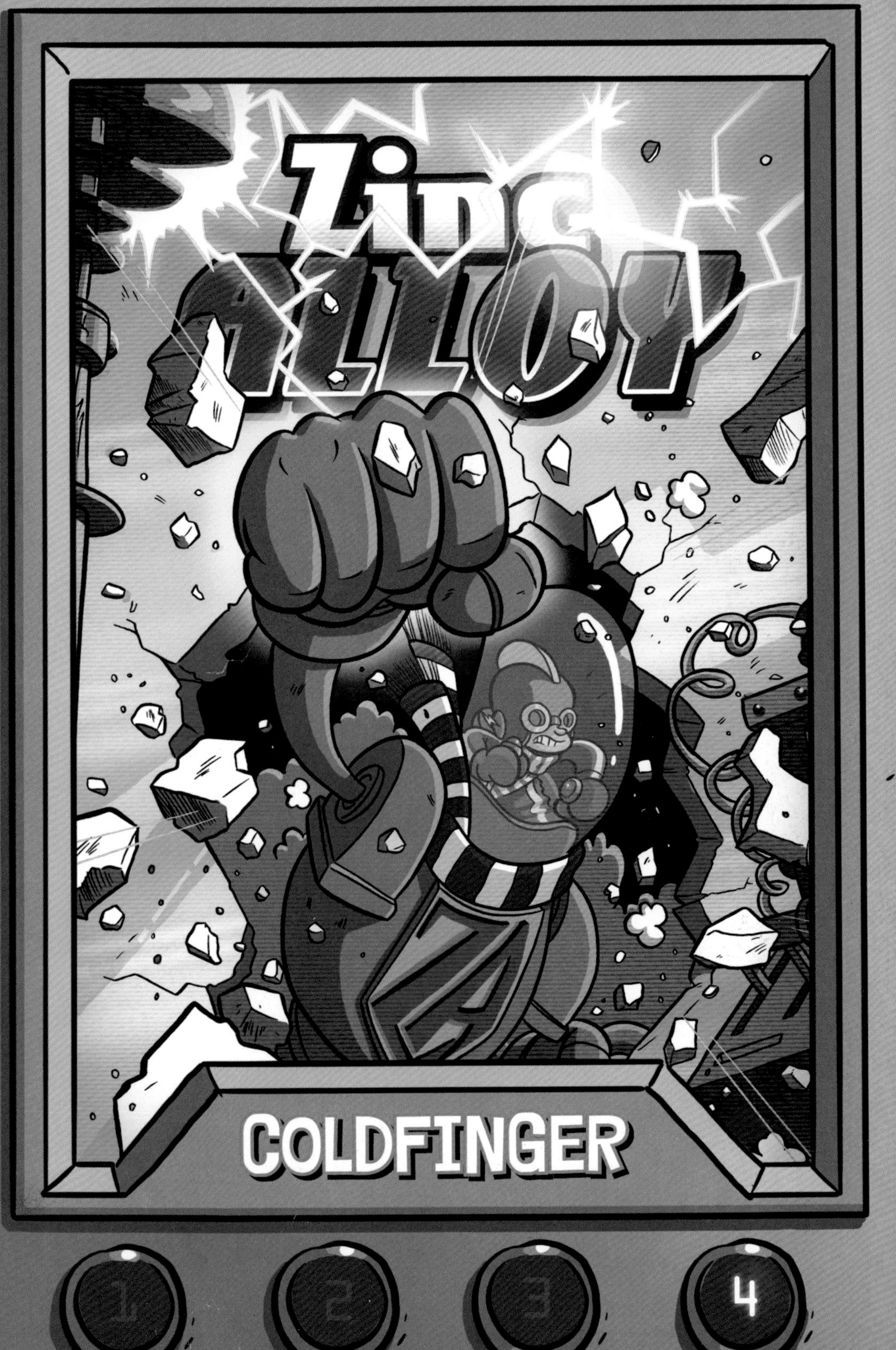
Zinc
ALLOY
COLDFINGER
1
2
3
4

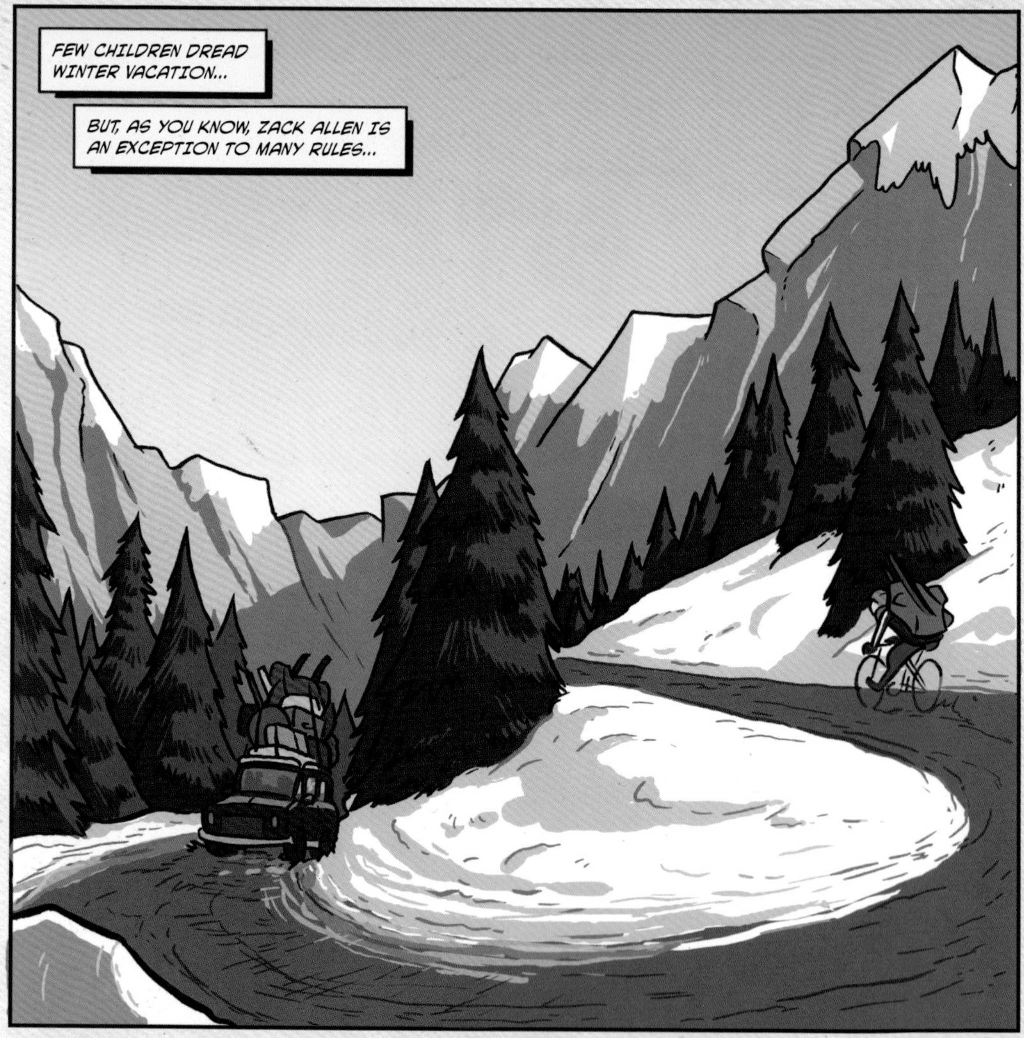
FEW CHILDREN DREAD WINTER VACATION...
BUT, AS YOU KNOW, ZACK ALLEN IS AN EXCEPTION TO MANY RULES...

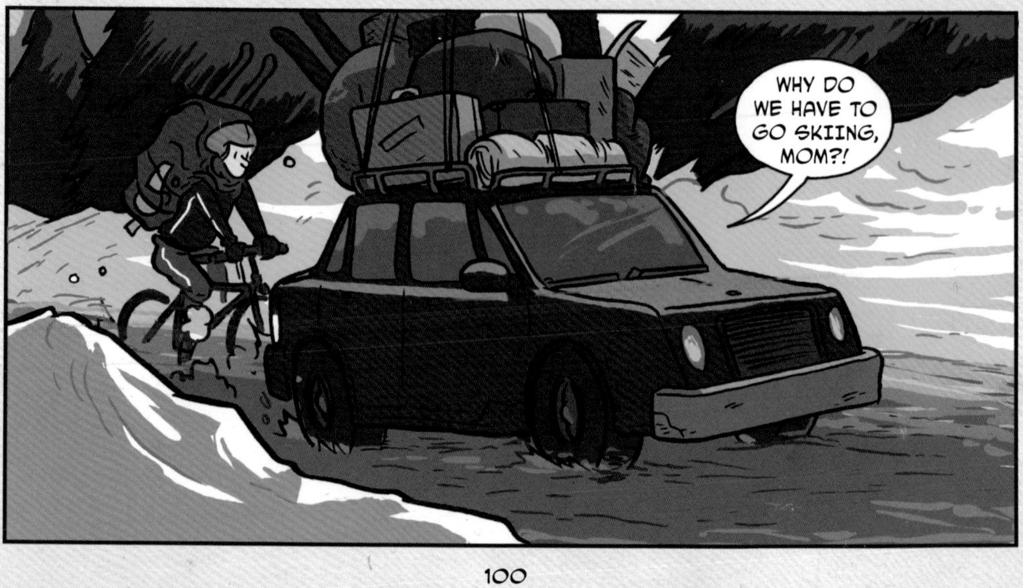
WHY DO WE HAVE TO GO SKIING, MOM?!

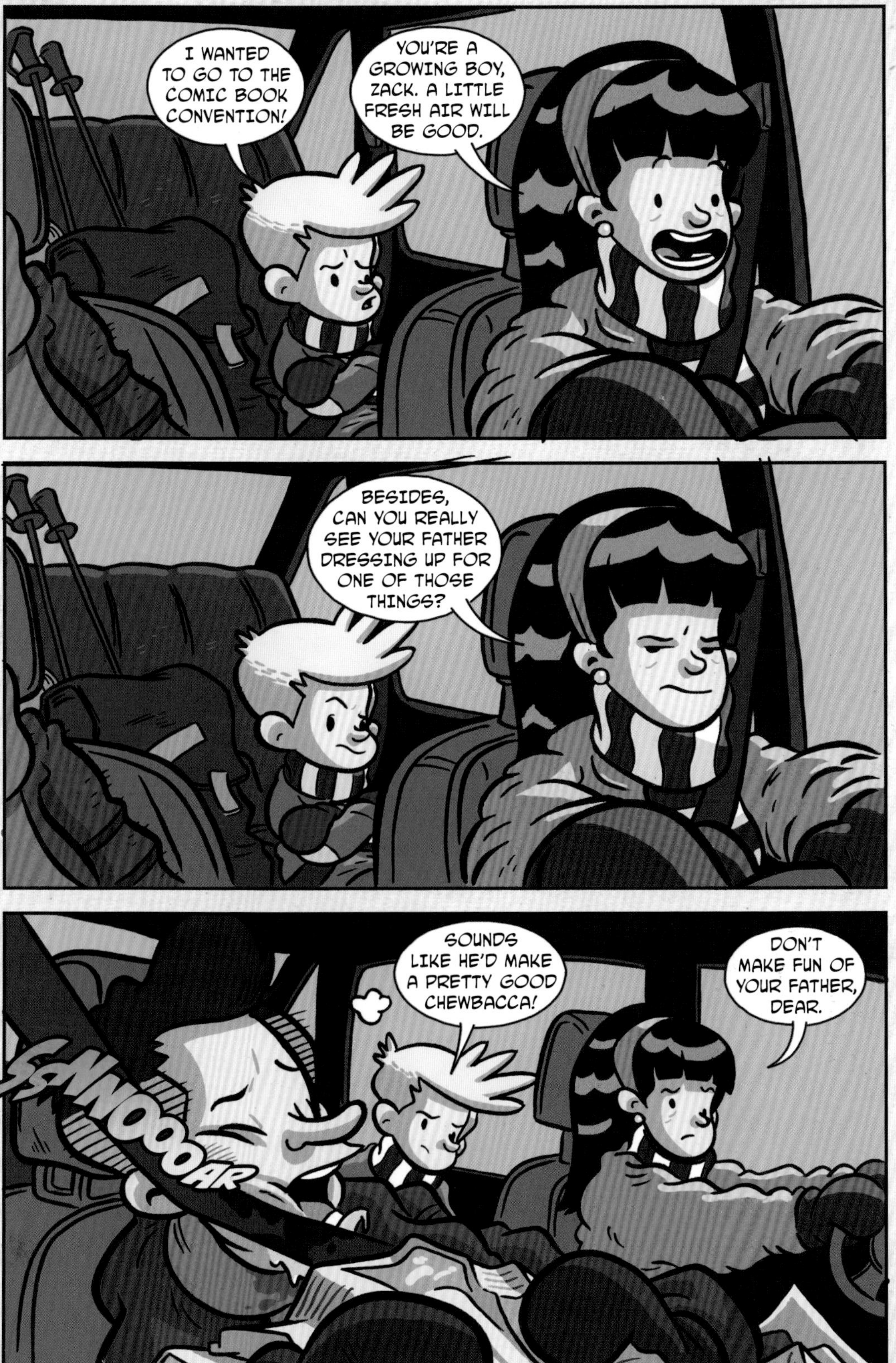
I WANTED TO GO TO THE COMIC BOOK CONVENTION!
YOU'RE A GROWING BOY, ZACK. A LITTLE FRESH AIR WILL BE GOOD.
BESIDES, CAN YOU REALLY SEE YOUR FATHER DRESSING UP FOR ONE OF THOSE THINGS?
SNNOOOAR
SOUNDS LIKE HE'D MAKE A PRETTY GOOD CHEWBACCA!
DON'T MAKE FUN OF YOUR FATHER, DEAR.

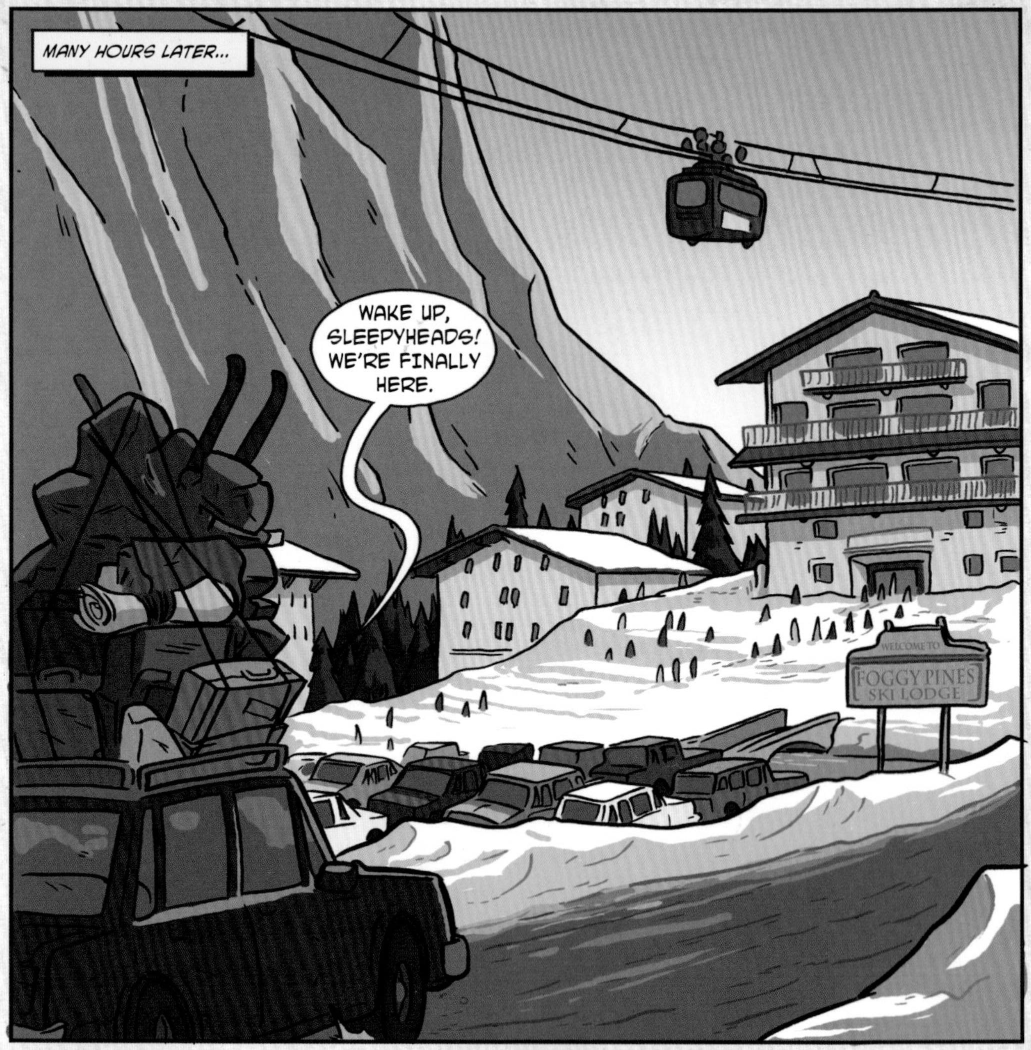
MANY HOURS LATER...
WAKE UP, SLEEPYHEADS! WE'RE FINALLY HERE.
WELCOME TO
FOGGY PINES SKI LODGE

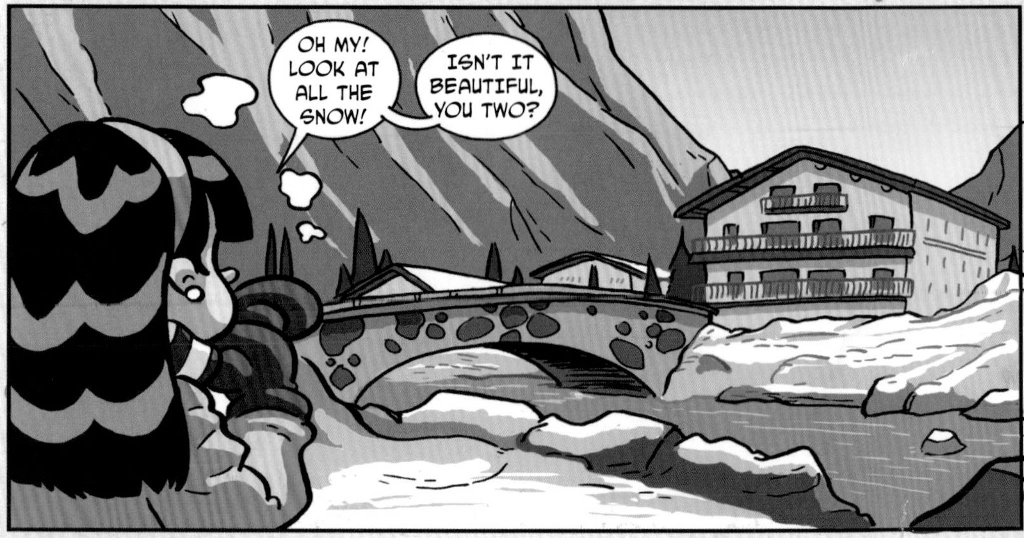
OH MY! LOOK AT ALL THE SNOW!
ISN'T IT BEAUTIFUL, YOU TWO?

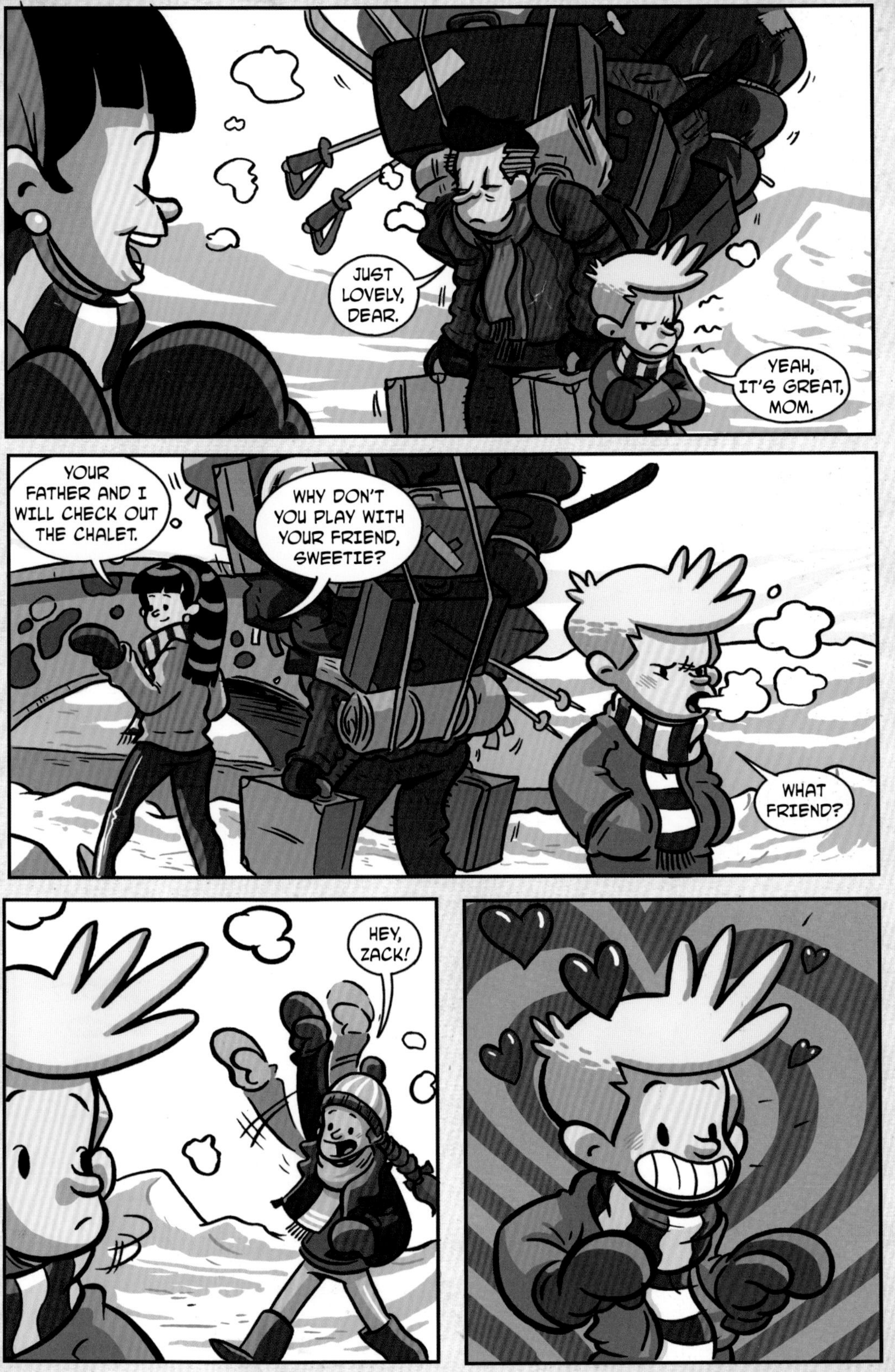
JUST LOVELY, DEAR.
YEAH, IT'S GREAT, MOM.
YOUR FATHER AND I WILL CHECK OUT THE CHALET.
WHY DON'T YOU PLAY WITH YOUR FRIEND, SWEETIE?
WHAT FRIEND?
HEY, ZACK!

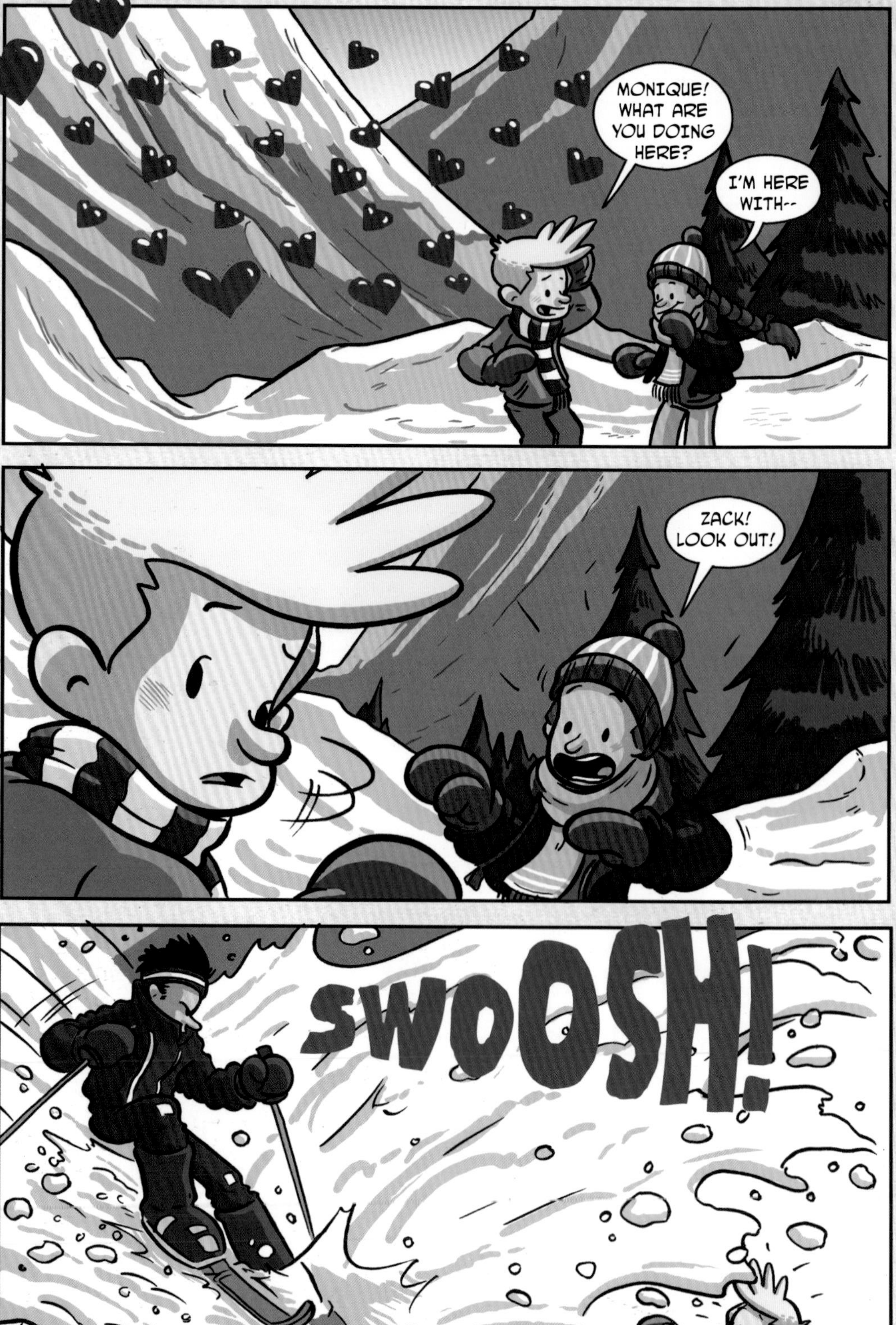
MONIQUE! WHAT ARE YOU DOING HERE?
I'M HERE WITH--
ZACK! LOOK OUT!
SWOOSH!

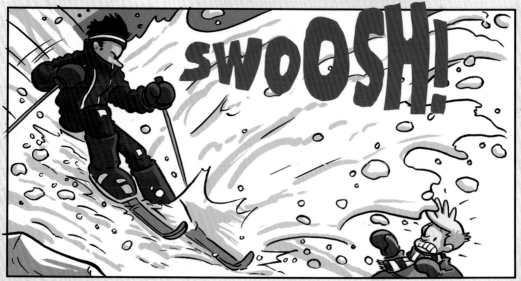

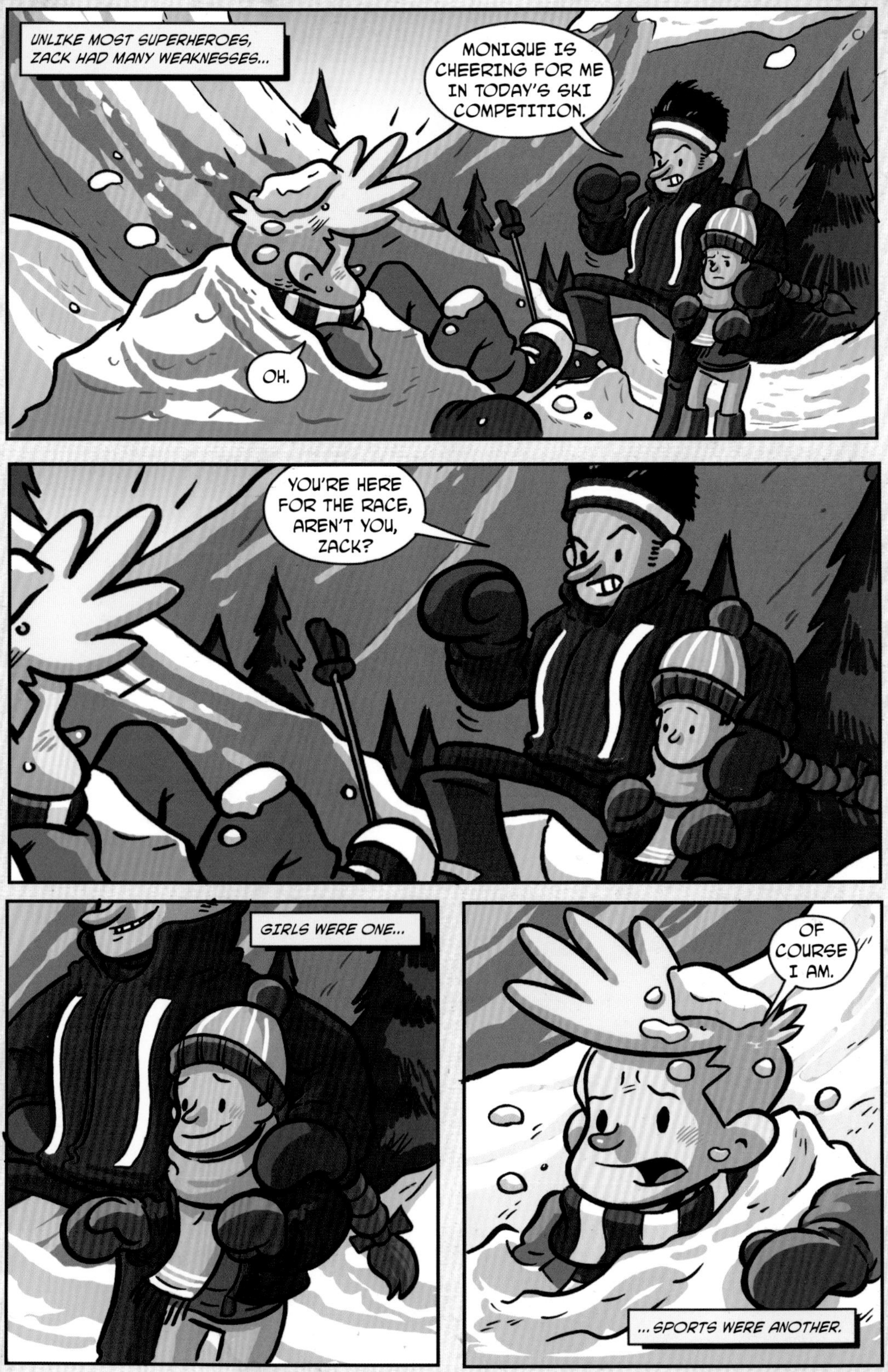
UNLIKE MOST SUPERHEROES, ZACK HAD MANY WEAKNESSES...
MONIQUE IS CHEERING FOR ME IN TODAY'S SKI COMPETITION.
OH.
YOU'RE HERE FOR THE RACE, AREN'T YOU, ZACK?
GIRLS WERE ONE...
OF COURSE I AM.
...SPORTS WERE ANOTHER.

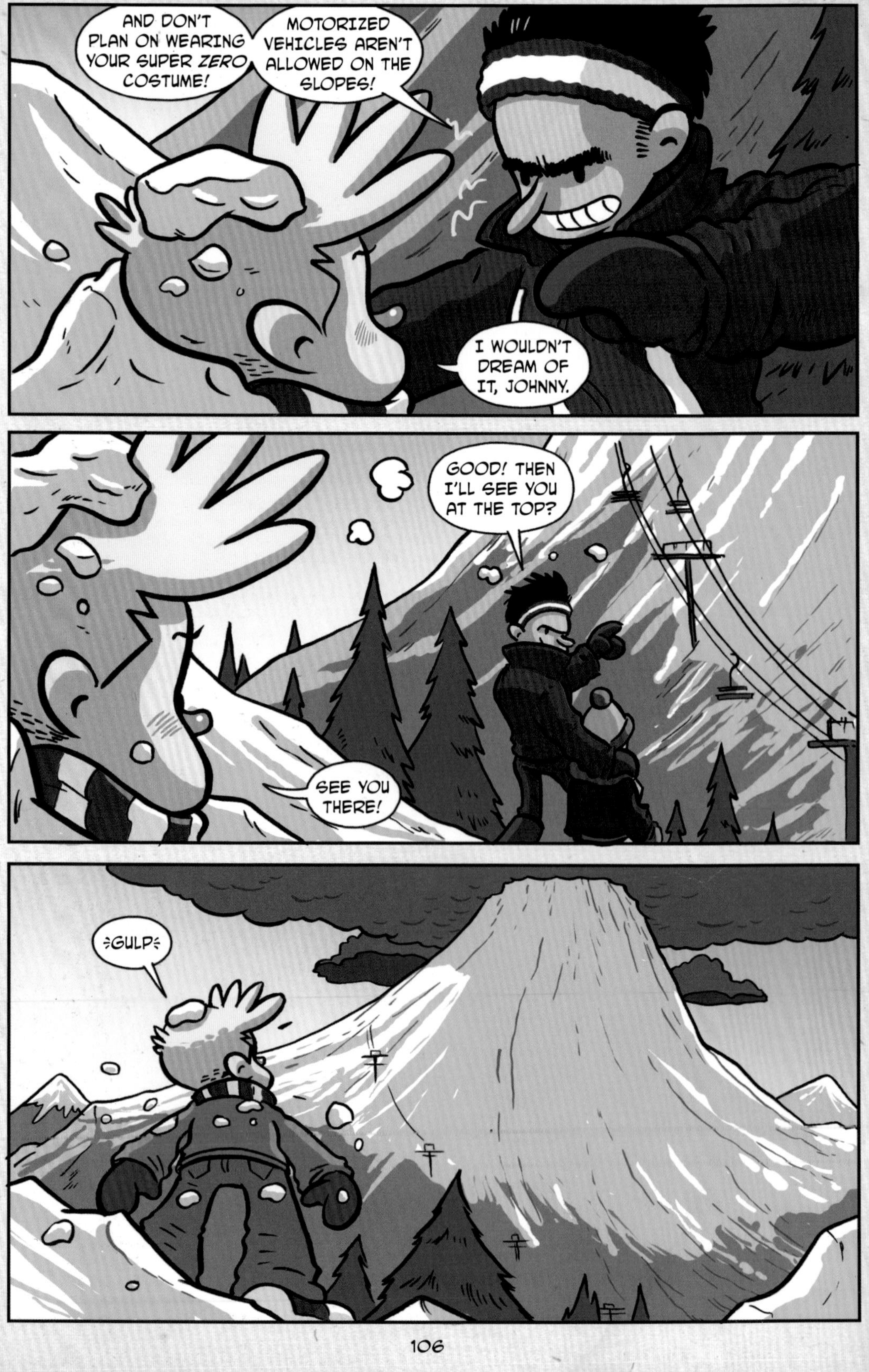
AND DON'T PLAN ON WEARING YOUR SUPER ZERO COSTUME!
MOTORIZED VEHICLES AREN'T ALLOWED ON THE SLOPES!
I WOULDN'T DREAM OF IT, JOHNNY.
GOOD! THEN I'LL SEE YOU AT THE TOP?
SEE YOU THERE!
GULP

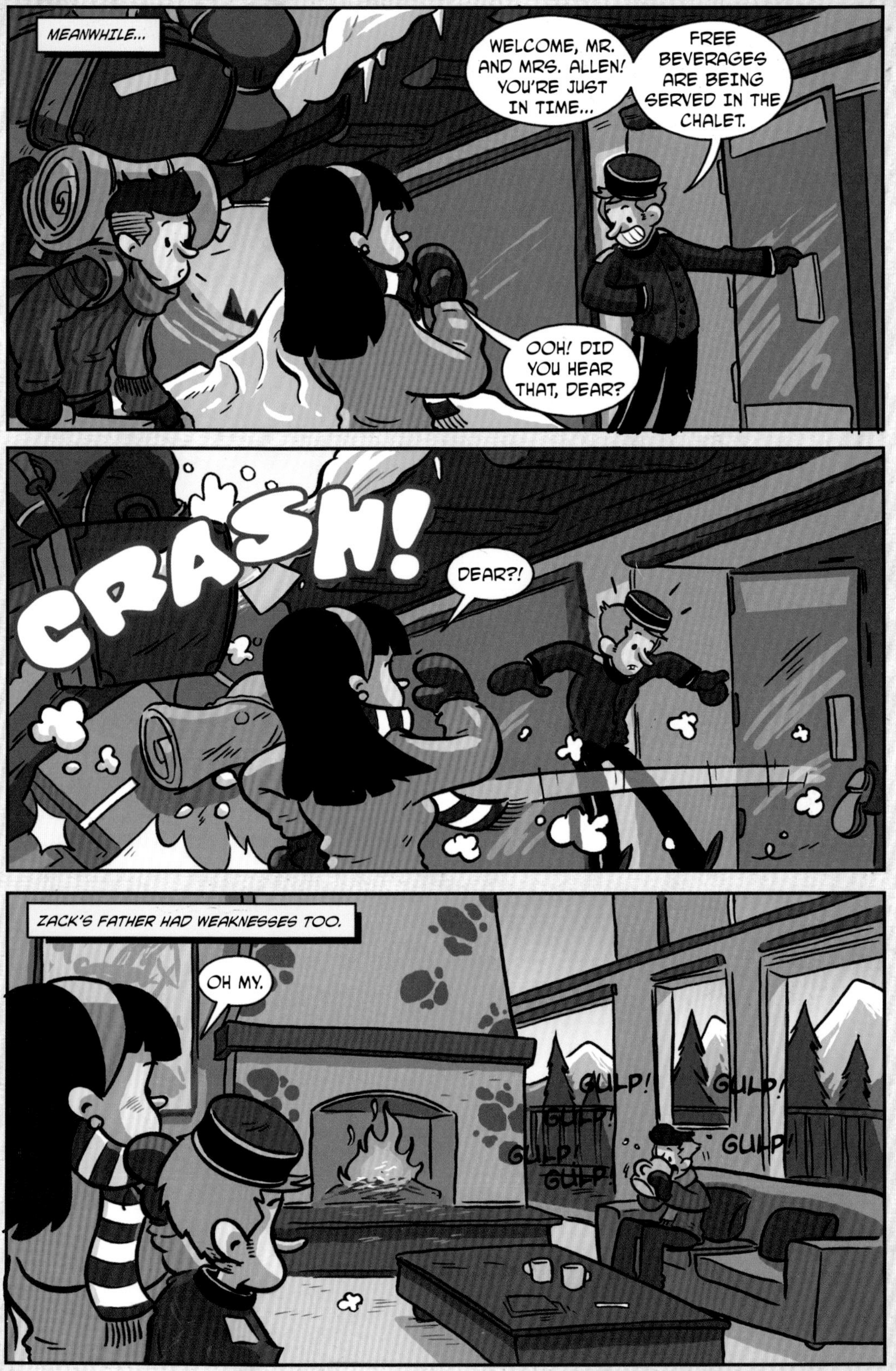
MEANWHILE...
WELCOME, MR. AND MRS. ALLEN! YOU'RE JUST IN TIME...
FREE BEVERAGES ARE BEING SERVED IN THE CHALET.
OOH! DID YOU HEAR THAT, DEAR?
CRASH!
DEAR?!
ZACK'S FATHER HAD WEAKNESSES TOO.
OH MY.
GULP!
GULP!
GULP!
GULP!
GULP!
GULP!

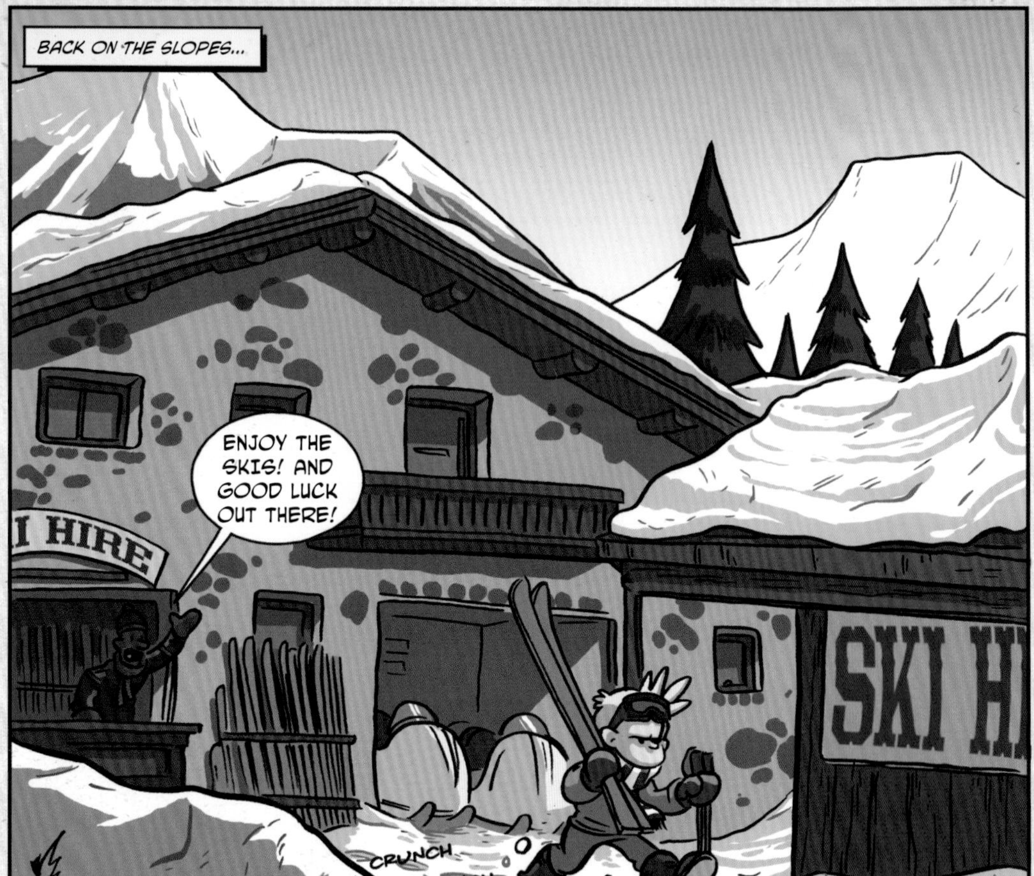
BACK ON THE SLOPES...
ENJOY THE SKIS! AND GOOD LUCK OUT THERE!
I HIRE
SKI HI
CRUNCH
CRUNCH
CRUNCH

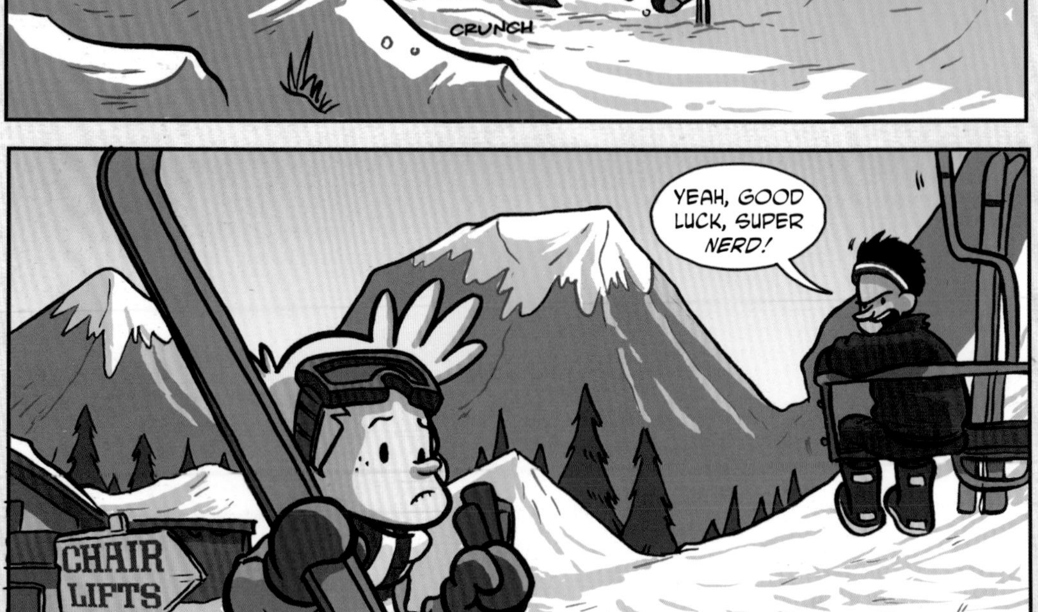
YEAH, GOOD LUCK, SUPER NERD!
CHAIR LIFTS

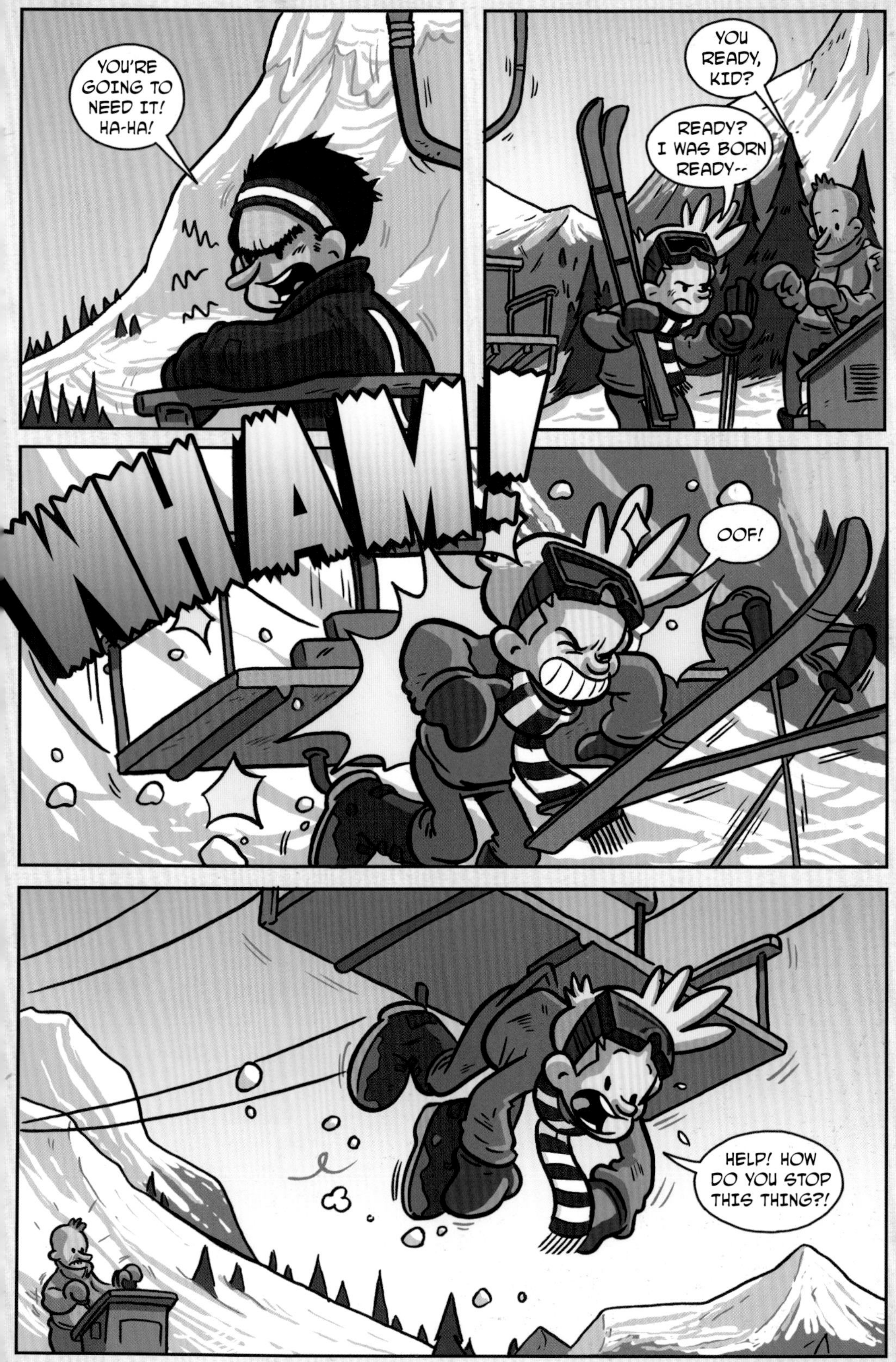
YOU'RE GOING TO NEED IT! HA-HA!
YOU READY, KID?
READY? I WAS BORN READY--
WHAM!
OOF!
HELP! HOW DO YOU STOP THIS THING?!

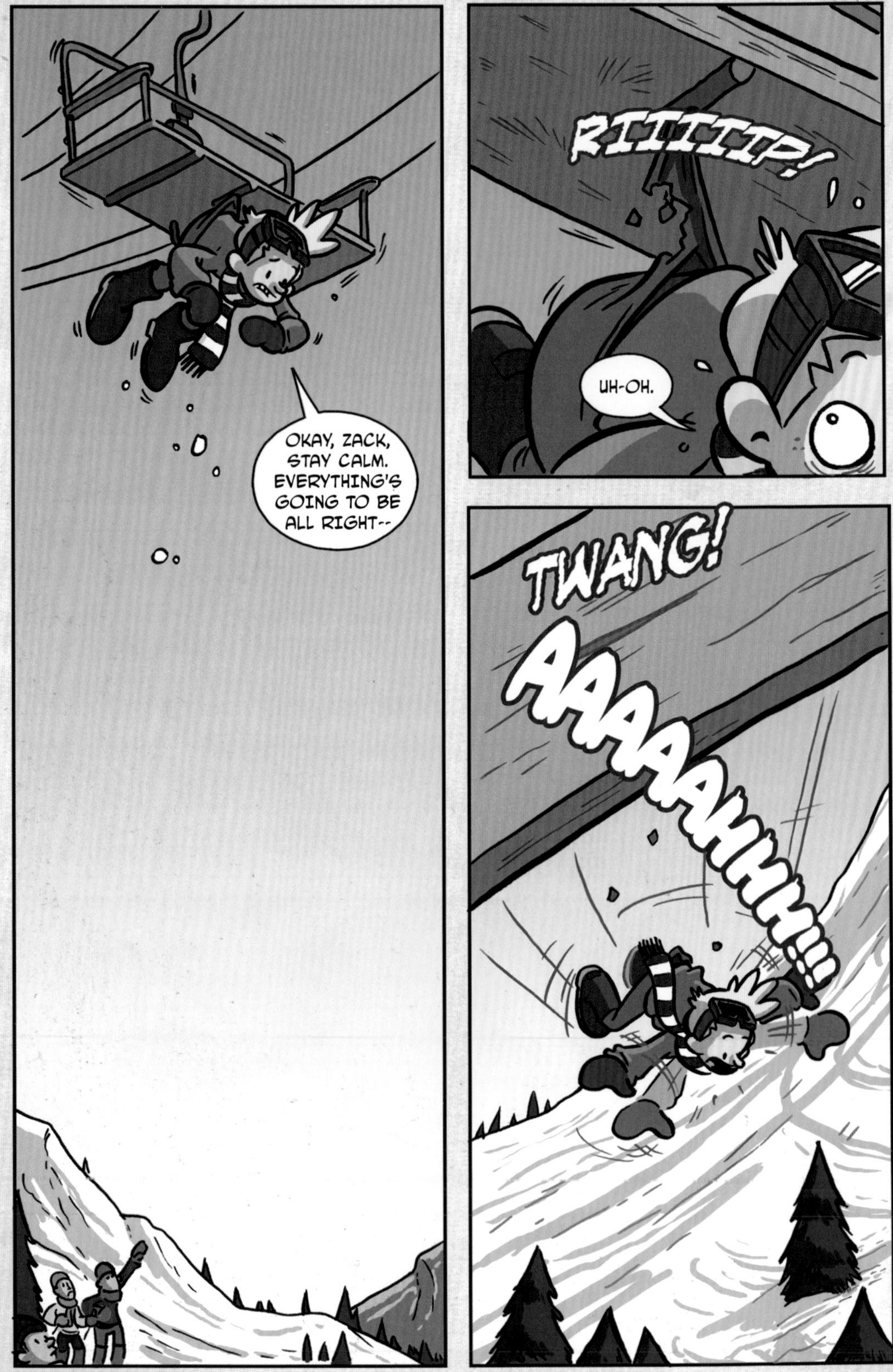
OKAY, ZACK, STAY CALM. EVERYTHING'S GOING TO BE ALL RIGHT--
RIIIIIP!
UH-OH.
TWANG!
AAAAAHHH!!!

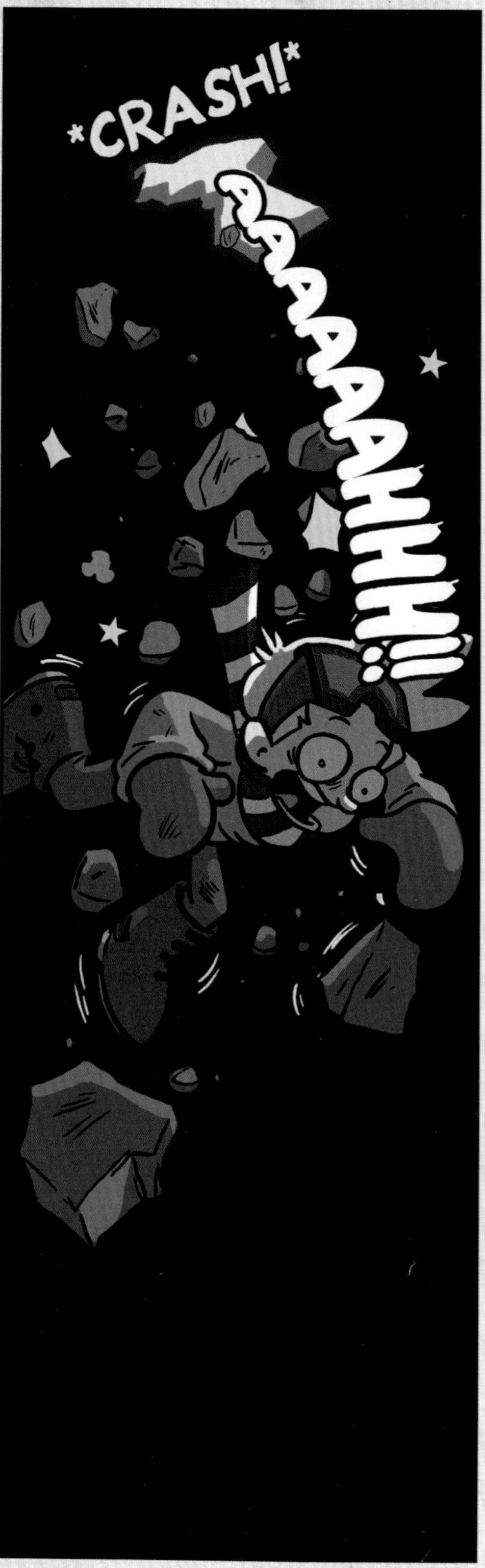
CRASH!
AAAAAAAHHHH!!!
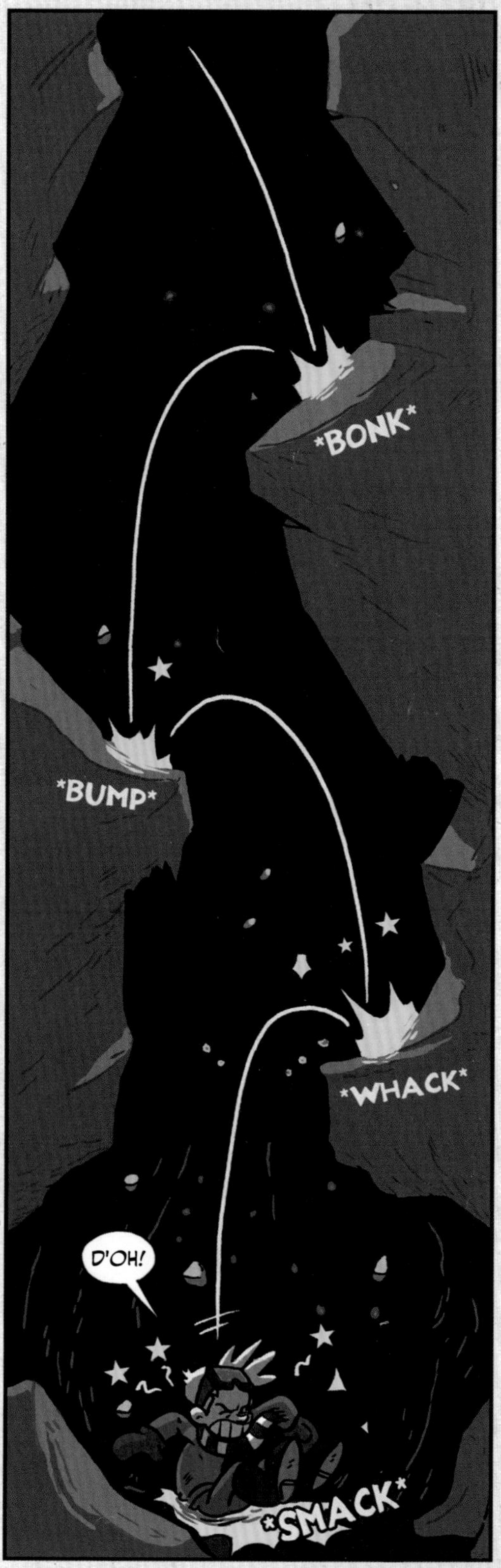
BONK
BUMP
WHACK
D'OH!
SMACK

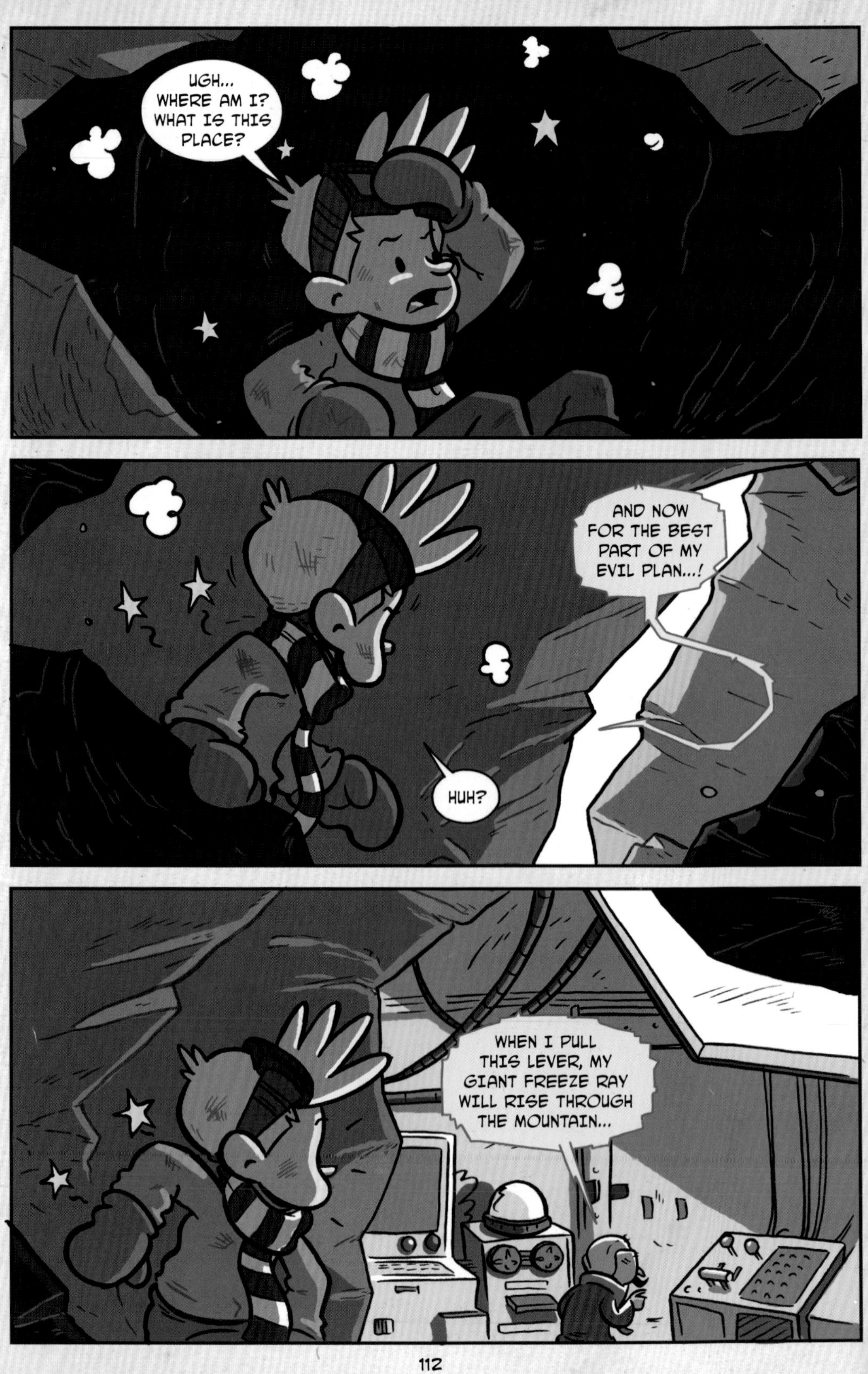
UGH... WHERE AM I? WHAT IS THIS PLACE?
AND NOW FOR THE BEST PART OF MY EVIL PLAN...!
HUH?
WHEN I PULL THIS LEVER, MY GIANT FREEZE RAY WILL RISE THROUGH THE MOUNTAIN...

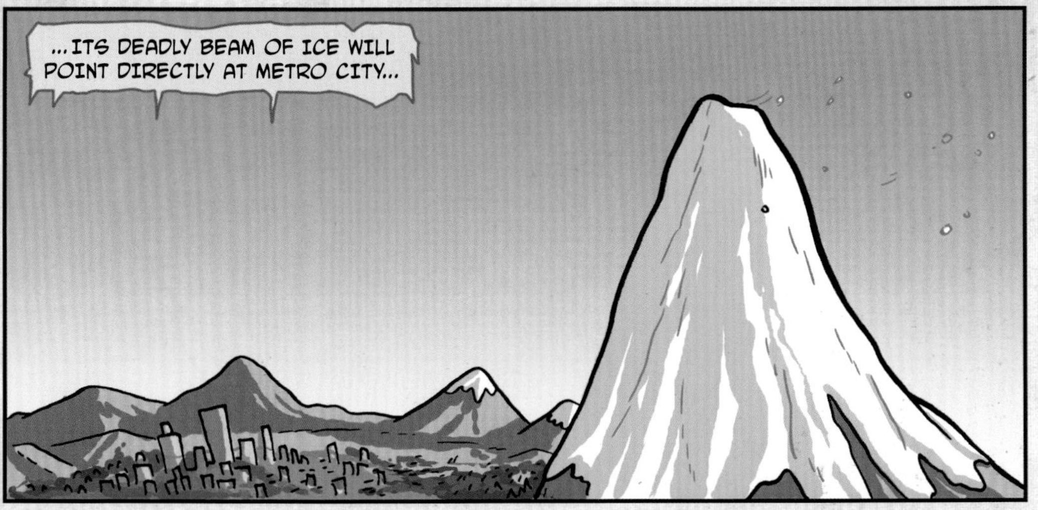
...ITS DEADLY BEAM OF ICE WILL POINT DIRECTLY AT METRO CITY...

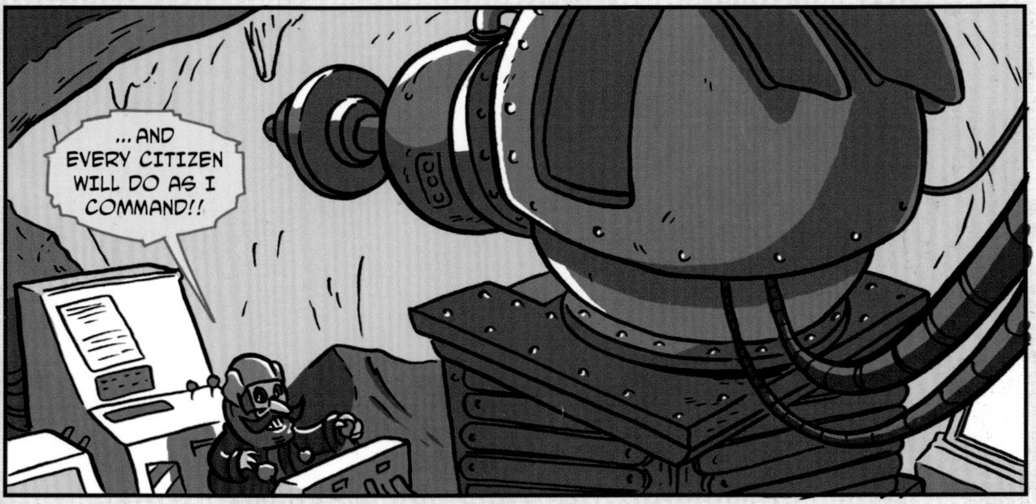
...AND EVERY CITIZEN WILL DO AS I COMMAND!!

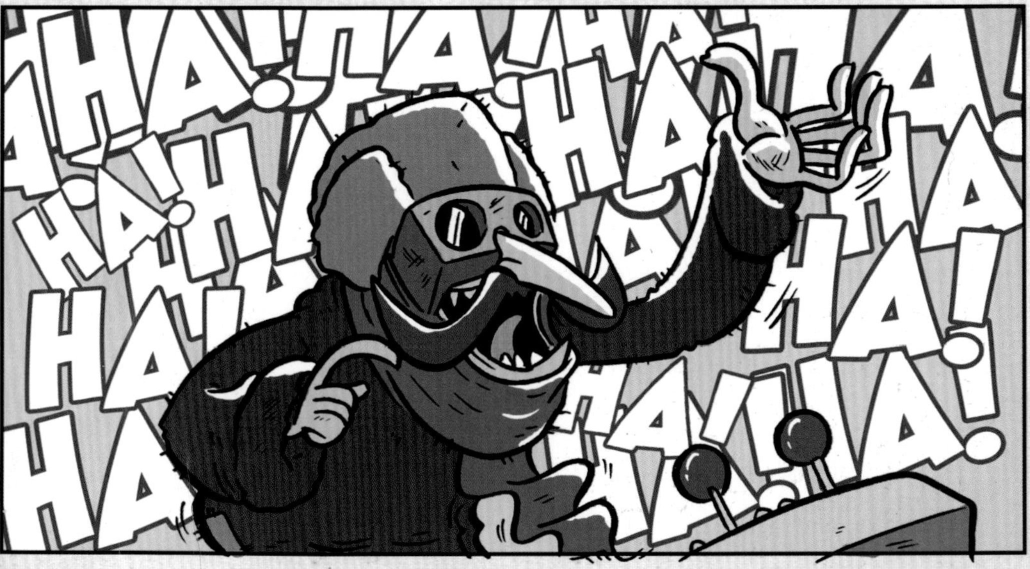
HA! HA! HA! HA! HA! HA! HA! HA! HA! HA! HA! HA! HA! HA! HA!

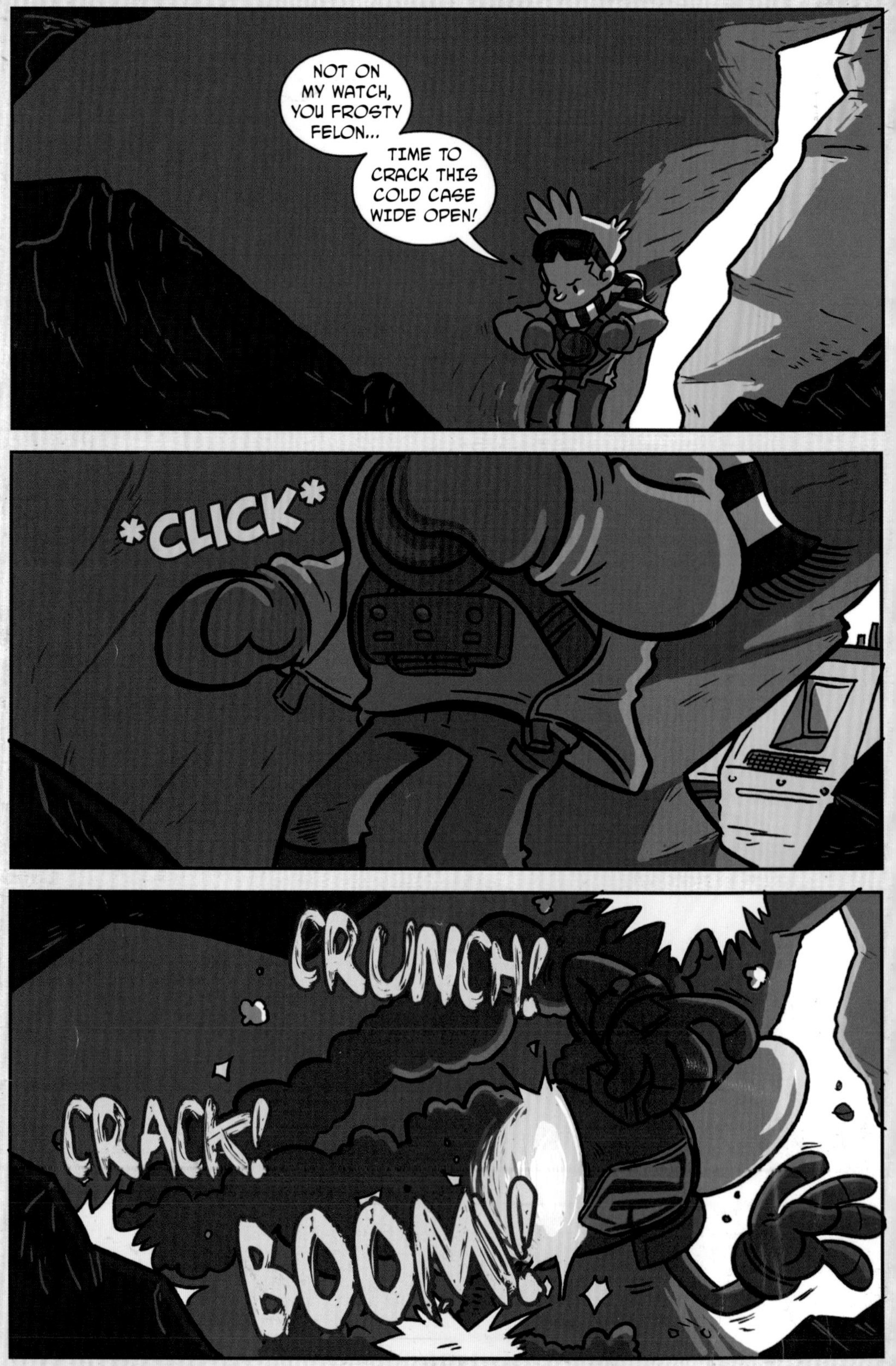
NOT ON MY WATCH, YOU FROSTY FELON...
TIME TO CRACK THIS COLD CASE WIDE OPEN!
CLICK
CRUNCH!
CRACK!
BOOM!

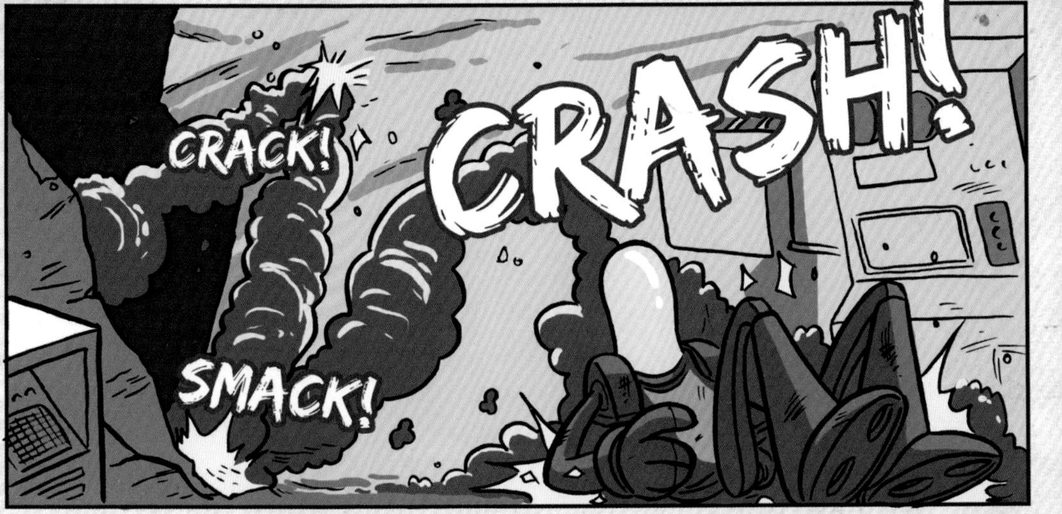
CRACK!
SMACK!
CRASH!

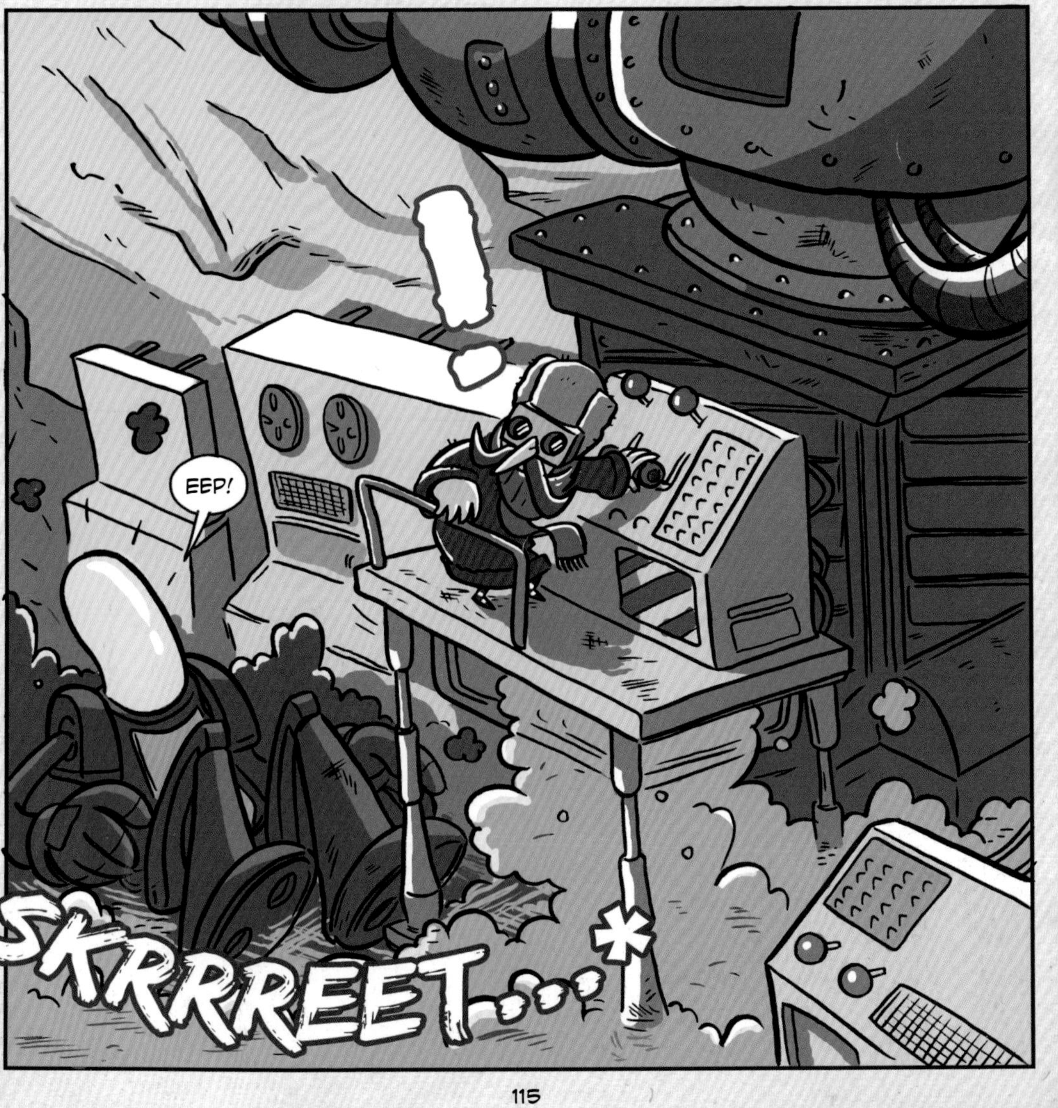
EEP!
SKRRREET...!

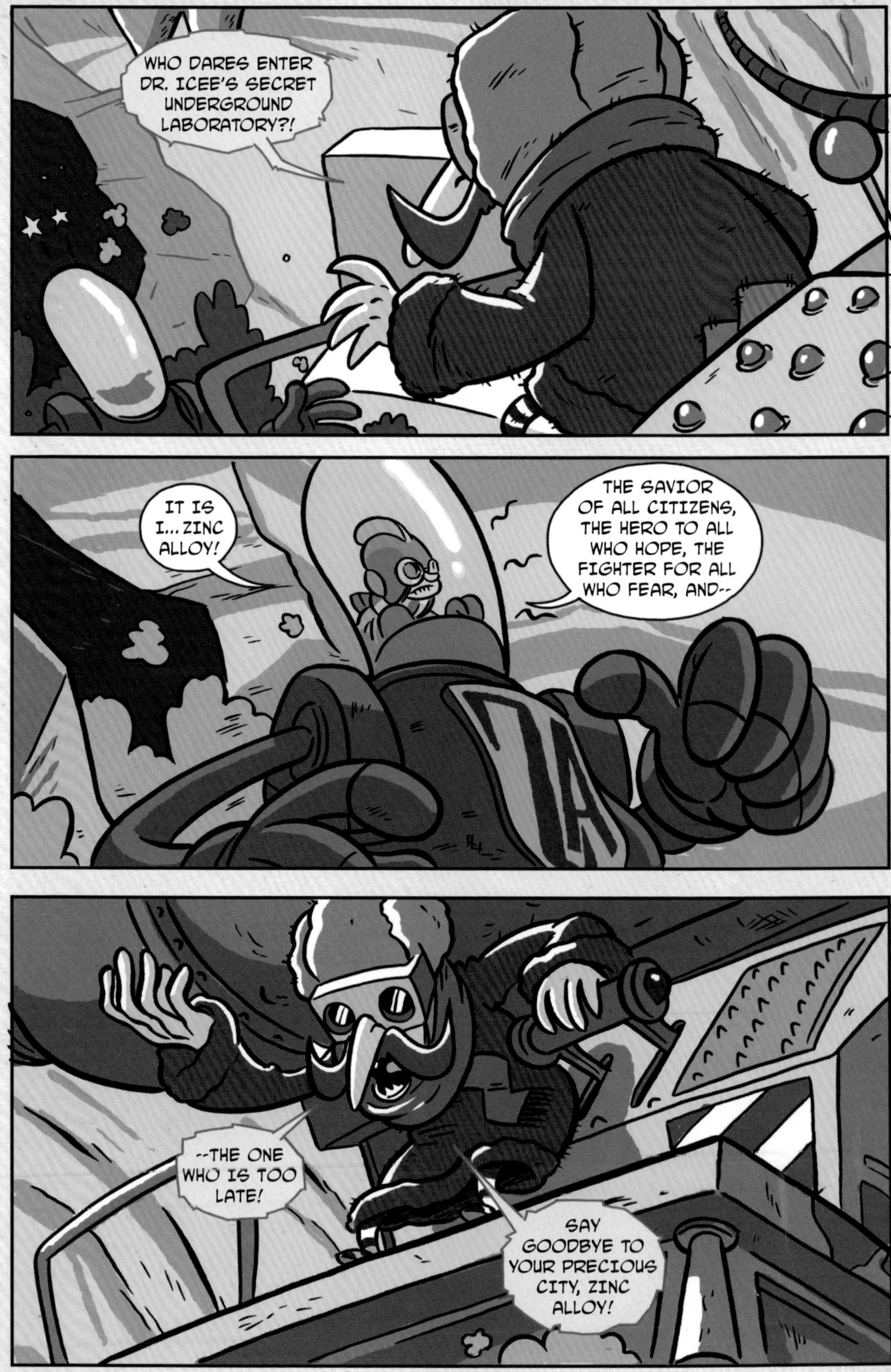
WHO DARES ENTER DR. ICEE'S SECRET UNDERGROUND LABORATORY?!
IT IS I... ZINC ALLOY!
THE SAVIOR OF ALL CITIZENS, THE HERO TO ALL WHO HOPE, THE FIGHTER FOR ALL WHO FEAR, AND--
--THE ONE WHO IS TOO LATE!
SAY GOODBYE TO YOUR PRECIOUS CITY, ZINC ALLOY!

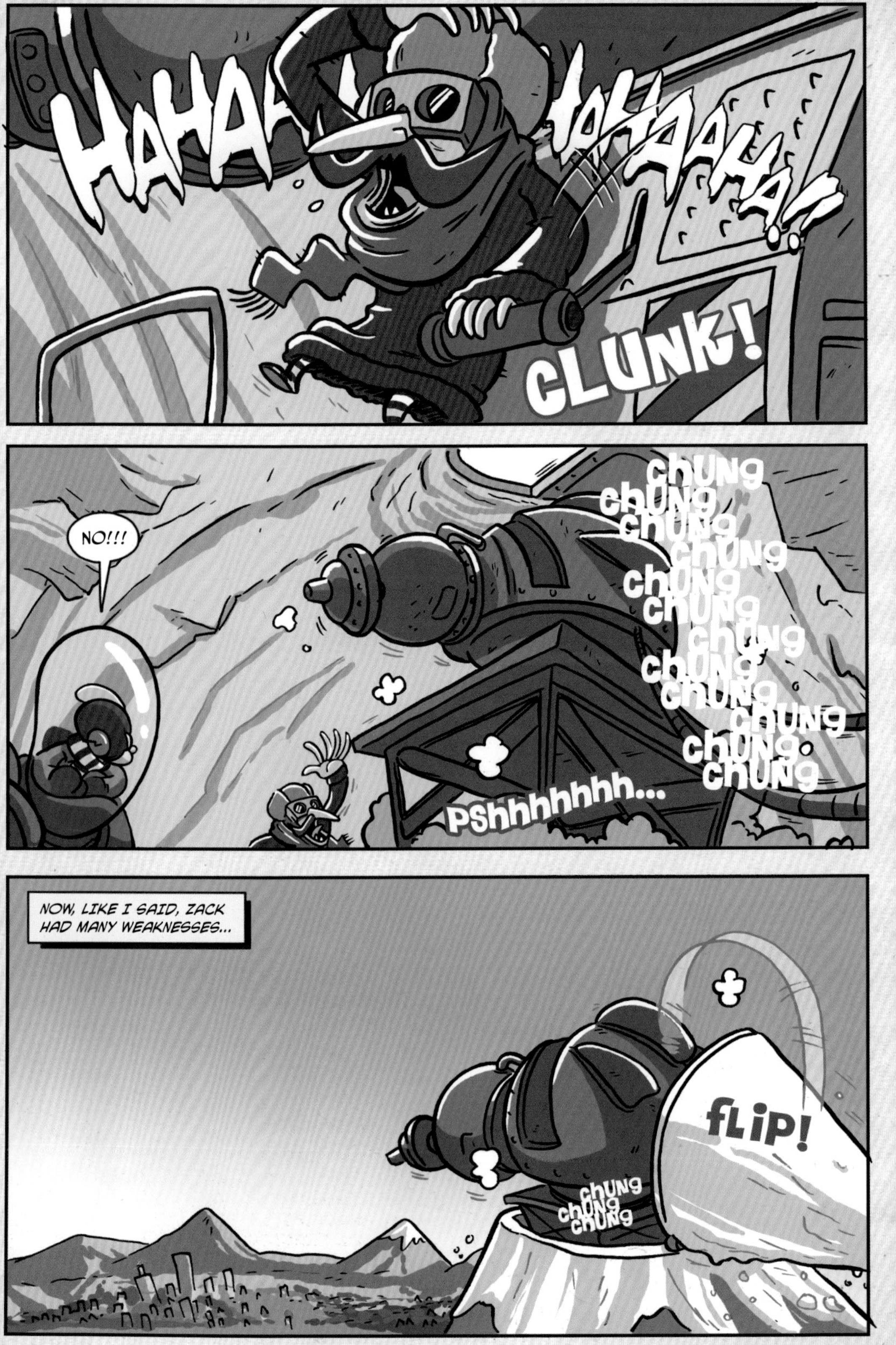
HAHAH
AHAHAHA!!
CLUNK!
NO!!!
chung
chung
chung
chung
chung
chung
chung
chung
chung
chung
chung
chung
Pshhhhhhh...
NOW, LIKE I SAID, ZACK HAD MANY WEAKNESSES...
FLIP!
chung
chung
chung

...BUT FAILURE WASN'T ONE OF THEM.

NOT SO FAST, DR. SLUSHIE!

IT'S DR. ICEE!!

WHY DO PEOPLE KEEP CALLING ME THAT?!

WHATEVER, MR. SLURPIE... I'M NOT LETTING YOU DESTROY MY CITY!

PUNCH!

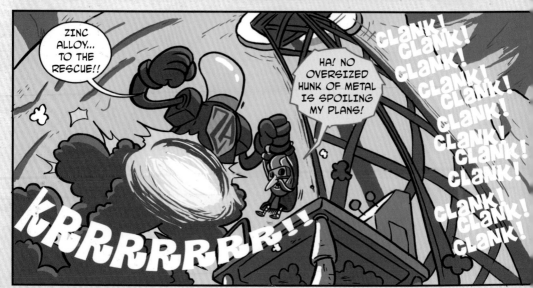

ZINC ALLOY... TO THE RESCUE!!

HA! NO OVERSIZED HUNK OF METAL IS SPOILING MY PLANS!

CLANK! CLANK! CLANK! CLANK! CLANK! CLANK! CLANK! CLANK! CLANK! CLANK! CLANK! CLANK!

KRRRRRRR!!

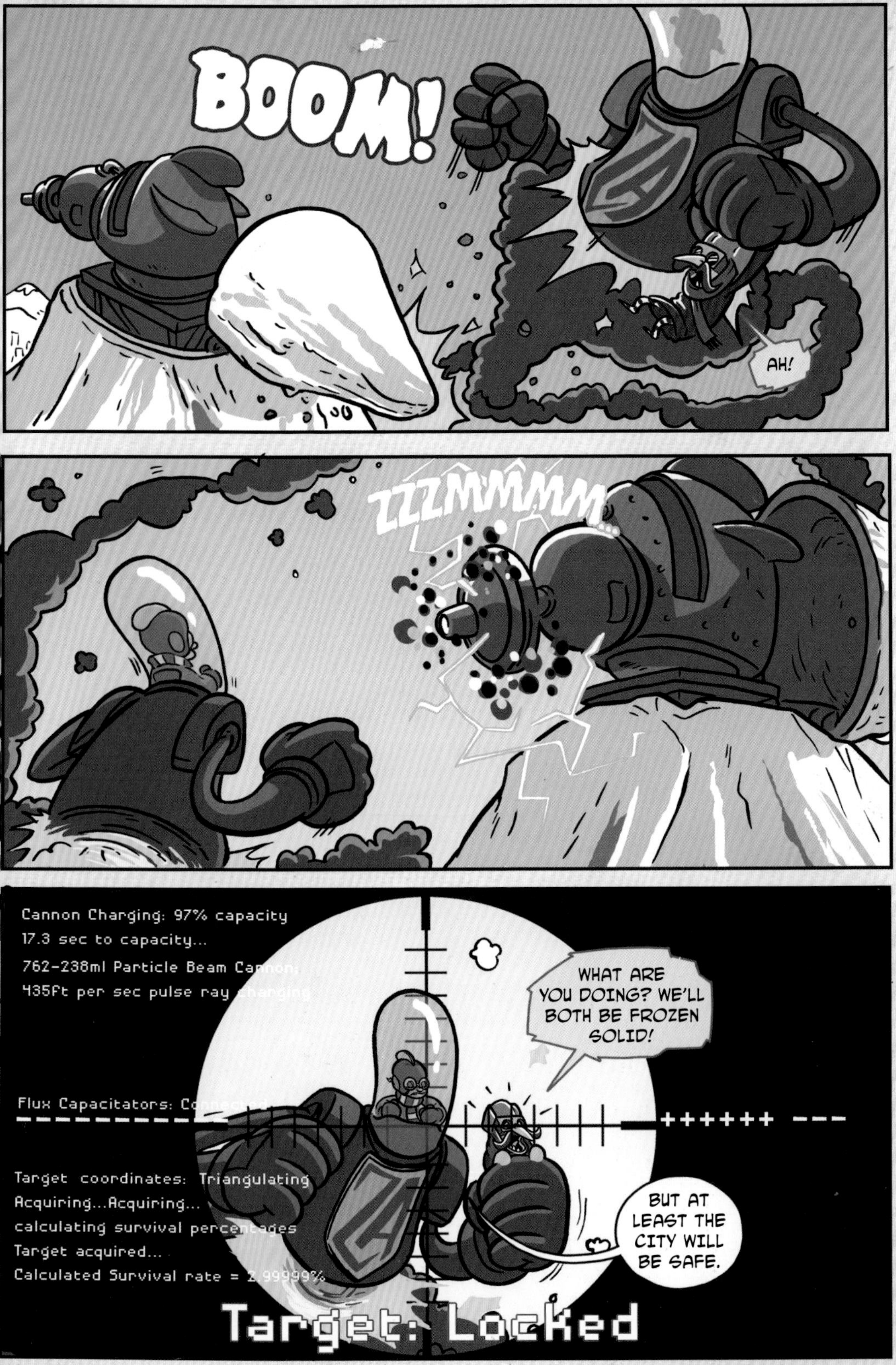
BOOM!
AH!
ZZZMMMMM...
Cannon Charging: 97% capacity
17.3 sec to capacity...
762-238ml Particle Beam Cannon,
435ft per sec pulse ray charging
WHAT ARE YOU DOING? WE'LL BOTH BE FROZEN SOLID!
Flux Capacitators: Connected
Target coordinates: Triangulating
Acquiring...Acquiring...
calculating survival percentages
Target acquired...
Calculated Survival rate = 2.99999%
BUT AT LEAST THE CITY WILL BE SAFE.
Target: Locked

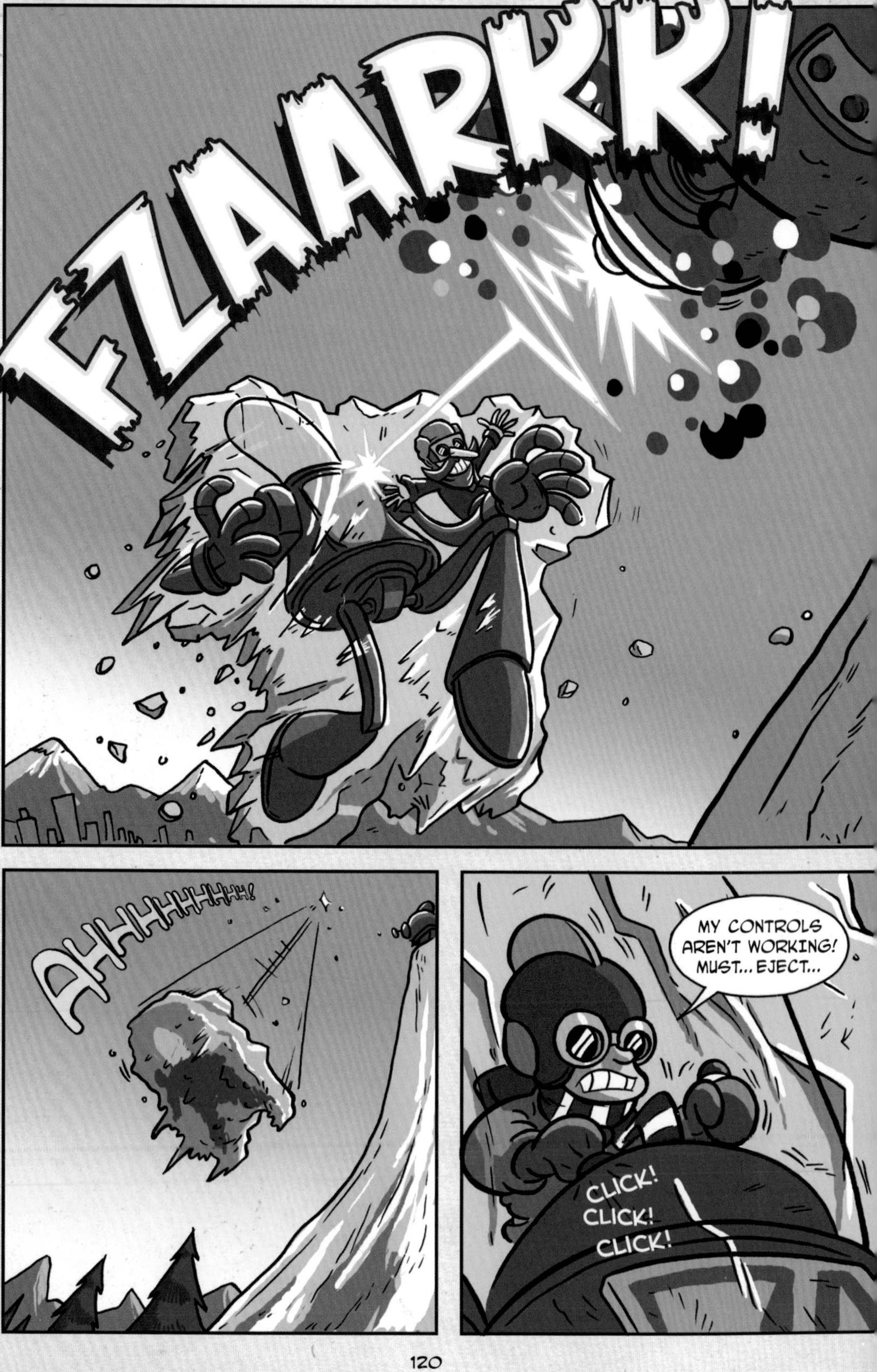
FZAARKK!
AHHHHHHHHH!
MY CONTROLS AREN'T WORKING! MUST... EJECT...
CLICK!
CLICK!
CLICK!

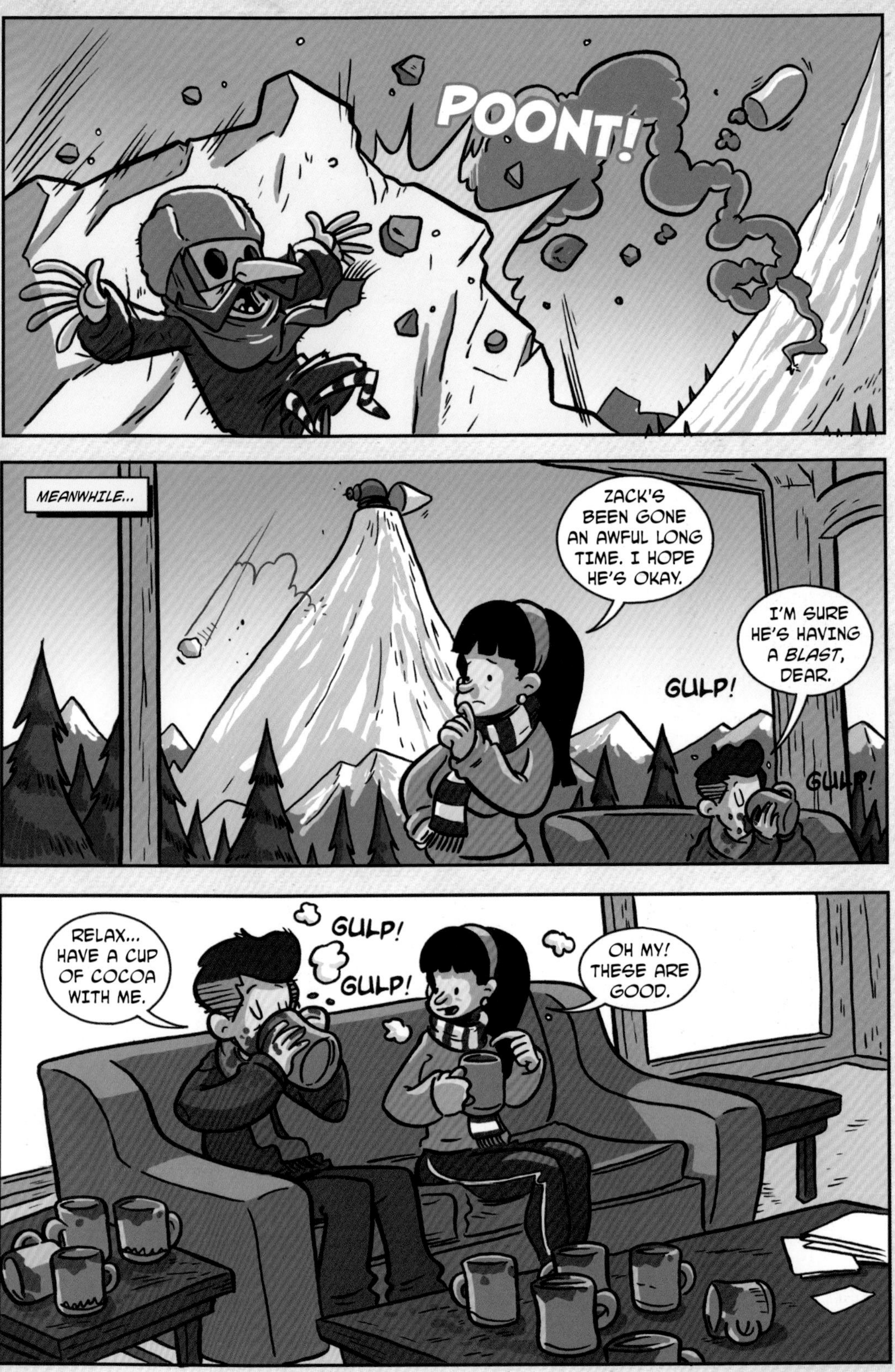
POONT!
MEANWHILE...
ZACK'S BEEN GONE AN AWFUL LONG TIME. I HOPE HE'S OKAY.
GULP!
I'M SURE HE'S HAVING A *BLAST*, DEAR.
RELAX... HAVE A CUP OF COCOA WITH ME.
GULP!
GULP!
OH MY! THESE ARE GOOD.

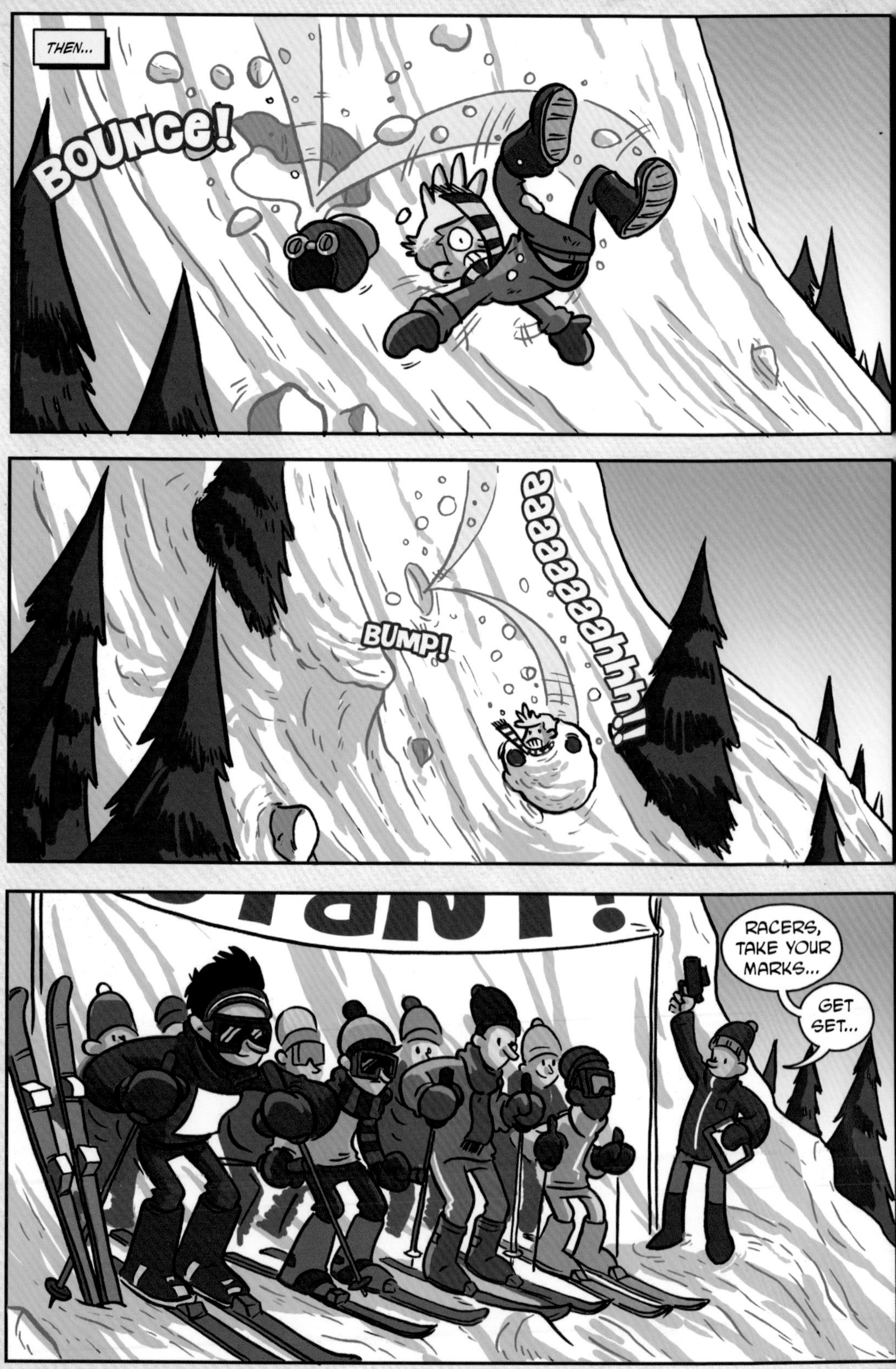
THEN...
BOUNCE!
BUMP!
aaaaaeeeeeahhhh!!
RACERS, TAKE YOUR MARKS...
GET SET...

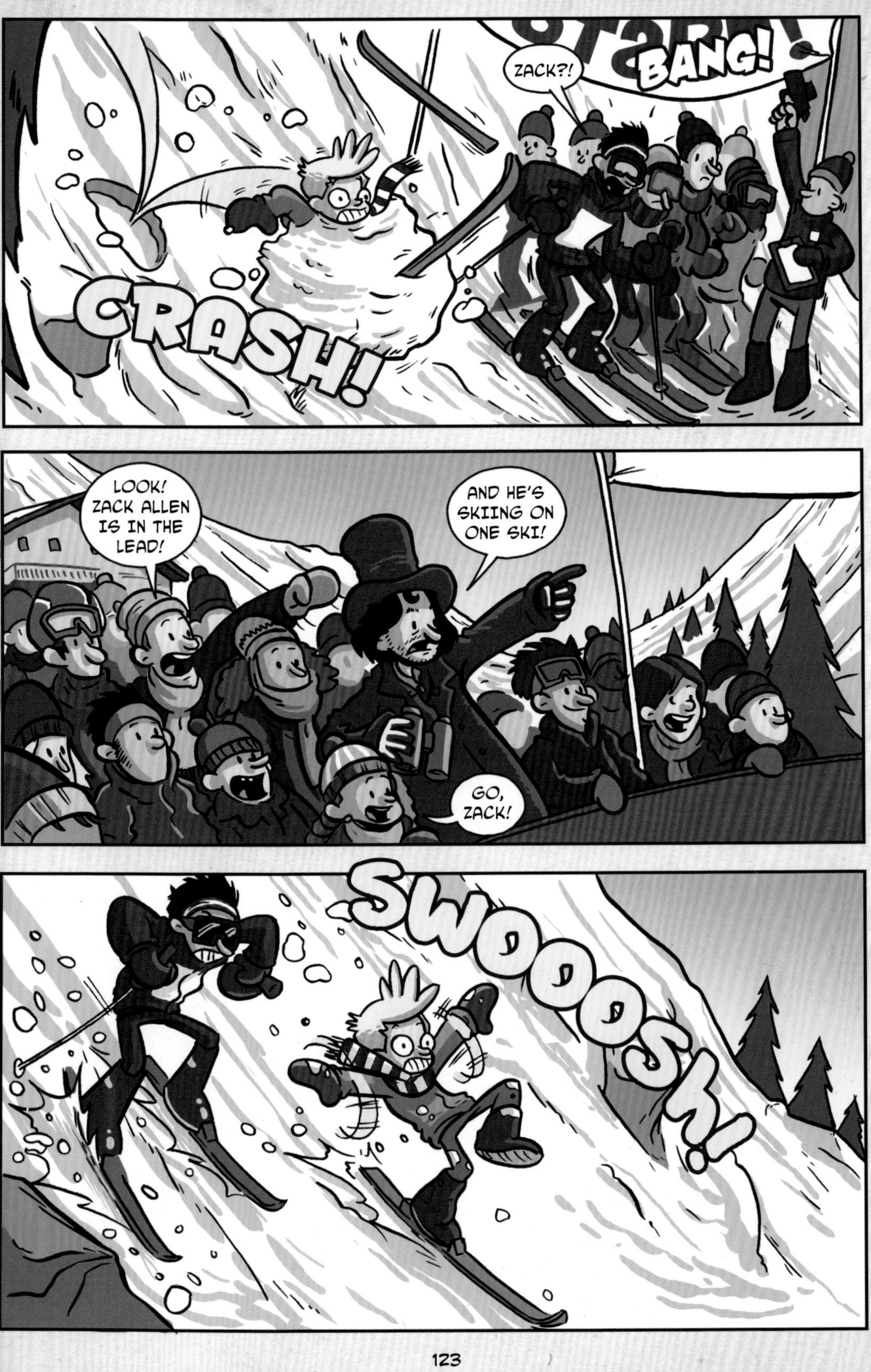
ZACK?!
BANG!
CRASH!
LOOK! ZACK ALLEN IS IN THE LEAD!
AND HE'S SKIING ON ONE SKI!
GO, ZACK!
SWOOOSH!

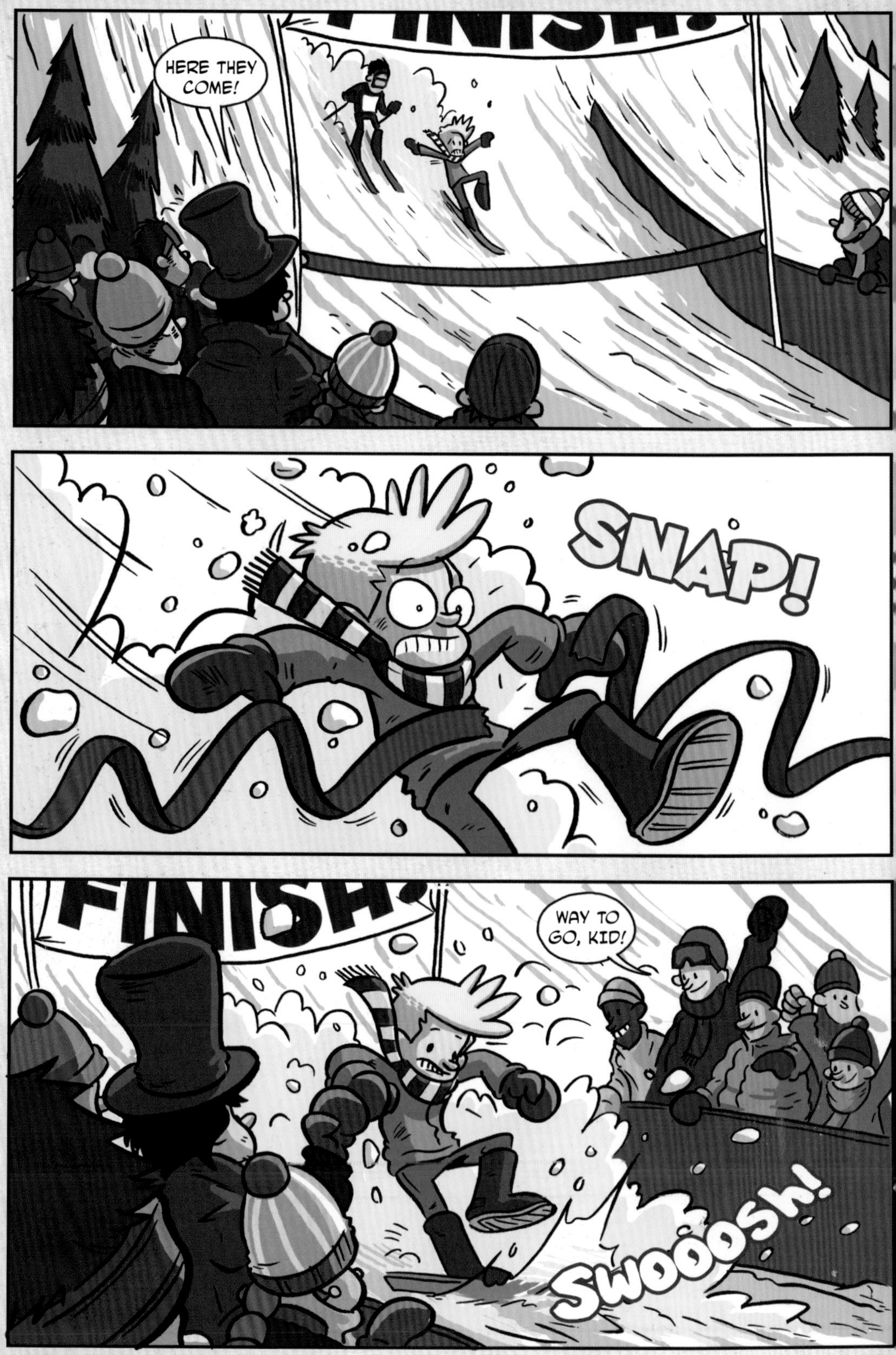
FINISH!
HERE THEY COME!
SNAP!
FINISH!
WAY TO GO, KID!
SWOOOSH!

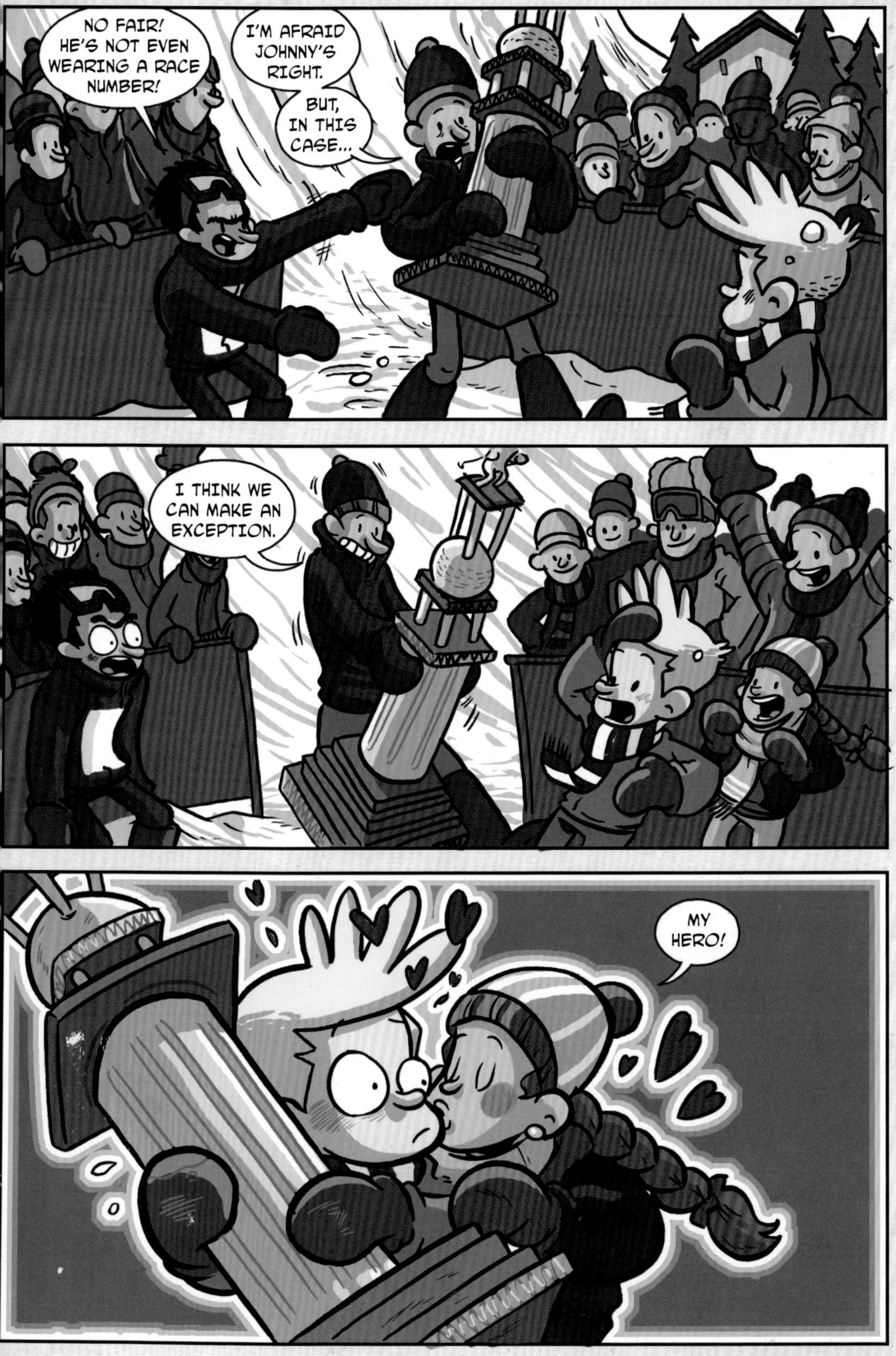
NO FAIR! HE'S NOT EVEN WEARING A RACE NUMBER!
I'M AFRAID JOHNNY'S RIGHT.
BUT, IN THIS CASE...
I THINK WE CAN MAKE AN EXCEPTION.
MY HERO!

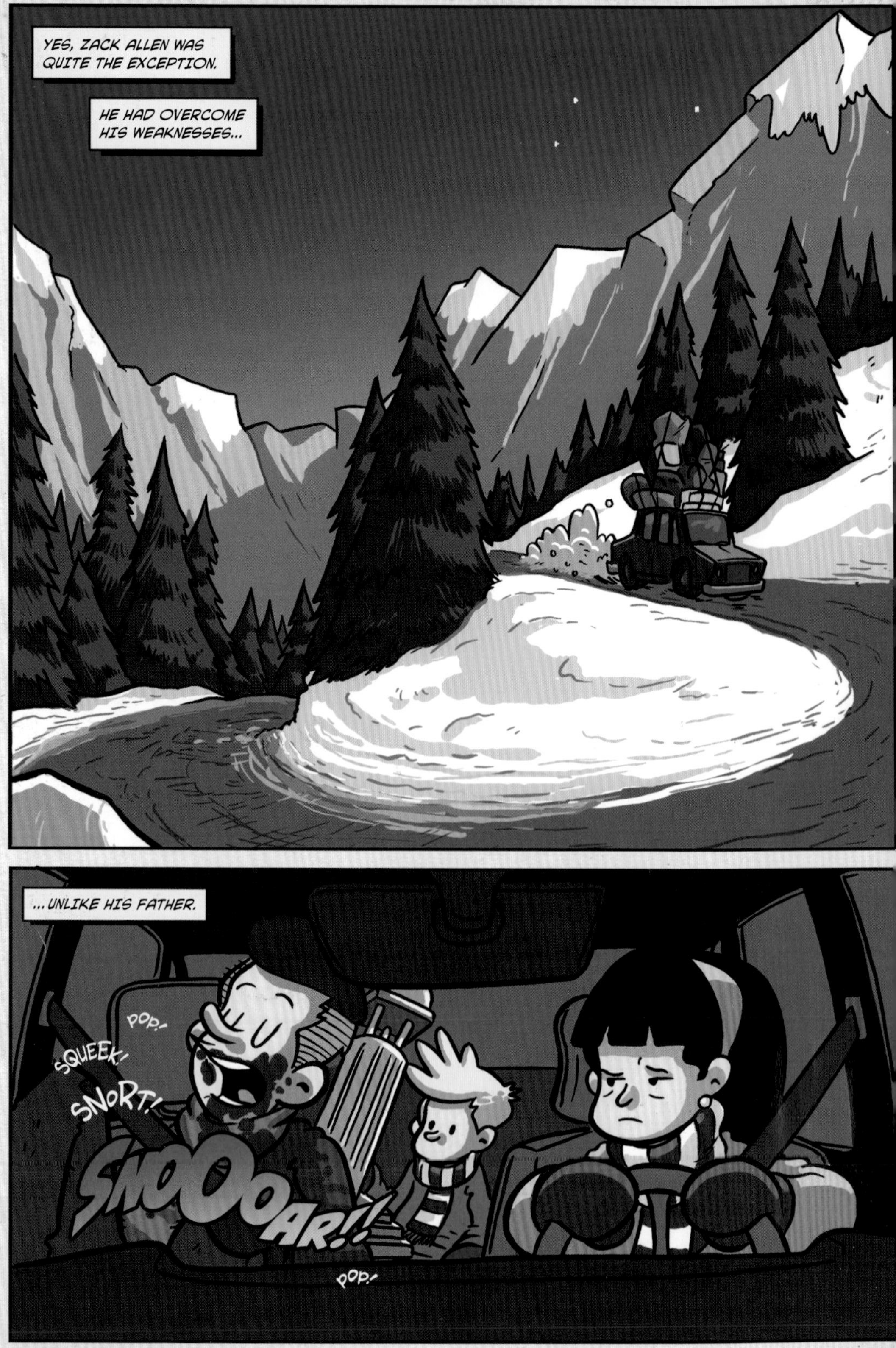
YES, ZACK ALLEN WAS QUITE THE EXCEPTION.
HE HAD OVERCOME HIS WEAKNESSES...
...UNLIKE HIS FATHER.
POP!
SQUEEK!
SNORT!
SNOOOOAR!!
POP!

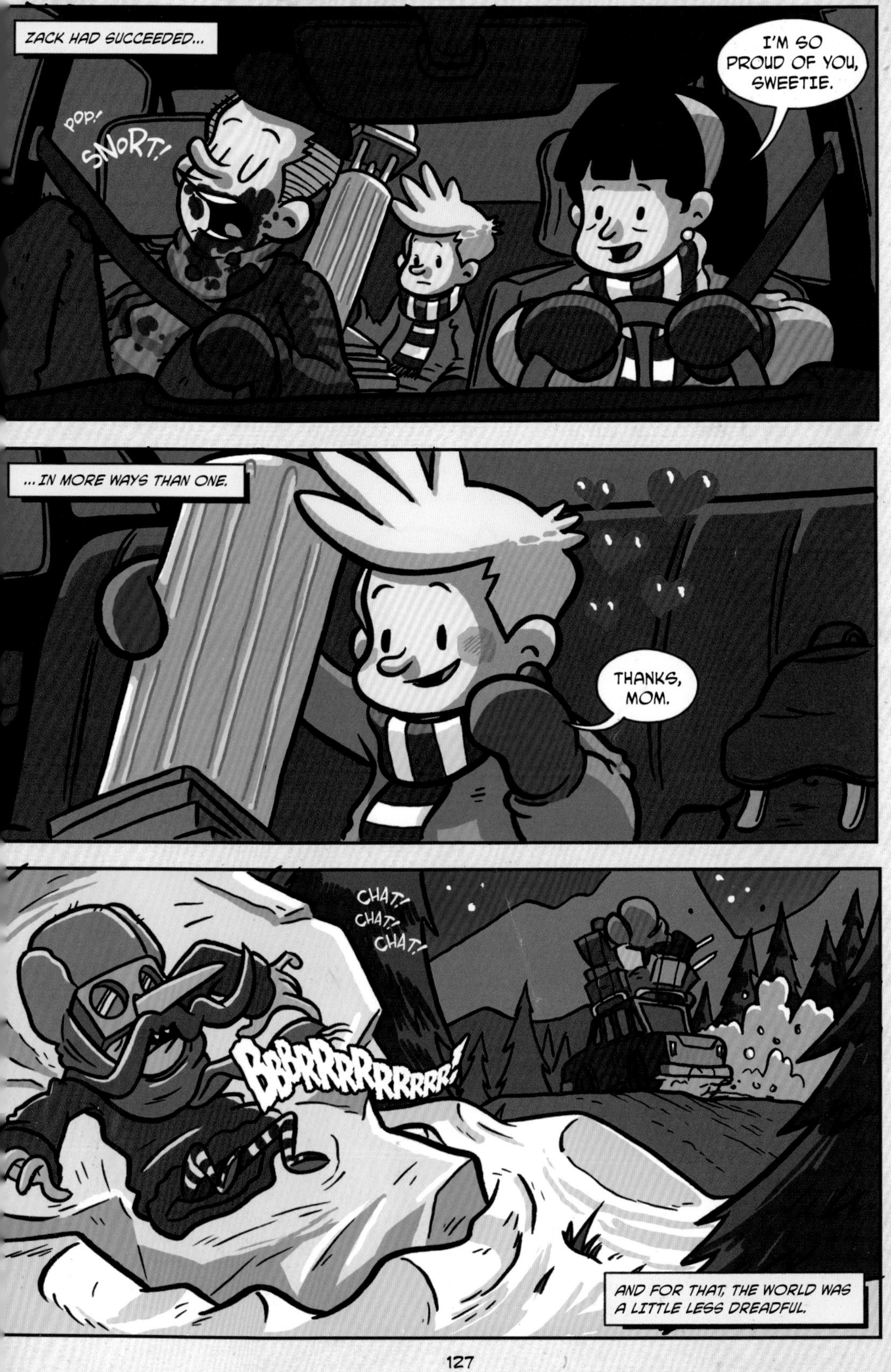
ZACK HAD SUCCEEDED...
I'M SO PROUD OF YOU, SWEETIE.
POP!
SNORT!
...IN MORE WAYS THAN ONE.
THANKS, MOM.
CHAT! CHAT! CHAT!
BBBRRRRRRRRRR!
AND FOR THAT, THE WORLD WAS A LITTLE LESS DREADFUL.

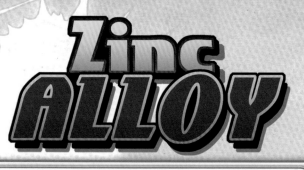

Zinc ALLOY

SUPERHERO SPECS

ZACK ALLEN IS JUST A REGULAR KID. WELL, EXCEPT THAT HE BUILT A TOTALLY INDESTRUCTIBLE ROBO-SUIT IN HIS BEDROOM. BUT EVERY KID NEEDS SOME BULLY PROTECTION, RIGHT? HERE'S A LOOK AT ZACK'S ALL-TIME GREATEST GADGETS--CREATED TO SAVE THE WORLD AND MAKE THE LUNCHROOM A SAFER PLACE.

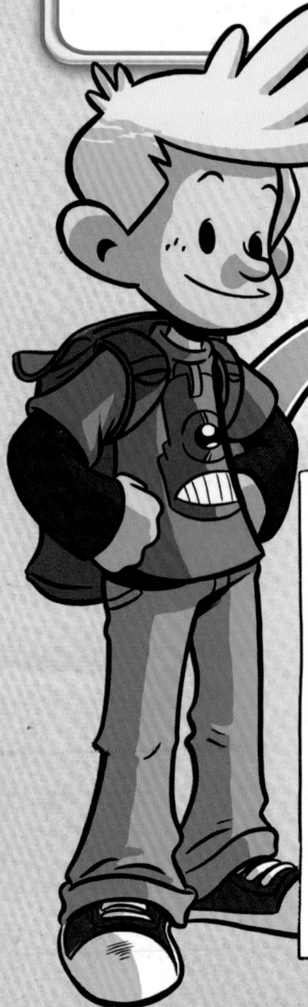

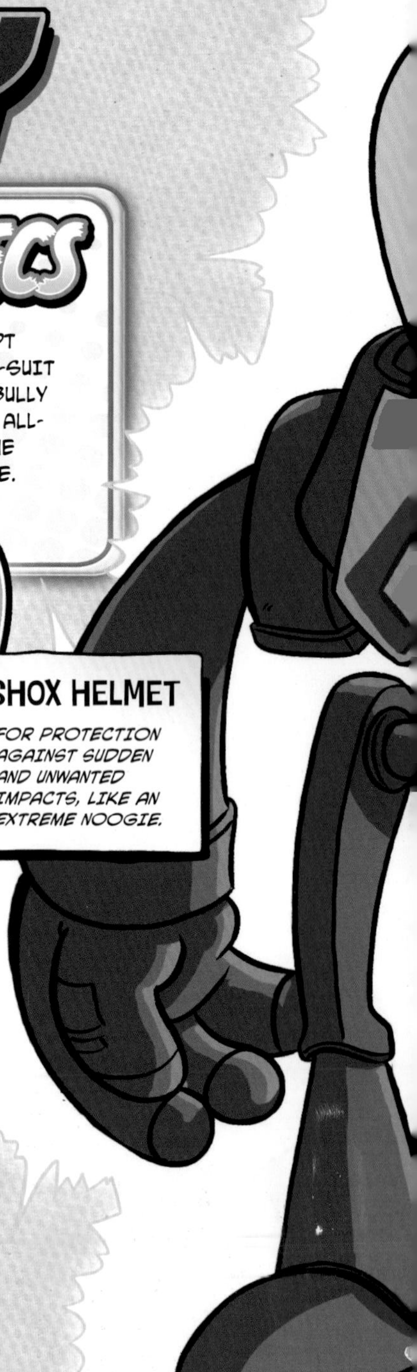

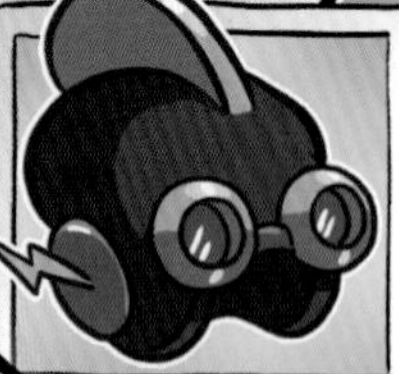

SHOX HELMET

FOR PROTECTION AGAINST SUDDEN AND UNWANTED IMPACTS, LIKE AN EXTREME NOOGIE.

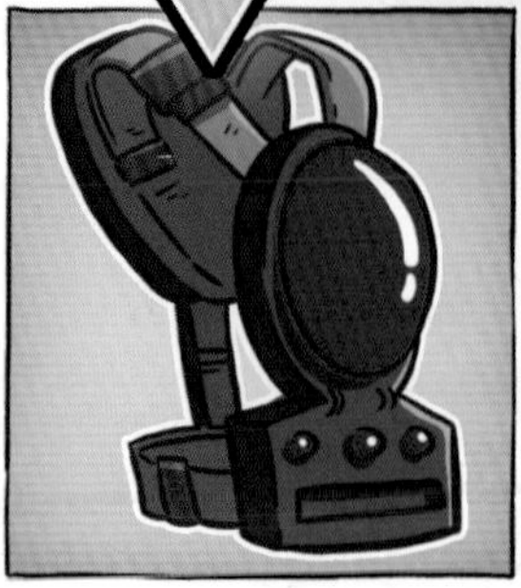

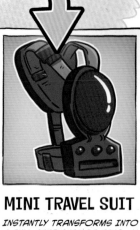

MINI TRAVEL SUIT

INSTANTLY TRANSFORMS INTO A FULL-SIZE SUIT OF ZINC ALLOY ARMOR. GREAT FOR ON-THE-GO EMERGENCIES.

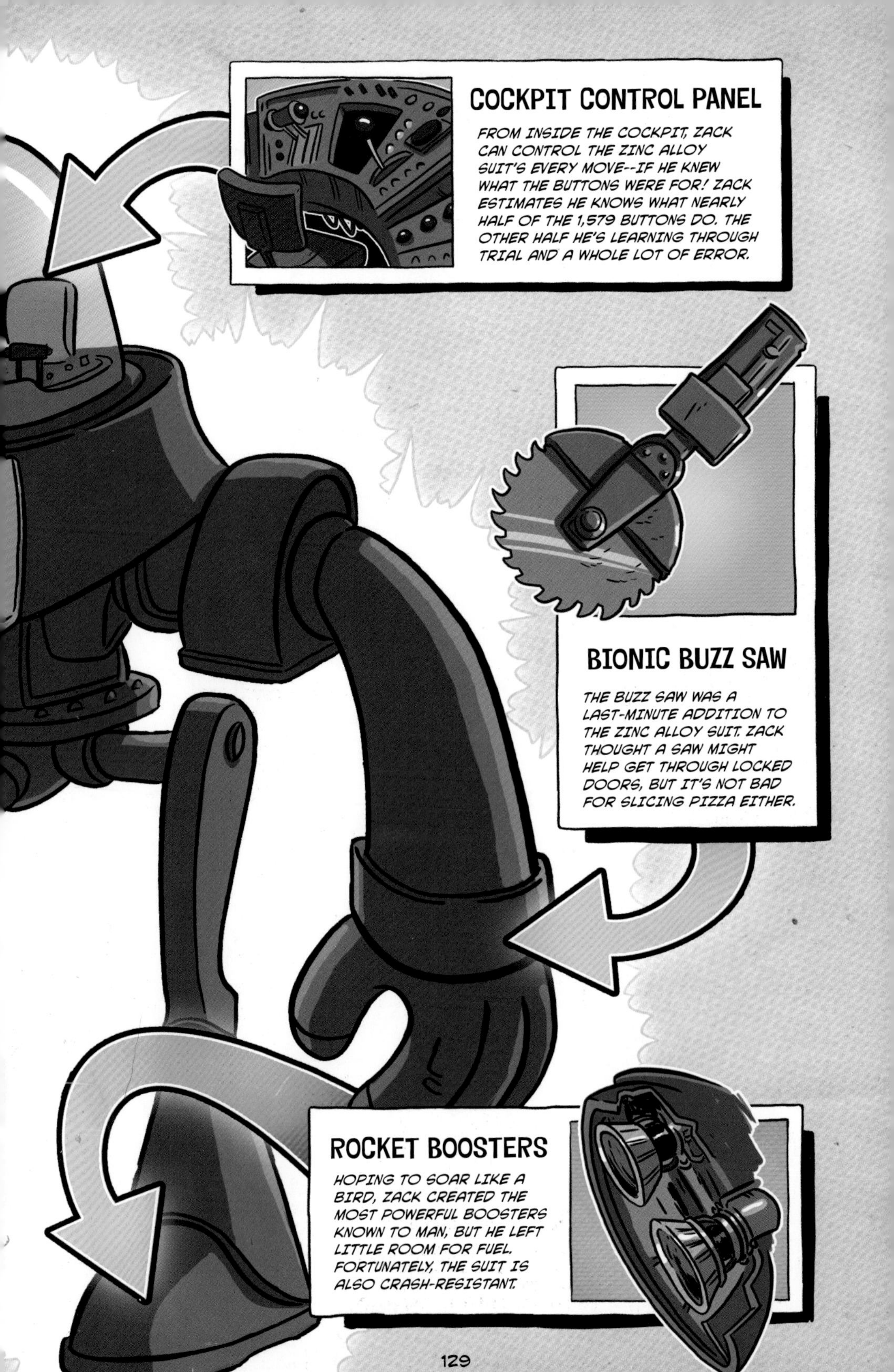
COCKPIT CONTROL PANEL
FROM INSIDE THE COCKPIT, ZACK CAN CONTROL THE ZINC ALLOY SUIT'S EVERY MOVE--IF HE KNEW WHAT THE BUTTONS WERE FOR! ZACK ESTIMATES HE KNOWS WHAT NEARLY HALF OF THE 1,579 BUTTONS DO. THE OTHER HALF HE'S LEARNING THROUGH TRIAL AND A WHOLE LOT OF ERROR.
BIONIC BUZZ SAW
THE BUZZ SAW WAS A LAST-MINUTE ADDITION TO THE ZINC ALLOY SUIT. ZACK THOUGHT A SAW MIGHT HELP GET THROUGH LOCKED DOORS, BUT IT'S NOT BAD FOR SLICING PIZZA EITHER.
ROCKET BOOSTERS
HOPING TO SOAR LIKE A BIRD, ZACK CREATED THE MOST POWERFUL BOOSTERS KNOWN TO MAN, BUT HE LEFT LITTLE ROOM FOR FUEL. FORTUNATELY, THE SUIT IS ALSO CRASH-RESISTANT.

BUILDING ZINC ALLOY

(SKETCHES BY DOUGLAS HOLGATE)

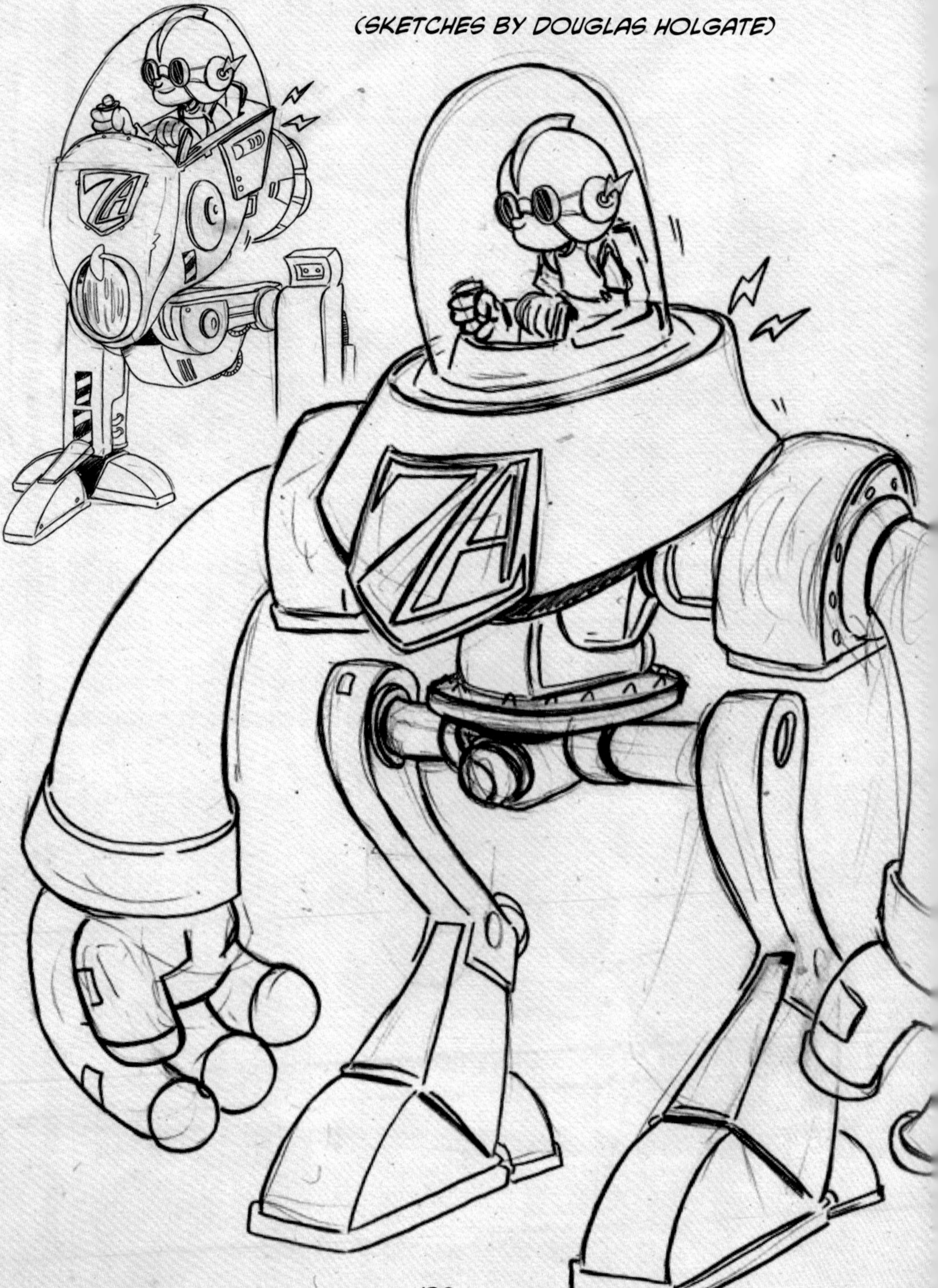

ZA
ZA

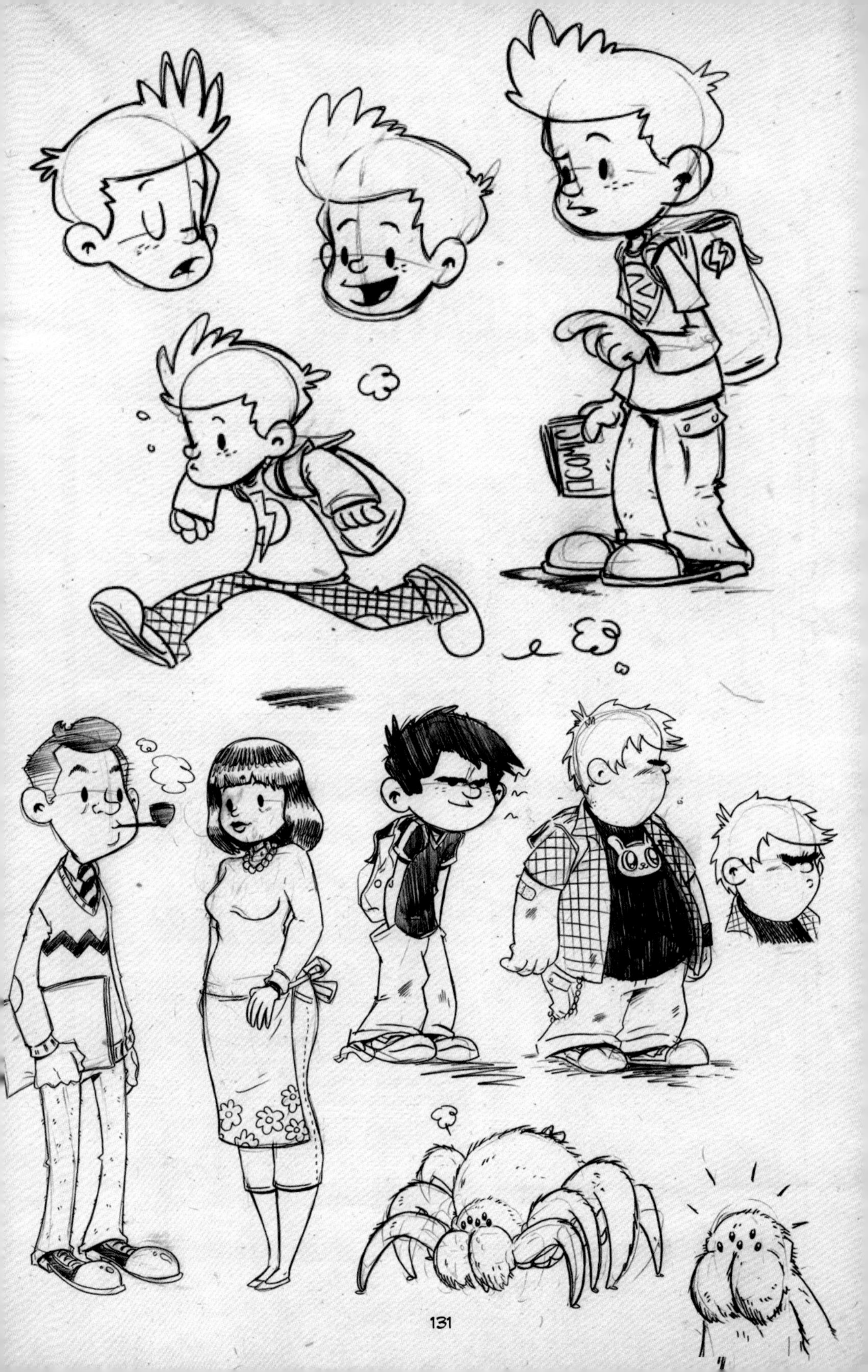
COMICS

Zinc ALLOY
CREATORS

ABOUT THE
AUTHOR

DONALD LEMKE WORKS AS A CHILDREN'S BOOK EDITOR AND WRITER. HE HAS WRITTEN MORE THAN 100 BOOKS FOR YOUNG READERS--FROM BOARD BOOKS TO MIDDLE-GRADE NOVELS-- FEATURING SOME OF TODAY'S MOST POPULAR CHARACTERS, INCLUDING BATMAN, SUPERMAN, SCOOBY-DOO, CHARLIE BROWN, HARRY POTTER, AND MORE. HE LIVES IN ST. PAUL, MINNESOTA, WITH HIS BELOVED FAMILY, WHICH INCLUDES HIS WIFE, AMY, AND THEIR TWO (SOON TO BE THREE) GROWING-UP-WAY-TOO-FAST DAUGHTERS.

ABOUT THE
ILLUSTRATOR

DOUGLAS HOLGATE HAS BEEN A FREELANCE COMIC BOOK ARTIST AND ILLUSTRATOR BASED IN MELBOURNE, AUSTRALIA, FOR MORE THAN 10 YEARS. HE'S ILLUSTRATED BOOKS FOR PUBLISHERS SUCH AS HARPERCOLLINS, PENGUIN RANDOM HOUSE, HACHETTE, AND SIMON & SCHUSTER, AND COMICS FOR IMAGE, DYNAMITE, ABRAMS, AND PENGUIN RANDOM HOUSE. HE CURRENTLY ILLUSTRATES THE NEW YORK TIMES AND USA TODAY BESTSELLING SERIES THE LAST KIDS ON EARTH, WHICH IS SOON TO BE A NETFLIX ORIGINAL SERIES.

Q&A WITH DONALD LEMKE

Capstone: Can you tell us a little about where the idea for Zinc Alloy came from?

Lemke: My personal desire to be a superhero, I suppose. I don't have any superpowers (at least not that I know of!), so I wanted to write about a kid who wasn't born with super-strength or heat-vision but found a way to be a hero anyway. Like Batman or Iron Man—two of my faves.

Capstone: What has been your favorite part of this character to tackle?

Lemke: I love how Zinc's robot suit gives him unlimited abilities. Unlike some superheroes, Zinc is able to adapt his superpowers to any situation—building new weapons, defenses, etc. The possibilities are endless, which makes it fun to write.

Capstone: What's your favorite part about working in comics?

Lemke: Getting to work with super talented people, like Douglas Holgate. Seriously, there are so many amazing comics out right now, developed by ridiculously talented individuals. I'm honored and humbled to work among them.

Capstone: What was the first comic you remember reading?

Lemke: When I was like 10 or 11, I had a subscription to *Sports Illustrated Kids*, which had a funny little reoccurring comic called *Buzz Beamer*. I remember eventually growing to like the comic more than the magazine.

Capstone: Tell us why everyone should read comic books.

Lemke: Because they're awesome! Whatever you like—fiction or nonfiction, superheroes or real-life stuff—there's something for everyone. You're never too old (or too young) to love comics.

GLOSSARY

alloy (AL-oi)—a mixture of two or more types of metal

chalet (shal-AY)—a small, wooden house with a sloping roof, often seen at ski resorts

convention (kuhn-VEN-shuhn)—a large gathering of people who have similar interests

cower (KOW-uhr)—to hide in fear or shame

exception (ek-SEP-shuhn)—something or someone that doesn't fit a certain rule or law

flexibility (flek-suh-BIL-ih-tee)—the ability to bend and change shape

freestyle (FREE-stile)—a swimming competition in which the swimmer may use any stroke

innocent (IN-uh-suhnt)—not guilty, or unworthy of punishment

noogie (NOO-gee)—rubbing one's knuckles on a person's head for a slightly painful form of torture

phase (FAZE)—a stage in someone's growth and development as a person

rocket booster (ROK-it BOO-stur)—a special rocket that gives extra power to an aircraft

rotating (ROH-tate-ing)—turning around in a circle

savior (SAYV-yor)—a person who saves or rescues others

thruster (THRUHST-ur)—an object that causes forward or upward force

zinc (ZINGK)—a blue-white metal used in many alloys

Share Your Ideas

1. In the first story, Zack Allen chose to stop the runaway train instead of getting back at the bullies. Why do you think he decided to use the Zinc Alloy suit for good instead of evil? Would you have made the same decision? Explain.

2. Robo Hero is Zack Allen's favorite comic book. Who is your favorite comic book character or superhero? Describe why you like that character the best.

3. In the second story, why do you think Zack chose to reveal his secret identity as Zinc Alloy? What effect did this decision have on Zack's life? Use examples from the story to explain your answer.

Write Your Own Stories

1. Imagine Zack Allen loaned you his Zinc Alloy suit for 24 hours. Write a story about your adventures. What would you do in the suit? Where would you go?

2. Zack used an on-the-go travel suit to turn into Zinc Alloy. Invent another way for Zack to turn into his alter ego. Be sure to name and describe your new invention.

3. The Zinc Alloy super-suit gives Zack amazing powers and abilities. Design your own super-suit. What powers does it have? Write about it. Then draw a picture of your new suit.